School Days, School Daze

ANGELA FERRELLI
ILLUSTRATION BY VICTOR GUIZA

outskirts press

DEDICATION

ALL TEACHERS AND PRINCIPALS KNOW
THAT THE TRUE POWER IN THEIR SCHOOL,
LIES WITH THEIR SCHOOL SECRETARY~
This book is dedicated to my favorite two secretaries,
Kathy F. and Lisa P.~Love and miss you both!

AND FINALLY...

I WAS A CLASSIC LITERATURE SNOB
MOST OF MY EARLY ADULT LIFE~
This book is dedicated to my dear friend, Sue
W., who on a trip to Ocean City, New Jersey,
told me to "Shut up, and buy the romance!"
I'VE BEEN HOOKED EVER SINCE!

ACKNOWLEDGEMENT

Grateful acknowledgements go to two people
in the preparation of this book:

- Lorelei Cudnik, who read, and reread a total of three times, and offered insights, grammatical fixes, and generally gentle guidance in the cleaning up of my book

- Michael Gorman, who I finally allowed to read my book after the fourth edit~he, too, offered insights (many I took, some I ignored)~he jokingly refers to himself as my MUSE, and after nearly 45 years of marriage, maybe he is!

PROLOGUE

His cell phone rang. Six-feet two, blonde and un-shaven Clay Mitchell, held his breath as he picked it up.

"Hey, Dad. Do you know anything yet?"

The rich baritone on the other end of the line replied, "You blew the competition out of the water with your video presentation. They've asked me to offer you the job!"

"Did you tell them that I'm your son?"

"I waited until they'd seen all the videos and it was a no-brainer. The School Board declared you the "best" candidate, hands-down. That's when I told them that you were my adopted son. Then I waited."

"Any questions about nepotism?"

"Hell, they've all worked with me for a long time. They know, and I reminded them, that no matter what connection you have with me, you will be treated the same as all the other principals in the district. After two minutes of talking and nodding, they voted you in... unanimously!"

"That's great! I can't wait to get started!"

"Well, here are the Board's expectations. They know that with the death of Thomas Hood, the teachers and families at Brandenburg Elementary need some time to work through their grief. They've asked you to communicate only with your school secretary, Kathy Tiffin. She's a great gal. She will know that you're the replacement; but they don't want to overshadow the town's mourning period for Tom, so we're going to wait to announce you at the Teacher's Opening Day."

"Point taken. All communication through either you or Kathy Tiffin. Got it!"

"Exactly. The Board figures that you'll have a lot of loose ends to tie up in Arizona; so they recommend that you and Kathy speak via email and phone for the next three weeks, while you're preparing for your move here. Kathy will book you a flight to Brandenburg on Thursday, and you can move into a rental in an area called Green Lakes. School starts on the following Monday with Teacher Opening Day, and the students start on Wednesday. So you're going to hit the ground running. On Opening Day, I'll come over and officially welcome you as the new principal and fill them in on some of your background."

"I'm really looking forward to getting back to the Midwest, Dad, even though it's not Barton. Will you be sending me info on Brandenburg--number of students, teachers, scores, past issues, and such?"

"Sure, son. In fact, I'm here at the office going through my files as we speak. I'll be attaching a bunch of stuff in the email I'll send along a little later today. Kathy is due in my office within the hour, and she'll contact you after we talk. She'll be able to help you through some committee selections of teachers, and issues that have arisen through the past year. They've done an amazing job with Tom out sick so much of the last school year; but having a principal back at the helm should really help relieve a lot of pressure on the staff. I think that this is the best way to handle a sudden boss change and deal with a long-distance situation at the same time. Any questions that you can think of as yet?"

"No, I don't think so, Dad. I'll just wait for the email information and get to work. I told my Superintendent that I was waiting for word and would call him immediately, one way or the other. They were really great to allow me out of my contract here. Some districts wouldn't have been nearly as supportive."

"You said a mouthful there, Clay. You're going to be fine, son. Just remember--do your job--and whatever else I tell you to do, just like when you were fourteen!" Jeff Graves, Superintendent of the Brandenburg, Indiana Local School District, chuckled.

"Gee, Dad, don't make me relive my teenage years! Once in a lifetime's enough!"

"By the way. Mom's expecting you for dinner on Sunday before school starts. Of course, she's making your favorite. I never understand why I have to wait for you to come over for that meal. But Mom says it's too much work and I don't appreciate it enough, so..."

"Well, there you go, Dad. Start appreciating more!" Clay laughed over the phone.

"Right, right...you go ahead and laugh." There was a pause and then quietly the words continued. "Hey, It'll be nice to have you closer to home."

"Thanks Dad. I feel the same way. I'll be in touch soon. Bye!"

Clay Mitchell, adopted son of Jeff and Caroline Graves, hung up his cell phone, and heaved a sigh of relief. *Brandenburg--here I come!*

1

Clay's flight had been delayed. He'd caught an Uber to his "new" apartment and found a note (and a case of beer) from his Dad. And Heaven Bless her! Kathy Tiffin, the angelic school secretary he had yet to meet, had left him a full-course meal he could nuke for dinner. Deciding to skip unpacking until the morning, Clay ate, showered, opened up a beer, and flopped down on the couch in the furnished apartment. He picked up a stack of paperwork to go through, but within a few minutes he was sound asleep. He awoke in the middle of the night, and pulled himself upstairs to the small bedroom, setting his phone alarm for 5:00 a.m.

When the cell alarm went off, he reached for it, rolled over in the slightly small double bed, and stretched. Today was the Friday before school started, but as much as he wanted to, he was not to go to see his new school. Today was the memorial service for Thomas Hood, beloved and long-time principal of Brandenburg, and according to his Dad and Kathy, the whole town would show up. Clay had decided to get all his clothes unpacked, and do his best to get settled by continuing to read through the packets of information about the district and the school, as he savored a cinnamon bagel and a third cup of coffee.

Later in the afternoon, he'd taken a long drive around Brandenburg, and then headed out of town, to become acquainted with some of the roads and byways along the way. Winding country roads with cornfields, cows and horses grazing, and some really beautiful old barns provided the scenery. A sense of quiet calm settled over him, and although it was still warm, Clay opened up his driver side window. There was a soft breeze blowing, and the humidity had dropped, signifying those cooler late afternoons that eased into the calendar by the end of August. *I'm so happy to get back to the Midwest. I've really missed it.* He decided to call his brother on Bluetooth. "Hey, Eric. What's up?" He listened, smiling.

"Yes, I've just been driving around the area, and being in Brandenburg reminds me of our growing-up days in Barton. I'm remembering all the trouble that we got into down there. Remember that night when we set those firecrackers in Mr. Johnson's barn? And the egg-throwing contest we had to see how many moving cars we could hit before Dad found out?" More laughter. "My ass hurt for days after that spanking...it was a weird coincidence that the lady whose car we hit happened to turn into our driveway to use the phone! And that Dad had made scrambled eggs for breakfast, so he knew exactly how many were left in the fridge. And we tried to lie our way through that! God, we were a handful!" Raucous laughter echoed over the line.

"Yeah. I'm actually heading to the local watering hole,

called Ojays. I guess it's the place to be in Brandenburg on a late August night. I'm looking forward to seeing you and Phyllis and Chelsea over the Labor Day weekend. Let's talk soon. Bye!" Clay disconnected the cell phone, as he pulled into the crowded parking lot about 7:30 pm. A neon blue sign over the building flashed OJAYS, and the large front porch was filled with people sitting out in rockers, and at picnic tables having a smoke. Everyone seemed to be in high spirits. As he walked in, he saw some summer softball league players gathered at the bar, as well as a row of pool tables in the back, behind the dining area. There was a lot of seating and the noise level inside was as loud as out.

Adjusting his eyes from the still bright light of the evening, Clay squeezed between two obvious regulars at the bar to order a beer. The crack of a cue ball into the rack drew Clay's attention to the pool tables. He sauntered back, placing two quarters in the queue for the next game.

Without looking up, the dark-haired guy at the table said, "You've got the winner. We play loser buys beers," and he proceeded to line up his shot.

"Great! I'm thirsty tonight!" replied Clay.

The dark-haired guy smiled confidently and proceeded to dispatch the balls into the pockets with business-like precision. Handing over the rack for the next game, he asked, "New in town?"

"Yeah, just last night. Moved in from Phoenix."

"Why would anyone move from Phoenix to Brandenburg?"

"An opportunity for change; I grew up in Barton and really wanted to be back in the Midwest." Extending his hand, he said, "I'm Clay. What about you?"

"Dave". Returning the hand shake, he tilted his head, and continued. "That loser over at the bar buying me a beer is Bobby."

Dave introduced Clay to Bobby, who returned with two beers, and the men traded jabs for an hour or so, taking turns on the pool table and enjoying the win or the loss, due to the unending rounds of drinks.

It was about 10:30 when Clay said, "Well, boys, it's been fun but it might be about time for me to be getting home. You know I really should ease into the 'wild' side of Brandenburg..." he shouted over his shoulder, and then stopped...dead in his tracks. A parade of women had just come through the front door of Ojays.

"You were saying...?" Dave chuckled, moving forward to poke Clay in the ribs. "Weren't you talking about leaving, Clay old boy? Or...maybe you'd like to meet 'em?"

Rendered speechless, all Clay did was nod.

"I thought so." Catching the eye of a redhead, Dave called out, "Hey, Sally, honey. Come on over with the gang. There's a new guy in town."

The sexy little redhead with the boyish haircut glanced up and waved her hand at Dave. She turned toward the others, pointed in Dave's direction, and they headed toward the tables.

"That's Sal. She's off-limits, so don't get any ideas. Behind her is Tammy, and the twins are Jennifer and Judy. They own the Twin Travel Agency here in Brandenburg."

But there was one left, and she was the one who had caught Clay's eye. The shortest of the group, a little honey-haired goddess tucked ever so nicely into a white pair of shorts and lime green and white polka-dot shirt, tied at the midriff.

"What about...?" Clay managed to get out.

"That's Sally's best friend, Olivia. She's a real piece of work, feisty and funny, and..."

Dave glanced over at the stupefied look on Clay's face and stopped the conversation. The girls had arrived.

"Hey," said Dave, giving the redhead a squeeze. "This is Clay. He's new in town, but I think he'll fit in just fine. He plays a mean game of pool, and doesn't mind buying beers for everyone. Okay, this one is Sally," motioning toward the redhead. Continuing, he introduced the brunette as Tammy, whose warm smile of welcome and softly quiet voice, told Clay that she was one of those shy, sweet girls.

The twins were a different matter altogether. Flanking Clay, and not in a shy way, they leaned in and whispered in their slightly breathy, identical voices, "Nice to meet you." Simultaneously pressing their business cards in each of his hands they encouraged him to give them a call when he was planning his next vacation. "We'll take care of you, double!". Then they pulled away, moving toward the softball players at the bar.

Dave was clearly taking liberties with Sally's butt, when Clay saw honey-hair slap the back of Dave's hand. She smiled and said, "Hey, fella, this is a public place. Get a room if you have to."

She'd arrived, and although Clay had noticed her from a distance, the up-close-and -personal was even better. She smiled at Dave and Sally and threw back her head, laughing in pure pleasure. "You are too much! Sally, what in the world is wrong with you, hanging out with this caveman?" she teased mercilessly.

Then she turned eyes on Clay--big brown eyes, with flecks of gold, long lush eyelashes, and the loveliest lips that Clay had ever seen. Extending her small hand, she spoke, "Hi. I'm Olivia. Welcome to Brandenburg."

Clay took the small hand in his, totally engulfing it, and smiled. "Glad to meet you. I'm Clay." He knew nothing about her, but there was some kind of mystical pull to that hand grasp, that sent zings of electricity up his arm--and further down as well. *Ah, Clay, my man, this one you gotta have.*

"Hey, Olivia?" interrupted Dave. "I've got a little business with Sally. Can you take my place on the table with Clay? We're playing for beers so bring your 'A' game against this guy. He's pretty good."

Honey-hair looked in his direction, hands on hips, and said, "Well, you heard the man. Rack 'em up!"

Clay racked the balls and instinctively knew by the way she positioned the cue for the break that she had spent considerable time on the tables. CRACK! Five balls were pocketed before Clay had a shot. It was not much of a shot at that. It was more of a miscue. Olivia got control of the table again, and as quick as that, Clay was heading to the bar, a loser.

Clay retrieved the beers, rewarded the victor and offered a toast. "To Olivia--a mighty fine pool shark!"

Both dropped their heads back for a generous swig of suds. When she looked up, a daub of foam remained on her upper lip. Barely losing eye contact, Clay motioned to wipe her lip off, laughingly saying "You mustn't waste!"

She shook her head, agreeing. "Another? Whose break?"

Clay positioned the balls for game two, but Olivia made short order of him again. He found himself at the bar ordering more beer, when Dave joined him. "Are you still getting beat by a girl? I'm going to have to re-think this friendship. I can't be hanging with a loser, bud!"

Clay laughed. "It appears that I'm getting a lesson at the hands of a very talented pool player!" They'd arrived back at the table, where Olivia and Sally were talking. He continued, "Hey, Olivia. How about upping the stakes for one final game?"

"What? You still want a piece of this?"

Oh, if only. "One game, loser buys a round for everybody in the bar."

Olivia looked around the bar. Most of the regulars were still there, but a lot of the patrons had gone home. "Okay, you're on," and she bent over to address the cue ball. Her break failed to pocket any balls, so Clay sized up the table. A crowd was forming, and several bystanders made private bets on the outcome. No one noticed as Clay lined up his shot right-handed. He had been playing from the opposite side all evening.

"Six ball in the side." In went the ball. "Three ball, one rail to the corner." And in it dropped. Clay circled the table, rechecking the lie. "Seven, off the two, into the corner." The purple ball tapped the blue ball and dropped in. The bar patrons were edging ever closer to the table to watch the action. "Four ball in the side." Another ball dropped, as Clay surveyed the emptying table. "One, down the rail to the corner," and the yellow ball hugged the rail and disappeared. "Five in the side." The plop of the orange ball into the pocket made Clay smile. He glanced over at Olivia, who was watching intently, shaking her head, as if in disbelief. "Two in the corner." It dropped. Now the table was empty save the eight ball, and all the stripes. Clay looked at the shot from two directions, reckoned the geometry of angles, and declared, "Eight ball in the corner, off two rails."

The crowd stood in hushed anticipation, trying to see the shot that Clay envisioned. He took aim and drove the cue ball into the moneyball, as the eight ball is called. It responded beautifully as it caromed into the end rail and then into the side rail at the opposite corner that Clay had called. The money ball rolled across the smooth felt, just missing the fourteen-ball. The eight lost speed as it neared the pocket. Had Clay given it enough? "Come on, come on..." Physics would say that a body in motion tends to stay in motion, with only the friction of the felt slowing it down. Closer and closer it got. Had time slowed?

Olivia turned to look at Clay as he watched the ball creep ever closer to the pocket. Then she noticed he held the stick in his right hand. Closer and closer, and then...

The black money ball disappeared into the pocket with a sweet thud. The crowd roared. Olivia placed her stick in the wall rack and headed for the bar, shaking her head. "Set 'em all up, Ojay, and give me two drafts, please."

Shouts of appreciation from the crowd rose up as people received their unexpected beverage. Olivia walked over to Clay, carrying two frosty mugs. "Nice little stunt switching over to your right hand when the bet went up," she said with a wry smile.

"Oh, you noticed," he chuckled.

"Here's to the winner!" announced Olivia to the

crowd. Clay smiled and turned to the cheering crowd. In the moment he acknowledged the cheers, Olivia lifted her mug in a toast and emptied the entire contents over Clay's head. He stood there stunned. Olivia was smiling as she turned to see the expressions on the faces of the patrons. Sally whispered under her breath, "Oh, my word." It was only then that Olivia realized she may have made a horrible mistake. And she knew it when she turned to see the frosty expression-- the cocked eyebrow and set line of Clay's jaw.

Olivia took a baby step backward when Clay grabbed her arm and pulled her close to his muscular body. "Not so fast." He held her tight. "What do **you** all think?" Clay asked, addressing the bar patrons while holding up his full mug. They all nodded. "I thought so!" Clay deposited the nearly full mug over Olivia's head. The suds splashed on the top of her head, soaking the beautiful hair. She closed her eyes as it cascaded down her face. Clay watched as the beer streamed down her face and gathered on her chin. A steady drip flowed into her fabulous cleavage. *Oh, to be a drop of that beer.* Olivia struggled in vain, trying to break free of Clay's grasp.

"Let me go, you big lug."

"Of course," Clay relaxed his hold on Olivia. "I guess that you're not used to being beaten on the pool table; but it's nice to give someone a taste of their own medicine once and awhile. Now that we've evened the score, would you like me to walk you home? I don't think either of us should be driving."

Olivia glanced at Clay, embarrassed by her show of bad sportsmanship. "I'm really sorry. I saw that you had been playing left-handed and switched over, and it made me really angry. And no...I'm not used to getting beaten. I've been the Amateur Pool Champ in Brandenburg for over five years."

"Apology accepted, Olivia. But what about that walk home I mentioned?"

"Well, it does make a lot of sense since we both smell like a brewery!" And she laughed--a silly laugh that made Clay laugh too. Waving good-byes to the remainder of the patrons in Ojays, Clay opened the exit door for Olivia as they left.

The night was still a bit balmy. The gentle breeze against Clay's wet shirt actually gave him a chill. *Or could it be the heavenly body standing next to me.* "Which way are we heading?"

Olivia pointed in the direction of the clock tower.

"You're a pretty good shot. Where did you learn?" asked Clay.

"Thanks. Coming from an obvious hustler like you, I'll take that as a compliment. I grew up with three older brothers and a table in the basement. All my brothers were pretty good. I guess I learned from them. Ojays has a big tournament every October, and I've won it five years straight."

"Very nice."

"What about you?"

"We had a pool table in the basement when I was growing up too, and my Dad and brother and I played all the time. My Mom used to scold us and remind us that there were girls sitting at home on a Saturday night, because we were playing pool in the basement with our buddies." He threw back his head and laughed, remembering.

Olivia smiled. *It's clear he's really fond of his parents.*

They walked companionably, enjoying the night breeze, when Olivia tripped.

"Damn!" he heard her mutter.

"Are you alright? What happened?" He crouched down.

"It's okay. I just wrenched my ankle. Looks like one of the Kelley boys left a toy out here on the sidewalk, and I didn't see it. I'm sure I'll be fine."

"Let's check it out. How does this feel?" He rotated her ankle gently. She cringed. "Here--let me help you up." His large fingers wrapped around her tiny waist and she leaned against him. She smelled of spicy perfume and beer, but her hair had dried in the warm night air and little wisps of it were blowing in her face. She looked up, grimacing slightly. His desire for her shocked him. He sat her down gently. "There now. Try walking on it," he suggested.

Olivia put her weight down and let out a little yelp of pain.

Clay frowned.. "It looks like those Kelley boys need a good talking to!" he said sternly.

"No!" she shouted, alarmed. "Those boys are two of the dearest boys in town, and their mother was just killed in a traffic accident, not two months ago. I won't let anyone yell at those boys."

The familiar pain in the gut rode in all at once, and washed over Clay. His body tensed as Olivia leaned against him. She felt him take a deep, slow breath, and watched him run his fingers through his hair.

"Is something wrong, Clay?" she asked quietly.

He sighed and stood for a moment. The anguished face turned towards her, but it was as though he was miles away in another time and place.

"Clay?" She reached up and touched his face.

Her soft touch brought him back to reality. "It's just..." he spoke, his voice raspy, "It's just that both my folks were killed in a car accident when I was ten years old. The pain is never really gone, you know. It lies just below the surface and then it just sort of boils up, even though it happened twenty-three years ago. Maybe I'll stop off one day and visit with the Kelley boys. It might help them."

"Oh, Clay. I'm so sorry."

"You just never quite get over the shock." He paused for a second, catching his breath. "Here--let's get you home. It's late. Lean on me and I'll hold you up." They tried a few steps that way, but he could tell by the way she held her breath, that she was really in pain. "Hurts bad, doesn't it?"

She nodded, grimacing.

"Oh, what the hell." In one swift movement she was off the ground and in his arms.

"Clay, put me down! You simply don't need to do this, I can manage."

"Not if I want to get home before five in the morning, you can't. You're just gonna have to relax and let me carry you. Anyway...you may be a heavyweight at the pool table, but there's not much to you in volume. Now quit fidgeting. Where am I going?"

"Not far. Just two more blocks down Main and take a right on Hennessey."

There was only comfortable silence then and the quiet sounds of a summer night--crickets mostly--and a bit of a breeze rustling through the trees.

"Do you like Brandenburg, Olivia?"

"I love it. I grew up here and decided to stay. I lived

for a year in Chicago, and I loved the excitement, but after a while I just wanted to be home where people knew me, and I knew them. I love all the cultural stuff a big city has to offer, but I miss all the "people" stuff that happens around here."

"You said you had brothers. Where do they live?"

"I've got three of the greatest brothers on the planet, but they don't live here anymore. My brother Jimmy and his wife, Susie, live up in Townsend, about three hours away. The others live out of state and get here twice a year for Christmas and Fourth of July. In fact, you just missed meeting them...I mean, if I'd known you on the Fourth."

"I would have liked to have known you on the Fourth. We could have made some real fireworks, I think," he said flirtingly, leaning in, coming ever so close to her upturned face. She looked a little like a deer-in-the-headlights for a second. Then the spitfire returned.

Pulling back, she said, "You can put me down now. This is my place." And she scrambled out of his arms, and hobbled up onto the front porch. "I've lived here for about two years and I really like the location and the amenities. My landlady, Mrs. Herbert, is a little nosy, but she really has a good heart...she just doesn't want anyone..."

Clay followed her up the steps, and stood right behind her. "Anyone ever tell you that you talk too much, Olivia?" He spun her around, his face lowering, his breath warm and intoxicating. For a split second their eyes met-- hers, brown and registering surprise, his blue, the long lashes shuttering. Then his eyes drifted down to her lush lips, and he said, "It's just that those lips of yours are so inviting...and I've spent all night looking at them...they just seem to be calling to me..."

Before even Clay knew what was happening, he was kissing her, his mouth warm and sensual, pulling her in, and tugging her body towards his.

She gasped in surprise, and the little rush of air opened her lips and allowed him entry. Their tongues mated, sampling the warm passion they found there. He heard her moan in reaction to the kiss, so he ramped up the "heat" level. It wasn't hard to do. *This woman feels so good.* She leaned into him, exquisite parts of her body touching parts of his, her fingers brushing through his hair as he bent to savor her. But when she sucked on his bottom lip, he pulled away from her, his breathing ragged. "Too good...too fast...and too late to let this go on, Olivia." He moved slightly away and turned his back to her.

"You're right, it is late," she said, feeling slightly embarrassed. *Wow! I really got carried away. He's irresistible.* Thanks for your help getting me home, and I promise I won't be such a poor sport **if** you ever beat me at pool again." She giggled.

He turned back in her direction. He didn't want her to go inside. Somehow he'd have to sample that delectable mouth of hers again. *There is a fire in this woman that I have to have.*

Grasping for conversation, he sat in one of the chairs on the front porch, and took her sore ankle in his hands, massaging it gently. He could feel her relax as he did so. "You know, it occurs to me that I don't even know your last name, or what you do for a living?"

She sighed as he massaged. "Oh--my name is Olivia

Sheffield. I'm a second grade teacher at Brandenburg Elementary."

Clay Mitchell felt as though all three of Olivia Sheffield's brothers had just kicked him in the gut. *Oh my God! One of my teachers?* He brushed his fingers through his hair and smiled, dropping her ankle gently, and said, "Well, it's nice to officially meet you, but it's late and I need to get going."

"Wait...?" She watched in surprise, as he backed formally away, and was down the porch steps in a second. He turned one last time, waved, and was off in the dark.

What just happened? The minute I told him my name, he was off like a shot. I thought I was going to get at least another of those mind-blowing kisses. And wait a minute--I don't know his last name either.

Disappointment made Olivia turn towards her front door, and as she unlocked it, she shook her head--*I've got to see him again. Maybe Dave knows his last name. I'll have to check tomorrow with Sally.*

2

Olivia had finally drifted off to sleep about three-thirty in the morning. And the reason? She couldn't get the image of Clay out of her mind. She rehashed their meeting over and over, and admitted that she'd been the one to spoil the easy camaraderie that they had established when she poured the beer over his head.

Please let him call or get in touch with me. She felt as though she was seventeen again, waiting for a call from Larry Adams asking her to the prom. She'd worried and waited and waited and worried, and finally he'd called. He said that he'd planned on calling all along, just hadn't gotten around to it. *Wasn't that the way it was with boys?* Girls agonized over every little detail of their relationships, and boys just "got around to it". It was infuriating. From that moment on, Olivia decided that she would never wait around for a man to call. Frankly, she hadn't had to. She had never been without a date for any function, especially ones in Brandenburg. Years before she had decided that there was no one in this town who would be a true love match. They all knew each other too well. But she had enjoyed flirtations and first loves with several of the local boys--some had stayed around, others had moved on to other towns or cities nearby. Those were easy, uncomplicated friendships based on past history.

And now this safe, predictable environment that she'd come to count on for so long, had been rocked off its foundation by the entrance of this new man in town, whose last name she didn't even know. She wasn't sure that she'd even heard it. *Maybe asking Dave would be too obvious? I can't do that. He's a blabbermouth, anyway. I'd never hear the end of it.*

Olivia just wanted to lay there in her bed reliving the memory of Clay's hot breath and seductive words that had led to that heart-stopping kiss. She had never felt so totally knocked off balance. *Lord, I'm embarrassed about how carried away I was. Thank God he couldn't read my mind. It would definitely get an R rating. Is he thinking about me in the same way?* There had certainly been a magnetic pull between the two of them. *Is he remembering the kiss? Or was I just another tipsy woman he'd met at a bar who'd responded to his fast wit and gorgeous face and body? God, I hope not! This is awful, Olivia! Pull yourself together--you are better than this simpering wimp of a woman. He'll call!* Finally able to talk herself into some semblance of reality, she fell asleep.

She was awakened abruptly by the ringing of her cell phone. She glanced at the clock. It was after 9:30 a.m. Olivia smiled, but she didn't pick up the phone until the third ring. Her heart thumped wildly as she answered. "Hello?"

"Hey, toots!" It was her brother, Jimmy.

She let out a sigh of disappointment. "Oh, hi, Jimmy."

"What kind of greeting is that for your favorite brother?"

"You're not my favorite, Jimmy. You're a pain in the rear, and you just woke me up from a rather delightful dream."

"What do you mean you just woke up? It's practically 10:00 a.m. Are you feeling alright?"

"Enough with the questions. I'm feeling just fine. I was out late last night, that's all."

"Well, maybe I need to move back to Brandenburg to keep an eye on you!"

"DON'T YOU DARE! Then you'll never be my favorite!" She laughed. "What do you want anyway?"

"Well, I just ran into Derek and he asked if I'd give you the details about the Gallery Opening tonight. He's swamped over there, so I'm going to pick you up about three this afternoon. Dress is business casual. I'll drop you at the gallery with Derek. Susie and I will meet you for drinks at Le Grande Pavilion at 7 p.m., and then attend the opening at eight-thirty. Derek will get you home afterward."

"Oh, Lord, I'd completely forgotten!"

There was silence on the other end of the line. "Olivia, sis? Are you sure you're feeling okay? Sleeping in so late, forgetting important events, and not telling me I'm your favorite when I know I am? It just doesn't sound like you." Jimmy sounded sincerely concerned.

"I'm fine, Jim, really. You know you're always my favorite, especially when the other two aren't around to hear! I've just had a lot on my mind with school starting Monday, the Memorial service, the new principal coming in, and, of course, the Opening. Don't worry. I'll be ready when you come to get me. Thanks for calling. See you later today..." She hung up the phone.

I can't believe it. Jim is right. I never forget important dates, and this Opening has been on my calendar for three months. In fact, if you'd asked me three nights ago, I'd have told anyone what I was doing Saturday night. What is wrong with me?

A six-foot tallish, blond-haired pool player named Clay, who kissed like there was no tomorrow.

I'd been so sure that Derek was where my path was leading--until last night.

3

Derek Donaldson stood in the Atrium of his soon-to-be opened Art Gallery in Townsend, Indiana. He had been lucky to find this space available after the bank had gone belly-up. He called to one of the many workers, swarming around like ants to get the place ready for tonight's Grand Opening. "Hey, Joe. That platform needs to be centered, so the view from the entrance is more impressive." Watching as the workers shifted the platform, Derek nodded, "There! That's perfect. Thanks, guys."

Derek moved through the gallery, looking with critical eyes for color combinations, composition, and placement for the four additional artists' works he would be featuring tonight. He had a multimedia artist in one room, a watercolorist in another, a sculptor in the lobby, a wood-worker who made custom furniture in the large room in the back, and a silkscreen artisan in the smaller workroom. He loved his job, and the creativity it brought to his daily planning.

Susie Sheffield hurried by, carrying a clipboard of

SCHOOL DAYS, SCHOOL DAZE

things to do. "Hey, Derek. It's looking great!"

"I think so too, Susie. Is Jim in yet?"

"No, he's picking up the remaining watercolors to be hung, and then he's heading over to Brandenburg to pick up Olivia. By the way, we just got a call from the caterer. They'll be here at 6:30 and Paul will be meeting them. I've gone over all the details with him in regards to the placement of champagne and hors d'oeuvres. One bar will be open at either end, and the dessert bar will be in the furniture display room."

"I think we've tackled every potential issue that could arise. I couldn't have done this without you and Jim being so involved. I'm glad we'll have some time this evening for relaxed conversation. I have an offer to make you both. And I want Olivia to hear it as well!" He smiled a mysterious smile.

"Well, now you've got me curious!"

"It'll just have to stay that way until this evening. We have reservations at Le Grand Pavilion at 7:00. Don't be late!"

"Sounds good. We'll see you later, Derek. I'm so excited!" She glanced over her shoulder and smiled as she waved goodbye.

Derek was excited too. He'd been waiting to get this gallery open and running, and if things went the way he thought they'd go he'd have more time to spend with Olivia Sheffield.

He headed back to his office, took off his suit coat, threw it on the sofa, and stretched out for an hour break from the hubbub.

Derek Donaldson, thirty-five, self-made man, who owned and ran two art galleries, one in Boston and the other in New York, smiled to himself, as he remembered the night that he had met Jim Sheffield's little sister.

Susie and Jim were entertaining a perspective artist, and Susie had invited both Derek and Olivia, against her husband's wishes. She was a bit of a matchmaker, and Jim knew that Olivia and Derek would not show up if they knew any matchmaking was being done.

But, of course, the rest was history. Derek had been totally taken with Olivia's sense of humor--well, hell, her looks first--then her sense of humor! To top it off, she knew about art and seemed to understand the degree of work and diligence it took to secure artists; she actually appreciated what he was trying to do in his galleries, and applauded the accomplishments that he'd already achieved in his career. In short they'd hit it off spectacularly. He'd asked her on a second date for tonight, the Townsend Gallery's Grand Opening. He spoke to himself, "I never thought I'd settle down before my forties, but maybe, just maybe, Olivia...?"

Derek dozed off with a smile on his face.

4

Clay awoke about six Saturday morning with Olivia Sheffield uppermost on his mind. *Damn, what a complete and total mess. I meet someone who I really want to get to know, and find out that she works for me!* If there was one thing that Clay couldn't stand it was trouble in the workplace..and boy, was this trouble. And, he hadn't even started working with her yet! Maybe a good jog would clear his head and help him decide how to handle this one. He pulled on his jogging shorts, white tee shirt, socks, and running shoes, closed and locked the door to his place, and ran.

It was a relatively cool summer morning, unusual for August, and Clay was grateful for the slight breeze in the air. He headed out going north, winding through the three parking lots surrounding the duplexes where he would live for six months. It wasn't a bad place at all, clean and well-kept, but he had already decided against extending the lease in January. He wanted a place to spread out a bit.

He liked the feel of Brandenburg already--its

hominess, the feeling of belonging somewhere, of finding and capturing a place from the past, where the hectic pace of life slowed down just a little. In short, it was a haven from the rat race he'd become accustomed to in Arizona. *I have time to think about where to live. There's a much more pressing problem to consider right now.*

Olivia. Who'd have thought it? A honey-haired, brown-eyed vixen, with a fabulous body, and the most kissable lips he'd ever tasted...*dear God, I have got to stop this! There is no way in hell I can carry on a relationship with one of my teachers.* He had visions of ducking into the custodial closet with her, where absolutely no cleaning would be taking place. He had images of the two of them on the desk in his office...*Get a grip, man! Just because she's got your libido up and running, doesn't mean it'll happen the next time you see her. I mean, those doublemint twins got your engines running too, and there's twice the fun to be had there.* Still and all, Clay knew that the doublemint twins weren't his type. *Hell, I don't know if Olivia Sheffield's my type either. But I'd sure relish the chance to find out.*

His breath was heavy from the running pace he was keeping, so he slowed down just a little, and began to take a look around. He had run to the center of town, where stood a city park, with a gazebo and the late blooms of summer, and an enormous pine tree. There were benches, a small playground, and walking paths where he noticed an older gentleman walking his little dog. He passed the florist shop, the infamous Twin Travel Agency, and then passed Kipley's Bakery, waving through the window, as someone pulled freshly baked doughnuts from the oven. Rounding the corner and heading down the neighboring street, he headed up the road toward "his" school, Brandenburg Elementary. The sign out front read, SCHOOL STARTS WEDNESDAY. WE CAN'T WAIT TO SEE YOU! The grounds looked freshly mown, the flowers around the sign were well-tended and in bloom, and the school looked as though it was ready to welcome the hordes of little girls and boys who were, by now, ready to return.

School had always been a place that Clay loved. From his first step in the door, as a kindergartener, all through his college years, learning had been his lifelong hobby. Clay had read early as a child, and had continued reading voraciously throughout his life. In fact, books were one of the few things that he could count on in those days following the death of his parents. He couldn't talk to anyone, not even his big brother. He'd just sit in total silence in his room, and read for hours, mostly sci-fi and fantasy, hiding in the characters' adventures, their perils, and their courage. He had needed their courage to find some of his own. Finally, after about two weeks of barely talking, sleeping, or eating, Clay had been able to begin the healing process. He had started to talk, and then to cry, and then to grieve. Eric, his older brother by four years, had sensed that he needed to have this time and had left him alone. But then, the two of them clung together, the little brother giving hope to the big brother. And Jeff and Caroline had been there throughout, moving into their friends' home to allow the boys time to transition. The bonds of family had grown strong that year. Eric lived in Wisconsin now, with his wife Phyllis and their little girl, Chelsea. Clay had been happy at the chance to return to the Midwest because he knew he'd be able to see his brother more regularly.

It was clear to Clay that Brandenburg was clearly a beloved school in the town and had always been well-maintained. Of course, looking at the school brought his mind back to his problem, namely one Olivia Sheffield. He would just have to tell her. He couldn't walk into the introductory meeting on Monday morning without speaking to her first. It just wouldn't be right. *I'll go over and see her later today, face to face. After all, I know where she lives.* They'd just talk about it, and he'd explain that it wasn't wise for a principal and teacher to be involved, and that they would just pretend that kiss hadn't happened. They'd be professionals in every way. After all, it had just been one kiss, not without its heat, granted--but just one kiss. They could erase that easily enough. *Sure, that's it. I'll go see her today.*

Clay felt a little better on the return jog to his place. Still, somehow in the back of his mind, he had a nagging feeling that he was lying to himself.

Clay hadn't called or come by all morning. Olivia was frustrated...and annoyed...and depressed. *Did I make that big of a fool of myself last night? He sure didn't seem to mind when he was kissing me, but then he practically bolted off the front porch. What was that about?*

Olivia stewed as she did the remainder of her laundry in preparation for Monday morning, knowing full-well that she wouldn't have the time once school began. She glanced at the clock and realized that she had been worrying most of the day about a stupid phone call from a veritable stranger. *What a waste of time! Just forget about it! I need to hurry and get ready! Jimmy will be here in an hour and a half to pick me up.*

Olivia showered quickly, and then worked on her make-up. She pulled the hot pink formal sundress out of her closet, admiring its casual elegance. She had loved it the moment she tried it on. It was knee-length and cinched at the waist, with a full-skirt and a layer of tulle underneath. She pulled it over her head, and then got her hair up in a French twist, fastening it with a pink and rhinestone comb. Strappy gold sandals that she'd paid too much for, but had to have, were the finishing touch to her ensemble. She was happy with what she saw in the mirror, even with a bandaged ankle... which then reminded her of the mystery man whose last name she didn't know--*I don't care if I ever see him again!* She headed down the stairs and picked up her cocktail bag, knowing full well that *that* was a total fabrication.

Clay had finished his jog, showered, fixed himself a huge breakfast, read the morning paper, and finished his laundry. He hated ironing, and had never really gotten the hang of it, so he'd taken to sending his shirts out. The Monday introductory meeting didn't demand a shirt and tie, so he'd be okay until Wednesday.

By the time his laundry was done, he stretched out on the couch to watch an old movie, and was asleep within minutes. He awoke at two-thirty and realized that he hadn't gone to see Olivia yet. He grabbed a fresh shirt, pulled on a pair of khaki shorts, donned his comfortable docksiders, and jumped in his car to head toward her house. He rounded the corner of Hennessy and drove up the road slowly, taking his time, so as not to miss her place. Strangely, there was a black BMW parked right in front. *Maybe this isn't her place. I don't know many teachers who can afford a BMW.* He decided to stay in his car and wait for a few minutes. These apartments all looked alike, and it had been dark when he'd left her last night. *Maybe someone will come...ah here she comes now.*

Down the steps she came--a honey-haired girl in a pink dress with her hair piled on top of her head. The dress was tailored to her tiny waist, and the full skirt swayed when she moved, showing off those incredible legs. She looked like a Barbie doll, accessorized to the hilt, and filled out in all the right places! *Wow!*

The guy in the BMW got out and met her on the sidewalk, giving her a big hug. Clearly they were comfortable together. He held her at arm's length and admired the view--*who wouldn't?* Olivia motioned towards the porch, and the man went up and picked up an overnight bag sitting out there. *Well, that seals it. She appears to already have game going with this guy--what do I care anyway? I came over here to tell her to be a professional and put that steamy kiss behind us. This makes it way easier. And, the hell with it! Let her just find out Monday morning that I'm her boss.*

As he watched the BMW, he noticed that Olivia had turned her head in the direction of his car. He quickly bent down as though to grab something on the floor and waited to be sure that the car had turned the corner before he sat upright again. *Damn!* Jamming his car into gear, he turned it around, and headed for home.

As Olivia climbed into her brother's car, she glanced with curiosity towards a car parked down the street. She noticed that the driver had blonde hair, but he looked as though he'd dropped something and had bent down to pick it up. She had a sort of unsettled feeling in her gut as she realized once more that Clay had never called her. *Darn him--well, I'm not letting that ruin my night!* She got in the car smiling, and within a minute, the BMW pulled away from the curb.

5

It was 8:45 a.m. Monday at Brandenburg Elementary. The teachers had come in fairly early for doughnuts and coffee, with the hope of seeing their new principal. Kathy Tiffin sat at her desk with a smug look on her face. A number of teachers surrounded her.

"I told you all, Dr. Graves will be here any minute to introduce you to the new principal. You're getting nothing from me except to say that I know he'll do a great job."

Most of the staff knew Kathy well enough to know that she would indeed say nothing else. A couple of the rookies, however, were still trying to get information from her, when Tom Moore, one of the fifth grade teachers, came running in and whispered, "Hurry up, everyone. Graves just came through the door!" The teachers scattered quickly then, taking an extra cup of coffee or grabbing a doughnut as they left, heading to the library. Sally and Olivia were the last ones to leave. They loved talking to Kathy and giggled about all the buzz over the new principal.

Olivia chimed in. "All this excitement over a new principal. I just can't imagine..." she said jokingly.

"Yeah," chirped Sally. "We've practically run this building on our own while Mr. Hood was so ill. As far as I'm concerned, we hardly need a new principal." She winked at Olivia.

"Well, girls, with Mr. Hood being out for so long, a lot of his work fell on my shoulders, and I for one, am glad to get rid of some of it"

"Oh, Kathy, we know you've been overworked and deserve all the help you can get," said Sally Litchfield. "Come on, Kath. How about just a few details?"

"NOTHING ELSE YOU TWO! Why don't you get on up to the library. Dr. Graves will be ready to start on time, and then you'll see for yourselves!"

Olivia laughed. "So much for our sleuthing abilities, Sal. Let's go!"

The office was quiet now, save for the sound of Kathy's computer keys clacking away. Clay Mitchell stepped out of his office with a solemn look on his face. "I couldn't help but overhear that conversation, Kathy. A couple of nosy ones, huh?"

She chuckled. "Not really, Clay. I call them the "field" girls because their last names both have field in them. Sally Litchfield and Olivia Sheffield are great teachers and the kids love them. But I think they'll really be surprised by how much help an engaged principal can be to them."

Clay smiled. "I'm banking on that element of surprise today, Kathy. Well, I better get up there. Jeff Graves...Dad... is not a man to be kept waiting...and I should know!" They both laughed. Clay climbed the stairway to the library. *Yes, the surprise element was going to be a little sweet revenge on Olivia Sheffield.*

Arriving at the library doors, he stood listening for Jeff Graves to introduce him to his staff. He could hear his dad's booming voice all the way out in the hall. When the superintendent spoke, everyone listened. To get a whole roomful of teachers to be quiet was, frankly, a miracle!. There was not a sound to be heard.

"We, over at Central Office, know that of all the schools in town, Brandenburg has been neglected in regards to providing leadership the past two years. I think you'd all agree that it was our most sincere wish that Tom Hood would rally and be back with us. But we know, unfortunately, that did not happen. I had a chance to spend some time with Tom near the end, and he asked specifically for us to find you the best principal in our power to find, and I think we have done just that. He also asked that you would support your new principal in the same manner that you supported him throughout his career." Several staff members dabbed at their eyes, and some of the men took out handkerchiefs, blowing their noses.

"So, we are starting a new chapter in Brandenburg history. By way of introduction, your new principal has a long list of achievements thus far in his career, including teaching college students while getting his advanced degree, and piloting a program to help teach both elementary and high school students in a more efficient manner, by partnering them. He is, by no means, a novice in administration either. Two of his years as principal were spent in a large inner-city school, so he has experience dealing with some difficult behavior issues. That is not to signify that we don't have some of those same issues right here in Brandenburg.

His final stint was for three years at an urban school in Phoenix, where the parent community, the education association, and the students lauded his work in helping to raise his students' proficiency test scores by thirty percent."

"He acts like the teachers had nothing to do with that," Sally muttered under her breath to Olivia. They were sitting at the furthest table back as they had gotten in late.

Graves continued. "Prior to his leaving, I had the opportunity to speak with his former superintendent, who let me know in no uncertain terms, that they would take him back at any time, if he wanted to return. I am happy to introduce you to your new principal...all the way from Arizona..."

Olivia had an annoying knot in her stomach. *Arizona?* "Sally, did he say Arizona?"

"Shh. I want to hear Graves."

"...Mr. Clay Mitchell."

Olivia Sheffield thought that she might throw up. She couldn't even bring herself to look up at that moment.

Sally gasped, grabbing Olivia's hand. "Oh my gosh, Olivia. It's...it's the guy you poured beer all over the other night in Ojays!"

Olivia looked up, trying to hide behind the other teachers in attendance. It was without a doubt the guy she had poured beer all over in Ojays. And the guy who'd walked (and carried) her home, and the guy who'd given her a kiss that she couldn't seem to forget, no matter how hard she tried. Standing there as large as life, and then some, he looked incredible. He was wearing charcoal gray trousers and a matching color textured sport shirt. His hair was cut impeccably. He smiled easily, glancing around the room.

The teachers began murmuring, talking amongst themselves quietly, and then he spoke.

"I'd like to thank Superintendent Graves for coming over here to introduce me, but I'm sure he has more pressing details to attend to now."

He shook Graves' hand, who then nodded and excused himself by saying, "Good luck on a new school year, ladies and gentlemen. If you have need of our help at Central Office, be sure to stop over anytime." He waved and was out the door.

Clay Mitchell spoke again "I cannot tell you all how excited I've been in anticipation of this first meeting today. It's been pretty overwhelming to read and hear about all the things that this staff has done under difficult circumstances in the past. I want to be able to assimilate myself into what appears to me to be a dedicated, hard-working group of people at Brandenburg. I hope you'll help me in making that transition, and that you'll feel comfortable in coming to me for help on any issues you may have."

Olivia heard the resident flirts over at the next table talking quietly under their breaths. Connie said, elbowing Melanie "I'd like to help him assimilate... personally." Melanie added, "My God, he is absolutely gorgeous!" Olivia rolled her eyes at them. They had this response to practically anything that wore pants, but without a doubt, Clay Mitchell, *so that was his last name,* was something to look at. He was speaking again.

"I've been anxious to meet you, although I have had the good fortune to meet two ladies here already.

SCHOOL DAYS, SCHOOL DAZE

Is it Sally...Litchfield?" he asked, glancing at a teacher roster.

Sally smiled, and said "That would be me."

Olivia wanted to go somewhere and hide, but of course he wouldn't let her off that easily, Clay spoke, "And then, although it's a little hard for me to see her, I believe that right next to Sally in the back might be our very own Olivia, aka pool shark extraordinaire, Sheffield?"

Olivia peeked around everyone blocking her, and without a word lifted her hand.

But Clay wasn't finished. "Funny thing about Brandenburg. The first time I decided to venture out into the social life of this town, I met up with the pool shark. It appears that everyone in Ojays knows that Olivia Sheffield is the amateur pool champ five years running, and they all decided that I should learn that on my own...to their great benefit, I might add. I do believe that I ended up buying a number of rounds that night. Right, Olivia? But maybe you want to finish the story?"

Oh no. Olivia stood up slowly, her face a curious ashen color, "Mr. Mitchell is right. I didn't give him a very nice welcome to town. I beat him twice...quite thoroughly, I might add!" She had gotten a bit of her spunk back. The rest of the teachers laughed, including Clay.

"Then what happened, Miss Sheffield?" Clay asked coaxingly.

"Well then...he...beat...me!"

There was a gasp that went up around the room.

"I know, right? No one has beaten me in five years! But he'd been playing left-handed before!"

"And then, Miss Sheffield?"

"And then, because I am an incredibly poor loser, as I'm sure some of you know, I bought everyone a beer. But, instead of just giving him his beer," and there was a pause, "I poured it over his head."

There was total silence for a split second, before the entire room burst into laughter.

Olivia was blushing, the color rising up her neck. "I did not, I repeat, did not know that he was our boss!"

The laughter grew louder, and someone shouted, "That's Olivia for you. Hope you won't take her temper tantrum out on us, Mr. Mitchell."

"Not a chance," Clay laughed. "I just thought I could rub her nose in it a bit more."

The teachers gave him a round of applause. Even Sally joined in.

"Thank you. Actually, I think that Miss Sheffield and I have declared a moratorium on pool playing of any sort. Would I be right, Olivia?"

"Ever and always," Olivia muttered as she sat down.

"Now that we've gotten through a few of the lighter details, I would like to suggest that we all speak privately. I think in pairs will be the quickest way to handle it. I'd like to get some perspective from each of you about our school--possible things to improve, as well as the things that have worked successfully. We'll also talk about your committee involvement. I know you want to get into your classroom, so I'll call you down to my office over the loudspeaker, two by two. I'll try not to take up much of your time. Tomorrow, we'll have a morning session of policy meetings, duty schedules, and safety and parents issues, then break for lunch. You'll have the afternoon free in your classroom. I hope you'll consider joining me in the cafeteria for lunch. Mr Henderson from Kipley's has agreed to cater a luncheon here for us all, on me. I think that socializing together as a staff is really important. You can plan on some other social events throughout the year, too. Thanks for starting my morning off so well. Particularly you, Miss Sheffield!" He glanced around the library, smiled, and left.

The cacophony in the library was deafening the minute Clay left. Connie made her way over to Olivia. "You really poured beer on his head, Olivia? You have all the luck; course I would have proceeded to lick it off if it were up to me," she giggled.

"Well, it wasn't, Con. Frankly, I'm declaring a moratorium on Clay Mitchell...period. I doubt I'll have any need for his services anyway!"

"Oh, right, Olivia. You never once needed the principal, I guess," Melanie threw in. "I'd do anything to employ his....what did you call them? Services!" Melanie and Connie walked off, chuckling. ,

Olivia fumed, but Sally grabbed her arm. "Come on, Olivia. He got his payback, and it's all over now. Let's get down to our classrooms, so we can get something accomplished. I have a ton to do!" Olivia nodded, and they both headed for their rooms.

Two hours later, Clay called for Olivia and Sally over the loudspeaker. They met in the hallway on the way to the office. Olivia was still in a tizzy over Clay's exposure of her somewhat childish behavior. *I'm surprised he didn't tell everyone about the kiss too. Oh, for crying*

out loud. Why can't I get that kiss out of my mind? She was deep in thought and hadn't said a word to Sally.

"Come on, Olivia. Shake it off and let's get this meeting done. I'm starving!"

Olivia nodded as they entered the outer office together.

"Well, what do you think, girls?" Kathy asked curiously. She had already heard about the session upstairs, and was anxious to see what kind of mood Olivia was in by now. Olivia just looked at Kathy for a minute, and then burst into laughter. "Well, actually, Kathy, he gave me my just desserts up there in front of everyone." She smiled as she reached back to smoothe her hair, turned, and ran straight into Clay. *Good Lord! He's kind of like walking into a wall--6'2" of solid...and gorgeous.* She took a step back, knowing that he had heard her comment. "But," she glanced up, smiling. "I think we're even now? Yes?" she nodded, her eyebrows raised.

"Absolutely. Why don't you and Sally have a seat in my office, and I'll join you in just a minute." Clay asked Kathy about a couple of forms he needed to submit, and then he joined the girls.

"Okay, ladies. Let's get down to a couple of details. First of all, I've heard very favorable things about the two of you and your teaching skills. I'll look forward to visiting your classrooms to see you in action. Secondly, I need to get a handle on some things that could be improved in the building. Any insights?"

Sally spoke first. "Well actually, Mr. Mitchell..."

"Call me Clay, please..."

"Actually, Clay, I think that lunch and playground duty assignment could be managed a little better.

People tend to be late fairly often, forget the day they're assigned, and some of us have to remind them, and we're not really comfortable doing that."

"That's always an issue. Any suggestions?"

"I think that we could go on a weekly rotation for each person. That way we wouldn't forget, and we'd only come up for rotation about twice in the year with the whole staff doing a duty. I could make a tentative schedule if you'd like," she offered enthusiastically.

"That would be great. Please don't hesitate to drop in if you need to talk about anything else. And by the way, would you consider being in charge of a Social Committee of sorts here at Brandenburg? You strike me as someone who enjoys a good time, and can get one organized. Actually, more than anything, I want the teachers to feel that their efforts are being recognized. Choose a few people you think would be of help to you on the committee. I consider this one of the most important committees in school, particularly because it's all about teacher morale. The committee can brainstorm about some things they'd like to do, and if I can help make it happen, I will. What do you say?"

"Sure. It sounds like fun!"

"Well, it is fun, but it's a lot of work as well. I think you know that teachers can be very opinionated!"

Clay was talking entirely to Sally, never even glancing in Olivia's direction. *Why doesn't he think I'd be good for the Social Committee? Not once has he even acknowledged my existence.* She looked at his profile, the thick, blonde hair, the intensity of the eyes. *He certainly could make a woman...no, a person feel as though they were the only one in the room. He is so incredibly...*

"Yes, Miss Sheffield? Did you want to say something?" He was staring directly at her, the blue eyes boring into hers. Olivia jumped about a foot out of her chair.

"No, I'm fine, Mr. Mitchell," she said as she examined the carpet.

Returning to the previous conversation, Clay questioned Sally. "By the way, I hope I'm not overstepping, but can I ask if you and Dave Garrett are an item?"

"Actually, you could say that." Looking at Olivia sheepishly, she said, "He asked me to marry him the other night. In fact, it was the night we met you at Ojays."

Olivia screamed and leapt out of her chair. "Sally, you awful girl! How could you not tell me?"

Clay watched smiling, as the girls jumped up and down like teenagers. *Awfully shapely teenagers.*

"Well, I wanted to tell you on Saturday, but we went looking for rings, and by the time we were done, you'd already left for your date with Derek. By the way, Mrs. Herbert told me what you wore and," she whispered, "when you got home. Truly, Olivia, that woman is so nosy she's a menace."

So there's someone named Derek in the picture. I wonder what time she did get home? Clay found himself clenching his jaw, and made a mental note to stop worrying so much about Olivia Sheffield's curfew.

"Oh, Sally, honey. I'm so happy for you. Dave doesn't deserve you, you know!" Olivia had risen and was hugging her friend, and both of the women had clearly forgotten for a minute that Clay was even in the room.

All the better for him to watch her. The honey hair that Clay so longed to touch again bunched up when

Sally wrapped her arms round Olivia's neck and returned her hug. They giggled, laughed, hugged, cried, and then giggled again. Her back was to Clay, but the camel-colored slacks she wore clung very nicely to her cute little rear. Clay caught himself drifting again and snapped out of it. He cleared his throat. "Ladies...I realize that this is a wonderful moment for you both, but I need to finish our discussion, and get onto some of the other teachers. Sally, why don't you head on out and start sharing the news with Kathy and the rest of the staff. I just need to speak with Olivia for a moment more."

"Yes, Sal, Get on out there and tell Kathy, or I'll tell her myself!"

"Alright." Sally stood, shook Clay's hand, and left his office quickly.

Clay walked around the desk to close the door to his office. Olivia sat, facing his desk totally quiet, feeling the electricity in the room. "And now, Miss Sheffield," Clay began. "I think that we need to talk about a few things."

She didn't look up, but kept her hands in her lap and waited, as the color rose up her neck.

"Would you agree that we've declared a truce of sorts, Olivia?"

She nodded.

"That's fine." *This is harder than I thought..* "Uh..." Clay stood with his back to her for a moment, and then turned around and brushed his hands through his hair. It seemed to be a nervous habit when he was stalling for time. Olivia looked up at him anticipating some kind of awkward conversation. "Well, there's no other way to say it, except to say it. That kiss. It was completely unplanned on my part...and I...wanted you to know that at that point, I had no idea you were one of my teachers. Nevertheless, it does put us in a rather curious...predicament, and I'm sure you'll agree with me when I say that that kiss..."

Olivia had turned beet red, but she was able to bluster out the words, "...that that kiss was...the result of too much drinking...and after all, you didn't know who I was, and...and...well, it was hardly...memorable!" *LIAR!* "I mean...that is...I'm sure that if you'd known who I was..."

"That goes without saying...that you're right, the kiss...meant very little...nothing, in fact!" *RIGHT, YOU JACKASS!* "Still and all, I don't think that it would be professional of either of us to...to..."

"...to...to let something like that happen again...in fact, it would be very silly...and totally unprofessional, and well...who needs problems in the workplace, I always say..."

Clay looked relieved. "Right you are. I couldn't agree with you more. Forgotten?" He held out his hand to her.

"Forgotten!" Olivia took his hand, rising. The spark was there the minute they touched. There was no denying this man did something to her.

The chemistry is powerful, and hard to ignore. IGNORE IT, CLAY. IGNORE IT!

They sat down again, slowly. "Well, good, I'm glad we got that cleared up." The blue eyes drilled into the brown ones, and for a second no one spoke. Finally Clay continued. "Would you be willing to sit on the Superintendent's Advisory Committee? Kathy thought that you would be a great representative for

Brandenburg and fight for our school when necessary. It's a meeting a month, and of course serving in whatever capacity Dr. Graves sees fit to assign you. There's been no one willing to do it from here for three years, and I think that it's important to have our school represented."

Olivia was pleased. He was willing to listen to other people's advice and input, and had asked her to serve on a committee where she felt that she could have a positive impact. "Yes, I'd like that very much, Mr. Mitchell. Thank you."

"Call me Clay, Livy. Is it alright if I call you that? It seems to fit so well?"

"That would be fine...Clay," she said quietly. Olivia stood, turned, and walked out the door. She shut it quietly behind her, and leaned against the door frame.

Kathy Tiffin, school secretary extraordinaire, looked up. Leaning against Clay Mitchell's closed office door stood Olivia Sheffield, eyes shut, whole body shaking. Kathy quickly looked down and continued typing. *It looks as though the fireworks have already started.* She smiled as she worked.

6

By the end of August, Brandenburg Elementary was up and running and pretty much under control. Clay made it a policy that as long as his office door was open, any staff member could just pop in. Sometimes they just peeked in to say "Hi." Other times they came with small problems that took a word or two of question or response. Only a few big problems had surfaced in the early weeks. The staff, the parents, and the students seemed pleased to have a new leader who was ready for anything and accessible to them all.

One of Clay's first priorities had been to meet with Jack Kelley, widowed father of Travis, a fifth grader, and Gus, a second grader. Jack seemed relieved to have someone to talk to about his own grieving process as well as that of his sons. He welcomed Clay's suggestion of meeting with the boys regularly to talk about their loss and to help them cope.

Olivia had received a note in her school mailbox, asking her to come to a meeting two days later regarding the Kelley kids. Gus was in Olivia's class, and the elder son was in Tom Moore's. The note indicated that the meeting would last about forty-five minutes and that there would be a Grief Counselor in attendance.

On the morning of the meeting, Olivia took great care in getting ready for school. *I think I need to dress up for a change. I've been entirely too casual lately.* When she left for school that morning she was satisfied with the results of her attention. She had donned a striking red dress adorned with gold buttons down the center. She also wore her trademark--shoes. Olivia loved shoes and she had scads of them. Even the youngest of her students loved to see the shoes that she wore to school each day. She'd chosen a pair of red kitten heels with gold trim. Her hair was pulled up into a French twist, and she'd applied her make-up more carefully than usual. Glancing in the mirror, she was satisfied with the results. *After all, I am meeting with a professional counselor, and Mr. Kelley, and...oh, for crying out loud. Admit it. You're dressing for Clay Mitchell, first and foremost.* She shook her head at the idea and left for work.

Ironically, the entire day passed without seeing Clay. He was out of the building all morning, and in the afternoon she had loads of school work to finish. Many of her colleagues had commented throughout the day about how nice she looked. Even her second graders had seemed appreciative. *There, just what I thought. It pays to get really dressed up now and then.*

The children had gone for the day, her room was picked up and ready for the custodians to clean. She gathered up some paperwork to take home, and headed down the hallway toward the office. *Oh my God. Why is my heart pounding so hard? I have absolutely no reason to feel nervous. I know how to handle myself in meetings, and I'm anxious to meet the counselor, and...I can't seem to keep my mind on anything today! Well, maybe one thing. It is absolutely ludicrous that a little meeting with my principal should have this effect on me.*

She walked into the office and headed straight for the conference room.The door was slightly ajar, so she knocked before entering. Everyone was there, but there was really only one face she saw. Clay stood from across the conference table and said, "Livy, come on in!" She let her gaze drift in his direction. *Wow!* Blue, gray eyes warmly welcomed her. The white of his dress shirt made his tan look darker. He had his sleeves rolled up to his elbows, and the tie he'd chosen had flecks of gray, blue, and green, making his eyes seem even brighter.

Clay hadn't really seen Olivia for several days, and he admitted that he hadn't been happy about that. But she'd walked in and smiled at him, and his heart had thumped in his chest. *God, she is dangerous. Look how that dress clings to those curves. It's a little on the short side. Short is good!* He had noticed oftentimes, that when Olivia Sheffield walked into a room, most of the eyes were on her. *And she doesn't notice it!* Nothing was different today.

"Miss Sheffield," Clay began, "I'd like you to meet Harry Jacobs, a grief counselor from Barton. He's been working regularly with the Kelley boys and Jack here. Mr. Jacobs, Miss Sheffield."

Harry Jacobs had risen from his seat, and taken Olivia's hand.

Apparently, he's a little dazzled, because he's having trouble letting it go ."Ahem...and of course, you know Jack Kelley."

Olivia finally pulled her hand from Jacobs' grasp and shook hands with Jack Kelley.

"Hello, Mr, Kelley. It's so good to see you again," she said quietly and sincerely. She noticed that Tom Moore was in attendance as well, and said "Hi, Tom."

"Let's get started, please," Clay said. "I felt the need for us all to be here together so that we could strategize on ways that will help the boys during the school year. Since both of you are the boys' teachers, Mr. Jacobs thought, as did I, that you would be important cogs in their healing process. I'd like to think that we can all keep each other informed of the various stages the boys will be going through this difficult first year. Mr. Jacobs, why don't you help by giving us some insights into what to expect from the boys in the next few months."

Harry Jacobs began to talk about Travis and Gus, as well as their father, and the tragedy that had changed their lives forever. Everyone in the room listened intently as Jacobs explained the phases and faces of grief and Jack Kelley asked a number of questions that had arisen in his interactions with his sons during this early period. They also discussed ways to help the boys navigate through those phases.

Clay rose, leaving the conference table area, to step away, knowing full well what would happen next. The dreaded cold knot in his stomach appeared, followed almost immediately with the uncontrollable shivers of fear, and the stinging of tears, when he was transported back to that moment when he and his brother had learned of their parents' deaths, He remembered how his brother and he had wailed and screamed at the policeman who'd come to break the news. He could picture his older brother punching the officer over and over again, until suddenly Jeff Graves had been there, pulling Eric off the policeman and taking him over to sit under a nearby tree. Caroline had been there too, and had pulled ten-year old Clay into a grasp that wouldn't let him escape. Together, the four of them in shock and mourning, held council as the neighbors looked on with sadness.

Olivia had watched as Clay left the table. Remembering what he'd told her about the loss of his own parents, she realized that he was in distress, and would not be able to initiate the end of the conversation. So **she** did. "Excuse me, Mr. Jacobs. I'm so sorry, but I simply cannot hear anymore of this right now. It is so emotionally draining. Would it be possible for us to continue this conversation via email?"

She glanced at Tom, and he nodded in agreement, adding, "I think I can speak for our staff, Mr. Jacobs. We will be supportive of your suggestions about the Kelley boys, but I think email may be the best way to handle it."

"Certainly. I'm sorry. I tend to ramble at times. I apologize for going on so long. I'm okay with email, but I'm always available to meet with you on an individual basis at any time, Miss Sheffield...er...and Mr. Moore."

That comment seemed to snap Clay out of his melancholy. "Yes, thank you, we'll keep that in mind, Mr. Jacobs." Clay was standing directly in front of Jacobs, shaking his hand, directing him toward the door.

Harry Jacobs glanced back over his shoulder

saying, "Please don't hesitate to call me anytime, Miss Sheffield...ahem...and the rest of you, of course...if you have additional questions about the boys' progress."

Clay was only slightly miffed with the poor guy. After all, it's tough to stop the effects of a steam roller. And right now, Olivia Sheffield was a steam roller and she didn't even know it. *I actually pity the poor slob... hell, not just pity him, empathize with him. She's quite a package.* "Goodbye, Mr Jacobs."

Next, Clay turned toward Jack Kelley. "Thanks for coming in, Jack. I know how difficult it is for you right now. We'll keep you up to date regarding the boys, and I know you'll do the same. It'll get easier...with time." He squeezed Jack's shoulder. The grieving man nodded silently and left the room.

Looking at Tom Moore, Clay asked, "How is Travis doing lately, Tom?"

"Pretty well, Clay. Better than could be expected, actually. He's got a lot of buddies, and when he starts to mope around, they're right on him, keeping him busy."

"He'll need to be alone eventually, but how great to know those kids are taking an interest in helping him get through this tough time. I don't want him to think that his younger brother can't see him cry, though. I know that my brother, Eric, had a difficult time trying to help me and didn't spend time healing himself. Just watch him and let me know if you need my input, okay?"

"Sure, Clay, and thanks for your support." Tom left.

Now he was alone with her, as he'd intended. "Before the opportunity passes me by, let me just say, that red becomes you. You look...incredible."

"Thank you," she said, the color rising on her neck.

"And, may I add, I think that' it's a safe bet that you'll be hearing from Harry Jacobs in the very near future."

Looking puzzled, Olivia asked, "Why would you say that?"

Shaking his head, Clay chuckled. "Livy, it never ceases to amaze me how totally oblivious you seem to be about the effect you have on most of the male population!'""

She was totally embarrassed now

"At any rate," he added quietly, the hand brushing through the thick blonde hair, "I want to thank you for getting him to stop talking."

"I just couldn't listen anymore. And I knew Mr. Kelley was...having a hard time as well. And you...well, I needed to clear my head," her voice trailed off.

His eyes met hers and she stopped talking. "For a feisty little pain in the rear, you've got a big heart, Olivia. Guard it carefully." The piercing, blue-gray eyes locked with hers, and drifted downward slowly towards her lips. *Oh, man, what I wouldn't give to...*

She held his gaze for a moment. It was all she could stand. She was getting warm, very warm in the room... in this space. She stood quickly to excuse herself. "You know, Gus is not at all like Travis. He's quieter, more introverted. He's a loner of sorts and will need more time, attention, and understanding. Thanks for re-membering about the Kelley boys."

"I...wasn't remembering for them...I was remem-bering for myself. Maybe I've still got some baggage to deal with...even after all this time."

"Maybe you have, Clay, but I'm sure that you'll find your answers here. Brandenburg's your home now. Let

SCHOOL DAYS, SCHOOL DAZE

it embrace you." She gently squeezed his hand, as she left the office.

Clay Mitchell wanted nothing more at that moment than to take Olivia Sheffield into his arms, and let her comfort him with those soft hands, those luscious lips, and that golden hair. Instead, he sat unmoving, and let her leave. *She said I was home. Maybe I am.*

7

Derek Donaldson was not at all pleased with the fact that he hadn't seen Olivia in almost a month. In fairness to her, he had been out of state for two full weeks; but she'd been so busy with the start of the school year, curriculum nights, parent meetings, lesson planning and on and on, she'd simply not been able to get away. He needed to find a way to change all that.

He'd been mulling over a lot of ideas, and finally felt that he'd hit on the right one. Putting a call into Susie Sheffield was step one. "Hey, Susie. It's Derek...Yes, I got in two days ago...It was a pretty fruitful meeting, but I can tell you more about that tomorrow at work. Are you possibly available for a conference later today here at the gallery?" When Susie responded in the affirmative, Derek continued. "Okay, why don't we say three o'clock this afternoon...alright, great! See you then!"

"If I can just put my plan into action, I'll be spending a lot more time here in Townsend. That way I'll only be three hours away from Brandenburg, and I can see Olivia more regularly," he stated enthusiastically as he crossed the room to his desk. He pulled out his records of all three galleries, and began working on the final details of the proposal that he was going to make to Susie Sheffield.

The Gallery was closed on Mondays, so the day passed very quietly. At lunch, he went out to grab a sandwich, then returned to work. When the knock came at his office door, he was actually surprised that it was already three. He got up, and went to the door, opening it with a smile on his well-rested face. "Hey Susie. Jim--you're here too? Come on in and sit down," he said, motioning to two seats at a small conference table in the tastefully decorated office.

"Sorry I didn't call ahead, Derek. But Jim and I were doing some errands, so I brought him along. We both have our own vehicles, so if you'd rather just speak to me, he can leave!"

She nudged her husband jokingly in the side.

"No...it's perfect that you're both here."

"I'm finding my naturally curious nature entirely stimulated," laughed Jim Sheffield. He was an affable young man, with dark hair and a goatee. He had a wealth of friends, a great sense of humor, and was crazy in love with his wife. "So...what's the buzz?"

Derek smiled and leaned back in his chair. "Okay, here goes. I would like to spend more time running the Townsend Gallery." He paused a moment for effect. "I would like to offer the two of you the job of Gallery Managers in Boston and New York. Now before you say anything, let me tell you the whole proposal. I have a large apartment in both cities, located within walking distance of each gallery. You are welcome to use those so that you don't have to sell your place here in Townsend for the time being. I know that you'll find them quite adequate for your needs. Secondly, it would be a sizable financial gain for you both, allowing you to do some serious saving. Thirdly, you'd be working in two of the most exciting cities in the world, and you'd be exposed to numerous new artists. I could concentrate on building up the Townsend Gallery...as well as being around the area more often. I find myself a little weary of the rat race. Well...what do you say?"

Susie and Jim sat absolutely dumbfounded, with their mouths agape. Suddenly, Susie jumped out of her seat and started screaming. "Oh, my God! Are you serious, Derek? I mean, truly serious? I mean do you have a crystal ball, or something?"

Derek looked clearly puzzled.

Jim added. "Just yesterday, Susie and I had considered coming to talk to you about a transfer of sorts. We'd like to try a big city for a change. But now you're offering us the management of two established galleries in two major cities? Do you really think we can pull it off?"

"I won't lie to you. It'll be a big job--but I have a lot of confidence in your ability to do it, and do it well. I'd want you to go over and see the places and speak to the other employees before you take the job; Susie already has working relationships with several of the curators in New York, and has spoken with a couple from Boston. Both of you bring different areas of expertise to the field, and frankly, I think this is the perfect job for you at this time in your lives. Susie has shared with me that you're not ready to start a family just yet, so I believe that this would be the perfect opportunity to place yourselves in a position to write your own tickets down the road." Derek sat quietly, watching their faces. The couple remained dumbstruck and silent. Finally Jim asked the obvious question. "What in God's name would Derek Donaldson do in Townsend, Indiana? You'll probably be ready to swing from the rafters after a week managing this small gallery. All the work will be done, and then what will you do?"

"Well, I could always take a drive over to... Brandenburg...or somewhere like that."

Susie squealed with delight. "Aha! I told you, Jim. Once Derek met your sister he'd be spending more time around town. You owe me twenty dollars!"

Derek laughed out loud. "You made a wager on your own sister?"

"Actually, Derek, it was more of a wager on you. With very positive rewards, I might add!" He winked at his wife. She hit him playfully on the arm. "So you're thinking that maybe my baby sister might be a new interest for you? Better look out, buddy. She can be a real handful!"

Derek grinned. "Actually, I've come to look at Olivia Sheffield as sort of a piece of art!"

The young couple looked at him questioningly.

"I might just do anything to acquire her!"

The three of them burst into laughter. The afternoon was spent answering questions, doing some long-term planning, and generally looking over the gallery lay-outs and financials. By the end of the afternoon though, the room was fairly bubbling with excitement. Friendships had become even deeper and Jim and Susie knew without speaking, that they'd take the job in a heartbeat.

"How about dinner and drinks to seal the deal, over Labor Day weekend?" Derek offered.

"That would be fantastic," Jim grinned. "Why don't I call Olivia, and give her the guilt trip about not seeing her big brother, and let her meet us here in Townsend next weekend?"

"I'll do you one better, Jim. Let's all head to New York for the weekend. You and Susie can take a plane to Boston, look over the operation there, and meet Olivia and me in New York City. We'll do some museums, help you get your bearings in the city, see a show, and then Olivia and I can come back to the calm reality of small-town life, while you and Susie stay a few days more and check out the New York operation. When you come back, I'll expect a firm answer."

Susie Sheffield was beyond excited. She was screaming. "A trip to Boston and then New York? Oh my gosh, Derek. You're not toying with us, are you? You really think we can do it?"

"Without a doubt. Do you think I'd leave my livelihood in the hands of inept managers? I've only just found something else that I'd prefer to spend my energies on, that's all. It just so happens that she has golden hair and the eyes of an angel."

"Her temperament isn't much like an angel, Derek. She doesn't like anyone to beat her...she's stubborn, and she'll drive you stark-raving crazy with all her activities and involvements at school."

"Frankly, Jim, stark-raving crazy already applies to me in regards to your sister. I'm crazy about her!"

Susie Sheffield looked smugly at her husband, held out her palm, and said, "Pay up, you big lug!"

8

Olivia had been more than a little surprised to hear from her brother, inviting her for a weekend in New York City over Labor Day. "Oh, Jim, I've only been in school for a few days, and I have so much to do already."

Jim, however, proceeded to shame her into coming. "Come on, sis. Derek's invited us all; Susie and I have great news and we want you to hear it! And anyway, I thought that we already established that I'm your favorite brother and we haven't seen you for two months."

She hesitated. *He's absolutely right. I just need to go and stop being such a stick-in the mud.*

"Olivia? We have rooms at the Waldorf!"

"The Waldorf?" she squealed. "The Waldorf's way out of your league, Jimmy. What's going on?"

"You'll find out when we see you next weekend. Say 'yes'"!

"Oh, of course, I'll come. Thanks for the invite...or thank Derek. I'll get a cab..."

He interrupted her. "No, a limo will pick you up at

home. I'll text you with the details as we get closer. See you next weekend!" and he hung up.

Caroline Graves had been cooking and cleaning all day in preparation for the evening visit with her "son". The aroma wafting through the kitchen made Jeff's stomach growl, as he walked in the door from work.

"Hey, darlin'. It smells great in here," he said as he began to lift lids off pots and reached his finger in to taste a sample of Boeuf Bourguignon.

"Oh, no you don't," Caroline said, smacking his hand. "Put that lid on right now; you're messing up the simmer!"

Jeff grumbled. "Why is it that the only time I get my favorite meal is when Clay's in town? It's been a year and a half since the last batch." He came up behind his petite, still attractive wife, giving her a squeeze and a kiss on the cheek.

"Oh, Jeff--you know how much time it takes for me to make this while I'm working. It's just for special occasions. And," she turned around and kissed him, "thanks for making it a special occasion, and getting Clay closer to our neck of the woods. I'm so excited to see him! The only thing that could be better would be if Eric, Phyllis, and Chelsea were nearby too."

"Now, honey, you know that they can't come here. Eric's started a great job, and they're really settling in up there in Wisconsin. We can't go up for Labor Day, but I promise we'll get up to see them for a long week-end later in the fall. And, anyway, Clay can fill us in after his visit with them."

"Oh, I know, I know." There was a pause, before Caroline gasped. "Oh, dear Lord. Why didn't you tell me what time it was? Clay will be here in an hour and I have to make myself presentable!" She pulled off her apron and started towards the stairway.

Jeff grabbed her as she started to walk by. "I think you look pretty fine right now, honey," he murmured, nuzzling her neck.

"Jeffrey Graves--now don't you go and get me off-track!"

He liked that. He knew if he put his mind to it, he still COULD get his wife of thirty-five years off-track, as she liked to put it. Conceding, he said, "Okay, I'll just wait for tonight!" and he winked at her.

"Oh, Jeff, you really are as ornery as ever," and she laughed as she headed upstairs.

Jeff reached for the lid on the simmering pot.

Without even turning back, Caroline shouted down the stairs. "If you want any treats later tonight, keep your hands off the Boeuf. If you're hungry, get yourself a cracker!"

A short while later, the doorbell rang at the Graves' home. Caroline was there instantly. She swung the door open quickly, and standing on her front step was her youngest, adopted son. "Oh, Clay, honey. I just couldn't wait to see you!" She grabbed him in a big hug, even though she had to stretch up high on her tiptoes to do it.

"Hey, Mama Caro. You're looking lovely tonight, and is that what I think I'm smelling? You made my favorite dish, didn't you?" He grabbed her, lifting her off her feet in a bear hug.

"Only the best for my boy..." They walked into the living room where Jeff was waiting too.

"Hey, Dad, How was the first week?"

"I'll ask that back to you, son?" reaching to shake Clay's hand. "What do you think of your new school?"

"I think it's going to be great, and so far my staff is really working hard to help me assimilate. You've got some really fine teachers in that building, and a great support staff. Kathy Tiffin is a treasure; she's really helping me to know the ins and outs of the school and the personalities, as well. They really did an amazing job holding that place together over those years that Mr. Hood was so ill."

"Yes, they did, Clay. We wanted to hire someone sooner, but they wouldn't hear of it. They wanted to see if Tom would rally, but unfortunately that wasn't the case. Anyway, son, you are going to be a real asset to that building this year. I have high hopes that all the creativity over there will finally have a chance to be unleashed. If you need to touch base at any time, don't hesitate to call. In two weeks, I'm having my first Building Advisory Meeting for all the teachers. Who'd you say was your rep?"

"Her name is Olivia Sheffield." *Little white shorts, rosy lips, honey hair...*

"Oh, I know Miss Sheffield. I've been aware of her for some time now."

My father is aware of Livy? Looking puzzled, Clay said, "Huh?"

"She came over to talk to me as a school rep when we tried to replace Tom. She had gotten the staff together to come up with all the reasons why we shouldn't hire anyone new yet, and they chose her to present those reasons to me. She is incredibly well-spoken, tactful, and meets you head-on with her ideas. I really like her, and clearly the staff respects her. I think she'll be a wonderful addition to the Building Advisory."

"Alright, you two. No more shop talk the rest of the evening, and I mean it!" Caroline had entered the room, carrying drinks. "I fixed you each a scotch and soda. Update us on things down in Brandenburg, and what you think of the town, and then it'll be time for dinner."

The three talked comfortably, sipping on their drinks, Caroline periodically excusing herself to finish the dinner preparations. Finally, they sat down to a sumptuous feast that clearly Caroline had put her heart and soul into making. "Dinner is fabulous, Mom. I really appreciate all the time you took getting it ready for my homecoming. Thank you."

"Dad and I are just so happy to have you back close, Clay, and we do expect frequent visits, you know." She smiled warmly, a look so filled with love that he had to turn away. *I'll never forget that look.* A lump formed in his throat, as it always did when he recalled these two people, his parents' best friends, taking in his brother and him, directly after the car accident. *There are no words strong enough to represent what these two have done for me and Eric. I only hope that one day I can be half the parents that they've been.*

Jeff watched the interplay between his youngest boy and the love of his life. He was so proud of his boys, and prouder still of the beautiful woman he had married so many years earlier. She had been a lioness in the protection of those boys, and a true nurturer. The boys had grown and thrived and they'd all become family in the face of tremendous tragedy.

When Thomas Hood had passed away, it had provided Jeff a perfect opportunity to extend an offer to Clay to come back to the Midwest to work. Jeff had recognized from things that Clay had told him, that he was simply not feeling a connection in Arizona, and simply missed his family. It worked like that with Jeff too. "Our bonds run deep, boy," he thought. "Thank goodness for that! Family really does matter!" Jeff brought himself out of his own reverie when Caroline brought up the "dreaded" subject. Women!

"Now, Clay," Caroline pleaded. "Just think about it. I've met the loveliest young woman, and she's about your age."

Clay and Jeff both rolled their eyes heavenward.

"I'm not kidding, you two. Jeff, you've already met her."

"I have? When?"

"At that fundraiser we attended three weeks ago. She's that gorgeous, leggy brunette you commented on. Her name's Nicole Marshall."

"Ahh. You're right, hon. I did notice her. She's really quite lovely, Clay...not the normal that your Mom tries to fix you up...Owww..." he grimaced as Caroline kicked him under the table.

Caroline continued. "Anyway, I thought that we might drag you along to the Keller's dinner party in two weeks. It's a must for all the employees, and I happen to know that Nicole does not have an escort at this time. She's a pediatrician and very busy. Do it for me, Clay. I really do think you'll like her."

Clay smiled. "Alright, Mom. How can I turn down a woman who cooks me my favorite meal and waits on me hand and foot?"

She kissed him on the cheek. "Don't get too used to it, dear. I have to listen to your father complaining then. Two weeks from Saturday at the Keller's. Now don't forget. I'll get back to you with the final details. Oh, and when you're visiting your brother next weekend, remind him that the phone works both ways...and tell him I love him," she smiled sheepishly. "I'm going to get going on the kitchen clean-up now."

"No, Mom. Not tonight. Let me do it for you."

"Absolutely not. Not your first dinner back. You can clean up the next time. Your Dad can help me now. You need to head back to Brandenburg. It's getting late, and you still have an hour's drive."

"Okay, this time only, Mom. Thanks so much for a great evening. Talk to you at work tomorrow, Dad. I love you both."

They walked him to the door, and waved as he left. Jeff held Caroline in front of him and she sighed. "Oh, Jeff, wasn't that wonderful? I'm so glad you brought him home."

"How glad?" he leaned down and whispered in her ear.

"Oh, now honey, we've got to clean up that kitchen. It'll be a mess to do tomorrow."

"I'll get up early to do it. You promised!"

"Oh, for heaven's sake, Jeff..."

"I mean it, Caroline. You promised and I'm not going to let you off..."

She pulled his hand. "Last one to the bedroom does the whole kitchen!" She ran up the stairs, laughing all the way.

9

The limo had arrived early Saturday morning to take Olivia to the airport. She'd tossed together an overnight bag with some mix and match ensembles, verging a little on the dressy side. *Why in the world didn't I think to ask Jimmy what we were doing this weekend?*

The limo driver got out of the car, and opened the door for her. "Hello, Miss Sheffield. I'm Rodney." He helped her into the plush back seat. "Can I offer you a drink? Or a coffee?"

"Coffee will be fine, please, Rodney."

Rodney poured a cup of coffee, handing it to her and pointing out how the tray table opened so she wouldn't have to balance. "There are some bagels and pastries there if you'd like, as well." Soon he pulled away and headed directly for the airport. He passed a ticket back to Olivia as he drove. "Here's your ticket, ma'am. There will be a driver to meet you at LaGuardia, as well. He knows where to take you."

Olivia gasped. "This ticket is first-class!"

"Absolutely, ma'am. Only the best for Mr. Donaldson."

The ride was brief, and companionable. Olivia sipped the delicious coffee, and enjoyed a glazed cinnamon pastry as she looked out the window. Before she knew it, they'd arrived at the airport.

"Here we are, Miss Sheffield." He was pulling out her overnight bag, and opening her door. "Head to Gate B, and you'll see the signs."

"Thanks again, Rodney." She handed him a twenty-dollar bill.

He returned it, saying "That's not necessary, Miss Sheffield. Have a great weekend."

She giggled, as she got out of the car. "Thank you." She headed into the terminal, but waved at him over her shoulder.

"Way to go, Mr. Donaldson. Only the best!"

Olivia had dozed off almost directly after take off, and awoke with a start as the plane began its descent. *Wow, I really needed that. Nothing like going full steam ahead this past two weeks. Now I think I can tackle the weekend, whatever it holds in store.* Arriving at LaGuardia, Olivia took her bag and met another limo driver, holding a sign with her name. He took her directly to the beautifully ornate Waldorf Astoria.

"Oh, my gosh. This is incredible. Thanks so much for the ride...Tony." She smiled and shook his hand, offering a tip.

He, too, turned it down. "It's all covered, ma'am. Have a great time!"

Olivia entered the beautiful lobby, working her way to check-in. *This place is amazing. What opulence--what wonderful, wretched excess. Enjoy it while it lasts, girl! This is probably the only time you'll ever be here!*

She was startled out of her reverie when she heard her name.

"Olivia! I'm so glad I caught you!" Suddenly, Derek was there, reaching her, wrapping her in an intimate hug.

"Oh, Derek. I have absolutely no words...this is unbelievable!"

"Wait until you see your room! It'll definitely be a highlight of your weekend!"

"C'mon, now, Derek. What is this all about?"

"Can't tell until this evening. Jim and Susie swore me to secrecy! But I promise it'll be a night to remember! I've got to go, now, though.

"But...but..."

"So...here are your instructions! Jim and Susie have the room next to you. All of you will be leaving here about 7:45 in my limo. You met my driver, Tony, already."

She nodded.

"He'll pick you up. Dress up for tonight. We're doing 8:00 dinner and the late show at the Oak Room! Until then, enjoy your room--you could visit the spa--or just put your feet up and relax. See you in a few hours!" And Derek was out the door.

It was like a whirlwind had just spun Olivia around and left. *But what an awesome whirlwind! Onward, Olivia Sheffield. Maybe a massage at the spa is on your afternoon agenda!*

That evening when Jimmy knocked on Olivia's hotel room door, she exited looking like a million dollars. "Wow, sis. You look fabulous...and rested!" He gave her a hug, and she greeted him and Susie.

"Turn around, honey. That dress has your name on it completely! I absolutely love it!" Susie exclaimed, twirling Olivia around.

"Thank you, Suze." Olivia had pulled together a black knee-length cocktail dress with crimped short sleeves. The dress clung closely to her trim, petite figure, and the skirt flowed freely. It was cut down low in the back, showing off her smooth, slightly tanned skin. She'd accessorized it with black dress shoes, laced at the ankles, giving her extra height, and a pair of faux diamond drop earrings and matching bracelet. It's very simplicity screamed class.

"I am with two gorgeous chicks. Come on--the limo is waiting!"

The three exited, talking together with excitement as they entered the limo, greeted Tony, and headed for the Oak Room. Once they arrived, they entered in awe. The dark wood and decor of the establishment spoke of times gone by, and they loved seeing all the pictures on the walls of so many famous entertainers. They were shown to their table where Derek was waiting. Derek greeted them warmly, pulling out the chair next to his for Olivia, lightly kissing her on the cheek. Jim and Susie took their seats as well.

"Okay, you three. I can't stand it anymore!" Olivia begged. "Time to come clean...what is going on? I'm dying to know what we're celebrating!"

At that moment her three tablemates all began to talk at once, and she could barely make heads or tails out of what anyone was saying. Finally, Derek held up his hand to get everyone's attention. I believe that I'll take charge of this conversation," he said laughingly.

He proceeded to explain to Olivia his plan to have Jimmy and Susie run the Boston and New York galleries. This was to be sort of a trial experience to expose them to both venues, the apartments, the travel, and the traffic. "They've already been to Boston, and just flew in to New York today."

Olivia had watched the delighted faces of her brother and sister-in-law, as Derek joyfully described his plan. Everything that she saw and heard made her smile, as well. "Derek, this is simply unbelievable. Are you actually thinking my big oaf of a brother can run two art galleries?" She swatted Jimmy affectionately.

"I'm certain he can with Susie being the mastermind behind him," Derek teased just as readily.

"Okay, you guys. Just keep talking like I'm not even at the table," teased Jimmy. "This is really helping my already bruised psyche. I know I have a genius for a wife. After all. I mean she married me, didn't she?"

"In all due seriousness, you two, I'm positively thrilled for you both!" Olivia stood up and gave her brother a kiss, and leaned across to give Susie a congratulatory hug and kiss as well.

"Mind you, they haven't given me a definitive answer yet, but I'm expecting one upon their return to Townsend," Derek offered.

"Speaking of that, Derek, whatever are you planning to do if your two largest galleries are being looked after by other people?" questioned Olivia.

Susie, Jimmy, and Derek all smiled knowingly. Derek cleared his throat and said, "Well, I thought I might focus on really getting the Townsend gallery up and running as well as looking for some promising Midwest artists to represent. I have a lead on a couple mixed media specialists and I want to see them in action. Then there would be the added benefit of being much closer to Brandenburg, where I might be interested in periodically seeing a certain overworked school teacher!" He gave Olivia a little wink.

Olivia blushed, "Oh my...I'm speechless."

"Jeez, Derek. That's <u>never</u> happened," joked Jimmy.

Susie laughed and kicked him under the table,

Their cocktails arrived and dinner was ordered. It included oysters on the half shell, calamari and shrimp for appetizers, steak and lobster with asparagus and mushroom in truffle oil, and flaming Bananas Foster over ice cream for dessert. The food was beyond delectable, and soon everyone had filled themselves completely. "Oh, my word," Susie announced. "I think if I have another bite, I am going to explode!" They all agreed. They sat companionably for a short time, and then the lounge show began and it was top-rate. At last, it was time to end the evening; Derek called for the limo and escorted them out to meet it.

"Are you staying in your apartment, Derek?" Olivia asked curiously.

"Yes, it's just around the corner...would you like to check it out?"

Olivia choked and sputtered.

"It's alright, Olivia. I'm just baiting you...a little!" He grabbed her hands and pulled her towards him. "I just want you to understand that I'm really interested in acquiring much more than artwork when I come to Townsend. I hope you'll let me see you on a more regular basis." He leaned in and lightly brushed his mouth over hers, kissing her sweetly.

Olivia allowed the kiss, lingering in it. "Oh, Derek,

you truly are a wonderful man. Of course we'll see each other more often. Thank you for all you've done for my brother and Susie. I know they're going to be just fine running your galleries. And thank you for this truly marvelous evening. Will we see you tomorrow?"

"Of course. I have another full day planned if you're game; shopping, a carriage ride around Central Park, a fabulous meal, and a Broadway show. How's that?"

"Oh...I don't know," Olivia said with hesitation. She held up her arm. "Go ahead...twist my arm!" She laughed, as she moved in for another light kiss.

Derek sighed, and put her away. "Enough, Olivia, give a guy a break...no more kisses unless you want to see my apartment!" His eyes sparkled with just a glint of a question.

"Come on, you two," shouted Jimmy from the car.

Derek opened the door for Olivia, helping her into the limo with Jimmy and Susie. "See you all tomorrow at ten sharp. Right, Tony?"

The driver said, "Sure, boss. Right on time. 'Night, boss."

Derek Donaldson smiled as he watched his future drive off.

Labor Day weekend had arrived for Clay, and he was ready for a break. The opening of the school year had gone smoothly, and he had already tackled a couple of big issues that had come his way. He had made time to get into some of the classrooms and was working hard at becoming familiar with his students and their families. Overall, he liked his new staff, and had made a number of notations about ways to help some of them improve their interaction with kids in the classroom. The school was running efficiently and there was a sense of boosted morale through the halls, if teachers' faces were any indication. Kathy had told him that it was partly due to his openness in accepting what they'd been doing in the past, and his willingness to give time to teachers and support them through difficult situations. Clay was pleased generally, but he knew he had a lot of plans for the future of Brandenburg, and that there would be lots of work upcoming.

For now, though, he just wanted to relax and catch up in Wisconsin with Eric, Phyllis and Chelsea, and try not to think of anything school-related. *Ha! Fat chance! Not a day goes by that I don't think about Livy Sheffield's lips, as well as other parts of her anatomy, and what I'd like to do with them. It was my idea to act like that kiss was nothing, so now who knows what she's doing this weekend. Quit talking to yourself, dumbass. Enjoy the airplane flight, and empty your head of the Sheffield dame.* Clay leaned back in his seat, closed his eyes, and in a minute he'd dozed off to sleep.

He awoke when the flight attendant nudged him, announcing that they'd arrived in Madison. Clay couldn't wait to get off the plane and see his brother. It had been two years since they'd last seen each other, although they usually tried to speak by phone every other week. Eric and Phyllis had moved to Wisconsin when Eric was offered a too-good-to-be-true job in the tech industry. Last year, they'd bought a house in a neighborhood with lots of kids and saw it as a great place to raise a family. Life was looking pretty good for Eric. Clay was really happy that he'd met such a great girl, and he was anxious to reconnect with his niece. Two years made a huge difference, when you were three years old, and all he'd seen of Chelsea were photos and FaceTime opportunities periodically. Clay grabbed his carry-on from the overhead, and left the plane hastily.

The moment he exited the terminal an adorable little girl came running up to him. "Uncle Clay, guess who I am?" her bright blue eyes sparkling, as she waited for him to guess.

"Gee, I don't know. How did you know my name was Clay?" He winked at his brother and sister-in-law over Chelsea's head.

"Oh, Uncle Clay, you're teasing me, I know, because I'm your only niece and you're my only uncle, and anyway, Daddy and Mommy pointed you out, and anyway, I just saw you wink at them so I know you're teasing!" It all came out in one breath, and Chelsea giggled.

"Uh-oh! Another brilliant woman in the family. How will we ever find the right guy for you, Chelsea?" Clay scooped her up in his arms and gave her a kiss and a hug.

"Ewww. Don't be silly, Uncle Clay. I'm too young for boys right now, right Daddy?" She looked over his shoulder in Eric's direction. "Daddy says I can have a boyfriend when I'm...what'd you say, Daddy? Was it thirty? I'm not exactly sure how long away from five that is but it sounds awfully far. Is it, Uncle Clay?"

Clay laughed as he carried her over to see her parents. "Probably not far enough to make your Dad comfortable, honey!" The three adults burst into laughter, greeting each other warmly. "Eric, Phyllis--am I ever happy to see you both!" He looked down when Chelsea yanked on his sportcoat. She stood with her hands on her hips, looking annoyed. "You too, doll face!" Clay added.

They picked up the car and headed home, talking all the way. Questions were asked all around about Clay's job, Eric's job, and what Phyllis was doing in her involvements with the school and the neighborhood, as well as with her volunteer work at the local hospital. Chelsea insisted on telling Clay about her new puppy, Cinnamon, and Clay kept teasing her about naming a dog after a spice. The twenty-minute drive to their home passed swiftly, and before he knew it, Clay had been shown to the guest room, deposited his stuff, and was making himself comfortable with a beer and some snacks before dinner. Phyllis and Eric had decided they'd stick around the house the first evening, but they already had warned Clay that Saturday was booked with picnics and parties, and they had a babysitter for Chelsea for Saturday evening. Phyllis entered the room with another beer and smiled at Clay. "It's great seeing you, Clay. We're so glad you're a little closer now and can get up to visit us periodically."

"I'm pleased too, Phyl. So what's with the babysitter for tomorrow night? If you and Eric have plans, I'm more than happy to watch Chelsea."

Eric had just walked into the family room from the kitchen. She looked over her shoulder at him, stuttering, "Well...uh...uh...we sort of planned on a double date," and she grinned with a hopefully expectant look.

"Oh, Lord, not more matchmaking! Mom got me to promise to go out with some woman she knows, and now you guys in Wisconsin, too?"

"Please, Clay. You'll love Monica. She's a teacher at Chelsea's school, where I volunteer. She's absolutely adorable, and well, she's in between men, and we, that is I, invited her to join us for dinner and dancing tomorrow night. Please say it's okay."

Clay looked at Eric and shrugged. Eric broke in smiling and said, "It seems that Phyllis is interested in helping you overcome your shyness in the romance department, bro."

"Well, if the truth were told, I would like Chelsea to have a cousin in the foreseeable future," returned Phyllis. "Now don't be stubborn, Clay. Just indulge me tomorrow night. If it's awful I'll never do it again."

"Sure, I'll go, Phyllis. One little double date won't kill me." *I wonder if she's got brown eyes and honey-colored hair?*

10

Olivia had decided over the long weekend, that she would really focus on building a relationship with Derek. He'd truly been a marvelous host, and was more than attentive to her. He'd made it very clear that he was bent on pursuing her, and although there weren't fireworks every time he kissed her, he had been a true gentleman. *Derek will do everything in his power to please me.*

She smiled remembering the details of Monday morning. After saying good-bye to Jimmy and Susie, she and Derek had enjoyed a sumptuous breakfast. They had talked about the weekend, and laughed a lot about the teasing comments they all had made about Jimmy, and what a good sport he was.

But then, Derek had shocked her by presenting her with a bracelet of lapis lazuli edged in small cut diamonds. "Oh, Derek. This is simply too much. I can't accept it."

"Now, Olivia. I want you to have something to keep your mind on me periodically, when you're bogged down with all those 'school' things. I'm going to be working here in New York and Boston for another month, but then I'll be heading to Townsend permanently. I'd like to see you. May I?"

"Of course, Derek. I'll plan on it. By the beginning of October." She looked down at the beautiful bracelet, which Derek had put on her wrist, touching and admiring the smoothness of the stones. "This is just incredible. Thank you. I'll wear it proudly, and I can't wait to show it to Sally, my best friend, when I get back home. Speaking of that," she glanced at her watch, "It's clearly time for me to head to the airport."

"I know, honey. Tony is parked out front waiting. He'll get you there in no time. Have a great flight back, and I'll call and check in with you tomorrow night."

The two said their good-byes as Derek walked Olivia to the waiting limo. He squeezed her hand, and pulled her in for a perfunctory kiss.

Olivia hugged him and whispered in his ear, "Derek, thank you so much…for everything."

She slid into the waiting open door, took her seat, and waved to Derek as the limo pulled away.

"Nice weekend, Miss Sheffield?"

"It was unbelievable, Tony. I feel like I'm living in a dream world, and this could never be happening to me. But it is!" She leaned back in the seat with a sigh, and looked down at the bracelet on her wrist, caressing the multicolored stones. *A relationship with Derek Donaldson would be like the courtship of a princess. No lust driving it, no sordid little sex comments, but true respect and chivalry.*

But there was that certain nagging feeling when she watched Tony brush his hand through his hair.

The movement so reminded her of Clay, when he was worrying over something; she smiled as she thought that she'd love to touch his hair just for a second. *Dear God. I am such an idiot. I have NO relationship with Clay Mitchell, and there is clearly not going to be one. Leave it alone,and get on with your life!*

The rest of the trip home, Olivia did everything she could to keep her mind off of Clay. It worked...sort of.

Clay returned from Wisconsin rehashing the evening double date with Phyllis, Eric, and Phyllis' friend, Monica. She was very sweet and attractive and she and Clay had a lot to talk about, being educators, but from the moment they met, they had both realized that there were no sparks between them, just simple camaraderie. That was fine with Clay. Long distance romances rarely worked out in his estimation. Anyway--he had no time for romance. Perhaps just a few wild flings, short-lived and passionate, with petite, voluptuous bodies with honey-colored hair. He rubbed his eyes, picturing it all too vividly. *Jesus, Clay, old man. Get back to business and focus on work, work, work! No time for women--especially a Sheffield woman.*

The Tuesday after Labor Day reared its ugly old head, and several of Clay's staff dragged in unceremoniously, a little on the late side.

"Rough weekend, huh, you guys?" Clay asked, chuckling.

Sally, who looked surprisingly chipper, laughed, and spoke for some of the staff. "A little too much partying from what I saw around town this weekend, Clay." Then realization struck her. "Hey, I didn't see you around here this weekend. Did you go out of town?"

"Yes. My brother and his family live in Wisconsin. I went to spend the weekend with them. That was one of the biggest perks of moving to Brandenburg. I can see them on a more regular basis."

"Nice. Glad you have some family relatively near-by." She started heading towards her classroom. "Oh, by the way. You asked me to coordinate a few social get-togethers. I thought that I might mention a happy hour this Friday over at Ojays. I think after a few days back, we'll all be ready to cut loose. Would that be okay, Clay?"

"Sally, you know these people far better than I do. If you think it'll fly, make the announcement, and I'll see you all at Ojays on Friday." He paused and turned back to look at her. "Do you think it's alright that I come? Sometimes happy hours are good venting places to complain about the principal."

"No problem. We'll just wait until you leave!" She tossed a droll look over her shoulder and walked off down the hallway.

Clay's laughter echoed down the hall with her. She would be great in the social department and an asset for teacher morale. He had made a good decision when he chose her.

Soon the students bustled in the door, ready and raring to go. Clay was in the lobby welcoming them as they and some of their parents came in. He had begun to remember a good number of students' names and tried to recall as many as he could, as they entered. The parents were suitably impressed, and some expressed surprise that Clay already knew their child's name. One mother even asked if her son had already been in trouble for Clay to know him, but he assured her that, thus far, Sammy had been a model of decorum.

"Well, don't get used to that," Sammy's Mom replied. "I'm certainly not!"

They both grinned and Clay took Sammy's hand and walked him to his kindergarten class.

Clay stopped outside of Livy's classroom, wondering why he hadn't seen her yet today. He peeked in, and there she was--struggling to keep a large stack of poster boards from falling off the top of a file cabinet right on her head. "Whoa, whoa, there! Let me help, Miss Sheffield. I really don't have time to call the EMT squad this morning for a teacher suffering from a concussion." He stood directly behind her, and with one hand easily returned the huge stack of falling poster boards to the position atop the cabinet. Then he looked down at her. She was out of breath and looking up at him. He felt as though he'd been punched in the gut. Her brown eyes caught his, and for a moment they both held each other's gaze.

Finally, Livy broke eye contact by looking downward. She stammered awkwardly, "Thanks. I do believe that I would have gotten knocked out by that huge stack of posters. Maybe I need to teach taller students, instead of second graders. Then the principal wouldn't have to rescue me." She laughed, easing back her head and smiling.

She takes my breath away. "I didn't see you come in this morning. Did you get here early?" he asked, directly.

"Yes, I got in at six this morning. I just had a full weekend, and needed to get my thoughts together before the kids came."

"Oh, were you here in town for Labor Day?"

"Uh...no...I was out of town...with my brother and sister-in-law."

"Aah--one of the infamous Sheffield big brothers. I hope you had a nice time," he said, hoping she'd elaborate. He had a strange feeling that there was much more to know about the weekend.

But there was no news forthcoming, and she began quickly preparing her classroom for the onslaught of kids coming in. Second graders started filing through the door, all shouting "Hello" to Miss Sheffield, and then to Mr. Mitchell. Clearly she couldn't say any more, and Clay decided to let it go. He didn't need to know where she'd gone, or what she'd done...*WHAT HAD SHE DONE?* He said lightly, "Well, I see you need to get back to classroom business. I'll leave you to it, then." He turned his back and started to leave the room.

"Mr. Mitchell," Olivia called after him. "Thanks so much. You were a great help a moment ago." He turned to see her smile, warm and inviting. The beautiful eyes met his again for a split second.

Clay smiled back and then nonchalantly said, "Sure.. "Have a great day."

The four-day week flew by, and it was, as Sally had predicted, time to cut loose. Almost every teacher on staff attended the happy hour gathering. O'Jay had set up two long tables and they all congregated around them, squeezing in close together. "Gosh," exclaimed Sally. "I'm always so glad that this is only a four-day week. I feel like I've been teaching for months already!" Most of the others echoed her response.

Tom Moore shouted towards the bar. "Hey, O'Jay, can you get a tab going for some more-than-eager teachers?"

"Sure," O'Jay responded. "I'm more than willing to help you all ease into the weekend. Remember--three of my own came through old Brandenburg. I always say teachers don't get paid enough. It's a wonder the building's still standing and anyone still wants to teach, after having my kids!" Conversation buzzed around the table, while O'Jay took their orders. Many of them remembered O'Jay's hellacious boys, who of course, were doing quite well as grown men. In fact, one of them was the Mayor of Barton.

Olivia walked in, waved at O'Jay and the others and stopped off to speak with Paul Browning, who was sitting at the bar. She and Paul had been friends for as long as she could remember. In fact, they'd even gone out in high school. But growing up together, living on the same street, and being in almost every class with him since elementary school, was just too much history to be involved romantically for the two of them.

"Hey, babe. How's it hanging?" Paul asked.

Olivia leaned in to give him a hug, and a peck on the cheek.

At that precise moment, Clay walked in the front

door of Ojays. The radar kicked in right away. *I have no idea why I seem to have this sixth sense about Olivia Sheffield, but there she is being manhandled by yet another guy I don't know.* After getting over his initial annoyance, he noticed that the guy was wearing a wedding ring. He also noticed that Olivia had changed into some very close-fitting jeans, and a turquoise cropped top. *Not that I'm complaining or anything.*

She fills out those jeans in all the right places.

Olivia had the strangest sensation that someone was watching her, and as she said good-bye to Paul, she turned towards the door. Clay was heading over to the teacher table, and although he hadn't seemed to notice her at all, she had certainly noticed him. *Oh, my God. How can anyone look that deadly in a pair of jeans? It should be illegal.* She watched as he joined the table where her colleagues sat. They were all laughing and responding to him. *He has a certain quality about him that makes him seem comfortable in his own skin, and puts everyone at ease. All except me, of course...I'm usually just flustered!*

Olivia glanced down at her wrist. She was wearing Derek's bracelet. No one had seen it yet because she hadn't worn it to school; and although she thought it was beautiful, she also felt uncomfortable having to explain what it signified around her colleagues...*and now Clay is here and it's even worse. Why did I decide to put it on now? Because it matches my top...and it is not something to be ashamed about! Get over it, Olivia!*

Sally had watched Clay and Olivia from her seat in the back of the table at Ojays. It was the funniest thing she'd ever seen, besides maybe her Davy in his long underwear. *Those two are going to have whiplash if they keep trying to ignore each other. Time to turn up the heat!* Sally stood and motioned for Olivia to join her.

Olivia walked over reluctantly, as Sally said, "Here, honey. I saved you the seat next to me!"

Dear God in Heaven, it was the seat in between Sally and Clay. "Really, Sal. Let me pull up a chair here across the table."

Clay smiled. "I wouldn't hear of it. Come on over and squeeze in next to Sally. It seems she's anxious to catch up, and anyway, you hadn't mentioned that you'd gone to New York City! What a great town!"

Olivia started moving towards the seat. "Excuse me...while...I...squeeze in here," she said as she tried to avoid even a brush with Clay's body.

Clay just smiled as that gorgeous rear end swept between his legs and the edge of the bench. *God, what I wouldn't give for a touch of that!*

Sally was all ears...and eyes. She smiled and coaxed. "Okay, girl. Spill the story. What did you do in the Big Apple? I'm dying to know," and she patted Olivia's hand. Then she saw the bracelet. "Oh my God, Olivia. Where in the world did you get that incredible bracelet?"

Olivia wanted to melt into the table. Of all the places for her big-mouth friend to announce to everyone about the bracelet this would not have been it. "Shh-Sally. You don't have to make such a big deal of it."

"Don't shush me. I want the skinny now!" And, of course, so did the rest of her friends at the table, who were leaning in, admiring the bracelet and commenting on its beauty. Questions were flying from everyone...except, Sally noticed, Clay Mitchell.

After more coaxing, Olivia was forced to tell her friends some of the details. "Well, I was invited to New

York City by Derek Donaldson." Everyone paused and looked at each other smiling and nodding their heads. "Oh, come on you guys. He invited me and my brother, Jim, and his wife, Susie. He's asked them to take over the running of his two galleries in NYC and Boston, and they've agreed to do it."

Kudos all around went to Jimmy and Susie who were well-known to everyone at the table. Tom said, "Wow, what a great opportunity for them both, Olivia!"

She smiled and nodded. "It really is, Tom. Anyway, we did a couple of shows and some great dinners, and..."

"Where'd you stay, Olivia?" Melanie interrupted.

"Uh...we stayed at the Waldorf."

"Oh, my God, Olivia. I'm extremely envious, and you know that rarely happens to me when it comes to you," Melanie laughed good-naturedly. "Get on with the bracelet story. Are those diamonds around the edge?"

"Really, you all. We don't have to get into all of this here, do we? After all, we're celebrating surviving the beginning of the school year. Surely someone else has something to talk about?" she asked expectantly.

They all shook their heads in the negative, and told her to go on.

Clay was taking it all in, listening and watching the interaction around the table and quietly drinking his beer. *Why is she trying to steer the conversation away from the bracelet? Any woman who received a bracelet like that would, and should, want to talk about it, dammit!*

"Oh, alright. Derek gave me the bracelet as a token of ...his...fond...ness for me, and well, yes, they are diamonds with lapis lazulis." All the women were reaching to touch the stones, or moving closer to see it at a better vantage point.

"Go on, will you, Olivia?" asked Connie impatiently. "Where exactly is Derek Donaldson now, and what will he do when his two largest galleries are being run by Jim and Susie?"

Olivia blushed from her neck to the top of her head. "Well," she continued, "Derek has already opened a small gallery in Townsend, and he's getting things started. He's currently looking for some Midwest talent, and plans on moving down in this direction in a month or so where he can be closer to..."

Tom offered, "...a certain school teacher we all know, perhaps?"

Olivia could not even look in Clay's direction. "No, now Tom, he needs to be around Townsend more and of course, he's looking to give Midwestern artists a better chance to display their wares..."

"Ha-Ha!" said man-hungry Melanie. "I wouldn't mind seeing his wares," and many of the girls around the table agreed.

Clay looked puzzled, glancing at Melanie.

"Well, really Clay, he's positively scrumptious in a Tom Selleck way, and rich as Midas, so he has definitely caught the eye of many of Brandenburg's women... including," and she patted Olivia's hand, "our little pool shark, Olivia Sheffield!"

"Sounds like a real catch," said Clay as he stood up to his full height. The need to hit something had come over him very quickly. *I think I might just hate that son-of-a-bitch and I haven't even met him yet.* The speed with which he rose, jostled the table and everyone's beer bounced around a little, spilling. "Sorry, you guys. Didn't mean to spill O'Jay's valuable merchandise, but I need to get going. It's been a great beginning. Thanks for all your hard work to get the school year up and running. O'Jay? The first round is on me." A cheer rose up around the table. Before he left, he smiled down at Olivia. "Congratulations, Livy. Looks like you've found yourself a keeper." He smiled, but the smile didn't quite reach those blue-gray eyes.

Olivia looked up at Clay. She was biting the corner of her lip and had a strange expression in her eyes. It almost seemed like regret.

Get a grip, Clay. Why would she regret Prince Charming? "See you all in school on Monday."

Sally Litchfield had been watching the scene play out. And surely what she was seeing was not a figment of her imagination. There were sparks as big as the Fourth of July display happening between her best friend and that gorgeous boss of theirs. Having a third in the mix was going to make getting those two together more challenging...and wild. They are both cut from the same stubborn cloth, and Olivia will never fess up to being attracted to her boss. She's all about following rules. Well, except when she threw that beer on Clay's head the night they met. There--that just goes to show that they're meant to be together! Wait'll Davy gets a load of the latest.

Olivia watched Clay walk out the door, and then answered the various questions that kept being thrown at her about Derek and the bracelet. But, the excitement that should have been evident in her manner, was nowhere to be found.

Clay Mitchell made the call to Caroline Graves the minute he got home from Ojays.

"Hey, Mom. Oh yeah, Eric, Phyllis and Chelsea were great. Wait until you see that little girl. She's a genius, I think...or so Eric tells me!" He heard his mother laugh on the other end. "Right. It's been a good week, but I haven't seen Dad once. Anyway, I wanted to get the final details for the fundraiser that the Kellers are giving next Saturday," He listened for a second, and then continued. "Right. Her name is Nicole Marshall--I'd like to give her a call. Can you text me her number, please? Right. Stanhope Country Club, cocktails at 6:30, and dinner at 8:00. Sounds great, Mom. I'll look forward to seeing you and Dad and meeting Nicole. Yes, I'll pick her up. See you then. Bye."

He hung up the phone and glanced at Nicole's number. *Well, Mom's got great taste in women. So it's time to go out and get back in the action. Who needs another school teacher?*

Clay went to sleep easily that evening.

Olivia didn't sleep well at all.

11

The month of September flew by at Brandenburg Elementary. Teachers were settling into new routines, and getting to know their students. Children were learning new and exciting things in their classes and making new friends along the way. Of course, there were always small confrontations, but nothing that wasn't easy to deal with by either the teachers or Mr. Mitchell. September was a month of adaptation all around, as well as a time when teachers could size up the work that lay ahead of them in regards to their new pupils.

By the end of the month, recess and lunchtime problems had smoothed out, and students generally came prepared to their classes. Clay was a regular sight around the school, popping into classrooms often to lend support for small problems or to interact with the students and the teachers. He never stayed long, because he didn't want to disrupt the teaching process or get the kids off track. Of course, he had plenty on his own agenda: meeting with the President of the P.T.A., speaking at the Rotary Club, planning the upcoming Open House, and meeting with the Teachers Advisory Committee for starters. He also attended bi-monthly meetings at Central Office with the other district principals. Staff meetings were usually twice a month, but were very short; Clay always had an outline of things to cover, but the meetings were mostly to keep the teachers informed of some of the things that would be happening over the next two weeks. Morale at Brandenburg was continuing to show improvement, and as always, Kathy Tiffin kept the school humming along.

Clay had begun to know his staff and their teaching styles--the ones he could joke with and the more serious ones who were there to get the job done and to leave. All in all the staff was very strong, not only in their teaching skills, but in their love of children and their dedication to their profession. He particularly liked stopping into Sally's and Livy's classes. They both taught second grade, as well as enjoyed some team teaching. But what he saw mostly when he visited their rooms were children who delighted in learning and were filled with curiosity and wonder. The women inspired the kids to be risk-takers and encouraged them not to be afraid of failing. They all seemed to be "cheerleaders" for each other in those classes and the students were always smiling.

That's why he was taken aback one afternoon when he passed Livy's class and heard the crying. The classroom door was open, so he quietly entered, seeing Olivia lifting up little Gus Kelley in a big hug. The pained look on her face made him react instantly. "Why hello, all you second graders? What's going on today in Miss Sheffield's class?"

Little Alex Curry shouted, "We're making a mural for Open House, and we all get our own section to color. We're allowed to draw anything that makes us happy!" Within minutes, several second graders had grabbed Clay by the hand to show him their portion of the mural and explain what they were working on; Clay listened closely and responded to their comments about their illustrations.

Then he quietly went over to Livy who was still holding the weeping Gus in her arms. "And who is this you're holding, Miss Sheffield? Aha--it's Gus Kelley. Miss Sheffield--didn't you tell me that I could do an illustration on your mural?" He made eye contact with Olivia and winked at her.

Puzzled, she replied, "Oh...of course, Mr. Mitchell."

"Well, there's a problem with that, you see. I'm just not a very good artist, and I could use some help on my portion of the mural. Gus--do you think that you could help me do my drawing?"

Gus looked up with tear-filled eyes in awe of the big man who couldn't draw. He nodded without saying a word.

"Great! Then come with me and let's get going, mister!" Clay grabbed him out of Livy's arms and swooped him over towards the mural. "Hey, Gus, maybe we can both do our drawings together if you want to? But you can help me first, and then I can help you. My drawing has to have lots of books and lots of kids because those things make me happy."

Livy watched as her students flocked around Clay and Gus, giving ideas and suggestions, but Clay was always careful to clear any other ideas with Gus. Soon Gus was drawing away with some help from other students and Clay was lying on his stomach coloring Gus' drawings. It was hardly what anyone would expect of a principal, and yet as Livy watched, it was the most natural thing in the world for Clay Mitchell.

Tears welled up in Olivia's eyes as she ran next door to get Sally, and show her what was happening on the floor of her classroom. Soon a number of the nearby teachers were also in the hallway admiring the "second-grade" artwork of their principal. When he heard chuckling, Clay, who had been totally engrossed, glanced up at the doorway, smiled wryly at the gathering of teachers, shrugged his shoulders, and got more crayons. After a few minutes, the teachers returned to their classes and Olivia cleared her throat. "Well, boys and girls, it's probably about time for Mr. Mitchell to go on about his job of being our principal. But, just so you're aware, Mr. Mitchell, we work on the mural every day from 1:00 to 2:00 after lunch and recess. Come in any time and you can finish your part."

"That's a great idea, Miss Sheffield. I do have some other things to do today." And he stood, brushing off his shirt and slacks. "Thanks for the help, kids, especially you, Gus. I'll try and pop in tomorrow!" Clay smiled and waved as he headed out the door.

Olivia mouthed, "Thank you" as he left. He nodded with an understanding look. She watched him go down the hall and that minute Sally popped over.

"Dear God, Olivia. If I wasn't engaged to Dave Garrett, I would so have the 'hots' for our boss."

Olivia had a sort of love-struck look on her face. "He is sort of irresistible. I could not get Gus calmed down today. He was so emotional. He just kept crying, and then Clay was there, and suddenly everything was great!"

Sally glanced at Livy's face and thought, "Boy, has she got it bad!

The last vestiges of summer were hanging on in Brandenburg, but the smell of autumn was in the air. School was running well. Open House had been a great night. Clay had been introduced by Superintendent Graves to the parents, although most had already met him. The Superintendent spoke of Clay's past accomplishments in other school districts, and several parents stood up in support of the help he'd given them already.

Jack Kelley rose from his seat and asked if he could speak. Travis and Gus were sitting with their Dad. The crowd got very quiet. "I'd just like to say thank you to Clay--Mr. Mitchell. He's been a tremendous influence on my boys over these past few weeks. He's come over at least once a week, and in a sense, he's been part of our evening life at home. Without too much information being given, Mr. Mitchell has lived through what the boys and I are experiencing. I'm fairly certain that I would not have gotten through these past few weeks without his help and friendship. Thank you, Clay."

Thunderous applause sounded in the room, and Jeff Graves' eyes filled with tears. He swiped them away quickly, but when Clay glanced his direction, he patted his chest as though to say I'm proud of you. Clay was suitably embarrassed as he shook hands with Jack

Kelley, and suddenly Gus shouted, "Yeah, Daddy, Mr. Mitchell's real nice." Then in a slightly quieter voice, he added, "But he can't draw too good!"

Raucous laughter filled the air, and Livy used that moment to unveil the second grade mural, lovingly colored and signed by all the kids and Mr. Mitchell. Adults crowded around the mural admiring their young artists' handiwork, and slapping Clay on the back for his lack of artistic ability. Everyone was enjoying themselves, and at that moment, Clay caught Livy's eye and quietly mouthed, "Help." He was absolutely surrounded by second graders and their parents. Livy just laughed and shook her head. She loved seeing him as the center of attention, and she wanted him to know how many people he'd affected already since arriving at Brandenburg.

The evening wore down after parents visited their children's classes, and a few of the teachers talked about running over to Ojays for some refreshment. Tom Moore invited Clay to join them and he agreed.

By the time Clay arrived, the others were already there and had ordered him a beer. Tom and the teachers raised their glasses in a toast to the evening going so well and to the new leadership that Clay had extended thus far. Even Kathy Tiffin and her husband Charlie, were there.

"Clay, I'd like you to meet Charlie," Kathy said.

Clay shook hands with the burly, gray-haired man in his mid-60's. "Finally...it's about time I get to meet you. I've heard so much about you at work."

"Not nearly as much as I hear about 'Mr. Mitchell' at home," said Charlie, pumping Clay's hand.

"Oh, stop it you two. Quit congratulating yourselves

and go and get me a nice vodka and orange juice. Not too strong, Charlie."

Charlie and Clay ambled over to the bar together. "Hey, O'Jay. How about a screwdriver...what, and a beer?" he asked Charlie.

O'Jay had already poured out the screwdriver and sat it down, and then asked, "Charlie--is this for you?"

"No, it's for Kathy."

"Oh, come on, Charlie," said O'Jay. "You know that woman can't hold her booze, and I poured a double shot."

Clay interrupted. "What's the big deal?" O'Jay and Charlie looked at each other.

"Well, you're new in town, Clay, so you don't know that Kathy doesn't really hold her liquor well," Charlie offered.

"Oh, come on, Charlie. A double can hardly do much damage, and Kathy has never come out to celebrate with us once. It's on me! What do you want?"

Shrugging, Charlie said, "You're probably right. I'll have a beer, please."

Charlie and Clay arrived at the table with drinks in hand. Kathy was talking to a couple of the teachers, and thanked them. Then she took a sip of her drink. She scowled at Charlie. "Charlie, this doesn't taste like a single shot. It's pretty strong."

"Well, honey. Clay made the order before I knew what he was doing." He tried for an innocent look.

"Jeesh, Kathy. I just wanted to celebrate with you, and after all, what can a double do? It's one drink."

A chuckle rose up around the table. Dave Garrett, with Sally on his arm, elbowed Clay.

"Look out, buddy. You just bought into a nightmare.

Kathy Tiffin is notorious for saying and doing anything under the influence."

Clay shook his head, doubting that Kathy would ever do anything inappropriate, but in a very short while he found out differently.

Everyone was in high spirits, drinking and laughing, and Clay and Dave were racking up the balls for another game of pool, when Clay just knew that Olivia had arrived. He paused for a moment and turned around to see her walk into the bar. Most of the male patrons noticed her too. Dave had glanced at Clay, as well, smiling knowingly.

Charlie Tiffin shouted out. "Hey, Olivia, haven't seen you in a long while. Come on over!"

"Oh, my gosh, Charlie. It's great seeing you!" She gave him a hug. "Kathy, you brought Charlie!"

Kathy shouted. "You wanna keep your hands off my man, Olivia!"

Shocked, Olivia looked at Charlie and whispered. "How much has she had so far, Charlie?"

"Well, Clay bought her a double to celebrate. And then I think someone else did too."

Olivia turned, and looked directly at Clay and Dave.

Clay shrugged and walked over with the pool cue in his hand. "What's the big deal? She's been fine so far. You guys are paranoid!" Then he heard the crash! He looked up to see Kathy Tiffin, his wonderfully sweet school secretary, plant a powerful right hook on one of the older guys in the bar. It totally unseated him.

Dave Garrett said, "That'd be Rich Oldham. He and Kathy went to school together here in Brandenburg, and everyone knows he still carries a torch for her. But instead of Charlie taking him on, Kathy just punches his lights out when he says something suggestive to her."

Clay watched, mesmerized, as Charlie ran over to grab Kathy and stop her from throwing another punch.

Kathy was on a roll. "Keep your hands to yourself, Charlie Tiffin. Rich and I are just having fun," she said as she struggled to get away from Charlie.

Rich scraped himself off the floor, rubbing his jaw as he stood. "Jeez, Kathy, you can't take a joke. Sorry, Charlie. You need to keep the liquor cabinet locked up good and tight." They shook hands and Rich waved goodbye to the customers. "Time for me to call it a night before Kathy knocks me on my ass again." Teasing shouts and goodbyes followed Rich out the door.

"Come on, honey. Time to head home," said Charlie.

Kathy started arguing about leaving, but at that minute her eyes lit on Olivia and Clay, Before Charlie knew what was happening, Kathy made a beeline to where they were standing, swerving just a little. "Now that we're after hours and I've got you both here, I want to know what's going on with the two of you?"

Olivia and Clay looked at Kathy and then each other. Sally, who was standing next to Dave, inhaled sharply, and then snickered.

"I...don't know what you're talking about, Kathy," stammered Olivia.

"Oh, baloney. You can't keep your eyes off each other when you're in the same room. It's a wonder that the fire alarms don't go off at Brandenburg!"

Olivia blushed from head to toe. Sally chuckled beside Dave. Clay was totally speechless. Kathy had a self-satisfied look on her face, and Charlie watched it all.

"Uhhh...well, Kathy, honey...I think you've succeeded in shocking everyone around here. Why don't we call it a night?" Charlie suggested.

"Not until I get an answer."

Clay jumped into the conversation. "Well, now, Mrs. Tiffin. You did come equipped for fireworks tonight." He looked at Olivia, who was still mortified. "I'm sure that you know that Olivia is seeing someone. I've never met him, but I overheard that he has plans to move closer to the area. And really, Kathy, we hardly see each other during the school day...and anyway, I'm seeing a young woman from Barton. You know that it's not appropriate for principals and teachers to be involved..." Clay rambled on digging deeper.

Charlie put a stop to it. "Okay, Kathy...time to get moving. I'm sure that this conversation can wait for another day." He grabbed her arm and moved Kathy toward the exit door. "Night everyone." Kathy was a little wobbly, but she smiled and waved over her shoulder as Charlie escorted her out. Once outside, Charlie said, "Wow, Kathy. You really lit a fuse under that situation tonight."

Kathy just smiled, and nodded her head, beginning to sober up. "I did, didn't I? Give me a high five, Charlie!" Charlie shook his head at her smiling...and raised his palm for a high-five.

Back in Ojays, the two pairs were quiet. Sally and Dave looked at Olivia and Clay. Dave cleared his throat. "Well, Sal, let's get a move-on. Work day tomorrow."

"Right," Sally said. "Olivia, don't forget the Building Advisory Committee Meeting tomorrow. Uhh...see you in the morning." Dave and Sally left together. Whispering as they exited, Sally continued, "That was kinda fun, wasn't it, Dave?"

"Oh, honey, now don't keep up with this matchmaking stuff. Clay and Olivia are smart enough to know that they can't have a relationship in their job capacities. Plus, you heard Clay say that he's seeing someone new, and Olivia has Derek 'Midas' Donaldson. She wouldn't be so stupid as to throw THAT away."

"Dave Garrett. If you're really that blind about chemistry, I have no idea how we got together!"

"Let me remind you, then, honey," and he patted her backside as she got in the car.

Dave walked around, and Sally yelled. "No, no, no. You're being deliberately obtuse about the fireworks between the two of them. You make me so mad I could scream!"

"Ah, Sally sweetie. I love it when you scream." He smiled, and leaned in, and gave her a kiss that sent sparks to her toes. "Why don't you come and sit on my lap, and I'll remind you of chemistry."

Sally giggled and moved onto his lap in the car, awkward though it was over the gear shift. "My, oh, my, Mr. Garrett. I think you get an A plus in chemistry." She wrapped her arms around his neck and kissed him right back.

Back in Ojays, Olivia and Clay were standing side by side at the table. Olivia was looking at her feet. "Sorry about that..."

"No, don't worry. I'll just remember not to ply Kathy with alcohol next time."

"So you're seeing someone from Barton now? That's wonderful..." Olivia smiled warmly. *What an actress I am!*

"Yes, her name's Nicole. And what's the name of

your...?" *Derek Donaldson, I know, I know.*

"His name is Derek."

"Well, I'm sure that we'll all get to meet in the near future." There was an awkward pause. "It's pretty late. Would you like me to walk you to your car?"

"No, thanks. I'll be fine. I need to stop off and talk to O'Jay for a minute, and then I'll get going."

"Okay. See you tomorrow." He wanted to take her hand in the worst way, but stopped himself. *No physical contact, buddy.*

Livy smiled as he left, but she remembered what Kathy had questioned. *Is it that obvious how attracted I am to him? I'm really going to need to be careful and keep my distance from Clay Mitchell.* She shook her head. *Who am I kidding?*

12

Nicole Marshall was a lovely, long-legged brunette, very soft-spoken with a Southern drawl. She'd grown up in Mississippi, and exuded class. Clay had liked her immediately. She'd been introduced to him by Mama Caro, and he and Nicole had enjoyed getting to know each other at the fundraiser at Stanhope Country Club. They'd had plenty of things to talk about--Nicole had done a lot of traveling, as had Clay. Her father was a Naval officer, so she'd moved around a lot in her early years. She spoke highly of her parents, smiling every time she mentioned them. She relayed that they'd supported her in her life-long dream of becoming a pediatrician, and Clay countered with all that his adopted parents had done for him as well.

"Wow! A pediatrician!" Clay commented. "I can only imagine the hours that you keep at your job!"

"Yes, it's really time consuming, building a practice. Right now it's only me and my nurse practitioner. I have another friend who is also on call for me in an emergency, but it's mostly just me. My social life is practically nil. I came out tonight because Mrs. Graves is hard to turn down," she said, smiling wryly.

"Don't I know that? She has a tendency to do match-making with her thirty-three year old son, and, I'm sorry to say, you're her next target."

Nicole laughed. "I figured that out rather quickly, Clay. I pretty much know your life story. Every time I speak with Caroline, she fills me in on more of your accomplishments and how excited she is to have you back close to Barton."

Clay groaned. "Sorry--but what can you do?"

"Actually," she took his arm lightly, "I'm rather liking the opportunity to finally meet you." She smiled genuinely.

"I feel the same way, Nicole. Let's take a look at the possibility of getting together again soon."

"I'd like that."

Clay headed home towards Brandenburg, after the evening was over. *Well, that wasn't bad at all, but it won't be easy getting together with her, considering the hour drive, and both of our schedules.* His thoughts drifted off to his work day on Monday...and as always, Olivia Sheffield pervaded them. He shook his head, upset with himself. *Get over that little spitfire. It's time to get on with life.*

Olivia had a date with Derek. He was driving in from Townsend and they were having dinner. It had been several weeks since the New York City trip. Of course, she'd written him and thanked him profusely for the beautiful bracelet, and let him know what was going on in Brandenburg.

He'd called her early in the morning, and had updated her on the progress of the Townsend Gallery, as well as readying Jim and Susie for their move into management. Then he said, "But I'm about as caught up as I can be right now. How would you feel if I drove over to Brandenburg and took you for dinner?"

She'd responded with a hearty, "Sure, sounds like fun!"

Olivia had faced the fact that, with Derek, attraction would grow and that, clearly, she needed to see him more regularly for that to happen. *Unlike Clay, whom I see almost daily, and let's face it, it's awfully hard to avoid that electricity. Derek will keep me busy, I'll have fun, and we can really get to know each other when he's closer.*

The plan was for Derek to pick her up at about 6:00 p.m. and head out to the local Mexican restaurant, Los Cabos. Olivia loved the ambience of the place with its mariachi band and bright decor, and the food was fabulous. She put on a pair of jeans and a multi-colored tee shirt, long dangly earrings, and the bracelet. Then she put on a pair of dressy denim heels, and she was ready to go. She was excited to see Derek face to face. When he arrived and rang the doorbell, she ran to the door, opened it, and greeted him with a big hug.

"Well, I could certainly get used to that every day!" said Derek, as he grabbed her and planted a quick kiss on her lips. "Are you ready then?"

"Whenever you are. You're the one who has driven three hours for dinner!" and she winked.

"Actually, I'm starving. Where are we headed?"

"My favorite Mexican place, called Los Cabos. Is that okay?"

Derek grabbed her warmly, saying "It won't matter where we are. I'll like it just fine if I'm with you."

They arrived at Los Cabos about 6:30. She'd talked the entire way, bubbling about school, and Open House, and all the students. He loved that her excitement just spilled out of her. Derek offered, "I think that Brandenburg School District is lucky to have you, Olivia. You're so dedicated, and you clearly love your students and the work that you do."

"Oh, I do, Derek. I'm so sorry that I've monopolized the conversation. Have you been able to get the mixed-media artists you were pursuing?"

"Well, keep your fingers crossed. I'm having a conference call with them tomorrow afternoon to work out the details."

They'd arrived at the restaurant and were seated. Derek liked the surroundings and decor in the restaurant and commented on it, A waiter arrived to take their drink order. "Would you like a...?"

"Margarita? Of course!" Olivia said, "They're fabulous, Derek!"

"How about a pitcher, then?" The waiter nodded and left to fill the order.

Conversation continued, margaritas arrived, and Derek began to pour. They toasted each other, read through the menu, and kept working on the pitcher. Livy finally got up to use the restroom, but she was a little wobbly on her feet. Giggling, she said, "We'd better order soon. That tequila is starting to work its wonders on me!"

"Okay, as soon as you're back, we'll order." He

watched her cute little backside head towards the restroom and thought about his long neglected libido.

They placed their orders after Olivia returned, and very shortly, the mariachi band began their set. It was loud, raucous, and everyone was singing and clapping along with the music. The band members moved between tables, taking requests. When they got to Olivia's table, they made a request of her--a shot of tequila for her favorite song. "Now, Pablo, you know what I get to do if I drink the shot!"

"Yes, of course, senorita. We know what we ask for, right, you guys?" The entire band nodded.

Derek was puzzled, but took it all in. The song was played, the shot arrived, and Olivia imperiously stood and swigged it down. She slammed the glass on the table. The cheers went up, then she walked up to the band. "Okay, Pablo...hand it over!" Pablo passed her one of the trumpets and the men put their hands over their ears. Olivia started playing the trumpet, blasting wrong notes, and generally creating a din. Derek's hands were over his ears by now, as were most of the patrons, but Livy just kept playing, if that's what it could be called. At that precise moment, the door of Los Cabos opened and in walked Dave Garrett, Joe Cartwright, Bobby Wilson, and Clay.

"Damn, what the hell...?" Joe shouted, grimacing while covering his ears.

"Oh, for crying out loud," grumbled Dave. "It's Olivia. She must be doing tequila shots again."

Clay looked up and saw Olivia Sheffield in form-fitting jeans and a tight little colored top, blasting the hell on a trumpet that the band player was wrestling from her grasp. She was fighting a little, and shouting, "You knew what you were getting into, Pablo. Be a sport!"

Everyone in the restaurant yelled, "NO!"

Then a dark-haired man stood up and gently pried the trumpet from Olivia's hands. *Damn, it must be the rich new boyfriend.*

Livy was laughing, but allowing him to manhandle her, until she looked up and saw Clay. The look of shock clearly registered on her face, so much so, that Derek turned around to see what had brought on her reaction. Livy calmed down and stopped wiggling, which up till that moment, Derek had been enjoying tremendously.

The guys from Ojays all wandered over to the table, with Clay at the end of the line.

"Hey, Donaldson," said Dave. "You feeding Olivia her shots of tequila?"

Derek smiled ruefully. "If I'd only been warned, I could have avoided the pain of hearing loss for the entire bar, but none of you gentlemen chose to tell me about this little problem."

"Well," said Dave, "we haven't seen you for a while. You remember Bobby and Joe?"

"Sure," said Derek. They shook hands. He looked expectantly at the fourth man in the group; tall, good-looking, blonde, and clearly someone that Olivia knew. His bristles were up, but as always, Derek knew how to act in public. "I'm sorry, I don't remember meeting you." He extended his hand. There was a pause, then Clay took the hand, and shook it. "I'm pretty new in town. I'm Clay Mitchell."

"Yeah, he's Olivia and Sally's boss," said Dave.

So this was the Mr Mitchell she'd gone on and on about. (Somehow I'd figured he'd be in the neighborhood of sixty years old...not this goddamn jock.)

Turning to face Clay, Derek offered his hand. "Well, it's good to meet you, Mitchell. Isn't it nice that your boss is here, Olivia?"

Quietly, and greatly subdued, Livy said, "Sure. Hi guys."

Derek protectively took her hand and led her back to their table.

*Keep your dirty rotten hands off...*Clay's jaw clenched.

Dave Garrett saw the reaction, smiled to himself, and thought, Sally, honey, you're going to be so proud of me. Following Derek and Olivia back to the table, Dave continued "Hey, Derek, would you mind if we pulled up some chairs and joined you guys?" Not even waiting for an answer, he said, "I'm starving. Let's order, guys!" and he promptly sat down.

The others joined him, as if on cue, conveniently leaving the only empty seat next to Olivia on the other side of the table open. Clay stood behind the empty seat and gazed down in Olivia's direction, as though asking for an okay. Stiffly, Derek looked over at her. She only shrugged her shoulders and glanced quickly away. Clay pulled the chair out and sat down.

Derek was the first to break the silence. "Well, Clay. How long have you been in Brandenburg?"

"I came in mid-August, just as school was beginning to start."

"Yeah, that was a night to remember, wasn't it, Olivia?" remembered Joe. "We got so many rounds of free beers that night, thanks to the two of them." The others laughed.

Derek noticed that Olivia and Clay did not. "Really, Olivia? Get me up to speed?"

"I can do that," said Clay. "Livy--sort of conned me into playing pool with her on my first night at Ojays."

Livy? Did he call her Livy? Derek's eyebrows raised. "I think I know where this is heading."

"Well, maybe a little," said Bobby. "It's just that she beat his pants off..."

"Now, wait a minute, Bob. It wasn't that bad..." said Clay.

"Hah! It was better! He was a total gentleman, never got his temper up; they'd bet a round of beers for the house, and he paid up both times..."

"Both times?" said Derek.

"Look," said Clay. "Have YOU ever played her?"

"No, I can't honestly say I have. Everyone warned me about her first."

Clay looked at the guys ruefully. "Thanks, you all."

Bobby continued. "Anyway, back to the story. After losing twice, Clay nailed her the third time!"

Oh, if only! Clay smiled at the thought.

Derek seemed surprised. "You actually beat her?"

"Yeah. By then I was aware of most of her moves, and I'm not a bad player myself."

"So," said Bobby, "now it's time for Olivia to pay up and buy a round of beers...which she did"...the boys were watching Olivia grow increasingly red by the minute. "But when she took the beer over to Clay, she poured it over his head!" They all guffawed, with the exception of Clay and Olivia.

Derek looked over at Olivia in total surprise. "Did you really do that?"

Mortified, she nodded. "Um-hum. I'm sorry to say that I did."

Now Derek was curious. He looked at Clay. "And

what did you do?"

Proudly, with a smile on his face, Clay threw in, "The only thing any man would do! I poured one over her head as well." He laughed outright at the memory.

Dave went on. "Yeah, the whole bar cheered Clay on for teaching her a lesson." Then Dave added the one-two punch. "Hey, Clay? Didn't you take Olivia home that night?"

"What the hell?" thought Derek.

Olivia was truly embarrassed. "Dave Garrett, stop that! We walked home together because we smelled like a brewery and had had too much alcohol to drive. It was not a big deal..."

Maybe not for you, but I'm remembering what it felt like with you in my arms. Clay continued, "Then she twisted her ankle and...I had to carry her the rest of the way to her house..." Clay let his voice trail off.

"But you're leaving out that neither of us had any idea that...you...were...my...boss..."

"That's right," Clay agreed

"Obviously, your boss must bring out your dark side, Olivia," Derek joked.

"Yeah, well," Clay added. "I think her dark side is hiding right under the surface..."

"Hey, could we all talk about anything but this, please?" Olivia pleaded.

"Actually, we've eaten and all. It's probably time to get you home. I still have to drive to Townsend to-night," Derek said,

Good. No overnights! I'm feeling pretty good about that. I don't think I like this guy much. Clay just had to offer. "Hey, Donaldson? I can get Olivia home if you want. Going back to her place is a little out of the way from Townsend, isn't it?"

"Clay...Derek and I are on a date. He can take me home, I'm sure?" and she glanced up at Derek.

"Well, of course, I'm taking you home, honey," and Derek pulled her towards his side.

"It's been good to see you all... I'll be getting to Brandenburg a lot more, when I officially move to Townsend. Come on, Olivia." And then he did it; he stood behind her with his hands on her shoulders and whispered in her ear. She smiled as he gave her a kiss on the side of her face.

Clay watched everything his jaw set. *One day I might just ram those perfect teeth down your throat!* Clay added aloud, as they exited. "Don't forget that we have a 7:00 a.m. meeting tomorrow morning with Jack Kelley about Gus, Livy."

Cavemen, the whole lot of them! "Yes, Mr. Mitchell," she added sarcastically. "I'm aware of my schedule. I'm ready now, Derek." She turned and they left together.

Clay watched their progress the entire way. "I don't think I like that arrogant son-of-a-bitch!" he said under his breath.

Dave, Bobby, and Joe chimed in. "We don't think he likes you either, big guy!" And the three musketeers laughed uproariously.

Clay had not slept well all night, wondering how long Derek had stayed with Livy. But then he corralled his disruptive thoughts and reminded himself that he had set the rules about no involvements, and that he would be seeing Nicole again soon.

He got into work early, about 6:15, and readied for the Kelley meeting. His back was to his office door when she arrived. He knew it without turning--her spicy perfume wafted on the air, and he felt her presence. *Why this woman?*

"Clay?" she said quietly.

He didn't turn yet. He needed to get his face in control. "Yes...oh morning, Livy..." *Now turn.* "How are you doing this morning?" *Mercy, she looks good enough to eat.*

Olivia was wearing an olive green dress that hugged her curves. She wore matching earrings and a green bangle bracelet. She moved towards Clay's desk and said, "Could we talk?"

"Sure. Have a seat."

"Well. Last night after Derek took me home, we talked. We both sensed some animosity towards him from you."

"Really? Well, I'd hardly say that he was Mr. Hospitable himself!"

"No, he wasn't, and he's the first to admit that."

"Well, isn't that just grand!" Clay spat out.

Livy looked up at him and started stammering. "I really...don't know how...to say this...I don't know what is going on with you...with us...and I'm having a terrible time understanding..." she looked down at her lap.

"What's going on with us?" He stood up, rounded his desk and placed his arms on either side of her chair. "I'll show you what's going on with us!" He grabbed her by her arms and lifted her in one movement; then his mouth claimed hers. He could feel the shock, the tension, but still he kept kissing her, all his pent-up emotions rioting out of control. Then his tongue forced her mouth to open for him, and he tasted her again and again until he could feel her melting in his arms. Livy's arms circled his neck, and he heard her low moan of pleasure. Suddenly she was kissing him back with all of the ardor he was exhibiting. It was as though no one else existed at that moment in time. *If I don't call a stop to this right now, I'm going to push her down on my desk and take her right here!* He broke the kiss. He put her away from him. They were both out of breath, their chests heaving.

"Dear God, Livy. Don't you know what you do to me?"

"If it's that, then I'm afraid you're a very big part of my problem. I can't seem to get you out of my mind... and the things I think...are..." she blushed.

Clay swallowed. "Trust me, no worse than what I think...and want..." He brushed his hand through his hair.

"But Clay, this just can't work and we both know it. You said it yourself!"

"I know. It's just not that easy having you so nearby. Usually my thoughts are taking shortcuts to find the quickest way to get you out of your clothes!"

Olivia was shocked and embarrassed. *And maybe a little pleased.* "Do you think that I should go to Superintendent Graves about a transfer to another school?"

"No way, Livy. You've been one of the strongest staff members who have kept this school running. You shouldn't leave! If anyone goes, it should be me."

"Don't even suggest that you should go. Staff morale has really improved here, and I don't want us to take a step back. Having another boss in here would be a horrible blow to the staff, and I don't think they could take that. Plus all the kids and the parents love you already."

They were startled by a knock on Clay's door.

"Yes?" Clay asked.

"Clay, it's Kathy. Are you alone or has Mr. Kelley arrived? I thought I heard you talking..."

Clay looked at Olivia as she straightened her hair, which was slightly mussed from the urgent kiss. She nodded.

"Come on in, Kath." He opened the door. "Miss Sheffield and I have been talking..."

"Hi, Kathy." Olivia Sheffield was flushed and beautiful,and Kathy knew that something had happened.

"Oh, well...I imagine you're getting ready for your meeting, right?"

"Right!" Clay and Olivia spoke at the same time.

Right! "I'm sure Mr. Kelley and Mr. Jacobs will be here any minute. Here are those papers you requested, Clay."

"Thanks, Kathy." Quietly he began to speak, but at that moment, they heard activity in the outer office. Jack Kelley, Tom Moore, and Harry Jacobs had all arrived. Soon their meeting was underway, mostly dealing with the progress that the boys were making, and more strategies for continuing to help them in their healing process.

Olivia excused herself a little early from the meeting, as it was almost time for the children to arrive, and she needed to get to her classroom. After saying good-bye she turned to go, but Clay interrupted. "We'll

continue our discussion at a later date, Miss Sheffield."
She nodded and left without looking back.

Tom Moore stood up to go too. "I need to get to my class as well. Nice to speak with you again, Jack. Travis is really doing alright, I think."

Harry Jacobs reminded Jack that it would be a long healing process, and Clay nodded in the affirmative. "I agree, Jack, although I'm not a trained psychologist like Mr. Jacobs. Don't try and rush Gus. He'll have to get there in his own time." Both men left the office directly afterward, and Clay was left alone.

What in the world am I going to do about Livy? Maybe I should speak with Dad. But something stopped him from picking up the phone. *Just get a grip, Clay. You're a grown man! You can work with Olivia Sheffield and keep your hands off of her! Just give Nicole a call and see when she's available to go out.*

At the end of the school day, Clay headed down to Olivia's classroom. Her door was closed, so he knocked.

"Come in," came her now-familiar voice.

Clay entered the classroom. She was sitting at the desk quietly grading papers. She looked up and smiled a sort of resigned smile. "Hi," she said, starting to rise.

"No, no, no. Stay in your seat. You look worn out." He paused, and then continued, "I thought that maybe we could talk for a minute before the day got away from us?"

She nodded.

"May I close your classroom door?" He did so, after she nodded again. As he walked toward her, he said apologetically, "I'm sorry about this morning, Livy. I know I told you that the first kiss was a mistake, and it appears that I've made yet another."

"It's alright, Clay. I was there too. I just don't know how to proceed."

"It's simple. I don't want to leave this school and neither do you, nor should you. We are just drawn to each other for reasons beyond our understanding. But we're grown adults, and we are both involved with other people. Surely, we can keep this relationship on a professional level?" He spoke with great conviction and solid commitment on his face. "What do you think?"

"Yes," she nodded. "You're probably right. I've been seeing Derek for some time now. I didn't know that you were seeing anyone regularly, but that's wonderful. You've convinced me. I'm sure that we're both adult enough to manage ourselves like professionals."

"Then it's settled?" Clay took Olivia's hand, ignoring the shocking warmth that he felt, as well as the tingle of desire. "Let's just do our jobs and we'll be fine!"

"You've got a deal!" said Livy, comforted somewhat by his confident attitude.

"Have a great evening, Olivia, and I'll see you tomorrow!" Clay waved.

"Alright...tomorrow it is," and Livy went back to grading her papers with her head down. After she heard her door quietly close, she looked up resignedly. *Please make it easy.* But somehow she knew that there was no chance that was going to happen.

13

Autumn came roaring in with those brisk October mornings and evenings; yet the Indiana fall was spectacular. The trees turned their varying shades of reds, oranges and golds and the last remaining mums were in bloom.

The children at Brandenburg Elementary were also blooming as they awaited one of their favorite events, the Fall Festival. It had been a long-standing tradition in Brandenburg. Each year it was held the third weekend of October, rain or shine. There were food stands of all kinds: French fries, cotton candy, elephant ears, ice cream, pizza,and caramel apples. There were also bratwurst and hot dog and hamburger sandwiches being grilled by the P.T.O dads. There was an inflatable castle where smaller kids could jump and play, and a merry-go-round and ferris wheel and other rides for the older kids to enjoy.

On the stage were visiting local performers. Even some of the high school choir and band kids came over to perform. A tent was set up for arts and crafts made throughout the year by church groups, senior citizens, and students; it included an art show judged by local dignitaries.

Fall Festival started early on Friday, so school was only in session for half a day. The kids were wired to the hilt and ready to have fun all weekend. It was one of those days when teachers generally pulled their hair out, and ended up playing games or doing review work with their classes. It was almost time for the bell to ring to signal the end of the morning. Olivia said, "Now ladies and gentlemen, I expect to see you all on your best behavior at Fall Festival. I know that you will make me proud of my second graders."

Little Melinda Robbins asked excitedly, "Are you coming tonight, Miss Sheffield?"

"I wouldn't miss it for the world! Remember--this is my hometown. I've been coming to the Fall Festival since I was in second grade."

"Gee, Miss Sheffield. You must be pretty old 'cause I don't think you've been in second grade for a long time," murmured Nathan Ellis.

"Nathan Ellis, you are not very nice!" criticized Melinda. "My mother told me you should never call a lady old, and anyway, Miss Sheffield isn't even married yet, are you, Miss Sheffield?"

"I know that, you sassy brat," said Nathan. "But my Mom says she might get married to that guy with the dark hair--what's his name, Miss Sheffield? Mom says he's really handsome--ick!"

Clay had just passed by Livy's room and had heard Nathan's question. He stepped quietly into the room. The children were all gathered around Olivia and her back was to the door.

Olivia was laughing and shaking her head, amazed at the direction of the conversation. "First of all, boys and girls, my personal life is my own and whom I choose to marry is certainly up to me; but in answer to your question, Nate, I do have a friend named Mr. Donaldson. I think that's who your mom was talking about."

Normally quieter than a mouse, Laura Brown took hold of Olivia's hand, and said, "I think that you should marry Mr. Mitchell instead, Miss Sheffield. He's much more handsomer than whoever that guy you said was, and he likes you a lot!" Clay heard the comment and turned to make a quick exit, but not before a number of the students had spotted him. They converged on him in a pack.

"Mr. Mitchell...hey, Mr. Mitchell...we think that maybe you should marry Miss Sheffield, so she doesn't marry that other guy!" Shouts of agreement were rising up from many of the students. They had pulled him back into the room.

Olivia turned around and watched the principal being dragged back into her classroom. The kids were barraging him with questions which he carefully deflected. "Now, boys and girls, this line of questioning is really not appropriate, and I know that I'm not comfortable speaking about it, and I'm sure that Miss Sheffield isn't either. Anyway, the bell's going to...."

And ring it did. The kids forgot all they were talking about, quickly grabbed their backpacks, and lined up in perfect order waiting to leave for the weekend. Shouts of excitement were blurted out, as Adam said, "Oh, please, Miss Sheffield? Can we go now?"

"Thanks for lining up so quickly, class. Yes, of

course. Go! I'll see you tonight!" she shouted and they raced out the door.

Clay watched as Livy's shoulders sagged and she heaved a sigh of relief. *Don't notice how great she looks in that shade of blue. Just stay calm.* "So you're coming to the Festival tonight, Olivia?"

She turned and smiled. "Oh, yes. I haven't missed the opening night of the Festival since I was a little girl. I can't start now."

"Is Derek joining you?" *Where did that question come from?*

"Yes, actually he is. Will you be bringing your... your...?"

"Yes. Her name's Nicole Marshall. Maybe the four of us..."

Civilized, isn't it? She interrupted. "Yes, that would be great. Let's arrange to meet somewhere this evening, then. Why don't we say 9:30 at the ferris wheel? We'll probably find some others to join us."

"It's a date...I mean a plan. See you tonight," and he was gone.

Sally came in a moment later. Livy had never told her about Clay, and she wasn't about to get into that discussion, now. *Nothing to talk about anyway.*

"Hey, was that Clay I just saw leaving?"

"Yes, he popped in for a moment. It seems he's bringing his girlfriend to the Festival tonight. Her name is Nicole Marshall. I told him that we'd meet them at the ferris wheel at 9:30."

"Sounds like fun. Mind if Dave and I join you?" Dave had filled Sally in on the evening at Los Cabos, but Olivia had never mentioned it. Sally knew that Livy told her everything, unless she was working through a difficult issue. Then she would veritably shut up like a clam. Sally couldn't help but think, " I'm dying to see the two of them together in a social setting." She realized that Olivia hadn't answered. "Olivia? Is it okay?"

"Of course. Why wouldn't it be?"

"Okay, then if we don't run into you and Derek before, we'll see you at the ferris wheel at 9:30. Toodle-loo! I'm so excited!"

I was too...a minute ago.

Dressed in her best jeans, a chocolate brown mock turtleneck sweater and jean jacket, Olivia led Derek through the Festival, meeting and greeting parents and students and old friends. Olivia was quick to introduce Derek to anyone that he had not already met, and she was pleased to see how conversant he was with everyone.

"Hey...I forgot to tell you. Jim and Susie are coming down to the Festival, too!" Derek offered.

"Are you kidding me? They're venturing out of the big city for a change? I haven't seen them since they took their new jobs. Oh, I'm so glad that they're coming! What time are they due in, or do you know?"

"I think that Jim said around 9:00 p.m. Let's see if we can meet them somewhere for a drink."

"No problem. A bunch of us are meeting at the ferris wheel at 9:30 anyway. I'll just leave a message on Jim's cell phone and have them meet there, too." She dialed Jimmy's number and got the machine. "Okay, big brother. Derek tells me you're heading for Brandenburg with Susie. Meet us at the ferris wheel at 9:30 or call if you're delayed. I can't wait to see you and get caught up on your new jobs." As she hung up, her excitement fairly bubbled out. "Oh, what a great evening!"

Derek agreed. "Okay, what's the first thing we need to check out?"

"Oh, I think the Fun House. Then we need to start eating our way through the midway."

"You like fair food?" Derek asked, surprised.

"You're kidding, right? I love it all and usually I'm sick to my stomach by the end of the evening. But what the heck, it's only once a year, so I go crazy!"

"Well, in that case, I'm dying for a big juicy brat, and I'm starving. Let's do the Fun House after we've eaten."

Olivia nodded and grabbed his hand. "Follow me, I know just where to go!"

Olivia pulled Derek over to a tent where the most mouth-watering aromas were wafting on the air. "Hey, Stan. How are you?"

"Great, Miss Sheffield."

"Oh, Stan, can't we lose the Miss title? It's so formal. By the way, this is Derek Donaldson. Derek, this is Stan Schuman."

The two shook hands, while Stan answered Olivia. "I'm sorry, I just can't do it...you've taught all three of my kids, and it was always 'Miss Sheffield this... Miss Sheffield that'. I just can't get out of the habit."

"How old are your kids, now, Stan?" asked Derek.

"Oh, Lord, let me be sure that this is right. I get mixed up sometimes. Let's see...Tommy is in 7th, Cory's in 6th, and Toby's in 4th, I think. But they all loved Miss..."

"Stan," Olivia used her 'teacher voice'.

Stan laughed. "They all loved Olivia when they had her."

"Not a surprise to me, Stan. How about a couple of bratwurst sandwiches? Those smell incredible!"

"On the house, Mr. Donaldson," he said, handing over the sandwiches. "The condiments are over on that table,"

"Thanks so much, Stan," Olivia smiled. "Say hello to Deb...and the kids. Of course, I do see Toby once in a while during recess or in an assembly."

She and Derek went to the condiment table. Derek watched Olivia pile on mustard, sauerkraut, pickle relish, some onions, and banana peppers. She looked up and watched his amused smile. "Now look here." she said. " I'm going all out tonight...so no kissing, I guess, because I'm not giving up the onions!"

He laughed. "Okay, then give me one now so I don't have to wait!" He leaned in and kissed her lightly on the lips, and she laughed too.

Sally and Dave waved them over to a seat under the big tent. "Already starting the Food Fest, Olivia?" teased Dave.

"What is it with all you spoilsports? Go on Sal. Grab a brat from Stan and get back here!"

"Great idea! Sally get me a brat, too. Come on, Derek. We need to grab some fries and a couple of beers." The men and Sally left and Olivia saved their seats.

"What a perfect night," said Sally when she returned from getting the brats.

"It really is! And guess what--Derek told me that Jimmy and Susie are driving over too. I haven't seen them since they took their new jobs, so I sent Jimmy a message to meet us at the ferris wheel too. Then maybe we can all head over to Ojays for a nightcap."

The girls were eating and dripping mustard and kraut and giggling when the guys got back, carrying two huge orders of fries with chili and cheese, and beers all around.

"I tried to stop him, Olivia. But he said you'd be fine with all this artery clogging tonight!" Derek wryly commented, with raised eyebrows.

"Oh, heaven. Chili-cheese fries, too." Olivia dove in.

Sally laughed at Derek's expression. "She tends to overdo at times, Derek. Haven't you noticed?"

All four looked at each other and burst out laughing. Of course, Olivia was the only one with chili dripping down her chin. Derek reached up with his napkin and wiped it off. She smiled back warmly at him, "Thanks."

Sally watched the sweetness of the gesture and took in the pair's interaction. He's a nice guy...but maybe a little too nice for Olivia? Then Sally said aloud, "Come on, you all. I want to get out to the midway and the Fun House!" They all quickly cleaned up their spots at the table and left in a hurry, joking and laughing along the way.

Clay had arranged for Nicole to come to town for the Fall Festival. Originally, she had expected to come on Saturday, but was able to get a colleague to take her emergency medical calls, so she had let him know that she would be available on Friday instead. Clay was pleased that they would have time together, and he'd

SCHOOL DAYS, SCHOOL DAZE

set her up in the nearby Inn of Brandenburg so that she could stay overnight. She had arrived in town at 4:00 and he'd given her directions to his apartment. He saw her car pull into the driveway and went out to greet her.

"Hey, hi," he smiled and hugged her. "Why don't you leave your car here, and we'll take your stuff over and get you checked in?"

"Sounds great. Oh, Clay, I have to tell you that I'm excited just to get out of town for a day and a half. The practice has been crazy lately, and my hours are certainly not my own."

Clay moved her suitcase to his car, opened the passenger door, and Nicole got in. He moved around to the driver's seat, and said, "Well, from what I've heard, the Fall Festival will be a great opportunity to relax and enjoy yourself. It's new for me too. And by the way--you may be overworked, but you look great!" She was really beautiful, her long brown hair pulled back into a ponytail, adorned with simple hoop earrings, and wearing a white sweater over jeans. "I think that you'll like the Inn. They've recently updated and remodeled from what I hear; I went over to check it out before I made your reservation. There's a nice hot tub down by the indoor pool as well, and that should help you unwind."

"Thanks for working it out. It sounds like Nirvana."

They arrived at the Inn and got Nicole settled, then headed out to the Festival. "I think that I'll park the car at my school and we'll just walk over, if that's okay with you."

"Oh, that would be fine. But would it be possible to see your school, Clay?"

He shrugged. "Sure, if you want to, I can give you a tour."

"You speak so highly of your job, I'd just like to see where you work."

They arrived at Brandenburg Elementary and Clay parked his car in the staff parking lot, which was pretty full already. Then he took her in for a quick visit, showing her his office and strolling through the halls. She saw the mural from the Open House in the lobby. "I positively LOVE the mural," she exclaimed as she strode over to take a closer look. Clay told her the story behind his illustrations and she listened attentively. "Well...it's nice to meet a man who is not afraid to admit his shortcomings. And looking at these drawings, they definitely are shortcomings!" she laughed.

"Oh, ha-ha. Another comedian in the group!" He locked up the building as they exited. "Let's get on over to the Festival."

Together they strolled through the midway, played some games, had a caramel apple, stopped at the Art and Crafts Building, and generally did a tour of the Festival. They rode a couple of rides and met some parents and students from Brandenburg, who were all anxious to speak with Clay. He would introduce Nicole, give them direct eye contact and lots of warmth, but he was also able to keep them moving on and not stopping in one place or with one person for too long.

"Wow. I love to watch you in action handling these people. You're a master of tactfulness, and yet we're not stuck too long anywhere. I need to take note to improve my "bedside manner..." Her eyes got big as she realized what she had said, and she turned bright red.

Clay winked at her. "Hey, now, we can talk about your bedside manner a little later this evening if you want." He chuckled. "We need to keep our eyes on the clock, though, because at 9:30 we're supposed to meet some friends at the ferris wheel. Then, if you're game, we'll probably go get a drink at our local pub, Ojays."

"Sounds great. Lead on!"

Jack, Gus, and Travis Kelley were walking down the midway, enjoying the fall weather and trying to do something that would take their minds off their recent loss. Travis was excited and rowdy, Gus, much more quiet and reserved, and Jack was just weary. *HOW DID NANCY TAKE SUCH GOOD CARE OF US?* The thought flitted through his head a hundred times a week, both at home and work. His employer had been so supportive. He was being allowed to get the boys off to school in the morning, then go to work, and then be there to pick them up after school. He was eternally grateful for that kindness. After taking the boys home, he'd do another two or three hours of work from home; at least the boys knew he was nearby. But he knew that he would need to get back to more regular hours eventually.

Somehow Nancy had managed the household, the boys, cooked, cleaned, volunteered at church and the school, and still held a part-time job. It was above and beyond anything Jack understood, now that he was walking in her shoes. *Oh, honey, I wish I'd told you how perfect you were so many more times than I did.* His eyes welled up with unshed tears, as he walked with the boys.

Suddenly Travis shouted and pointed ahead. "Hey,

Dad, look over at the fishing lake. There's a bunch of my friends. Can we please go over, please, please!" he pleaded.

"Well, it's getting pretty cold to catch any fish, but... Gus, what do <u>you</u> think?" He looked down at his little boy, who so resembled his wife.

"I think that would be fun, Dad. Let's go."

Jack wiped his eyes, threw off his melancholy, and said, "Last one to the lake's a rotten egg!" All three of them took off like a shot. Of course, Jack slowed down on the way; he noticed that Travis held back too.

"I won! I won!" shouted Gus.

"You sure did! What do you say to some fishing, and then some dinner, and then a trip to the Fun House before it gets too crowded?"

"Woo-Hoo!" said Travis. "Give me fivers, Gus." And they high-fived. "Come on, let's go get a fishing pole."

"Hey, wait a minute, boys. Do any of <u>you</u> have money to rent a fishing pole?"

The boys looked at each other. "No! Come on Dad! We need you!" and they both grabbed a hand.

And I need you too, boys. "Okay, fellas, let's go catch some bass!" he yelled, as they grabbed their poles, and headed towards the lake.

The evening was perfect, one of the nicest October evenings that anyone could remember. The place was packed with lots of townspeople and their out-of-town relatives who made their yearly fall trek here for this weekend. Everyone seemed in high spirits, the aroma of all the foods was wonderful, the barkers were hawking their wares, the rides were running non-stop, and the performers were playing to big crowds. All in all it was a great night. By 9:00 p.m. the stars had come out and the evening was getting crisp and much cooler. Suddenly, Jack Kelley came running up to some friends at the Festival. He was in a panic. "Hey Vince, Karen, Joe? Have any of you seen Gus? Somehow he got away from me."

The trio answered in the negative, instantly showing concern for Gus. "Where were you last, Jack?" someone asked.

Speaking quickly, his eyes darting everywhere, he said, "Well, we'd gone fishing, then went to get a bite to eat, and then went over to the midway. Gus was holding Travis's hand and I was walking alongside. Suddenly, Gus just pulled away from Travis and ran. I spotted him for awhile, but then I lost him in the crowd. "I've been calling and calling, but he hasn't answered, and Travis and I are going crazy."

"Stay calm, Jack," said Vince, who was a policeman in Brandenburg. "I'll call the Chief and we'll get everyone in the park to look for him. We'll get an announcement over the loudspeaker."

Karen patted Jack's hand consolingly. By then Travis had caught up with his Dad, and it was evident that he'd been crying. "Hold on, honey, I'm sure we'll find your little brother," Karen soothed.

"But it's my fault he's gone!" Travis wailed.

"It's not your fault. Just stay right here with us, and Gus will turn up. I just know it." She pulled Travis towards her in an embrace.

"Please, Karen, can you keep an eye on Travis? I just can't stand around," Jack asked.

"Go! Go, Jack! It's okay. We'll be fine."

Suddenly over the loudspeaker, the announcement came blaringly. "ATTENTION ALL FAIRGOERS! WE HAVE A MISSING CHILD TO REPORT--PLEASE KEEP AN EYE OUT FOR GUS KELLEY. HE WAS LAST SEEN ON THE MIDWAY ABOUT THIRTY MINUTES AGO. HE IS 7 YEARS OLD, WITH LIGHT BROWN HAIR, AND WEARING A BLUE SWEATSHIRT AND KHAKIS."

From all corners of the park, people stopped and listened to the announcement. If they lived in Brandenburg, they knew little Gus; immediately, groups split up heading in different directions. Panicked shouts were heard everywhere, as people searched and called Gus's name.

Clay was stunned as he listened to the announce-ment. He turned to Nicole and said, "Oh, my God, I've got to find that boy! He lost his mother just a couple of months ago and well, I don't know what his Dad and brother would do if something happened to him."

"Go ahead, Clay. I'll catch up soon. Just meet me when you can at the ferris wheel."

Clay's frown showed Nicole how concerned he was as he waved and left her at breakneck speed.

Olivia, Derek, Sally and Dave, had just met Jimmy and Susie when they heard the announcement.

"Dear God, Sally! If something's happened to that little boy, I'll just die! I know where I'm going first, though!" And Olivia was gone, without another word.

Derek shouted, "Olivia?" But she was too far ahead to even hear him. "Where do you think she went, Sally?"

"I have no idea. Just stick with us, and we'll start hunting too."

Derek nodded in assent.

Olivia Sheffield was angry as she ran all the way to the bandstand where the announcements were made. *Oh, please God, keep him safe.* She arrived at the speaker's booth, followed almost instantly by Clay.

"Livy!" Clay grabbed her hands. "Do you know anything?"

Tersely, she answered. "Not yet." But somehow she felt a little better that he was there. "Hey, John? Could I possibly get on the loudspeaker and say something? Gus is in my classroom."

"Of course. Anything if you think it'll work." He moved out of her way.

Olivia spoke sternly over the loudspeaker. "GUS KELLEY, IT'S MISS SHEFFIELD. YOU PROMISED ME TODAY THAT YOU WOULD BEHAVE TONIGHT AT FALL FESTIVAL. AND NOW WE CAN'T FIND YOU, AND I'M REALLY GETTING SCARED..." a sob escaped her voice. Clay motioned for her to turn over the microphone.

"GUS KELLEY, IT'S MR. MITCHELL I'M NOT SURE WHERE YOU'RE HIDING OR WHERE YOU'VE GONE, BUT WE'RE ALL GETTING REALLY WORRIED. I THOUGHT MAYBE IF YOU WERE LOST, YOU COULD SEE THE TOP OF THE FERRIS WHEEL AND GO OVER IN THAT DIRECTION. YOU CAN ASK ANYONE FOR HELP THAT YOU MEET ALONG THE WAY. I WAS THINKING THAT WE COULD TAKE A NICE RIDE ONCE YOU GET THERE. I'M GOING THERE NOW. I HOPE THAT YOU CAN HEAR ME AND YOU'LL COME AND RIDE. FERRIS WHEELS MAKE ME A LITTLE NERVOUS, AND I'D LIKE YOU TO BE THERE WITH ME. MISS SHEFFIELD WILL

BE THERE TOO.

"Oh, Clay, I'm so scared."

"I know, honey. Hang on..." and he took her hand and they headed to the ferris wheel.

Little Gus Kelley was mad. His brother, Travis, had been pushing him around when they were fishing, and then he made fun of him when he'd dropped his ice cream cone, and well, he had just been bossing him around all the time, and Gus was tired of it. Finally, when Travis and he were walking on the midway, and his big brother told him that he couldn't fish too well, and that he was a baby who needed his hand held, well, Gus just exploded. He pulled away from Travis and ran as fast as he could.

In the beginning, Gus wasn't afraid. He just ran to get away from his big brother. But as he was running, everyone was so big, and there were so many walkways, and so much noise, and so many people, that finally he slowed down to look back and see where Travis was. But he didn't see him anywhere...or his Dad...or anyone else he knew, as he looked upwards towards the faces of the men, women, and children who were passing. He didn't want to ask for help because he knew Travis would only call him a baby again, so he quietly wandered around keeping his eyes out for a familiar face.

As time went by and he didn't see one, Gus began to get scared. His heart was pounding hard and he couldn't help himself; he started to cry. He didn't hear the park announcement because he was watching some big kids shoot the pop guns at the rubber ducks; and he was so confused he didn't know what to do or where to go. Now he began to cry even harder--*maybe I am a baby*--but he didn't care and couldn't help it. Then he heard a voice he recognized. It was Miss Sheffield... oh, no, it sounds like she is crying! Then he heard Mr. Mitchell's voice too. He had to find a way to get to the ferris wheel, so Mr. Mitchell wouldn't be afraid. I'll ride it with him...if I can find it! Maybe if I hurry, Miss Sheffield will stop crying too. He wiped his eyes and rubbed his dripping nose on his sweatshirt, and turned around to look up high. There it was--the shiny ferris wheel all lit up. It was the biggest thing out there. He knew by now that he might get lost, so he went up to some of the big kids and asked if they would help him get to the ferris wheel.

Senior Ted Young turned around and looked at the little boy who was talking to him. Clearly he'd been crying. Ted had heard the announcements and knew instantly that this was the missing little boy. "Hey, is your name Gus?"

The little boy nodded.

"Well, sure, little buddy, I can take you to the ferris wheel," and in one big movement he picked Gus up. "See it right over there!" He pointed to the big ride. "It's pretty big so you can see it. But it's pretty far away. I'll take you there now. Do you want to ride on my shoulders? Think how cool that would be. You'd be taller than everyone!"

Gus smiled through his tears, and nodded happily.

"Hey, guys. This is Gus, and I'm taking him to the ferris wheel. I'll meet you over at the ring toss when

I get back." Ted knew he needed to get word to the crowd that Gus had been found. He went up to one of the barkers and asked, "Do you have any way of calling the main office to tell them that the missing boy's been found?"

"Sure do, young man," said the barker as he shook Ted 's hand. "Good job, son."

"Well, he sort of found me," said Ted, modestly.

Ted hurried off with Gus riding high on his shoulders, his hands on Ted's head. "You okay up there, buddy?"

Gus smiled down and nodded at his new hero.

"Well. come on. Let's get you to that ferris wheel," and off he went as fast as he could safely go with his cargo.

A minute later an announcement came over the loudspeaker. ATTENTION EVERYONE: GUS KELLEY HAS BEEN LOCATED AND IS BEING BROUGHT TO THE FERRIS WHEEL AS WE SPEAK!

Great sounds of applause and laughter erupted through the park. Gus heard it, but he didn't know what the fuss was about . He couldn't take his eye off all the sights from his new perspective.

"Almost there, buddy," said Ted, smiling.

And sure enough, there was the ferris wheel. The first people Gus saw were his Dad and Travis; right behind them were Mr. Mitchell and Miss Sheffield. Oh, oh...I might be in trouble.

Ted sensed Gus's fear. "Hey, what's going on up there, mister?" Gus's eyes were round. Ted lowered him down off his shoulders. "Hey, are you scared or something?"

Gus nodded, eyes growing even larger.

"Word to the wise, little buddy. Those people aren't mad...they're just glad. You wait and see!" and he grabbed Gus's hand and led him over to the crowd.

The second Gus arrived, Jack Kelley knelt down and grabbed him up in a fierce hug; then Travis came too, and HE was crying. Then Miss Sheffield came and she was crying too. Finally, Mr. Mitchell was there, and he bent down and shook Gus's hand. His new friend, Ted, had been right. No one was even yelling at him, and everyone standing around was smiling.

Gus knew his manners. He said to everyone, "This is Ted. He helped me."

Now handshakes went all around with Ted, slaps on the back as well, and profuse thanks from Gus's dad. "Son, I can't thank you enough for helping Gus get back to us."

"Oh, it was nothing. I have a whole slew of brothers and sisters and..."

"Gus, what do you say to Ted?" urged Jack.

"Thank you for helping me, Ted. Maybe you could come over..." he looked up at his Dad, "and hang out with me at my house sometime."

"Sure, buddy."

Jack shook his hand and said, "How about we take you out for dinner one evening this week, Ted?"

"Oh, that's not necessary..."

"I think it is for us, Ted. Can you give me your phone number, and I'll give you a call this week?"

"Sure, I guess." As Ted and Jack exchanged information, a local reporter took some photos of Gus and Ted and the crowd hanging around them all.

Even Travis got in a picture. "I'm really sorry I

made you mad, Gus; and I'm glad you're okay. Would you like to play with my new computer game when we get home?"

Sensing opportunity, Gus replied, "That would be cool!" Then he looked at his brother, and suddenly they were both hugging. The photographer snapped another picture.

Jack Kelley exhaled. "Well, I for one, am totally done in. Let's get on home, guys," he said, as he took Gus's hand.

Gus pulled away instantly. "I can't go right now, Dad. I have to ride the ferris wheel with Mr. Mitchell!" Under his breath he added, "You know he's a little scared to ride it."

Clay caught Jack's eye and smiled. He bent down towards Gus, and said, "You know, Gus, I can wait to ride the ferris wheel until another time."

"No, no, no." Gus glanced at his Dad. "I don't think that Did will bring me back here until next year. It's got to be NOW."

By now, an ever-growing crowd of people were in the vicinity, including Derek, Sally, Dave, Jimmy, Susie and Nicole. They were all milling around and listening in on the conversation; they just couldn't help it. "Go on, Clay," Dave chortled. "We know how scared you are to go that high..."

"Okay, okay, I give up," responded Clay, throwing his hands in the air. "I'll ride the ferris wheel with you, Gus." He held out his hand to Nicole. "Gus, I'd like you to meet Miss Marshall. Could she go on the ferris wheel with us as well?"

Gus looked at Miss Marshall. She was pretty and all that, but he didn't know her. He could see Miss

Sheffield smiling at him. Gus considered the request for a moment, then said, "No, thank you. I want to take Miss Sheffield on the ferris wheel with us," and he ran and grabbed her hand.

Olivia was surprised and embarrassed. "Oh, Gus, dear, you're so sweet. But I don't need to go...and Mr. Mitchell has his nice lady friend to take, and..."

Gus was pulling on her and wagging his head negatively. "No...it's you and Mr. Michell...now! Come on!"

Clay looked apologetically at Nicole, and she smiled and shrugged. "No problem, Clay."

Olivia glanced in Derek's direction as she was being pulled towards the ride. His mouth was tightly set, but he nodded. He really had no choice. Derek stood there a minute watching Clay, Gus, and Olivia climb into the bucket of the ride. *Well, at least the kid is in the middle.* Then he felt a tap on his shoulder. He turned around, and was face to face with the brunette. "Hi!" She held out her hand cordially. "Looks like our dates are double-booked! We might as well get to know each other. My name's Nicole Marshall."

"It appears so," Derek agreed, as he shook her hand. "I'm Derek Donaldson. They watched the progress of the ferris wheel for a minute.

Sally glanced over. "Hey, Derek and Nicole. Let's head on over to Ojays for a nightcap. It's been a long evening!"

The crowd dispersed and the four of them headed for a drink at Ojays. Derek and Nicole walked together, smiling and talking. Sally kept an eye on the two of them and linked her arm with Dave's and headed down the street, talking quietly.

The ferris wheel rose slowly in the air; Gus was the first to speak. "I don't really get why you're afraid of this, Mr. Mitchell."

Clay looked over at Livy and smiled. "Well, it's not so much fear, as I don't really like being up this high."

Livy was giggling. "To be really honest, Gus, neither do I, and it seems we're getting higher and higher." She was looking down.

"Well, yeah. They have to load all the people on. You know what's really fun?"

"No, what, Gus?" they both asked.

Gus began to kick and rock his body. "When you make the bucket rock back and forth like this!"

How can a little boy make this movement so quickly? I'm not feeling so well...what with all that fair food and the fright..."Could you please stop, Gus? I think I might be sick!"

Gus was joyfully rocking when Clay looked over at Olivia and saw that her face was a peculiar shade of green. "Gus...stop that right now!" he commanded.

Recognizing the voice of authority, Gus quit instantly. He looked up at Miss Sheffield and apologized. "I'm sorry. I won't do it anymore."

Clay watched as Livy patted Gus's head. "It's okay. But you know, Gus, you had us all so worried, that suddenly I'm very tired. I'll bet you're tired too." She began to stroke his head.

Gus denied it. "I'm not tired at all!" But the comforting motion of her hand and the ferris wheel succeeded in putting Gus to sleep within minutes.

When she realized that Gus had fallen to sleep, Livy sighed. She looked up and saw Clay staring at her, the intense eyes full of compassion.

"You look a little done in too," he murmured quietly, nodding towards the sleeping boy.

"Oh, Clay. I was so scared. All I could think about was finding a way to speak with Gus or get his attention. And then you were there too. It gave me such comfort. Thank you."

Clay reached across to Livy's shoulders. "No one can see us up here. Just lay your head down on my shoulder and close your eyes for a minute." His left hand reached across the back of the bucket seat and began twirling loose strands of her hair. It felt so good that she closed her eyes and totally relaxed on his shoulder.

When the ferris wheel returned to its starting place, all three inhabitants were out cold. Gus was asleep in the middle of the seat, Livy's head was on his shoulder, and Clay's head was lying peacefully on top of Livy's head. The two adults were holding hands, as if to keep the boy safe.

The photographer shot that final pose, and said to the reporter. "Here's your wrap up for the article on the kid. Now let's get it to the newsroom."

14

The jolt from the ride operator pulling on the safety bar of the ferris wheel, woke the trio up abruptly. Clay and Olivia were even more unsettled to find themselves holding hands, which they quickly unclasped. Clay helped Gus and Olivia off the ride.

"Gee, I think we were all tired, Mr. Mitchell...Miss Sheffield. We were all asleep. But I saw you two holding hands. I'm going to tell the kids at school now that you'll be getting married soon; they'll be real happy."

"Gus, I hardly think that holding hands is a reason to get married. We were just being sure you stayed in the car safely. Right, Mr. Mitchell?" She looked at Clay beseechingly.

"Right!" he said assuredly. "Now look here, Gus, you don't need to be telling the kids anything about Livy..." he cleared his throat, "I mean Miss Sheffield and me getting married. We work together and came on the ride because you asked us to."

"Yeah, but you two were the ones who didn't like the rocking when I wiggled around in the car, and you two were the ones holding hands, and the kids told you that they want you to get married..."

"Okay, okay, Gus. Let's drop the subject now. We need to find your Dad and brother. It's getting real late, and I imagine that it's way past your bedtime."

Suddenly, Jack and Travis were there and Gus made a beeline straight to them, chattering away. His Dad said something to him, then he turned and waved goodbye to Olivia and Clay.

"Thanks for taking me on the ferris wheel. See you in school on Monday!" Gus turned his back, grabbed his Dad's hand, and father and sons headed off toward the parking lot.

"Well, that was certainly interesting," chuckled Clay as he and Livy watched the three walk away.

Livy agreed. "Do you think that we'd better get over to Ojays and meet the crowd?"

"I do. Let's get a move on."

They began to walk quickly. Livy couldn't stand the quiet. "That Gus is something else. You don't really think that he'll talk to the kids about..."

"Nah," Clay interrupted. "He'll have forgotten it all by tomorrow morning. Just wait and see."

Olivia nodded in agreement. *Fingers crossed!*

They entered Ojays to cheers and greetings and went directly over to Derek and Nicole who were standing together at the bar.

"Hey, you two. How was the ride?" Derek asked.

"Alright, if you don't get motion sickness. That

little boy was rocking the car like crazy. We practically had to hold him down," said Olivia, glancing in Clay's direction.

Clay nodded in agreement. "He's a piece of work, but you can't help but like him. Those gears up there," pointing to his head, "never quit working."

Nicole chimed in. "I just thought that he was adorable, and when he asked you two to ride with him, that was priceless." She grabbed Clay's arm and smiled up at him. Clay looked at her and returned the smile, patting her hand.

Ooo-she might be just too sweet! At that moment in time, Olivia did not like her reaction to the situation. *Get a hold of yourself! You're here with Derek.* She took Derek's arm and steered him away from the group, whispering, "How about a glass of red wine, Derek? I'm a little chilled from the night air."

Clay watched Olivia whisper into Derek's ear, and it bothered him, but for once he kept control of his errant thoughts, and asked Nicole what she'd like to drink. The crowd at Ojays enjoyed lively conversation, and each other's company until the wee hours of the morning. Finally, O'Jay shouted, "Last call, everyone. I need to get home and get some rest."

The crowd agreed as they settled up tabs and began to disperse. "What a great night for the Festival," Dave commented to Sally, as they took their leave.

"Yeah, it's been one of the nicest. Now while I've got you alone...tell me again about that night at Los Cabos. You didn't get to finish the story, and I've been watching Olivia. It's obvious to me that she hasn't been comfortable tonight seeing Clay with Nicole."

"Now, how would you know that?" Dave glanced

over at Olivia. "She looks fine to me."

"Dave Garrett, Olivia and I have been friends since sixth grade. We <u>know</u> each other; I'm here to tell you that every time Nicole Marshall so much as looks at Clay, Olivia wants to wring her neck!"

"Okay, okay, I get it. But frankly, I'm not so sure that Clay is keen on the way Derek looks at Olivia either."

"That's what I'm talking about. I think that there are fireworks just waiting to blow between Olivia and Clay, and I'm going to be the one to light the fuse!" Sally wore a satisfied grin.

"What about Derek and Nicole? They're really great people," said Dave.

"I agree; but maybe not for Clay and Olivia...so spill...we need to work on the details of a plan to get those two together!" They walked out with their heads together, hand in hand.

On Monday morning, the kids piled into Brandenburg Elementary, tired, but exhilarated all the same. They chirped excitedly about the rides, the food, the games, and all the friends they'd seen at the Festival. Basically, the teaching staff did the same. They all had great stories to tell about friends and relations who only came into town for the Festival, and generally spirits were high that morning.

Olivia was running late to school. On the front page of the Brandenburg Press was a telling photo of her and Clay, asleep in the ferris wheel car, holding hands across Gus Kelley.

They looked so...so...domestic...and kind of sweet. The headline read: SCHOOL DAZE--ASLEEP ON THE JOB, and then went on to describe pretty accurately what had happened with Gus. She could have killed Eddie Frantz, the photographer. He'd graduated with her, *Ohhh, that Eddie! When I see him, I'm going to give him a piece of my mind! Not that it will matter. The photo is good, and it'll sell papers!* Eddie had been a jokester in school, and was always trying to embarrass someone. He knew she'd been dating Derek and Clay was her boss. He'd deliberately taken the photo, to stir the pot. All that she could think about was the questions that her second graders would be asking, and the teachers, and her friends, and...oh, it was just too embarrassing to think about. *And what if Derek gets hold of this? What will he think?*

It turned out, though, that no one said a thing. *That's a good sign. Hopefully no one has read the paper yet.* But when she dashed into her classroom, the first person she saw was Clay. He was waiting for her...standing and talking quietly to the kids who came on the early bus. She quickly pulled off her jacket, hung it up, and turned around to make eye contact with him.

Dear God...she is beautiful. All flushed from the morning air and rosy with her hair tousled like that. I wonder if she looks like this every morning? "Well, good morning, Miss Sheffield."

"Good morning, Mr. Mitchell. Is there something you need?"

An open-ended question that I'd like to answer... with just the two of us in the room. "I've been speaking to some of your students, and they have been so excited to talk about the Festival...and their friends...and the food...and...us." He smiled sheepishly.

Livy was mortified. "Oh?" she said quietly.

"Yes. I think that I will take care of morning announcements, then head back in here, sit down with the kids, and have a little talk after they all arrive. After all, as the principal, I think it would be best if I met this little issue head on, and cleared up any questions. Are you okay with that?"

"That will be fine, Clay. I'll let the kids know that you'll be coming in soon." She looked at him and rolled her eyes.

"Don't worry. I'll take care of this once and for all."

Livy watched him leave, thankful that he would talk to the kids, but a little wary about the questions. Second graders--no, all kids--were pretty intuitive. They had no filter whatsoever. They said whatever was on their minds...oftentimes, to the consternation of their parents...or others.

Clay was back within a half hour, ready to sit down and speak with Livy's class.

"Alright, alright, quiet down now, class. Mr, Mitchell is here to speak with you, and I would like you to give him your attention, please."

"Hello, second graders."

Lots of responses came back. "Hey, Mr. Mitchell," and shouts of "Hello," and laughter and smiles.

"For the time being, I want you to just listen, and then I'll give you time to ask me some questions later.

Pay close attention, because I want you to get the story right."

"What story?" shouted Angie Robinson.

"The story of Miss Sheffield and me."

Giggles and smiles appeared on all their faces, and a couple of the little boys murmured, "Yuck!"

Livy sat at her desk, quietly listening. She knew that a lot of little eyes were on her.

"First of all," Clay began, "Miss Sheffield is a teacher in this building, and I am the principal." The kids nodded in agreement. "Without going into a lot of detail, I must tell you that Miss Sheffield and I are friends. Many of the other teachers here at Brandenburg are my friends, as well. I have a lot of friends...here, where I work...in my hometown...and people I don't get to see much anymore who live in other places. Just because people are friends, does NOT mean that they are linked in any other way. Men and women can be friends...but not..."

"...boyfriends and girlfriends?" shouted Missy Owens.

"Right! Now some of you have gotten the impression that Miss Sheffield and I are..."

"...boyfriend and girlfriend...and getting married... really soon..." offered Joanie Coswell.

"That's exactly what I'm talking about, Joanie," continued Clay. "You are starting something called a rumor when you say that Miss Sheffield and I are getting married. We are NOT getting married. In fact, Miss Sheffield has a real boyfriend and I have a real girlfriend already. We ARE friends though...and only friends...so we need to stop this conversation about marriage. It embarrasses Miss Sheffield...and it embarrasses me.

Principals and teachers work together to help their students...but they are not boyfriends and girlfriends. Do you all understand?"

The students were nodding, and whispering quietly. Livy looked around at them. They were listening closely to Clay. He had presented his argument in a serious manner, not speaking down to the kids. It was working well.

"Now, do you have any questions?"

A little hand in the second row rose. Clay peered around the student in front.

"Gus Kelley?"

"Well, I think that you and Miss Sheffield should get married...if you like each other...and if you're friends... and anyways, I saw you two holding hands." He looked around at his fellow classmates and nodded. "Yep, they were holding hands on the ferris wheel with me the other night." A collective buzz went around the class.

"Now, Gus. We already explained that we were nervous about you falling out of the ferris wheel car, and that's all there was to it about Miss Sheffield and me holding hands."

"Well, aren't you s'posed to marry someone you like?" asked Kelly Douglas.

"Of course you are. In fact, you're supposed to marry someone you love. And I'm sure that when Miss Sheffield meets someone she loves, she'll be ready to get married; and she'll want you all to know. She'll want me to know too, because that is the kind of good thing that you share with your friends. But it is simply wrong to keep talking like something serious is happening between Miss Sheffield and me; I'm asking you to stop talking about it, and to explain to other kids...

or even grow-ups...if discussion arises, that nothing is going on between the two of us. Do you understand?"

Murmurs of understanding and nods went around the classroom. Gus looked a little forlorn. "But we like you and Miss Sheffield, and we think that you would have fun if you got married!"

Clay looked at Olivia, sitting behind her desk. *I'm fairly certain that I'd have fun.*

"Nevertheless, Gus, it is not in your power, or anyone else's to simply wish that two people would get married. It has to be a decision that they make. Are we clear on this?"

The kids nodded in understanding.

"Alright then. I think it's time for you and Miss Sheffield to get back to your school work, and I have plenty to do myself. Thanks for being good listeners. I'll see you around school, boys and girls."

Shouts of "Bye" and "See you later" rang through the class as Mr. Mitchell got up to leave. He stopped at Miss Sheffield's desk and quietly said, "Hopefully this talk will put all this nonsense to rest, Livy." Clay took his leave.

Livy watched him go.

Joanie and Gus watched Miss Sheffield watching Mr. Mitchell-- they each turned and smiled at each other.

15

As all children and their teachers know, the time and space between the end of October and the holidays is a mere wisp of breath. The youngsters at Brandenburg Elementary knew the excitement of those days well, as the autumn waned and the first week of December arrived. Teachers everywhere know that December is basically a roller coaster, one where you hold on tight, and just let the ride take you.

One of the school's favorite traditions followed for as long as anyone could remember, was the decorating of the large blue spruce that ruled majestically on the outer edge of the school grounds. The decorating theme was chosen by the fifth graders, as they were the upperclassmen of the school. When the theme was announced in November, all students could work to create ornaments of any size and shape that would be placed on the tree the first Monday of December. The goal was to keep everyone working diligently on their classroom subjects, but when they finished, they were permitted to work on their ornament design in their regular class, or in the art room with supervision by the art teacher. Some of the designs were very simple, and others, very intricate. Some students even had help from parents or siblings; but all ornaments were accepted and placed on the tree by Mr. Walker, the afternoon custodian, with help from parent volunteers.

Clay had been involved in all of the planning for the upcoming holiday programs, but this one was the one that reminded him why he loved being in a small town again. The evening was crisp and cold; you could see your breath as dusk began to fall. No matter how chilly it was, kids were running around giving adults directions as to where to hang their ornaments. People were starting to congregate around the tree in preparation for the lighting ceremony. He'd invited Nicole over for the ceremony, and he would be the one to give the signal to light up the tree.

"Wow, Clay." marveled Nicole. "I've never seen anything like this."

"Yes, I know. It seems like small towns have some great traditions."

Sally and Olivia wandered over, admiring the tree from all sides.

"Hi, you two, " said Nicole Marshall, as she and Clay approached Olivia and Sally. "This is pretty amazing."

"Yes, we were just saying that," said Sally. "How are you doing, Nicole? I haven't seen you since Fall Festival."

Nicole replied. "I know. Life in a pediatric office is just plain crazy, and this is the first time we've actually seen each other since then," and she squeezed Clay's arm, "even though we do have random phone conversations."

Livy realized that she was secretly pleased. "The lighting of the tree is such a special moment in town. I know that you'll both love it." She glanced at Nicole, smiling, and then lifted her eyes towards Clay. Clay and Olivia had kept a respectful distance since the Fall Festival and continued to work professionally, but did nothing to be alone together. At the moment their eyes met, there still seemed to be a kind of electrical charge that connected them. It was difficult to ignore it, and they both turned away quickly.

I'm glad it's almost dark and no one can see me blush. "Look!" she pointed. "Tom Moore is lifting Travis up to put the topper on the tree. According to Tom, Travis has been working three solid weeks on a very special angel he designed to look like his mother."

All eyes went to the scene, and were clouded by tears. Quietly, Travis Kelley lifted the angel up, and with the help of Mr. Walker, his teacher and his dad, he attached the angel to the top of the tree. Everyone applauded.

Clay stepped forward and spoke in a strong, steady voice. "This has been quite an evening for me, and I want to give a big thank you to all of our students, teachers, Mr. Walker, and parents who have helped to make it possible. What a remarkable town this is; I'm so happy I live and work here! Now...if you're all ready... we're going to light this baby up?" Everyone cheered. "Here goes!" Suddenly the tree lit up with thousands of colored lights; it was as though Fourth of July had returned with all the "ooo's" and "ah's" echoing over the schoolyard and in the town square. People were shaking hands, patting each other on the back, and hugging friends and neighbors. Kids were jumping up and down, cheering and applauding and generally acting as boisterous as if it were a snow day. The music teacher got up and led the fourth graders and everyone else in a chorus of "Jingle Bells" and "Santa Claus is Comin' to Town". Everyone sang, even if they didn't know all the words. When the excitement started to ebb, Mr. Kipley reminded everyone about the hot chocolate and cookies.

"Shall we?" Clay asked Nicole. "It's not spiked, but what the heck...I'm getting cold out here!" Nicole agreed. The two of them started to leave, when Clay turned around to speak with Sally and Olivia. "Are you two coming?"

Sally nodded her head in agreement and started to pull Olivia with her. "Sure...," when she felt a squeeze on her arm. She looked at Olivia who was shaking her head ever so slightly.

Olivia spoke up. "Uh...we...we were already over there earlier, and we need to get home and..." she glanced at her friend, "...meet Dave and Derek. Thanks for the offer though. See you in the morning," she finished.

Sally waited for Clay and Nicole to leave, and then said, "Why did you say that about meeting the guys? You know they're not here tonight!" She sounded a little cross.

"I think it's time for you and I to sit down and have a real conversation. No men invited...", said Olivia.

Sally looked at Olivia with a raised eyebrow. "No questions avoided?"

Olivia nodded in the affirmative.

"Okay...Let's go over to my place, open up a bottle of Baileys, and throw in a little coffee. Then we can talk!"

Olivia Sheffield had known Sally Litchefield for a very long time, and she knew that there was no way to avoid this conversation. Maybe Sally hadn't even noticed her reactions to Clay and could give her some perspective about the nagging attraction that kept popping up at unexpected times and places. "Okay," Olivia said. "A little spike of Baileys sounds great, and so does your company." The two friends headed away from the town square arm in arm, the same way they'd done since they were schoolyard chums.

After arriving at Sally's apartment, they took off their shoes and wrapped up in warm robes that Sally kept in her bedroom. Sally started a small pot of coffee, and Olivia lit the gas fireplace and settled in.

"Coffee's ready. I'm coming out with the Baileys, but I warn you. I've been known to be a little heavy-handed," Sally chuckled, winking.

Olivia laughed as her friend carried in a tray with two large mugs, steam rising, Each taking a cup, they sat back, put their feet up on the coffee table, bumped their mugs together and said "Cheers!" Taking a sip, there was a simultaneous sigh, and then laughter. For a moment, no one said a word, and they just enjoyed the companionable silence. Finally, though, Sally spoke up. "Okay, Olivia. Time to talk. I've known you almost all my life and you're not telling me anything lately. So what's going on?"

"I know. It's been so awkward, and you know me... when I've got problems, I clam up totally. But I really need to talk...so here goes. When I met Derek I thought that he was the man for me. He's handsome, smart, so incredibly polite, and I admire him in his work relationships and all he does at his galleries. He couldn't be more supportive of my job, he showers me with gifts, and he even hired my brother and sister-in-law. He's flown me to New York, and wined and dined me at the best places."

Sally interrupted. "I know all those things, honey. Derek is an unbelievable catch. But let's get down to brass tacks. How is the sex?"

Olivia rolled her eyes. "Is that all you think of?"

"Well," Sally thought a minute. "Yeah, I think so," and she smiled her dazzling smile and giggled. "It's just that you're making a list of Derek's attributes, almost like an excuse. Where's the 'hot'? How does he kiss? What does he say to you in bed? Come on, girl, we've talked about all this type of stuff before, and you sure don't hesitate to ask me about Dave. What's the scoop?"

Olivia looked puzzled. "I honestly don't know. We have a great time when we're out, and his kisses are pleasant--but no real fireworks there; and he has yet to make a pass or cop a feel. He's a total gentleman. When I think about it, I don't understand why all his fabulous qualities don't seem to be enough! I don't have a logical answer."

"Oh, Olivia. I can answer that for you. I couldn't have, though, until I met Dave. No matter how many wonderful attributes they have, if there are no sparks, then it's not the right man for you, honey. I know that it would be very easy to accept Derek. He's a great guy and would take care of you well and always provide for you. Some woman will really love all that he has to offer. But it's not you."

Olivia frowned and nodded. "That's what I've been thinking too. But I like him so much that I think maybe

I should go to bed with him and see if anything happens there."

Stunned, Sally gasped, "You mean that hasn't happened already between you two?

"No, it hasn't. From the moment that I met him, there's always been a conflict. He had to drive all the way back or catch a plane, or I had deadlines to meet. We've shared some very sweet kisses, but every time it seems that it might be getting a little more involved, it's time for one of us to leave."

"No way, hon. If you guys had real chemistry, no deadline would keep him from trying to get in your pants...and you know it!"

Olivia sat silently, nodding. and took a big gulp of her coffee. "I know you're right," she continued, stammering, "And...then...there's..."

"...Clay?" Sally finished with eyebrows raised.

Olivia looked up at Sally with rueful eyes and nodded. "Yes, and then there's Clay. Oh Lord, Sally, I don't know what I'm going to do about that!"

"Keep going."

"Well, from the moment I met him at Ojays and poured beer on his head, it has been spontaneous combustion between us. He kissed me that night...a kiss that curled my toes. We argued and yet there was a feeling of pure excitement and adventure, and I wanted to take a leap. Hell, if he hadn't heard my last name, and practically sprinted off my front porch, I might have gone to bed with him that night, and you know I'm NOT that type of girl. Anyway, we try to keep away from each other. We've only shared one other kiss, but talk about chemistry...and he's admitted that I affect him too. But we're both trying to act like the professionals we are.

He's made it very clear that as principal and teacher, we can't pursue a relationship ...of any kind. It's driving me crazy! I see him almost every day and I can't get over that standing in front of me is a man I'll really like to get to know better, in every way, and it just can't happen." She sat back on the couch and sighed.

"Have you thought about having this conversation with Clay?"

"No, It's embarrassing. Then he met Nicole, who I must say is absolutely beautiful, and nice on top of it. He even came into my classroom and told the kids that we were both seeing other people, and that we just worked together and there was nothing between us."

"Bummer. But Olivia, I have to tell you that both Dave and I think that Clay feels the same pull that you're describing. When you're in a room together, he can't take his eyes off you. I've seen it. So has Kathy. I think that despite Nicole being in the picture, you still have a shot at Clay Mitchell."

"Are you crazy? How would that work?"

"Frankly, I don't know. But I do know that if you don't pursue some kind of connection with him, you're going to always wonder what could have been and that will keep you from any serious relationship with Derek. Working out the principal/teacher thing is an issue, but not one that can't be figured out some way. After all, Olivia, it's only your life path that you're talking about!" she said sarcastically.

"Okay, okay. I'll think about it and maybe I'll come up with an idea of how to get close to Clay Mitchell."

"Are you forgetting the staff Christmas party at the Field's estate a week from Thursday? What better opportunity than that? All you have to do is show up looking drop-dead gorgeous, put the moves on him, and then see what happens! Speaking of that...have you found anything to wear yet?"

"No, not yet. I was planning to go out this weekend to look. I could always wear something in my closet if I had to."

"Let's go shopping. I'm wearing my cowl neck emerald green dress and I need a new belt and shoes to go with it. Maybe you'll find something...provocative... sexy, to catch our principal's eye."

"Now, Sally. Don't play the matchmaker here. Chances are, nothing will come of this all, and he'll ignore any flirtation. But I think that I am ready to pull out a few tricks, and see if maybe he'll take the bait."

"Great idea, Olivia. I don't think Nicole has it over you in the charm and maneuvering department, plus I don't think they see each other much anyway. That certainly works in your favor."

Shrugging her shoulders, Livy said, "Right. Just like Derek and me." She sat quietly for a moment. "Okay. Let's go shopping Friday after school. Maybe we'll have some luck in the clothes department."

"It's a deal. Drink it down. I'm getting really tired all of a sudden and morning comes early, girlfriend."

"You're right." Livy gulped the rest of her coffee, slipped out of the robe, put her shoes back on and stood up to get her coat. "Thanks for the girl-talk and the coffee, sweetie. I really needed that!"

"And now you need to quit talking and act!" Sally walked Olivia to the front door.. "Do you want me to run you home?"

"No way. I need the exercise, and maybe it'll give me some time to clear my head and figure out how I'm going to get some time alone with Clay." Olivia waved good-bye and headed down the street, walking at a brisk pace.

Sally watched her go, smiling to herself. When she closed the door, she immediately called Dave on her cell phone. "Hey, hon. Wait till I tell you about the conversation I just had with Olivia. We were both right about her. Let's hope we're both right about him too. Anything that we can do to push them together we do. Is it a deal?"

Dave smiled on the other end. "What's my payment for helping Cupid?"

"Oh, baby. I can't say it over the phone. But if you come over right now, It's not that late..." and she hung up, with a smile on her face.

Dave sat down his phone, and grabbed his coat. "Bye, guys. Pressing issue over at Sally's. Gotta go!"

"But it's your hand..." his buddies shouted.

"Keep my money. I've got a better deal elsewhere!" Guffaws sounded all around, as Dave rushed out the door.

16

Mr. and Mrs. Emmett Fields, a school board member and his wife, hosted the annual Christmas party for the staff of Brandenburg Elementary. They were an elderly, wealthy couple who joyously opened their home to all the teachers and their spouses. But they drew the line at only spouses. Significant others of either persuasion were not invited, due to the size of the crowd.

Party attire was dressy, and all the women used it as an excuse to put on their finest cocktail dresses, many going to the salon beforehand for a fancier hairdo as well. The men wore dress suits and ties. Everyone looked wonderful, and actually enjoyed dressing up, if only to please Mrs. Fields. She was an absolutely lovely lady with silver hair, a beautiful wardrobe, stunning jewelry, a regal bearing, and a quiet voice. Mr. Fields was her total opposite. He was large, imposing, balding, loud and his laugh was infectious.

Olivia and Sally had ridden together, both taking extreme care to get dressed to the hilt. Sally had found the perfect belt to circle the hipline of the emerald green cowl sweater dress she loved. The belt was gold with pearls intertwined. She had lucked into a pair of amazing shoes, pearl colored with gold brocade stitching. With her short red hair, pearl and gold drop earrings, and beautiful green eyes, she looked like a million dollars. When Olivia saw her, she gasped. "Oh, my Lord, Sal. You look incredible!"

"Don't I though?" Sally laughed happily. "I can't wait for Dave to see this outfit."

"How long do you think you'll stay in it when he sees you?" Olivia teased.

"I hope not long!" A raised eyebrow and a grin graced Sally's face. "And what are you talking about? You look fabulous!"

Olivia's honey-colored hair was done up in a French twist with a gold clasp that caught the light. She had found a dress that looked like it came from a designer's collection. It was a clinging black underdress that hugged every curve, with an overlay of gold lace and a tulip hemline. Her shoes were black with gold trimming, and her earrings matched the hair clasp. Olivia had great legs and the dress was the perfect length to show them off to perfection. She giggled at Sally's compliment. "I love getting dressed up like this! It's so much fun!"

Sally looked over at her friend fondly. If that outfit doesn't knock Clay Mitchell off balance, I don't know what will. I hope there's mistletoe tonight!

The valet parking at the front door of the palatial mansion made it really easy to make their way up to the front door. It was decorated with a huge swag of fresh pine boughs wrapped in gold and silver draping, red holly berries, and white lights. Beside the front door stood two life-sized toy soldiers, also in shades of gold, silver, red, and green. "Oh, my gosh, Sally, can you believe this?" Olivia asked, awestruck. The door opened.

"Hello, Miss Sheffield, Miss Litchfield." Mrs. Fields welcomed them warmly as they approached the front door. "Emmett, please take the ladies' coats, dear. Now turn around and let me see you, dears." Mrs. Fields inspected them both with a critical eye. "Marvelous choices, girls. I do believe that you have outdone yourselves this year."

"Thank you," they both replied in unison.

Mr. Fields handed them each a glass of champagne and directed them down to the sitting room. His loud voice boomed. "So glad you girls came tonight. I tried to talk Florence into letting me sit down at your end of the table, but she doesn't like me flirting with the single ladies." He laughed uproariously.

Mrs. Fields smiled at him with adoring eyes. "That's right, Emmett. No flirting with any of the women, especially the single ones!" She smiled back at the girls and quietly said, "It's always wise to let them think that they know our every thought. It knocks them off kilter when we surprise them. Then they usually can't get their footing until we've already gotten our way. A word to the wise, ladies: follow that rule and you'll come back next year with husbands in tow."

Olivia and Sally moved on down the staircase, taking in the beauty of the home, decorated in its finest Christmas wrapping. "Look at that tree!" gushed Sally. "It has to be fifteen feet high and every inch covered in light and gold and silver. It takes my breath away."

"It's unbelievable," Olivia agreed, and her eyes looked upward to the landing. In a very quiet voice,

Olivia said, "Speaking of taking your breath away... oh...my word..."

Sally glanced up to see Clay Mitchell being divested of his overcoat. He wore a black suit with a dress shirt of starched crisp white with a very narrow black stripe running through it. His long frame, broad shoulders, and slim waistline made the suit fit as though it were created just for him. His hair had been freshly trimmed, and he was leaning in towards Mrs. Fields, taking her hand in his and smiling. "Wow!" was all that Sally said. "Dear God, is that man beautiful!" She looked at Olivia for agreement, but apparently her friend had been struck deaf and dumb, but certainly not blind. Sally grinned to herself. Okay--here we go. Let's see how often I can get these two in the same vicinity.

Clay Mitchell was walking down the stairs with a glass of champagne in his hand. He was smiling at the other guests below, as they were calling greetings to each other. His eyes scanned the crowd and came to a dead stop at Olivia who had quickly turned her back, so that he hadn't seen the look in her eyes.

Sally saw the look of pure lust, before Clay propelled himself to the other side of the room, as far away from Olivia as he could get. "It's not going to be that easy for you, big guy. You're going to have to face the music soon enough," she said under her breath. She smiled and headed directly for Mrs. Fields. Sally waited until there was a break in the arrival of quests, then whispered in Florence Field's ear. "Mrs. Fields. I know that you've known me and my family for years. Could I ask an incredible favor of you? I'm sure that you've already planned the seating arrangements for tonight, but if I could persuade you to seat Olivia next to Clay Mitchell,

I'd really appreciate that."

Mrs. Fields looked down her nose a bit, as if a little put out with the request. Raising her eyebrow she asked, "Would you now, my dear?"

Sally stood quietly with her head down. "I'm sorry, I overstepped the bounds of etiquette, I'm sure. There's just a little...chemistry there and you talked about us bringing husbands next year..." Sally rambled.

Mrs. Fields held up her hand. "No need to go further. Kathy Tiffin called me to request the same thing over two weeks ago. Clearly, it should make for an interesting evening. That's the real reason why Emmett is sitting at the other end of the table. I want to be down on that end with all of you!" She laughed quietly and nodded her head. With a finger to her mouth, she indicated silence. "Now get on your way. Everyone's arrived and it's time to take our seats."

Mr. and Mrs. Fields stood handsomely at opposite ends of the massive mahogany dining table, as she said, "If you would please find your seats via the place cards now and raise your glasses for the first toast of the evening. Does anyone need more champagne?" Several nodded yes and they were served straightaway. Olivia was one of them. The minute she saw that her place card was next to Clay's, she gulped down the rest of her glass. Her heart started pounding as he began to come around the table looking for his seat. When he saw where he was to sit, he paused a minute, and then looked over quietly at Olivia and shrugged with a slight smile on his face.

"Alright, glasses up, please," said Mr. Fields. "Tonight we are here to recognize the work ethic, dedication, and involvement of all of you to Brandenburg.

Both Florence and I attended Brandenburg in its earliest days, and because we were not blessed with children of our own, we decided to take on a project that had something to do with children. Of course, we're involved in many ways with the school district. But this one night we applaud you...and your tireless efforts in working with the children of this town, helping them to love learning, and encouraging them to reach for their highest goals. Now sit back and enjoy your special evening! Cheers to you all!" They raised their glasses, and the clinking of crystal on crystal sounded throughout the room as everyone drank.

Clay's seat was toward the very end of the table. He moved quickly to pull out Mrs. Fields' chair, and then went directly to Olivia's on his side of the table and did the same. Both women smiled and said, "Thank you." The minute he pulled his own chair out and sat down, his leg brushed against Olivia's, sending a frisson of excitement down her spine.

"Excuse me," Clay uttered.

"No problem," said Olivia, without making eye contact.

He looked over at her. "Livy...you take my breath away."

Sally was sitting across the table watching the two of them and thinking, Oh dear Lord. It's going to be a long night if they act like this, all shy and quiet. "Mrs. Fields, would it be rude if I asked you how you and Mr. Fields met? I don't think that I've ever heard that story."

All eyes at the end of the table turned in Mrs. Fields' direction. She smiled, threw her head back in a quiet laugh, her eyes twinkling. "Of course it wouldn't be rude. I love to tell that story. When I was in first grade, I was out at recess. The school had just installed a jungle gym on the playground. We were all so excited to get our turn to climb and hang on it, and we were all giggling and acting like monkeys climbing higher and higher. But I got scared and came down to one of the lower bars and got my friend's attention. I was hanging upside down swinging, and making monkey sounds. Before I knew what happened, this big boy was right in front of me; he grabbed my shoulders and he kissed me! That was Emmett!"

Those who'd overheard the story began laughing around the table. It was so silly picturing the proper Mrs. Fields hanging upside down on the jungle gym! Any tension at the end of the table disappeared; everyone started talking at once, and passing the story along to those who hadn't heard. Tom Moore commented that Mr. Fields certainly knew how to pick them.

"Mr. Fields," Clay asked, "how old were you at the time?"

"I was much older than Florence...I was in third grade, and a very worldly boy, at that!" Mr. Fields howled. "From then on we were friends, running around playing games at recess. She even took me home for lunch one day, when I'd forgotten to bring my lunch to school."

"Yes, and Father reminded me that I was much too young to bring home a boyfriend," Florence reminisced happily. "Anyway, I followed Emmett all through school, even when he went into the upper grades. We seemed to have established a bond."

Conversation continued around the table about the Fields' love match, with Mr. Fields taking over the story again. "Well, of course, I knew I would marry her. We were friends first, and knew everything about each other."

Clay laughed out loud. "Hah! Friends first, huh? How many guys kiss a girl the first time they meet?"

Livy choked on her champagne. "Excuse me, I need to use the ladies' room." She tried to scoot her chair out, but couldn't' get it to budge on the thick carpet.

Clay stood to pull it out for her. While she was in earshot, he whispered behind her, "Actually, I do remember kissing someone the first time I met them. I recall that kiss quite well."

Olivia blushed, and quickly turned towards the ladies' room. She was definitely feeling the effects of the champagne, and the man next to her. She had a little trouble navigating.

"Are you alright? Do you need help?" Clay asked, touching her arm.

"I'm fine...just fine..." *Why is he touching me, whispering in my ear, talking about that first kiss? My stomach is churning with all these mixed messages.*

Olivia returned to the table, as the meal was being served. First course was a creamy lobster bisque with crusty French bread to accompany it. The waiters brought around red and white wine and began serving. Conversation died down a little as the guests sampled the bisque, and sighed with pleasure after their first taste.

"Oh, Mrs. Fields," Olivia exclaimed. "This is heavenly. If this is only the beginning of dinner, I think that by the end of the evening, I'll be so full that my dress won't fit me." Others around the table agreed.

Clay's imagination went wild. *I'd be happy to see you out of that dress.*

He snapped out of his reverie, however, when Mrs. Fields' spoke. "Since you are, after all, the new man on the block, Clay, what do you think of Brandenburg and your staff?"

"It's been a smooth beginning, and frankly, I've never seen a staff work harder than this one has. They're very willing to do almost anything I ask, and they have tremendous ideas and strategies to continue helping the kids. Cheers to all of you!" He raised his wine glass and the whole table took a sip.

Olivia felt the need to continue. "Mr. Mitchell has done a tremendous job taking over after Mr. Hood's passing, boosting the morale in the building, and spurring us all onward. The kids love him too, don't they?" she asked various teachers nearby. "So...I'll propose a toast to Mr. Mitchell, as well. To new beginnings and future excitements. Cheers!"

Mrs. Fields chimed in. "What's this I hear, Miss Sheffield? Aren't all of you on a first-name basis when you're not at work? I understand it's Mr. Mitchell when children are around, but I hardly think that's necessary here."

"Of course, you're right," Olivia blushed. "It's just that we always try to stay professional, and I'm just used to calling him that."

"Professional?" added Mr. Fields. "Of course, but after all, you are colleagues, and I imagine friends as well. No other teacher has called him Mr. Mitchell this evening that I've heard. Isn't that right, Florence?"

"Right you are, my dear. Clay, you don't mind if Olivia calls you by your first name, do you?"

"No, of course, I don't mind. You know you can always call me Clay, Livy," and this time he touched her fingers and slid his palm down to rest on hers.

Olivia nearly jumped out of her skin.

Clay continued. "Since we're trying to lighten up the evening, and not be so professional, can I offer anyone another glass of wine?"

Sally, Tom, Olivia and Mrs. Fields all held their glasses up. Clay poured two whites, and three reds, as he included himself, and dinner proceeded. There was an arugula salad with sun-dried tomatoes, walnut, and feta cheese, then a vodka sorbet for cleansing the palate. Dinner continued with salmon with pistachio and cilantro chutney and a rolled chicken breast filet stuffed with three cheeses and spinach. Saffron risotto and fresh green beans finished off the main course.

The entire room was silent when dinner was over, too stuffed to move.

"I can't possibly hold another bite, but Florence and Emmett, you have certainly outdone yourselves this evening!" congratulated Jerry Foust, another school board member. "Thank you!"

There were echoes of appreciation throughout the room.

"Well, as many of you know, that woman over there, my little Florence, is the class of our union. I stay out of her way when she plans the decorating and the meal, and I just do what she tells me. Right, honey?"

"Of course you do, Emmett." Mrs. Fields commented sweetly

"But now she has to do what I tell her. And so do all of you. Every present under the tree has a number on it. You are to draw a number from this bag, and go and search for your present. Then wait for further instructions."

They drew their numbers, and made a mad dash to the Christmas tree, in search of their package.

"Alright--now does everyone have their package? Here's the deal. When I blow my whistle, you are to trade the next four gifts that you receive, to someone else. You cannot turn down a gift. No limits...not in order...you can run across the room...or toss it to someone. But when I blow my whistle again, you must stop, and open the present you're holding, no matter what! Do you understand?"

Everyone laughed and nodded. The whistle sounded. Gifts were flying in different directions. People were dashing across the sitting room bumping into each other, passing presents around like crazy. Laughter and calls like, "Hey, I want that one!" and "No, that isn't big enough for me!" and "Hurry up, I want to keep this one," echoed through the room. Finally, Mr. Fields blew the whistle again, and everyone stopped. Folks were breathing hard and shaking their heads.

"I turn into an animal when we do this every year," said Charlie Tiffin.

"You've always been an animal, Charlie!" Kathy laughed. Everyone laughed as well and joined in teasing Charlie and Kathy.

"Come on, Kathy. That night in Ojays when you went ballistic was a major education for me!" Clay shouted.

"Is that right, Clay Mitchell? You're the one who fed me double shots that night, I found out later that you were warned! If you've noticed, I've strictly been drinking water this evening. I know my limits!"

"Hah! Not another episode with you and your temper, Kathy?" Emmett Fields joked. "Kathy's older brother and I graduated together so I've seen her in action!"

Kathy smacked Emmett on the shoulder. "Don't you dare start with that, Emmett. How do you put up with him, Flo?"

Across the room, genteel Florence Fields smiled and said, "I let him get his way all the time, of course. Don't you do that with Charlie, too?" All the women at the table chuckled. It was like girl-speak. The guys all looked puzzled, and knew better, but Florence was so convincing that they dropped it.

"Oh, please," Sally pleaded. "Can we open our presents? I'm dying to see what's in here."

"GO!" yelled Mr. Fields.

They tore into ribbons, tissue, and wrapping, throwing it into the center of the room. No trades were allowed. You had to keep what you got no matter what--at least until you left the party. There were gifts that seemed perfect for the receiver and others that were as far off-base as they could possibly be. Livy got a set of beer mugs, accompanied by hoots of laughter about her throwing beer on people. She rolled her eyes, but not until she and Clay made eye contact and had a good laugh. Sally got a new serving platter that happened to work well with her kitchen colors. Melanie got a gas card and car-washing kit, and Clay got a little peach nightgown, size. 4. It left little to the imagination. When he opened the box and held it up, everyone in the room laughed uproariously, "I'm fairly certain this was meant for someone else. I don't think this color does me justice!"

Conversation was light and easy, as people compared their gifts and worked out trades later that evening. Sally pulled Olivia aside, and said, "I was hoping that you'd end up with the peach lingerie. I know peach is one of your favorite colors."

"I DO covet that."

"Well," Sally said, and nudged Olivia. "Maybe this is your chance to plan a trade and to get a little closer to the boss. Come on, Olivia...you're supposed to be making moves on the guy!"

She's right! If I don't do something, I'll never know what's happening between Clay and me. She nodded, and headed in Clay's direction. "Hey, Mr....Clay?"

She'd appeared out of nowhere, when he was talking to a school board member; but he'd known she was at his elbow. Clay turned.

Big brown eyes were looking up at him.

Clay looked at the school board member, and excused himself. "Let's get together next week, and discuss that. I'll give you a call." As the school board member moved on, Clay waited, looking at Olivia expectantly.

"I just wanted you to know that I have these lovely beer mugs...and I do think that peach lingerie would look better on me--your coloring just doesn't work. So I thought...that maybe...we could take it out in trade?"

Clay's mouth went dry.

Olivia stammered a little. "Now... I'm not exactly sure how it would work...us being professionals and all," she cocked an eyebrow, "but I'm willing if you are!"

Oh...my...God...yes! Caution goes out the door... and I can't wait. Clay looked into her gorgeous eyes, and grinned. "Well...I'm certain that we can make some kind of a deal...those beer mugs are, after all, quite a gift. And maybe seeing you in that peach lingerie would work for me...I think that's professional behavior, don't you?"

Olivia blushed and nodded.

He leaned in and whispered in her ear. "How did you get here tonight, Livy?"

"I rode with Sally."

"What would you think if I gave you a ride home?"

"I think I'd like that very much."

Dessert was announced and served in the sitting room along with coffee and hot tea. It was a perfect Baked Alaska, and because no one was sitting in marked places, everyone milled around and had time to catch up. Olivia moved towards Kathy Tiffin and Sally who were speaking in the corner.

"Hey, Sally, hon. Would you mind if I rode home with Clay tonight?"

Sally's head popped up, a smug smile on her face. Kathy had heard the question as well. They both smiled at each other and then looked at Olivia. "FINALLY!" they both said simultaneously. Kathy threw in, "You might want to suggest a trade for that peach nighty. Sally tells me it's just your size!"

Olivia's eyes grew large, and she said, "Hush, you two!"

Kathy and Sally just laughed and laughed.

Clay appeared with Livy's coat, which she had described, and held it for her as she put it on. "Mr. and Mrs. Fields," he began, "this has been a wonderful evening. Thank you so much for your hospitality," and he shook both of their hands warmly.

"You are so welcome, young man," smiled Emmett, who slapped Clay on the back. "I mean that for tonight and for coming to Brandenburg."

"Thank you, sir. I'll see you at the next school board meeting. Goodnight now."

Olivia said her goodbyes as well, and Clay escorted

her up the staircase. They were just getting ready to leave, when Mrs. Fields came up the stairs as well. "Hold on, you two. May I remind you that there is mistletoe directly above you, and no one leaves my house without taking advantage of it!" She stepped back and crossed her arms, waiting.

Clay and Olivia stood there for a minute looking up at the mistletoe. Sally and Kathy stood at the foot of the stairs looking up at the couple. "This should be good," Sally said under her breath.

"Un-hum," Kathy murmured. She made eye contact with Florence Fields at the top of the steps, who had a smug grin on her face. They both nodded.

Clay took a quiet breath, as he lowered his face toward Olivia's. Her brown eyes were almost closed as he lifted her chin, and lightly kissed her lips, as though they were delectable morsels. It was a sweet and gentle kiss, yet somehow it was enough to get Livy's heart racing. Then it was over. Clay put her away from him slowly, and though she didn't say anything, he turned again to the hostess and said, "Assignment, completed, Mrs. Fields. Thanks again!" He opened the door, and he and Olivia stepped out on the front porch.

17

Outside the Fields' home, Clay handed the valet the stub for his car. He breathed in the crisp winter air scented by Olivia's perfume. Neither of them said a word, until Olivia broke the silence, and uttered softly, "Oh, look, it's snowing! It's the night before Christmas break. The kids will be so excited."

"What does it take to get you excited, Livy?" Clay looked deeply into Olivia's eyes, and then his gaze drifted to her lips. Leaning in to sample them was utmost on his mind until the harsh headlights of his car rounded the curve, circling to the front porch. The valet bolted out to open the door for Olivia. With a sigh of resignation, Clay pulled out a five-spot, handed it to the valet, and got into the car.

Quietly Clay repeated, "You didn't answer my question, Olivia? What's going on here? We've been really good avoiding each other since the Fall Festival. What's changed that tonight you're allowing me to take you home?"

Olivia didn't answer directly, because she wanted to

get the words right. "Oh, Clay...I know what we've both said to each other on and off since we met. I know that we're both seeing other people periodically, and that we've been trying to avoid any close encounters since October. But I can't keep away from you anymore, and I don't want to. I have no idea how this will work, or won't work, but I'm not willing to miss a chance that's staring me in the face. When I'm near you, I..."

Clay picked up the conversation, "...I just want to... touch and kiss you all over. I want to feel your hair in my hands, feel your body close to mine, want to make you weep with loving, and I don't give a damn if we work together, or we're not supposed to be with each other. I don't want to waste more time, pretending that you are not in my waking thoughts daily, even when I don't see you...or even when I'm trying to avoid you. Does that sum it up?"

The car had never left the driveway, and people were beginning to come out the front door. As Clay put the car in gear, all that Olivia could say was, "Yes."

Clay maneuvered the car out of the lengthy driveway, and headed down Main Street, turning left on Hamilton.

Livy noticed and said, "Where are we going?"

He smiled. "You said I could take you home. I didn't say your home. We're going to my home. Come up and have a drink with me, honey." The voice was soft, mellow and very persuasive.

Olivia overrode all her good sense, and nodded. "I shouldn't have much more to drink. It's been champagne and wine all evening. I still have a roomful of second graders to see tomorrow morning."

"I know, I know." Clay parked his car in the carport

ANGELA FERRELLI

of his apartment and escorted Livy up the sidewalk to his front door.

She was making nervous conversation. "I've never been to any of these apartments. Are they nice? Do you like living here? I've been living in my place for three years, but my landlady is a piece of work. Her name is..."

Clay inserted the key in the front door and placed his hand on the small of Livy's back as they went through the portal. "A little chatty, aren't we?" He stood behind her and began to take her coat off her shoulders. As he lowered it, he whispered quietly in her ear, his warm breath on her neck. "I have to be honest. I'm not much interested in talking, unless of course, you're begging, Livy. I can barely stand being this close to you without..." and he began to nuzzle her neck; then his teeth lightly tugged at her earlobe.

Olivia Sheffield got chills over every square inch of her body, and she leaned back into solid man, sighing. Her arms dropped out of her coat, which fell to the floor of the foyer, as Clay turned her around and pulled her towards him, his mouth covering hers in heart-wrenching kisses.

Her arms twined about his neck, playing with the hair at his nape, reveling in the feel of her body against his, sighing as his tongue entered her mouth and tasted, savored, tugged at her bottom lip and drove her crazy with desire. Livy sank into the kiss, loving the feel of his hands on her back, caressing her lightly, at the same time the pressure of his kiss was becoming more intense. She groaned, and began to move her body closer, her hips swiveling against the front of his trousers. What she felt literally took her breath away.

"Oh, God...that feels,,,!" His manhood was rigid against the front of the little black dress, and he reached down and took her bottom in his hands and lifted her harder towards his rampant erection. When the contact was made, he growled low in his throat. Clay picked her up as though she were a feather and carried her into the living room, setting her gently on the couch. He took off his suit coat and threw it down on the nearby chair, loosened his tie and unbuttoned the top button of his shirt, never taking his eyes off her.

She lifted her arms toward him and he came down to the couch, lowering himself above her. He stroked her neck and felt her rapidly beating pulse and started tracing her lips with his finger. His smile was predatory. "Well...I guess by now, you have an idea about how much I like you." He brushed away a tendril of her honey-colored hair from her face. "I've wanted you here since that first night in Ojays, and I can't tear my eyes away from this beautiful mouth," He leaned down and kissed her. "In fact, I'm having a terrible time not touching you all over every inch of your perfect body." His hands skimmed up and down languorously over her sides until his palms found her lovely breasts, squeezing the nipples lightly, until they puckered under his touch.

She allowed him free reign over her body, as she closed her eyes and let him worship her with his hands.

"Open your eyes, and show me what you want me to do to you, Olivia."

She slowly sat up and undid the clasp in her hair, and the French twist fell away. Her hair tumbled down to her shoulders. She couldn't look away from the amazing gray-blue eyes of the man who'd haunted her dreams since August. "I want you to kiss me wherever I tell you," she invited, smiling seductively. She pointed to her lips.

He kissed her, drinking in the taste.

But Olivia gave as much as she got. She lightly pushed him away. "Now here," and her hands touched the sides of her neck below the earlobes.

He kissed her, starting with the earlobes and worked his way downward.

She shuddered as chills ran up and down her spine. She reached back and unzipped the top of her designer lace dress and slowly lowered it off her shoulders. "Now here," and her glance covered her shoulders.

Clay trailed light kisses over both shoulders that ended in little love bites.

The flame was burning in both of them.

"Where should we head next, Liv? I'll do whatever you say." He stood, his feet spread apart, waiting. His fingers itched to grab her, but he tried to control the raging desire that threatened to undo him.

Olivia Sheffield, proper second grade teacher, sister with three brothers, finally decided to take this bull by the horns. She stood up slowly only a little wobbly from the alcohol, and began to unzip the entire length of her dress.

Clay watched the whole thing, slowly unfastening his belt, and his mouth went dry when she stepped out of the little black dress, wearing nothing but a black lace bra, which covered very little of her fabulous breasts, tiny black lace panties, and a garter belt with black hose.

Clay looked his fill, but kept his distance. "At this moment in time, Miss Sheffield, I'm not feeling the slightest bit professional, and I've just realized that I've given myself an impossible task. I can no more stay away from you, than I could stay away from a kid who needed help. It's not possible for you to stay here, unless I have you naked in my arms. I don't know what you're feeling for me, but either I take you home right now, or you won't go home until morning." The direct look he gave her made his message very clear.

She looked down for a moment as though working things out, and then looked directly back at him, her smile curving up on one corner. Coyly, she shrugged her shoulders and delivered a line that Clay had never really expected to hear. "I think I won't go home until morning."

Clay took that as the best of invitations, stepped towards her, and drew her in against the length of his body. His mouth took hers in a searing kiss as Livy's arms encircled his neck and she leaned into his hot body. He tasted the depths of her mouth and their tongues performed a mating ritual as old as time.

Clay's top shirt button was undone, but Olivia wanted him out of the shirt. As she began unbuttoning the buttons, she would plant a kiss on each square of bare skin that was revealed. When the shirt was completely unbuttoned, she slid it off his shoulders. As it dropped to the floor, she looked her fill, and then she touched his chest and rubbed her fingers in the light hair. Her eyes followed the path of blonde hair trailing towards his waistline. She licked her lips in anticipation. He was every bit as perfect as she'd imagined, and as she touched him, she leaned forward and ran her tongue around his nipples.

Clay stood frozen, his eyes shut, his breath coming

faster, clearly enjoying her hands on his body.

Olivia looked up at the handsome face, and loved that she had the power to elicit this response from him. She fanned her hands across his chest and ran them down the front of his rock hard abs, and murmured, "Ummm." She looked up and smiled at the golden Adonis in front of her; then she moved forward and sank her teeth into his shoulder giggling.

Clay's eyes snapped open. He lifted her off her feet, saying, "Oh, you want to play rough, do you?" Before Livy knew what was happening, Clay had set her in the high back navy armchair. She was breathless with laughter until he knelt before her, and lifted her right leg, and began to undo one of the silk stockings from the garter belt. He rolled it slowly down the length of her leg, feathering kisses all the way to the bottom of her foot. Then he repeated the same with the other leg. Olivia leaned back in the chair still breathless, but no longer laughing. She was lost in his kisses, feeling his hot breath on her legs. She felt tingles all over, and her very core felt like molten lava.

"Oh, honey," Clay said huskily. "If you could only know how often I've thought of this...and more." With her hose gone, he placed his large hand under her sweet bottom, feeling the lace of those little black panties. He tilted her bottom upward and touched the front of her panties right at her luscious center. "You're so wet, but I want you wetter." He pulled the lace back and let his finger do magic--in and out, in and out, rubbing, circling. Livy was mesmerized by his touch, and knew that she could barely keep herself from climaxing right then. She threw back her head and tightened her muscles, and pushed his shoulders away. "Too fast, big guy. It's been awhile for me, and I want it to last."

"Oh, sweetie, it's gonna last," and before she could stop him, he'd pulled off her panties and garter belt, and his mouth was supping on her most private place.

She moaned and dropped her arms on either side of the armchair, unable to do anything but surrender.

"Not to worry, honey. I'm going to give you more than one orgasm, so let it go."

And Olivia did. She slid further down the chair, her legs spread, his shoulders embraced between them. Clay circled and licked, his tongue darting in and out, the same path his finger had traveled. She was getting closer and closer to the peak, and he knew it. He watched her as she let him claim her with his mouth, and then he leaned in and let his tongue lap her from the bottom to the top of her womanhood. Her shout was one of ecstasy, and he could feel her throbbing in his mouth, as she climaxed.

Clay stood for a minute while Olivia basked in the afterglow, and then he lifted her in his arms. "I'm not proud of myself, starting this in the chair. But those little black underthings were too much. I wanted to pleasure you first. It's frankly all I've thought about for a long time. Let's go upstairs to my room and continue this. I'm getting pretty uncomfortable in my slacks and shorts."

Olivia reached down and felt his shaft through his dress slacks. "Oh, my," she swallowed. "I think I understand why. That feels...simply amazing."

"Speak for yourself! It's not feeling that great to me, just uncomfortable as hell." He carried her up the stairway to the room on the right. The door was open, and she had her first glance of his bedroom. Everything about the room was masculine, yet somehow seductive, all forest green and warm cherry wood. The king-sized bed was made, but with one pull the bedspread went flying. Clay laid her down on the sheets, and he began to unzip his slacks. She waited and watched the goings on with that little teasing smile on her face. But the moment that he started to pull his slacks down over his clearly protruding erection, his cell phone rang.

Olivia jumped.

Clay sent a puzzled frown in the direction of the phone, as he reached over and saw that the caller ID said GRAVES. "Oh, no. This can't be good," he said, picking up the phone quickly.

"Clay," Jeff Graves' voice came over the line.

"Dad? What's the matter?"

"Your Mother's being taken to Barton Memorial as we speak, and I need to get over there."

"What's wrong?" Clay asked anxiously.

"They think it's appendicitis, but they're really moving fast. They're afraid it's going to burst, so they took her in the ambulance. I just wanted you to know...can you call your brother?" his voice said, trailing off.

"Of course, Dad," Clay's hand brushed through his hair. Olivia was watching worriedly. "I'll be along right away, Dad!"

"Your Mother will be furious that I called you."

"I'll be there, whether she's furious or not, Dad. Give her my love. I'll call Eric too...don't worry. Just get to Mom." He hung up the phone. "Olivia," he looked at her pleadingly. "I have to..."

"Clay, go!" Olivia's hands raised squarely in front

of her. "Don't even explain. I can call Sally to pick me up..."

"No, I'm heading right by your place on the way to Barton. They think my mom is going to need an emergency appendectomy. I hope you understand, but I just have to go!"

Olivia nodded, "Of course. Let me get my things. I'll be ready in a second"

Clay nodded curtly, and pulled on his shirt and grabbed a couple of items out of his closet. "If I'm not at work tomorrow, will you let Kathy know? I'll call her as soon as I can!"

"Of course. Please don't worry about school. Get there and be with your folks. They need you."

"Thank you," he said, his brow furrowed. They were heading down the stairs. He opened the outside door, they exited the house, and got in the car. Clay drove swiftly through the neighborhood, clearly preoccupied. "I'll give you a call when I'm able," as he pulled up to her house. "Let me get the door."

"No, no, no Clay. Just go. I'll get in just fine. Be safe and drive carefully. I'll see you later."

He nodded, and the car drove away into the darkness. She stood for a minute on the sidewalk, racking her brain, trying to remember if Clay had ever told her about his second set of parents. All she could remember was about the horrible accident that had taken his birth parents away from him. *I'll have to ask Kathy tomorrow morning. Maybe she knows the details by now.*

She turned and slowly walked onto her front porch, and let herself in for the night. *I think I'll sleep well tonight. I'm a pretty satisfied woman...too bad I couldn't do some satisfying as well. That leaves next time, doesn't it? Definitely something to anticipate! I'll await your next visit, Clay. Then we'll see who gets pleasured first.*

18

Clay wasn't at school in the morning, and Olivia let Kathy know as many of the details as she could, without indulging anything personal. Puzzled, she continued. "Kathy, I guess Clay never told me about his adopted parents. I only knew about the accident because of the Kelley boys. Do you have any idea who the people are who adopted Clay? Did they adopt his older brother as well?"

Kathy was busy at her computer taking care of morning attendance issues. Without looking up she said, "Sure, I know. Clay's adopted parents were his biological parents' best friends, Jeff and Caroline Graves."

Olivia's stomach lurched. "Do you mean Superintendent Graves?" she asked haltingly.

"Yep. They loved those little boys, and by that time in their lives, they knew they would be childless. It took them all of five minutes to decide to adopt Eric and Clay. The reason that I knew these details is that Caroline and I have served on some charitable committees together. They were thrilled to be able to interview

Clay for this position, after Mr. Hood passed away."

"Didn't the school board throw a big fuss about conflict of interest or nepotism or something?"

"No way. Anyone who knows Jeff Graves, or has worked with him as long as this school board has, knows that he wouldn't give anyone preferential treatment, even if they were related to him. Mr. Mitchell was the best of the five candidates, hands down, from what I heard. I was a little concerned when I saw how young he was, but I think that he's taken Brandenburg to a whole new level already; these kids and the staff love him. Don't you agree?" she asked, her eyebrow arched.

Olivia didn't make eye contact with Kathy. *Well, he's certainly taken me to a whole new level.* "Well, of course I do, Kathy. The staff really appreciates his willingness to help through crises, and the way he backs us up when there is a dispute with parents. He's clearly explained the necessity of bringing up our test scores, while still allowing the kids to make choices about their electives and continuing to have fun in a learning environment."

"I agree, and if Clay made a poor decision or was involved in anything less than professional, Jeff Graves would have his hide, just like he'd have anyone else's."

Olivia nodded half-heartedly. *Dear God, what have I done? I've gone off and let him turn me inside out when there can't be any resolution to this. I've got to cut this off myself before Clay has to deal with the situation. I would feel awful if he were fired because of our behavior.* "Well, thanks, Kathy. I need to get to my class now before the kids start arriving. Let me know if Clay...I mean Mr. Mitchell calls about his mom."

"I'm going to call the staff together straight away to let them know why he's not here, and hopefully, before the day is out, we'll have a better handle on Caroline's health that I can share with everyone."

"Good idea. It's the last day before Christmas holiday and the troops are due in about fifteen minutes. Do you want me to do the all-call for teachers?"

"That would be great, Olivia. I just have to finish this. Have everyone meet me in the library, and then we'll get on with the day."

The all-call was sounded and quickly the teachers converged in the library. Everyone was talking and laughing about the party and several of them looked a little worse for wear, but they were all in high spirits. Kathy came in and told them the details about Clay, and she promised that the minute she knew anything, she would let them know. They all nodded their heads, looking concerned and headed back to their classrooms.

Sally waited for Olivia at the back of the room. "Hey, sweetie. How are you today? Got anything juicy to tell me?" she smiled suggestively.

Livy tried to smile, but it wasn't too convincing. "Only that I've gotten myself into a real fix. Did you know that Superintendent Graves is Clay's adopted father?"

"What? No way. Are you kidding? If I'd have known, Olivia, you know I would have told you." she said seriously.

"Well, according to Kathy, Clay and his brother were adopted right away after the accident and have been with them since they were little boys. Apparently, they were Clay's biological parents' best friends."

"Wow, what an incredible sacrifice and gift." Realizing there was more, Sally added, "But this isn't good news, is it?"

"Oh, Sal. Last night was amazing, and it's all I've thought about. But, when I got in this morning and asked Kathy about Clay's adopted parents, well, dear God, there's no way I can be romantically involved with my principal! Let alone when he's the son of our school superintendent! Can you imagine the gossip? I'm going to have to find a way to cut it off, and it makes me sick, just thinking about it."

"I'm so sorry, Liv. But wait until you and Clay talk. Don't do anything drastic. You're both adults and you shouldn't make that decision for him. Maybe you can work it out."

"Maybe," Livy said hopefully. But she doubted there was any good way out of this mess.

Caroline Graves had indeed needed an emergency appendectomy, and Jeff and Clay had stayed through the night at the hospital to be sure that the surgery went alright. Caroline's doctor had just appeared and spoken with them both. "She's doing just fine now. You can go in and see her, but not for too long. She's still groggy from the anesthetic. I'm keeping her an extra day due to the level of severity of the infection, but she'll be ready to head home tomorrow evening, I think, right in time for holiday events."

"Thanks so much, Dr. Kuhn," Jeff sighed as he shook the doctor's hand.

He and Clay headed past the nurses' station to Caroline's room. "Hello, sweets," cooed Jeff. "How are you feeling?"

Caroline looked up and smiled wanly at Jeff and Clay. "I'm fine," she responded slowly, her words a little slurred. "It was just an appendix. Clay, dear, isn't school in session today?"

"Now, Mom. You know that I was just waiting for a reason to take the last day before vacation off, and you gave it to me. Thanks so much!" He squeezed her hand and bent down to plant a light kiss on her forehead.

Caroline chuckled, but she was clearly drifting off again. "Jeff," she called, holding out her hand.

He took it, patting it lightly.

"Go home, dear. I'm so tired. I just need to sleep... and so do you. Come back tomorrow. You too, Clay. Love you." And she leaned her head totally back on the pillow and was out.

Jeff and Clay were discussing if either should stay overnight, when the attending nurse arrived to check in. "She's just coming off the anesthetic. Believe me, there's no reason to be here until morning. She should sleep through the night. Go home. She'll be much more rested tomorrow."

Together, father and son headed down the hospital hallways to the bank of elevators and then to the parking lot to get their cars. "You okay to drive, Dad?" asked Clay, concernedly.

"Yeah, I'm fine. See you at home. I know that I need a shower and a good shot of Scotch."

"I'm right there with you, Dad. See you at your place." Clay headed on to get his car, pulled out of the garage, and paid the parking fee. *I'm so tired I don't even know what time it is.* He checked the car clock and it read 1:00 p.m. Clay pulled out his cell phone and dialed Brandenburg.

"Clay, is that you?" Kathy answered on the first ring.

"It's me, Kath. I just wanted you to know that Mom is doing fine and making a good recovery. Dad and I are heading home to clean up and sleep; then in the morning we'll head back to the hospital. They think she'll get out tomorrow night, if all continues to go well."

"That's fabulous, Clay. I'll pass the news onto the staff. They're all concerned and asking."

"Thanks, Kathy." He started to hang up the phone. "Hey, Kath, would you tell Livy--Miss Sheffield--that I'll call her in a few days, please? I know she's still in class, and I don't want to interrupt her. By the time I get home, I'll probably pass out. I feel like I could sleep for a week!"

"Sure, no problem. Take care and give my love to your mom and dad. I'm so glad that Caroline is well. Have a great break and I'll see you in January!" and the phone went dead.

Clay headed the car toward the Graves' home. *Damn! What have I gone and done?*

He continued on the interstate heading for his parents' home. The afternoon was gray and overcast and even though he was pleased with his mother's prognosis, his mood was as gray as the day. *Maybe once I get cleaned up, have a Scotch, and hit the sack, I'll be able to tackle this relationship thing with Olivia and talk it over with Dad. Maybe I'm overthinking this whole professional thing, and once I tell Dad he'll understand why I need to see Olivia. If we're discreet, we could pull it off without much trouble. Then next year, I'll ask for a transfer and Livy can stay at Brandenburg.* Clay pulled into the driveway just five minutes ahead of his Dad.

"Go ahead and let yourself in, son. I need to get some of your mom's things out of the trunk. Fix me a Scotch on the rocks, will you? I need a good shot before I hit the shower."

"Will do, Dad. I'll be joining you."

By the time Jeff entered the kitchen, both drinks were ready and waiting. Without a word, Clay and Jeff picked up their glasses and downed the golden liquid in one gulp. Wiping his mouth with the back of his hand, Jeff Graves commented, "Well, I doubt I'll have trouble sleeping, but if so, this should put me over the top. I'm going on up to the shower. You know where the towels are, son. Make yourself comfortable."

"Thanks, Dad. I'll be up soon." But Clay fixed himself two more drinks before he dragged himself up the stairs and passed out on the guest room bed. The last thought he had was of Olivia Sheffield in black lace.

19

Christmas vacation had begun, and everyone was caught up in the hubbub of seasonal excitement. The malls were crowded, people met for holiday lunches and dinners, and most everyone had a secret or two they were keeping for Christmas morning! Olivia jumped into the holidays like she did everything else-- full steam ahead. She had been so busy that she had done little shopping, less decorating, and no wrapping. Friday night she made calls to Sally and Donna Puckett, a long-time friend from high school, firming up their breakfast plan and shopping excursion for the next day. Olivia knew that Caroline Graves was on the mend, and Kathy had told her that Clay said he would call later. *Whatever happens, I need to keep busy today. I don't know what I'm going to say or do when he calls, but maybe Sal is right, and we can talk through this mess.* She shivered just thinking of his touch and enjoyed the euphoric anticipation of seeing him again.

The girls met and started their marathon morning with an oversized breakfast before the early bird sales began. Sally stuffed in the last bite of pancake and leaned back in the booth. "Oh, my Lord, I am filled to the gills. But we need to build up our strength for all this upcoming shopping, right?" she chuckled.

"Right!" Olivia and Donna echoed in unison.

"Does everyone have their list so we can get a move-on?" Donna questioned. She was the best shopper of the three, and they allowed her to lead the troops.

Sally and Olivia nodded.

"Great! I'll pick up the tab for breakfast; then you guys can handle lunch and happy hour later!"

Sally was bundling up. "Okay. I'll go get the car and pull up front. It's a little icy. Be careful when you walk out the door. No time for injuries. Too much to do!"

Before they knew it, Donna and Olivia were piling into Sally's car. The threesome drove to Brandenburg Mall to begin shopping. They stayed close together for a while, then decided to split up to make better time. "Okay," suggested Donna, "how about we meet at Boxcar's around two, and we can grab an appetizer and a drink? We'll see how much more we have to do at that time. Then, if we're all done, we'll make a plan for the rest of the evening."

Sally said, "Sounds great, but Donna, would you mind if I tagged along with you a little while longer? I've been racking my brain for something special for my niece, and I'm sure you'll know where to go."

"Oh, I've got the perfect place. Your niece is six, right?"

Sally nodded.

Olivia said, "Okay, you two. Looks like you've got a plan. See you at the restaurant this afternoon. Whoever gets there first, grab a table. You know how crowded it gets! It's sure to be a crush!" Olivia waved her goodbye as she headed off in search of gifts for her brothers and their wives. She had made a list of what they needed as well as their sizes and she was able to find some really great bargains as she moved through the aisles of her favorite department stores. Her mind wandered peri-odically, realizing that she hadn't yet heard from Clay. *Keep focused on your shopping list, Olivia. He'll call...*

Caroline Graves had gotten home from the hospi-tal the evening before and was resting upstairs in her bedroom. Jeff had been hilarious. He'd gotten her an old school bell from his office and told her to ring it anytime that she needed anything. The bell had been ringing non-stop and Clay and his Dad had been rush-ing upstairs all morning. Suddenly, the bell sounded again, for what seemed the fiftieth time.

"Uh-oh, Dad. Your turn, now. I've done the last two!" Clay laughed outright.

Jeff Graves rolled his eyes. "What do you suppose she needs now? We've taken her blankets, food, drinks, the television guide, and her phone charger. What's left?"

"I have no clue, but the mystery will be solved soon... when you get upstairs!" Clay laughed, tapping his foot. "Uh--she's still ringing!"

Jeff ran up the stairs two at a time, mumbling to himself about throwing the damn bell out the window. Clay watched him fondly. *I'm so glad that Mom is feel-ing much better. I think she's paying us back for all the times she's waited on us.*

Clay finished ironing the clean shirt he'd just washed. It had gotten cold through the night and he debated throwing on a sweater before he left for the airport to meet Eric, Phyllis, and Chelsea's plane. He shouted up the stairs. "Hey, you two. I'm heading over to get Eric. Do you need me to pick up anything from the store?"

Jeff came halfway down the stairs. "Buy some more beer, and Mom says to grab a couple of boxes of macaroni and cheese. That's Chelsea's latest craving. Apparently, Phyllis says that she eats it almost every day, and I guess we have to cater to a five-year old."

Clay laughed. "I guess she takes after her Uncle Clay. Didn't I scarf down at least four boxes a week when I was about twelve?"

"Yep. We debated buying stock in the company," Jeff recalled, jokingly, "but about that time, you quit eating it altogether and wouldn't touch it for over a year."

"Anything else we need?"

"No. We're doing take-out tonight, and she hopes she'll be able to do her homemade vegetable soup for tomorrow night, even though I told her that I could do it."

"Gee, Dad...I don't know..." he glanced up the stairs at his dad.

"Alright, alright...so I'm not the best cook...but I can follow directions...Oh, great! There's that damn bell again!" Jeff headed up the stairs, still talking. "Better get a move on, son. I checked earlier and the flight was on time."

"On my way. See you later." He opened the door

and got in the driver's seat. He was really anxious to see his brother, Phyllis, and Chelsea. He put the car in reverse and headed toward the airport, thinking about what the next few days looked like. *Apparently, Mom has every night planned for the next week. How am I going to arrange to see Livy?* Little black lacy things filled his memory, as well as the sensual sounds Olivia made when she was aroused. *Damn! The mere thought of Olivia Sheffield makes me hard. I've never felt so in touch with a woman, and so happy to give her pleasure. I've got to find a way to see her, to touch her, and to finish what we've started. I need to talk the issue through with Eric tonight. I value his opinion and think that' he'll understand what I'm dealing with. He was a bit of a player in his dating days. I'll figure it out, and then talk to Dad.*

Clay neared the airport and pulled into the lane for arriving flights passenger pick-up. The car was warm and waiting. *Focus on your family right now, Clay, old boy, and put Livy on the back burner. Burner being the key word. Once I've worked out how and when to see her, I'll give her a call.*

Satisfied with his decision, Clay watched for his family to emerge from the airport, spotting them coming out the door. He opened his car door, stood out, and shouted and waved, so they would see him. "Over here, you guys!"

Eric, Phyllis and Chelsea headed in Clay's direction with suitcases, bags, and Christmas gift bags. Little Chelsea had her backpack, and a stuffed monkey with long arms. "Hi, Uncle Clay! You're not allowed to look in the blue bag, because it's not wrapped yet!"

"Alright, little girl! I'll be good...but only because

Santa is probably watching. Get on in the car!" and he held the door open for his niece. He greeted his brother with a pat on the back, and hug, and then kissed Phyllis on the cheek.

"Everything okay with Mom?" Eric asked, as he threw bags and suitcases in the trunk.

"As good as can be expected. But hold onto your hat--Mom has an agenda that never stops. You'll all need a vacation from your vacation!"

"So what's new, right?" All three of the adults groaned, and agreed that it would be a vacation to remember.

Caroline Graves adored Christmas. And this year she had both of her "boys" home as well as her two "girls", Phyllis and Chelsea. And she had her dream man beside her. Somehow that emergency squad that had carried her to the hospital had reminded her of the fact that life can change in the blink of an eye and that moments spent together were the ones that mattered the most.

She encouraged everyone to spend time together, awaiting Christmas morning, preparing for sharing the day with Chelsea. She had planned some special event practically every night that Eric and his family were to be in Barton, and they all barely had time to get from one event to the next each day. No one dared oppose her. She was a true matriarch, and you just didn't mess with powerful, driven women, especially at Christmastime.

Late one evening after Chelsea had been tucked into bed and Phyllis and Caroline had fallen asleep early, Jeff, Clay, and Eric sat by the bonfire down by the lake, behind the Graves family home. Clay had tried numerous times to get Eric alone to speak with him, but Caroline's schedule had not allowed for that to happen. Now he was sitting alone with his Dad and brother, all of them wrapped up in heavy jackets, smoking cigars, and swigging beers. *It's now or never.*

"Hey, Dad, Eric, can I ask you a question?"

"Sure, son," Jeff Graves said smiling, as he leaned in and poked at the fire. His prodding caused the flames to rise up momentarily and Eric dropped another log on the fire, saying, "Yeah, what's up?"

"Well...there's a bit of a problem at work..."

Jeff glanced up, puzzled. "What are you talking about? I've only heard rave reviews over there from everyone."

"This hardly would hit the radar...at least not yet."

"Well, what is it?" Jeff and Eric both waited for Clay's reply.

Stumbling for the right words, Clay jumped into the fray. "Well, two people on my staff are...well...involved in what one would term a romantic liaison of sorts..."

Jeff groaned. "Oh, God, don't tell me that Tom Moore finally nailed Melanie? Son...you have to nip this in the bud before it blows up in your face."

"But Dad--I don't see what the big deal is as long as they're discreet and keep it private. After all, they're grown adults and you really can't stop them from whatever..."

"Clay. I've dealt with this when I was a principal. It's just not good, and it sets a terrible precedent. Two people driven by lust who see each other daily, are NOT focused on children, only on their own unbridled desires. And let me tell you, they <u>can</u> be unbridled, as they were during my tenure. I couldn't keep the two apart; they were seen in many parts of the building, and they would leave their students unattended to find a place to be together. It really got bad, because even the kids noticed their behavior and pretty soon they had gone home and told their parents. Then I had all kinds of people up in arms at the unprofessional behavior being modeled at the school by my "staff". Before long, the parents were forcing me to either fire one or the other, or transfer both to other buildings."

Clay listened to the whole thing with a sensation of dread. 'What happened to the couple?"

"Well, I ended up suggesting to my superintendent, that they both be transferred to other buildings. They were both good teachers, after all; they left very quickly after my recommendation, and I had to replace them in the middle of the school year. Not the best scenario for them or for their students, I might add."

"Do you know what happened to them?" Clay inquired, quietly.

"Sure. They kept trying to keep their relationship going. But part of the allure was sneaking around, so that excitement wore off quickly. Over time, they grew apart; eventually they both married other people."

Eric added. "Yeah, we had a similar fling in our office too. It was a nightmare, mostly because the two salespeople weren't selling anything to anyone, but each other, if you get my meaning!" He smiled, jabbing Clay with his elbow.

Jeff continued. "Look, Clay. Handle it the way you

think you should. But the first phone call that hits my desk from a disgruntled parent or townsperson, well, then the problem becomes mine. And I can assure you, that both of them will be gone before you can blink your eyes. Do you understand?"

Clay glanced up at his Dad and brother, eyebrows furrowed, the shadow of the flames dancing on one side of his face. He nodded and quietly said, "Sure, I understand." When he caught his Dad's gaze, he quickly dropped it and changed the subject. At that moment in time, Jeff had the strangest feeling that he only knew some of the story, but Clay had risen and was shaking his brother's hand, and saying his good-nights. "I'm bushed. I need to get to bed, so I can have energy for whatever Mom's got planned for us tomorrow." After a pause he asked, "What DOES Mom have planned for us tomorrow?"

"Who knows!" they both echoed, laughingly.

Clay smiled ruefully and waved good-bye as he turned and quietly headed up towards the house. *What an incredible mess! I don't want to call Olivia without knowing what I'm going to say, and the days of this vacation are flying by. She's probably wondering why she hasn't heard from me by now.*

He got to his room and sprawled out on the queen-sized bed trying to puzzle through the whole thing. But try as he might, no answers jumped out at him. He didn't want to jeopardize either of their careers, or their mutual friendship, as well as lose the respect of his father and his staff.

Face the facts. I may not be strong enough to overcome the magnetism between the two of us; and I'm not even sure I want to. But right now, I guess I just need to take a step back and listen to Eric and Dad. I'll get through the Holiday break, and give Olivia a call when I've worked through a plan. Clay stifled a yawn, and was sound asleep within minutes.

Most of the holiday break had passed, and as the days sped by from busy mornings to evenings, Olivia's mood darkened. *Perhaps he isn't going to call, after all.* She'd always felt Clay was a man of his word, and somehow this lapse of hearing from him had disappointed her no end. But still she had given him the benefit of the doubt because of his mom's surgery. *Maybe family matters have really kept him busy.*

But when the second week passed without a phone call, Olivia had a sinking feeling in her soul that it...*what it?*...was over. And she began to put up barriers around her heart, as most people do when they've been hurt. She began to think it all through and realized that no matter the pull he had on her, she would just have to fight it...and move forward with her life. *I guess there will be no second night of pleasure with Clay Mitchell. I just can't put myself through the disappointment again when "things" don't work out.*

Resolved, am I? It's easier said than done. The hardest part will be when I see him again, looking all sexy, and have to explain that I'm not interested anymore. I won't be able to look him in the eye, or he'll see that I'm lying. That's it! I'll write him a note explaining that I want to end it, and he'll have to honor my wishes. Then we don't have to talk about it at all when school starts.

So on that chilly, gray evening, Olivia sat down at her desk, pulled out a sheet of stationary, and began composing a letter that was a complete fabrication of what she really wanted.

Dear Clay,

I hope this note finds you well over the break and that things are good with your family, particularly your mother.

I don't want to be rude, but the more I've thought about what happened between us the night of the Fields' party, the more I've realized that I don't want it to happen again. I'm putting it down as too much alcohol and the holiday spirit.

We've both agreed that no close interaction is the best way to handle our situation, and I plan on abiding by that philosophy. Please respect my wishes.

I hope that you understand my need for being comfortable in my place of employment.

I will certainly remain one of your staunchest allies in regards to your job and leadership.

Respectfully, Olivia

When the note was finished, Olivia read and reread it three more times before she placed it in an envelope, stamped, and addressed it. She sighed as she closed the drawer of her desk. *This is the only way I can think to handle this situation. Now I've just got to avoid him at all costs and move on, somehow.*

She bundled herself up in her warmest jacket, walked outside to the mailbox, inserted the letter, and flipped the flag up. Then she looked up at the moon in the cold night sky as the snow fell quietly and headed out on a long walk. Her thought was to go over to Sally's, but as she rounded the corner, she thought better of the idea. *No point in continuing to talk about something that's over. All it would do is rub salt in the wound right now, and I'm not up to that.*

So she kept right on walking until she was numb, and then she headed home, wrapped herself up in her warmest pajamas, poured herself a glass of red wine, and fell asleep, staring at the fire in her fireplace.

New Year's Eve was on a Friday that year and Eric, Phyllis, and Chelsea were leaving that morning. Clay had taken them to the airport, promised a summer visit, and wrapped little Chelsea in a big bear hug.

"Oh, Uncle Clay. I'm going to miss you!" Her sniffles warmed his heart.

"Me too, little one, but we'll still talk every week. You can let me know what's happening at school and home, and if Dad and Mom are doing everything you want them to." He glanced up smilingly at his brother and sister-in-law. "I want to hear from you if they misbehave! Is it a deal?"

"Yep," Chelsea fairly shouted as she nodded her head sharply. The impish look on her face as she snuck a look at her parents had them all giggling.

Clay shook his brother's hand and gave Phyllis a hug and kiss on the cheek. "Take care, you two. It's been great spending so much time together!"

Clay waited until they boarded the plane before heading out of the airport to his car. When he got to it, he unlocked the driver's side, and sat in the front seat. It HAD been great seeing his brother and his wife and child. He loved to watch the three of them, celebrating the intimacy of a family life. In truth, Clay had begun to yearn for that, too. The connections they all shared, as well as the relationship that he'd seen growing up with Jeff and Caroline had made him value the partnership that marriage created. He smiled, reliving some of the jokes that Phyllis had played on Eric over the length of their stay. He knew that he wanted that same easy camaraderie with a wife of his choosing. And somehow, the face of that person, that wife, that had begun formulating in his mind's eye was Olivia Sheffield's. In the beginning it had been a bit of a shock. Sure, he wanted her sexually. That was a given.

But suddenly, he'd been flooded with lots of little memories that had happened since he'd met her. *The first night I met her when she started out adorable, became a pain in the ass throwing beer on me, and then defended the Kelley boys walking home. Or her rescue of me in the session with the therapist.* He recalled the pain in her eyes when Gus Kelley cried on the mural making day. *I can still feel her quaking when she was afraid that Gus was missing at the Festival. And oh my God--that awful trumpet playing in that Mexican restaurant!*

Olivia was a package that invited opening every day.

She was a bundle of contradictions--adventurous and cautious, carefree and rigid, tender and brash, worldly and innocent, and the list went on and on. *A life with that woman would never be boring...and to top it off, she's incredibly hot! She'll need a man with considerable daring to keep her excited. And Clay, my man, you want to keep her excited!*

And then it hit him as though he'd walked into a wall. Their times together, and now their time apart, had shown it to him just as the adage stated....as plainly as the nose on his face. *I am in love with Olivia Sheffield! I don't know when or exactly how it happened, but I've never felt like this about any other woman. And I don't care if Dad doesn't want us together--we'll just have to work it out.* He smiled in his new-found knowledge, secure that he could convince Olivia that his feelings were hers as well, and that whatever the obstacles, they could and would overcome them.

He'd said his good-byes to his parents before he drove to the airport, so he'd pulled out of the parking garage and headed down the interstate towards Brandenburg, ready to get home and call Olivia right away.

Sure, I should have called her before this, but the private time was scarce and I didn't have a clue what I was feeling. Now I know, and I'm going to set the path forward for a perfect partnership as soon as I talk with her.

The trip from Barton to Brandenburg only took about thirty minutes regularly, but the roads were a little icy, and the extra holiday travelers slowed down travel on the freeway, so it took him an hour. He'd wanted to go right over to her house, but he hesitated calling her. He needed to see her face to face instead. He'd decided to run home, drop off his suitcase, and knock on her door unannounced. The element of surprise would be with him that way, and Olivia wouldn't have any warning he was coming.

He left his car out in his driveway, pulled his suitcase out of the trunk, and went in through the garage door. He quickly walked through his house, turned up the heat a little, and checked to be sure everything looked alright. When he'd known that he wasn't coming home, but would be staying up at his parents' place after the surgery, he'd called his neighbor, Bill, asking him to bring in the newspapers and mail. All of that was waiting on his kitchen counter.

He thumbed through a couple of piles of bills and set them aside. He went to the refrigerator and pulled out a beer, untwisting the top and taking a long swallow, glad to be back in town, in his own space.

The pile of junk mail got bigger as he went through the ads and mailers, but then he spied a small handaddressed envelope. He recognized the handwriting. It was hard not to. It was from Olivia. He smiled as he opened it, noticing the beautiful penmanship before the words began to take focus. Then they did take focus, and he read the letter slowly, over and over, shocked at its contents.

Finally, he set the letter down on the counter. He stared at it, the envelope, and then took a long draw on his beer. The disappointment he felt was palpable. *How could she have written that letter, just when I've finally figured out that I want her, and that we need to be together? Why doesn't she know that we're a perfect match for each other? That we're destined to be a pair?* Once more, of the many times since meeting Olivia Sheffield, Clay Mitchell was at a loss as to how to proceed. He didn't like it one damn bit, either. Particularly with women, Clay always knew what to do. *I'll just have to convince her that that letter is total BS! But how?*

On Monday, school starts up again. She's made it clear that a professional relationship will be all that exists between us. I need a plan, and I need one fast! Clay sat down at his kitchen table, beer in hand, and resolved to find a way.

20

It had been with a gnawing sense of loss that Olivia had written the letter to Clay. She had stayed away from everyone in order to work through her feelings and yet even after three days, she was still in a total mope. Somewhere over the holiday break she'd realized that she was a little in love with Clay. *Who am I kidding! It's more than a little. I am head over heels in love, and he hasn't even bothered to call me once in all that time.*

She'd had a few relationships and knew when she was being "dumped", so she'd decided to be the one to do the dumping. When Clay read the letter he'd know it for sure, and hopefully, he'd leave her alone. That was all she could expect under the circumstances. She was having her third cup of tea and still sitting around in her pajamas when the doorbell rang.

"Hey, girl, where have you been?"

Olivia recognized Sally's voice. *Might as well answer. There'll be no holding her off.*

Getting up from the table, she walked over to the

door and let her friend in. "Hey, Sal, how are you doing?" She wrapped her arms around her friend in a gentle hug.

Sally pushed out of the embrace. "What the hell is going on with you? You look terrible, and I've been calling for three days, and you haven't even bothered to answer. I was getting worried!"

Olivia saw the concern on her friend's face and felt horrible. "I'm so sorry. I haven't felt well, and I didn't want to have company. I just needed time to regroup,"

Sally watched her face. "Bad news from a certain boss?"

"No news, Sally; nothing--not a phone call or email or text. It's as though he dropped off the planet and didn't bother telling me where he went. Anyway, I'm done with it. I wrote him a note telling him that I want to keep our relationship totally professional from now on, and I expect him to abide by my wishes. Hopefully, that'll take care of the problem!"

"Hopefully...?"

"Yes, I'm finished with Clay Mitchell and don't you dare try to shame me into anything else!" she snapped, as she pointed her finger in Sally's direction.

"I wouldn't dream of it, honey...What a total slimeball, even though he's a good boss."

"And that's what he's going to stay!"

For a second Sally looked at Olivia's pasty white face, questioning her friend's decision; but then she brightened and said, "Okay, then. How about we get you out into the real world again? You look like an absolute fright. Let's take in lunch and a movie...after you clean up, of course!"

"I get it, I get it. I'll get a quick shower and be ready

as soon as possible. Help yourself to anything in the 'fridge while you're waiting." Olivia exited the kitchen as she spoke.

Sally opened the refrigerator, and rolled her eyes. Two cups of yogurt, one egg, and a loaf of half-opened bread was all that greeted her. "Scrumptious!" she muttered under breath. "You're sure convincing me that you're over Clay Mitchell, Olivia Sheffield."

Olivia took about twenty minutes to clean up. With a shower, clean hair, and a bit of make-up, she looked closer to her old self. Picking up a mirror she glanced at her reflection. *My eyes are still puffy--that's what comes from three days of a sobfest! Get your act together, Livy.* She headed downstairs to meet her friend.

"I'll bet you feel better! You certainly look better." Sally added snidely.

'That's what I love about you, Sal. Always so sympathetic!"

"Oh, hon. I get it, really I do. I'm sorry things didn't work out with Clay. But you'll figure it all out, I know. What do you think about going to see that new detective film that opened on Christmas Day. Are you game?"

"Sounds great. But can we get some lunch first? I'm starving!"

I wonder why? "Of course. Where to?" Sally asked as she grabbed her car keys.

"You pick. I'm not prepared to make any decisions today."

"You're on!" Both girls barreled out the door and headed towards Sally's car.

The curtains parted ever so slightly in the kitchen window directly across from Olivia's apartment, as the girls drove off. It was Mrs. Herbert's unit,

Olivia's landlady. "Boy, I'm glad she's surfaced," she said to herself. "I was getting really worried! If two more days had passed without seeing her, I was going to have to get my pass key and check if she was dead! What a relief!"

Priscilla Herbert owned several units of apartments in Brandenburg. She was sixty-eight and after the death of her husband, she just couldn't bear the thought of leaving Brandenburg and starting over somewhere else. So she'd stayed and lived vicariously through her renters. She had to admit to herself that without a question, Olivia Sheffield was her favorite. Not that she'd ever let Olivia know it! None of the others really gave a care about her. But she remembered when Olivia brought her those daisies and put them in that pretty vase, when she was sick. And she always asked me about the family and my houseplants.

Of course, Tommy, her late husband, had taught her that too much emotion just got in the way, so she stayed on the fringes of her tenants' lives; but she knew a lot about them all anyway. She paid attention to their comings and goings and was not shy about asking them questions, if she was unsure what they were doing. Most of her clientele stayed on, because she always corrected any problems in their apartments in a timely manner, and all the units were expected to be kept well-tended inside and out. Mrs. Herbert did her part keeping up with the needed exterior work and the apartments always looked nice and well-cared for from the street.

Priscilla hadn't seen much happening at Olivia's place for several days, and she hadn't liked it. That man with the mustache hadn't been around for awhile, but she wasn't crazy about him anyway. She just didn't think that Olivia Sheffield "fit" with that perfect looking guy. She'd watched them interact through her window of course, surreptitiously, a number of times. And she'd even seen him give Olivia a couple of goodnight kisses. But they didn't seem too exciting. "She needs a little "wild" in her life, instead of a perfect specimen. A little like you, Tommy--feis*ty* and driven and well, sexy." She smiled, picking up a framed photograph of her and Tommy in ages past, when they were celebrating New Year's Eve in Florida. "What a night that was!" she sighed.

And here it was--almost New Year's Eve again. "I wonder if Olivia has any plans for Friday night?"

Olivia and Sally had a good day of lunching, talking, movie-watching and window-shopping. Not one word was mentioned about Clay the entire day, but when Sally brought up something about school, Livy just changed the subject quickly.

"Oh, let's not talk shop, Sal. We only have a few days left of vacation, and I want to savor them."

Sally acquiesced, knowing full-well that Olivia was avoiding conversation in that direction. She'd never known her not to want to talk about school-related topics, but she let it go and asked her if she had plans for New Year's Eve.

"Sure. Derek called after his trip to Belgium, and left me a message. I haven't actually spoken with him, but I did tell him that we could go out on Friday; he

SCHOOL DAYS, SCHOOL DAZE

said he'd get back with me on the details."

"Great, girl. I'm sure he'll plan something elaborate and amazing!"

"You're probably right. Sometimes, though, I would just like to spend an easy evening out without a lot of show, Sal."

""You know, girlfriend, you're a kook! Most girls would love that fairy-tale thing that Derek seems to always give you."

"Oh, I know," Livy said apologetically. "I don't mean to seem ungrateful; Derek always plans the most unbelievable surprises. I guess that down-the-road when we see each other more often, I'll be able to tell him that he doesn't need to do that all the time."

"Down the road? Am I hearing about something more permanent, Olivia?"

"Well, Sally, I have to admit that I've been putting up barriers in regards to Derek and ignoring so many of his great qualities...but no longer! I'm moving on with my life, and if that means that Derek will be part of it, I'm resolved in that direction."

Sally looked into Olivia's eyes and heard her words; but she had an unsettled feeling about the whole thing. Sally and Olivia dropped the conversation, and headed out for dinner.

Now pulling up to Olivia's complex, she watched as her friend gathered up her shopping bag, and the carry-out bag from the Boxcar. Olivia spoke. "I'm totally done in, Sal. Thanks for rescuing me from my funk and getting me out in the world again!"

"No problem. I had a nice time and it was good seeing you more like yourself. I guess I'll see you on Monday at..."

"Don't say it, Sally. I'm not ready to hear the S word yet!"

"Okay, okay. You're absolutely right. Happy New Year, hon." Sally waved good-bye as she drove off from Olivia's place.

Olivia rearranged the plastic bag she was carrying as she crossed the road over to Mrs. Herbert's place. As she came up the front porch step, she thought she saw the curtains move, but couldn't swear to it. She knocked on her landlady's door. It took two sets of knocks to get a response.

"I'm coming, I'm coming! Hold your horses!"

The door swung open and there stood her landlady, decked out in a blue and purple robe with purple slippers. Surprise and annoyance registered on her face.

Livy was used to the annoyance, but she didn't buy the surprise. "Hello, Mrs. Herbert. It occurred to me that I haven't seen you for some time, so I brought you some dinner and dessert!"

Now the look of surprise was genuine. Gruffly, Priscilla Herbert said, "Uh...uh, I don't need any dinner! I made myself one of those microwave meals and..."

"I'm not listening!" Olivia slipped through the front door right past her stunned landlady, asking, "Where are your TV trays? Oh, there they are...now you just set one of those up, and I'll go and get some silverware from your kitchen...what do you want to drink? I see some milk here, or do you want a cup of coffee? I think I'll have one, if you don't mind." Olivia came bustling out of the kitchen, armed with napkins, silverware and two cups of coffee.

Mrs. Herbert was flabbergasted. "Now, see here, Olivia..."

"Now, Mrs. Herbert. No arguments. Why don't you sit down here, and I'll bring you your dinner. Sally and I went to the Boxcar and you know...well, maybe you don't...how big their portions are. I've brought you this wonderful chicken piccata with vegetables and mashed potatoes, and then I bought a dessert for us to share. I know you'll love it! We can get all caught up!"

Before Priscilla knew what was happening, she was sitting behind one of her TV trays, with a fabulous plate of food that smelled like heaven under her nose.

"Eat up, now, while it's still warm. We'll have dessert later!"

The aroma of the meal in front of her stopped Priscilla's protests. The first forkful lingered in her mouth, and the look on her face spoke volumes. Then she opened her eyes and noticed Olivia watching her, smiling; she swallowed that bite and tried to put on her sternest face. "I truly don't know what you were thinking barging in here at this time of night, Olivia!"

Olivia kept the smile plastered on her face. She knew what the biddy was really about, so she continued to ignore her sour demeanor. "Oh, it's not that late, and I took a chance that you'd be home. I think you need to eat more anyway. Tell me what you've been doing lately? Did you go and visit your kids for Christmas?"

The two of them talked, Priscilla harping on her two kids and the unruly grandchildren; but she produced some newly framed photos of the "brats", as she referred to them, talking about them both, and what they were doing in school. Olivia watched her face soften as she talked about the kids, and she knew that Priscilla loved seeing them and having the company of her own children as well. Olivia filled Priscilla in on her Christmas doings, as well.

During their conversation, the food had disappeared, and Olivia got up from the couch where she had been sitting. "Alright, great! You must have liked that chicken! Now let me clean this up, and I'll bring us out a plate of that carrot cake. You're just going to die, it's so good!"

Priscilla tried to argue, but Olivia was having none of it. When she left the room, Priscilla sighed with pleasure. "I don't think my stomach has been this satisfied in a long time." But when Olivia reemerged with two plates of the largest slab of carrot cake she'd even seen, she groused, "There is no way I can eat that! It's a monstrosity!"

Livy laughed. "I know, isn't it ridiculous? We'll just have a bite or two...it's so rich! Then I'll wrap it up and you can finish it later!"

Mrs. Herbert shook her head emphatically. "I told you I don't want it...and..."

On that word, her mouth being open, Livy shoved a bite of the warm, gooey carrot cake into her mouth.

This time she said nothing until she swallowed. "Oh...my.,..word, Olivia. That is...the best...cake I have ever tasted!"

Olivia chuckled. "I told you so! I usually have one piece of this a year; otherwise, I would have to get all new clothes to make up for my expanding waistline."

The two of them ate four more bites apiece; then Mrs. Herbert called a cease-fire to the feeding frenzy. "Enough! Go wrap that up right now!" Olivia did as she was told, smiling to herself.

A few minutes passed before Priscilla shouted,

"What are you doing in there? I don't want you snooping through my kitchen, you know."

Livy came out, drying her hands on a dish towel. "I was just cleaning up a little. I love the new curtains you got in your kitchen. They're so...sunny!" Olivia wondered about a seemingly crotchety woman who would have bright yellow and blue kitchen curtains.

"My daughter brought those over. She likes to decorate, but I told her they were too bright!"

"Oh, I don't think so. I absolutely adore them. Well, I best be going for now; I've got some things to do before I go to bed." Olivia began to put on her coat.

"Where's your slice of carrot cake? Don't you dare leave the whole thing here."

"Oh, right...right." Livy stepped back into the kitchen, and brought out a plate. "Can I bring back your plate later this week?"

"Of course. But don't break it! Those dishes are from my wedding." Then the interrogation began. "By the way--I haven't seen you out and about much. Are you going out for New Years' Eve? You're not planning a big party here, or anything like that?"

Olivia knew she was fishing. "No...no party for me. I have a date with a man I've been seeing. I'm not sure you've met him. His name is Derek Donaldson."

"Is he the one with the mustache? Not bad looking, I guess, if you like them perfectly pressed. Does he live around here?"

"No. He lives over in Townsend. He is opening a new art gallery there, so I haven't seen much of him lately."

"Well, I hope he's a gentleman. You can't be too careful these days!"

"Oh, he's a total gentleman." *In fact, I wish he wasn't such a proper gentleman. What did she say? Perfectly pressed?* Her thoughts hovered on a face with blonde hair and blue-gray eyes. *No, Olivia. You're not going there!* "I'll be careful, Mrs. Herbert. Don't worry." She bent to give the woman a hug.

Priscilla Herbert stood at once, avoiding most of the physical contact. "Well, even though I didn't invite you...I...I'm...thankful for dinner and the dessert. It was...very...nice..." A half-smile appeared on her face.

"No problem. I'm glad you enjoyed it. You take care, now, and if you need anything, just give me a call. I'll let myself out."

Olivia closed the door behind her quietly, smiling to herself. *That was a job well-done, if I do say so myself. I needed to get my mind off of my petty problems and think about someone else.*

Mrs. Herbert returned to her regular perch behind the front curtains and watched as Olivia unlocked her front door, and closed it behind her. Then she shuffled over to lock her own door. That's when she saw the plate of carrot cake, sitting on her end table. "Oh, well, maybe I'll go and get a fork!" And she smiled all the way to her kitchen.

21

Clay had returned to work after the Christmas holiday, prepared to win over Olivia, to cajole her, to prove to her, to make her realize that they were meant for each other. He would make arrangements to speak with her, despite any protests that she might have in the beginning. *I'm not going down without a fight, Miss Sheffield--no matter what you wrote to me.*

But within an hour of the school day beginning, the buzz started going around. The unthinkable had happened! Olivia Sheffield had gotten engaged on New Year's Eve! There was rumor to the effect that she'd almost swallowed the ring, it being placed by the waiter at Derek's request, in her glass of champagne! It was all anyone was talking about in the halls and at lunch.

And to top it off, Kathy was gushing about it as well! *Traitor!*

"Oh, Clay, isn't it great about Olivia? Derek is a wonderful man who will take good care of her. Have you met him yet?"

Son-of-a... "Yeah, I've met him. He seems perfectly

alright, but I think, a little bland for my tastes." Clay brushed his hand through his hair.

"Your tastes? What do they have to do with anything? He's not marrying you!" Kathy commented, puzzled at the surly response from her normally jovial principal.

His head snapped around in Kathy's direction. "You're right, it's nothing...just ignore me. But we need to get back and focus on education around here. This engagement conversation has gone on long enough. I'm closing my door for awhile, Kathy. I need to get my bearings after break and get back to business. Excuse me, will you?" he asked as his door closed sharply. *Jesus--what am I going to do now? I can't lose her.*

Kathy heard the door slam, but kept on typing, thinking, "Oh, boy. He's got it bad! Wait'll I tell Charlie I was right all along."

The restaurant in Townsend where Derek took Olivia for New Year's Eve, was called The Peak. It was a popular site overlooking the small town, with its all-glass dining room and gourmet menu. Olivia had been the surprised one, when Derek had proposed after quickly pointing out that there was something in the bottom of her glass that she was getting ready to swallow. He'd even gotten down on one knee in front of the other restaurant patrons. It seemed as though time stopped, as she stared down into his expectant eyes, with everyone watching her, before she answered. At that moment, the face of Clay Mitchell slid through her mind; but she cleared it away, smilingly looking around the room, and nodded "Yes" to the applause of all those in attendance. Derek rose and kissed her hand, as he slid the ring on her finger.

"Olivia, this is the greatest night of my life! I hope that you feel the same way!" He kissed her ever so gently for all to see.

Olivia could only smile through her tears, as a lump formed in her throat. Finally, glancing at the ring, she squeaked out the words, "Thank you. The ring is just lovely. Oh Derek, it'll be just wonderful, I'm sure!" *Am I trying to convince myself?*

They talked over dinner, and she watched the obvious pleasure on Derek's face as he began to make plans aloud. *I've made the right decision. Derek and I will have a good life together.*

"Hey!" Derek said, excitedly. "Let's call Jimmy and Susie and give them the news!"

They dialed Jimmy's cell, and actually spoke with the couple, who were ecstatic. Jimmy asked, "Have you set a date yet? I need to clear my calendar!"

"Heavens, no," Olivia laughed. "We're not rushing things; but we wanted you two to be the first to know. I'll call the other brothers and Mom and Dad tomorrow."

After the conversation ended, Olivia and Derek went into the restaurant bar to listen to the piano player and see in the New Year. Overall, it was a heady night, full of excitement and high spirits.

When Derek began to talk about details, and the timing, Olivia said, "Derek, would it be alright if we waited for a formal announcement? I'd like to tell my parents and Sally and my colleagues, before we go full steam ahead."

"Anything you want, Olivia. You've made me the happiest man in the world tonight!" They toasted again and stood companionably as they watched the ball drop in Times Square on the big screen television. Then everyone in the bar raised their noisemakers, using them with glee, kissing and hugging everyone in their reach. Derek turned to her and kissed her again. The kiss was heartfelt, she knew. *But it doesn't stop my heart.* She wiped out the memory of the kisses that had. *There's so much more to this man than just his ability to make me weak in the knees. I can live without that, especially compared to all that he brings to the table.* She vowed to convince herself of that.

Clay was beside himself. He knew in his heart and soul that Olivia was making a mistake and that he and she should be the ones engaged. But how to change the course of the latest events totally baffled him. *The only option I can think of is to talk to Sally, and tell her everything. Maybe she can help.* He called her into his office at the end of the day on Tuesday.

"Hi Clay," she greeted as she entered his office. "Happy New Year. How is your mother doing?"

"Fine, Sally, fine. Thanks for asking. Hey, could you please close the door?"

She nodded, wondering what was up. She turned and looked at him, eyebrows raised, a question on her face.

Clay's hand brushed through his blonde hair, which was a little shaggier than normal. "Sally," he broached hesitantly, "...I'm not sure if this is the best way to handle this, but...well...what the hell do you think about that engagement?"

Sally didn't let the grin that bubbled up inside her show. Nonchalantly she said, "Oh, you mean Olivia and Derek?"

"Well, of course that's what I mean!" he spat out belligerently.

"Well, Clay. What exactly are you asking me?"

"Dammit! He's not right for her and you know it! He's too friggin' perfect, and she'll be bored to tears in a matter of days!"

"As opposed to being bored to tears by a man who didn't even call her during the Christmas break...a man who can't see the opportunity standing in front of his face?" she threw out sarcastically.

It was as though she'd slapped him. He sat down in his chair begrudgingly nodding. "You're absolutely right. I've been a total ass; and the thing was that when Mom went into the hospital, Dad and I were all caught up in that drama. Then my brother and his family came into town for the holiday. At that point in time, I knew I wanted a relationship with Olivia; but frankly, I saw it as a ...well, to be as crass as I can think...a wham-bam-thank you, ma'am sort of a fling where we could let our inner demons out and all, and then be done with it!"

Sally listened, watching his face, with not even the hint of a smile.

Clay continued. "I decided to talk to my Dad and brother about it, in light of the fact that Olivia and I work together."

"Are you telling me that your Dad, our Superintendent, knows that you and Olivia have the hots for each other?"

He glanced up, hopefully. "Does she have the...?"

Sally interrupted. "Answer my question?"

"No, Dad doesn't know who it is. In fact, he doesn't know it's me either. He just assumed it was someone else on the staff, when I spoke to him about two people who wanted to pursue a relationship. Will you sit, please, Sally?" He gestured towards a chair in his office. 'This might take a bit." Sally found a chair and Clay continued.

"You see, I'm not sure that you're aware of my past history. My parents were killed in a car accident when I was young; Dad and Mama Caro took me and my brother in from the moment it happened. They had been my parents' closest friends. They raised Eric and me as though we were their own, and I've always thanked God that I had the good luck to have two amazing sets of parents." He paused, clearly remembering back.

"Dad's love for teaching inspired me through the years, and as you know, I followed in his footsteps, so to speak. I love and respect him beyond measure and would do all in my power not to embarrass or disappoint him...Mama Caro too."

Sally nodded, caught up in Clay's story.

He went on. "When the subject came up that evening, I truly thought that Dad and Eric would see it my way. Two consenting adults, after all, interested in pursuing each other? I was dead wrong. Dad told me about the problems that he had encountered as a principal with two of his staff members when they had a fling; and then Eric told of some issues in his office that occurred under similar circumstances. Anyway, when it was all over, Dad assured me that if I let the problem continue and he received any news whatsoever of this fling, both of the parties would be fired instantly." He grimaced, and nodded at the worried look in Sally's eyes. "So you see, I had decided that maybe I'd better step back and get some distance between Olivia and myself, and see if the desire sort of went away. What a laugh that was!" he looked up, ruefully.

She waited, as he seemed to take a big breath, and regroup. "So--what's changed, Clay?"

"Well, the rest of the vacation passed, and I took my brother, wife and niece to the airport. And then it just hit me...I didn't want a fling with Olivia! **I wanted a life with Olivia!**

Hell, besides one very heated evening, which ended too soon, and a few hot kisses, we've never been together...and I don't care! I just know that I have to have her! I also know that no matter how perfect that son-of-a-bitch is, he's not a match for Olivia! But I am...I'll drive her crazy at all the right times! Sally, do you think you can help me? I...love...her."

Sally looked up with a quirky little smile on her face. "Well, it's about time, you idiot! Sorry for that, by the way, but only because you're my boss. Yes, Dave and I will help in every way we know how. For some strange reason, I think that you're totally right. Olivia needs to pass on Prince Charming, and dare I say it? Settle for Mr. Toad!" She giggled as Clay's face lit up, and then sank quickly. "Oh, come on! I'm teasing you...but you deserve it for being so stupid. Anyway, the truth is...I think Olivia Sheffield is in love with you already, in spite of the fact that you've been clueless through most of this. Can you come over to my place tonight? I'll call Dave and we'll see what strategies we can set in motion."

Clay stood from behind his desk, walked out and around, and grabbed Sally up in a bear hug, lifting her off her feet. "Yes, tell me what to do, where to go, what to say...I'll do it!"

"Put me down, you big lug!" she said, laughingly. "Here's my address," she said, scribbling on a post-it from his desk. "Come over at seven tonight and be ready to work for your prize!" Sally turned and smiled happily. "See you later!"

Clay watched her go with a little cautious euphoria creeping into his heart.

22

The evening spent with Sally and Dave was a good one for Clay. They ragged him endlessly about his stupidity in becoming aware of his feelings for Olivia, but in the end, he knew that they were on his side. The three of them talked about Olivia and Derek, and Sally made it very clear that she wouldn't stomach anything bad being said about Derek. "After all, he's a good guy in every way. Way nicer than either of you two," she added with a grin.

Dave wrapped his arm around Sally, pulling her close. "Let me remind you, honey. I can be <u>very</u> nice, when you want me to."

She slapped him on the shoulder as she pulled away, giggling. "Later, big boy. Right now we need to help my boss here nail my girlfriend...in the nicest of ways, of course."

Over beer and pizza, Sally and Dave talked about Olivia and growing up in a small town together. Clay asked questions, but later said, "You know, I picked up a lot of information about Olivia the night we met at

Ojays. My biggest problem now is that she is avoiding me at all costs, and I'm not sure how to change that."

"Well...I <u>do</u> have one idea that I think might help you get close to her, although I hesitate to subject you to it."

"What is it?" Clay and Dave both asked.

"Well, I overheard you telling Dave that your lease expires at the end of January, and you know you don't plan on extending it."

"Right."

"Well--you probably know that Olivia lives in those townhouses on Hennessey...and they're really nice, considering what she pays. The only drawback that I can see is the landlady, Mrs. Herbert. Livy likes her, but I think she's a snooping busybody; she spies on everyone over there. I also happen to know that there are two townhouses available, and one of them is directly behind Olivia's place!"

"No kidding?" Clay remarked, the gears in his head already turning. "She'd have to talk to me eventually, if she kept bumping into me all the time...and it'd be away from work, so there'd be no pressure to behave! I like it...a lot!"

"Wow, hon. That's a great idea!" Dave added as he patted Sally's hand.

"Maybe I'll pay a visit to Mrs. Herbert tomorrow," Clay announced. "If she's willing to have a new leasee, I'll give my notice now at my current place."

Sally nodded in agreement. "Look, Olivia and I are running around tomorrow after work, so I'll keep her away from home until later in the evening. Hopefully, you'll have time to meet with the Dragon Lady while Olivia's away and get things settled. I'll call you on your cell if those plans change. We wouldn't want her to see you over there. It would ruin the element of surprise."

The guys agreed.

"Secondly, I'll talk to Kathy about the whole thing... if that's okay?"

"Kathy Tiffin? Why...do you think she needs to be involved?"

"You're kidding, right? Sometimes guys are so dense! Not you of course, Davy"

Clay and Dave looked at each other, clearly puzzled.

"Well, for heaven's sake. Kathy's already involved. How do you think we arranged for you and Olivia to sit together the night of the Christmas party at the Fields' house? Do you really think that was happenstance? Kathy talked to Florence Fields beforehand. She's seen the way you two look at each other...Don't you remember the night she said you two could set off the fire alarms at school?"

Dave and Clay laughed, remembering Kathy's night of being overserved.

"Kathy will find other ways to help you and Olivia meet each other; she's sneaky...in a good way, of course! But Clay, you have your work cut out for you! Olivia is stubborn, and now that she's agreed to this engagement--though I don't understand why--she will do all in her power to convince herself that she wants it. Also, she won't tolerate anything that would hurt Derek."

Clay nodded, with full understanding on his face. "That's one of the reasons I love her."

Sally and Dave stood together arm in arm, watching the look on Clay's face, knowing that he meant what he said.

"Okay, then. All for one and one for all...raise your

glasses for Operation **GET OLIVIA UN-ENGAGED!** Time to get to work on changing Olivia's mind...and Clay, you'd better do it fast! I really don't know how much time you have," she warned.

The knock on Mrs Herbert's door, at four in the afternoon, startled her. She took her time, thinking that maybe her ears were playing tricks on her. But then the doorbell rang as well, and she went cautiously towards the front window, peering out to see who was on the front porch. It was a man! One she didn't know...but my oh my, isn't he handsome? And blonde like Tommy.

She spoke through the door in her gruffest voice, while double-checking the lock. "Who are you and what do you want?"

"Mrs. Herbert? My name is Clay Mitchell. I'm the new principal at Brandenburg Elementary. I've been living over at Green Lakes and my lease expires soon. I'm looking for another place. A friend told me that you had a couple townhouses available; I was hoping that I could take a look."

Of course. I remember now. I've seen him around town, at the tree lighting ceremony, and jogging around the streets. Still curious, she questioned, "Who told you about the vacancies?"

"One of my teachers, Sally Litchfield."

Ah, that's Olivia's friend--the sassy one. "Well, I'm not promising anything, Mr. Mitchell, but come on in."

The sound of locks being opened greeted Clay's ears as the door opened slightly. Before him stood a woman in her late sixties, he guessed, with gray curly hair, wearing a bright orange robe with orange slippers.

"Well, hello, Mrs. Herbert. I certainly like your bright colors on such a gray day." He took her hand and shook it.

She was surprised at his forward behavior...secretly, loving it. "I don't make it a habit of shaking hands with total strangers. Now, Mr, Mitchell, why don't you tell me why you want to leave Green Lakes? Those are fancy apartments...much fancier than these places."

He smiled, summoning up his ready charm. "May I sit, Mrs Herbert?" he asked, indicating the nearby chair.

"Yes, sit." She didn't offer to take his coat, but he took it off, and laid it across the back of the chair. He looks real nice in that blue suit.

"Well, I moved here from Arizona within days of school starting. The school district got me a six-month lease, because they knew I wouldn't have time to house-hunt. Right away I knew that I didn't want to stay at Green Lakes long-term. You're right, they are fancy places...actually, a little too fancy for my tastes. I prefer something a little," searching for the word, "homier."

Mrs. Herbert listened, nodding.

"Anyway, it came up in conversation the other night that I needed to move and Sally mentioned your townhouses. Is there any way you'd consider renting to me? I'd be happy to take a year-lease if that's what you need."

"Without seeing the place?" she asked skeptically.

"Well, no, I'd want to see the place, of course. But when a friend recommends it, well, I'm willing to take her word."

"Alright, then, I'll show you the unit over to my left. I think that you might like..."

"But don't you have one directly next door and adjacently behind?"

"Uh...well, yes. But that's not as nice, and it needs some work."

"Could I see that one instead? I'm fairly handy. Maybe I could help and do some of the work that it needs."

"Well, alright. You can follow me. I'm just going to pull my coat over my robe and step into my boots."

"Let me help you, Mrs. Herbert." Clay held her elbow as she struggled into her boots. Then he held her coat up so that she could slide her arms into the sleeves.

"Thank you, Mr. Mitchell; I'm not much for fussing over..."

"I'm not fussing, Mrs. Herbert. Just helping a little," he said, grinning at her.

"You ARE a charmer, aren't you, Mr. Mitchell? That normally doesn't work for me!" she said sharply, pulling her elbow out of his embrace. She turned and looked him square in the face. "Well, what are you waiting for? Let's go!"

She shuffled through her kitchen to her back door, stepping slowly down the stairs in front of her and turning left, following the sidewalks to the townhouse in the back. "Every one of these townhouses has its own carport. The one for this unit sits directly behind the drive over there." She pointed indicating the direction. "At least you don't have to clean snow off your car much, unless it's really windy."

"Sounds good," Clay nodded.

They mounted the front steps, and Mrs. Herbert

unlocked the door. "The place may be a little dusty, because you didn't call and make an appointment!" she groused.

"Gee, I'm sorry. It was hectic at work today, and I just didn't get a chance to call ahead. But please don't worry--a little dust doesn't bother me!"

"Well, it bothers me! You'll see what I mean when we get inside the living room area." They walked into the open room, Mrs. Herbert turning on the overhead light.

Clay looked around the room. It was a decent-sized living area with lots of old cherry woodwork that looked really inviting. "This is great, Mrs. Herbert. I like the woodwork and the old-fashioned fireplace."

She smiled slightly. "Come on," she said, motioning towards the kitchen. "Now the kitchen here really needs the cupboards re-stained, but I haven't had anyone look at these units for so long, that I've let it go." She looked into Clay's face with an almost apologetic frown.

"It's okay. I could do that for you actually, and I would be happy to help. It wouldn't take me more than a couple of days to finish."

"The bedrooms are upstairs." She proceeded along, gesturing towards the bathroom on the main floor. "Oh, and here's the powder room. There are just two bedrooms and they share a full bath, but it's enough."

Clay climbed the stairs behind her, thinking about what Olivia would look like in his bedroom--without any clothes on. *Whew! I'm getting a little warm in here.* Once at the top of the stairs, he peeked into the smaller room and then glanced towards what would be the master bedroom. It had more than adequate floor space and a good-sized closet. "I'll take it, Mrs. Herbert!"

"Wait a minute! You haven't even asked what it costs, and I haven't even decided if I like you. You're awfully pushy!"

Clay retreated. *It would not be right to alienate this woman. I need her help.* At that point in time, Clay decided that honesty might be the best policy. "Uh, Mrs. Herbert. Could we go and sit down and talk? I have a little story to tell you."

That caught her ear. She glanced over her shoulder, nodded, and headed for the staircase. When they returned to the living room she turned out the lights, and stepped back outside onto the porch, locking the door behind her.

They walked, without conversation, back to her home, where she quietly took off her coat and boots. Clay hung her coat back on the coat hook in her living room. She motioned to the chair again, and Clay lowered his large frame into the little chair, while she sat on the couch.

"Go ahead and get to this story. I'm curious!"

He looked up and prayed he'd made the right decision. "Well, it's true that Sally told me about the two vacant units you have here. The thing that I haven't told you is that the most pressing reason I have to live here is Olivia Sheffield."

Her eyebrows shot up, and she motioned for him to continue.

"It's kind of an awkward story, actually. I'm thirty-three years old, a grown man, and I just realized last week, that I'm in love with Olivia. We've never really dated, because I was trying to avoid the chemistry between us...being her boss and all. But over break I decided that I didn't care about that and that I need to do everything in my power to convince her that she feels the same way for me. The only problem is..."

"...the rich, polite, and entirely handsome man that she's engaged to?"

"Yeah," Clay said, rolling his eyes. "I don't think he's that handsome!" he snarled.

Mrs. Herbert just raised her eyebrows.

"Oh, alright. He's handsome. That would be the problem...but I have to say to you, he's just not right for Olivia. He's too damned perfect! Olivia needs some-one...flawed...and stupid, like me! She needs someone who can't keep their hands off her, and someone who can keep her busy for a lifetime of re-training!" He'd said it almost proudly. He looked up at the gray-haired woman across from him, smiling sheepishly. "I'd treat her well--and we'd have fun together, all the time."

Mrs. Herbert still hadn't spoken.

He looked her square in the eye. "Would you help me, Mrs. Herbert? I'm in love with Olivia Sheffield, and I just can't imagine life without her, now that she's stepped into mine. Anyway, she'd be bored silly with that son-of-a..." Clay caught himself before he finished the profanity.

Priscilla Herbert smiled inwardly. *He's absolutely right about Olivia. She would be bored with that magazine cut-out; and anyway, I like his eyes.* "I believe your motives are honest, Mr. Mitchell. I'll let you rent the unit you want. But mind you, if I see that Olivia doesn't have feelings for you, I won't discourage her from Mr. Donaldson. And understand, if you do anything--and I mean anything--to hurt Miss Sheffield, I will personally evict you, and tell everyone in town that you're a disreputable lout! Now let's shake on a six-month lease. If you haven't won her by then, you're not the man I think you are!" She held out her hand.

But Clay ignored the outstretched hand and smiled, wrapping her in a big bear hug. "Thanks, Mrs. Herbert... when can I move in?"

"I'll do some tidying up over there this week. You could move in as early as this weekend, or whenever it's good for you."

"Fine, that'll be just fine. What do I owe you for a deposit?" He pulled out his checkbook.,

"We'll work all that out later, Mr. Mitchell. I want to turn on the evening news now; and I'd like to have some quiet around here."

Clay grinned at his new landlady. "Mrs. Herbert. I think that you deliberately don't want anyone to know what a 'softie' you are."

"I beg your pardon, young man!"

"Okay, okay, I'm going. I'll call you...may I call you to let you know when I'll be moving in?"

"Yes...yes; now get going!" she said, as she reached for the television remote.

Clay pulled on his coat, and turned around to look at his new landlady, as he cleared his throat. "Ummm... Mrs. Herbert?" he asked, in an expectant voice.

"What, what, what?" She was already engrossed in the five o-clock news, not even looking at him.

"Could you not tell Livy that I'm moving in? She might not be too happy to find it out right now."

She glanced sharply in his direction. "Have you already upset her then? I'm telling you, if you've lied to me..."

"No, no, it's not that. She just THINKS that she doesn't want to see me; but I'm going to change her mind!"

"Alright, Mr. Mitchell. We'll wait and see how things work out. Goodnight!"

Without another word, Clay showed himself out the front door of his new digs, and jumped off the top step, with the enthusiasm of a little boy.

Priscilla Herbert had watched it all from behind her living room curtains, chuckling at the childish show of delight that she'd just witnessed. "Oh my, Mr. Mitchell, you do my heart good. Let's see if you can work your wonders on Olivia's heart as well!"

23

Since her engagement, Olivia had avoided Sally. It wasn't that she was ashamed, really, it was just that she didn't want a lecture about her choice. She knew that Sally would encourage her to rethink her response, and Olivia just didn't want to rehash the whole thing.

Derek wanted to take Olivia to meet his parents as soon as possible; they'd set aside a mid-January visit to Townsend together, but then the storm came. Winters in Indiana were unpredictable. In fact, there were some winters that Olivia remembered having no more than an inch of snow; this January was different. The winter storm warning came unexpectedly on the news, and within two hours the snow was falling and falling hard. Snow plows could not keep up with the barrage of heavy white snowflakes and cars were getting stuck everywhere, slip-sliding off the roads into the rapidly rising snow banks.

Still and all, Olivia had heard the news, had a pretty stocked pantry, and had gotten in from school before the bulk of the storm hit. The television newscasters were having a field day forecasting the gloom and doom scenario, but Olivia didn't really believe that they'd ever get the amount of snowfall that was forecast. This time she was wrong; by five-thirty, they'd already cancelled school for the next day, and as she gazed out the window, she just shook her head in disbelief.

Her phone rang. "Hey, little sister! How are you doing over there in Brandenburg?" Jimmy inquired.

"Oh, my gosh, Jim, you cannot believe the amount of snow here. I don't ever remember this much on the ground, and it's blowing around something awful! They've already cancelled school for tomorrow; but I have everything I need, so I guess I'll open a bottle of red wine and read my book and enjoy the quiet."

The conversation continued and Jimmy asked about the engagement news. "Have you gone up yet to meet Derek's parents?"

"No, not yet. In fact, that was to happen this weekend, but, well, here we are. I just spoke with Derek a little while ago, and he's stranded too, as I'm sure you've heard on the news. We'll just have to reschedule. Are you and Susie okay?"

"Actually, Boston isn't bad at all right now. The storm seems to be sticking over the Midwest, so we may escape the mayhem for a while. Anyway, I just wanted to check in on you. Take care, Sis. Hopefully we'll get to see you sometime during the thaw--it if ever comes!"

"Okay, Jimmy. Thanks for calling. Love you!" She hung up, happy to touch base with her big brother.

She didn't really feel like watching the television anymore, so she went into the kitchen, opened a bottle of Cabernet, then went into her bedroom to change into her favorite flannel pajamas. As she was changing, she thought she heard voices outside. *Who in the world would be outside on a night like this?* She moved her bedroom curtains to the side, and peered out the window. The snow was really blowing hard. *Oh my gosh, someone is moving into the back townhouse! What a terrible night to be moving!* There were several guys with heavy coats on, trucking up and down the front step carrying furniture and boxes. Everyone was wearing a hood and gloves and she couldn't see anyone's face. They moved quickly, though, and she could tell that they were relatively young. At that moment one of the guys' hoods blew off and she saw that it was Dave Garrett! *What in the world is Dave doing over there? And who is he helping to move in?* As if someone read her thoughts, in front of her very eyes were two men carrying in boxes, covered with snow. One of them was Bobby Wilson and the other one was...she strained to see...a blonde god...Olivia gasped, pulling away from the window. *Dear Lord, it's Clay! What in the world is the meaning of this?*

Before she even knew what she was doing, she picked up the phone and dialed Sally. The phone rang four times before Sally answered.

"Hello?"

"Sal--it's me!"

Right on cue! Nonchalantly answering, Sally said, "Oh, hi, Olivia. How are you over there? Bundled up in your warm snuggies yet, or...?"

"Sally, do you know what's going on over here? I just peeked out my bedroom window, and Dave and the guys are over here carrying in boxes...and Clay is out there too."

"Oh, yeah, I know; but I guess you didn't. Clay's

lease expired, and he decided to rent over there in your complex. I guess it hasn't come up, since you and I haven't really spoken in a while!" she added scoldingly.

Olivia heard the harshness of the comment as though she'd been slapped. Quietly she said, "I know...I know, Sally. I'm sorry we haven't talked lately; there's just a lot going on in my life right now, and well, you know I'm like a clam when I'm working through stuff--I just shut up and hide. I'm sorry, honey, I didn't mean to hurt your feelings."

It was quiet for a minute, and then Sally said, "Apology accepted. Anyway, I don't really know much.,..except..." forgive me, she thought quietly... "that Davy found out that Clay's lease was almost up and told him about the units over by you. So I guess he went over to talk to Mrs. Herbert and she's letting him rent it. Of course, he'd given his notice, and Green Lakes found someone to move into his place, so he was stuck and had to move today. I'm making sloppy joes and they're all heading over here for a late dinner when they're done. Do you want to come too?"

Olivia was taken aback totally. *Clay will be right under my nose at school and after school! It'll be harder than ever to avoid him now!*

Sally continued her badgering. "Hey, Olivia? Do you want to come over too, hon?"

"No...no, but thanks for the invite. I'm not leaving my place tonight. It's too bad outside!"

"Okay, sweetie. Well, enjoy your day off tomorrow. I, for one, am sleeping in!" Sally's line went dead.

Olivia stood looking at her cell phone, and then looked again out the window.. The snow had stopped blowing just a tad, and she could see more clearly.

Clay was shaking hands with the guys on the front porch, obviously thanking them for their help. As she watched, he reached into a cooler, and pulled out four beers, handing them around, They all toasted Clay and his new quarters; then he opened the door, motioning for them all to come inside. Within a minute, the front porch was empty of beefcake. Olivia sat down in shock on her bed, head in her hands. *What a mess!*

Over at Clay's house, Dave's cell phone vibrated in his pocket. He pulled it out, saying, "Hi Babe. What's up?" He listened for a moment and added, "...that's great! See you soon. We're all starving!"

When he disconnected, he looked at Clay and quietly said, "She knows, and right now she's not taking it well!"

Priscilla Herbert had hatched her own plan to get Olivia Sheffield around Clay Mitchell more often. The storm had dumped almost fifteen inches on Brandenburg that night and nothing was moving outside this early in the morning. She started up her favorite crock pot recipe--her famous chicken and noodles. It would simmer most of the day. She took her time watching the morning news, since the paperboy hadn't been able to get out with papers. It was likely that the snow would keep coming, according to the news, for at least two more days.

Clay's phone rang about eight-thirty in the morning. He answered quickly, as he'd been up a couple of hours, unpacking boxes. "Oh, hey, Mrs. Herbert. Yes, I got in last night...no, nothing is dripping on the floors over here. The guys were a great help; and we basically got it all in before the worst of the weather."

"Mr. Mitchell? I think that since you said you'd help around here, I have the perfect job for you."

"Yes, and what is that?" Clay asked, hesitantly.

"Well, I'm thinking that with all the snow and maybe more coming, it would be really good to have someone shovel the sidewalks between all the units, so that people could at least get out to their cars if they need to. The snowplow driver will come and do the front sidewalks on the street side, and the parking lot, so there's no need to worry about those. What do you say?"

"Sure. Let me work here a couple more hours, and then I'll get out and shovel. I'll probably be ready for a break by then anyway."

"Wonderful. And Mr. Mitchell? I'd like to invite you to dinner this evening. Could you come? I've put on my chicken and noodles, and they're my specialty. My husband, Tommy, dearly loved them."

He chuckled and teased her. "Are you asking me for a date, Mrs. Herbert?"

She sputtered, as he was laughing.

"I'm teasing you. Of course, I'll come to dinner. It sounds great! I have to warn you, though. I have a pretty big appetite--especially when I've been shoveling."

"There will be plenty. Let's say about six this evening?"

"Will do, Mrs. Herbert. See you tonight!"

Okay. That's half of the problem. Now for part two.

She rang Olivia next. "Hello, Olivia. It's Mrs. Herbert. I was wondering if you'd consider coming over for dinner? I started my chicken and noodles in the crock pot. You know it IS my best dish, and I know that there will be way too much for just me. I want to thank you for bringing me dinner a few weeks back."

Olivia was delightfully surprised at the invitation. *Usually she's a veritable hermit.* But Mrs. Herbert seemed insistent and actually sounded excited, and Livy's stomach growled at the thought of a home-cooked meal of chicken and noodles. "Sounds delicious! What can I bring?"

"Oh, nothing. I've got the whole meal planned. Shall we say six-fifteen?"

"I'll be there! Thank you!" Hanging up the phone, she remembered Sally's constant complaint that Mrs. Herbert was a busybody. *Tonight, I'm going to be the busybody, and get the scoop about Clay moving in.*

Olivia couldn't help but look out her window when she heard the scraping sound of a snow shovel in the center of the complex. She moved aside her curtains and saw Clay shoveling all the sidewalks leading to the carports. Watching him, as she was, surreptitiously, there was simply no other way to describe it: *He takes my breath away! Why, oh why, do I have to see him regularly, even when I'm not at work? How am I going to get on with my life?* Deep down, Olivia knew that she was not yet over Clay, not by a long-shot.

He'd been shoveling a while already, but his broad back muscles did not seem to even hint at fatigue as he lifted shovel after shovel of heavy snow. She so wanted to call him in for something warm to drink, but

she just couldn't chance it. Having him in her place--
his presence so big in a room, would engulf her and
she was afraid--not of Clay, of course. *Of how I would
react around him. I just need to keep busy today doing things around here, until he goes inside his place.*
So she kept busy, catching up on laundry, and doing
some ironing and cleaning the bathrooms. Finally, the
shoveling sound stopped, and she looked outside to an
empty walkway. *Okay, now I can relax.* But the tension in her shoulders and neck didn't abate, and she
was keyed up the rest of the afternoon.

Clay was famished. Not only had he done all the
shoveling of the internal sidewalks, he had unloaded
almost all of his boxes, and started to get things in
place where he wanted them. He actually loved his new
place. It reminded him of the house that he had lived
in with Eric, and his Dad and Mama Caro, all warm
and inviting, not super big, but cozy; a place where
you could put your feet up on the hassock and drink
a beer in front of the fireplace. Green Lakes had been
way more contemporary, and he never had felt at home
there.

He'd showered and put on a pair of jeans and a deep
green sweater, running a comb through his thick hair,
and splashing on a little after-shave. *I think maybe
Mrs. Herbert secretly likes me a little already. Not
that she'd ever truly show me...or say it!* He grabbed
his coat, locked his front door, and crossed the newly
shoveled walks, heading for her place. The snow was

taking a breather, but was due to start up again later in the evening. He knocked at the front door, and heard Mrs. Herbert's voice.

"Let yourself in. I'm tending to dinner!"

He entered to an aroma that made his mouth water and his stomach churn. "Oh, wow, does that smell great!" He'd stopped without even taking his coat off.

She came out of the kitchen, a slight smile on her face. "I told you this is my specialty. Don't you listen? Go on, now, hang your coat in the hall closet and have a seat. What would you like to drink? I have coffee...or coffee."

Clay laughed. "I guess I'll have the...did you say, coffee?"

She poured him a cup waiting expectantly for further instructions.

"Oh, two teaspoons of sugar and some milk, please!"

Mrs. Herbert handed the coffee to him. "Mr Mitchell, I must tell you that you did a mighty fine job on those sidewalks today. It'll sure help people get out tomorrow because you made a big dent in it today."

"No problem. Mrs. Herbert, could you call me Clay? It seems awfully formal when you're always calling me mister. And since I'm sure you'll be calling for help now and again, we might as well fix that right away."

"Alright, Clay it is."

"Hey, how about I help you set the table? My mom always gave me that job when I was a kid, and I'm happy to do it." He bounded up and headed towards the small dining nook. When he saw the table, he stopped. "Oh, it's already set, and I see it's not just the two of us!"

She stood staring at him, her gaze strong and steady. Then the doorbell rang, and she winked at him.

"I'll get that!" she said as she hurried over to the front door. "Come on in, now. It's cold outside!" her voice said loudly.

He knew without looking who was there. *Wow! When I took Priscilla Herbert into my confidence, I hadn't expected such an instant payback. Jesus, my heart is racing and my palms are all sweaty. I feel like a junior high kid again. Okay, buddy, time to turn on the charm.* He started to step out into the living room, but thought better of it. *It might be good if Olivia gets a little warning.* So he called out to the living room, "Hey, Mrs. Herbert? Do you want me to fill the water glasses?"

Olivia stopped in her tracks. She looked up at Mrs. Herbert with a stunned look on her face. She was able to muster up a few words, "Oh, my, you have other company?" she exclaimed, passing her coat to her landlady.

"Yes, yes I do. Mr. Mitchell, well, you know him, he's your principal. He moved in just last night. He'd volunteered to do some work around here, so I called him this morning to see if he'd shovel the walks in the complex, and of course, he did. I had to offer him dinner! That's only fitting. Besides, I always make way too much of this recipe. I didn't think you'd mind, dear. Do you?"

Blushing, Olivia swallowed and said, "Of course, I don't mind. It's your house and your dinner. You can invite whomever you'd like."

"Good. I'm glad that's settled! Clay? Come on out here and hang up Olivia's coat, please."

Clay, who'd stayed busy in the dining room and kitchen, stepped out drying his hands on a dish towel. He walked into the living area and felt as though he'd been punched in the gut. *Why does she always have this effect on me?* She had on a pair of form-fitting black stretch pants, a black turtleneck sweater that clung to her breasts and black flats. Her honey-colored hair lay softly on her shoulders and shone as though it had burning fire in the strands. She was also wearing big hoop earrings. It was simple, comfortable, and damned sexy. He couldn't take his eyes off her.

They both stood a moment in total silence, taking in the other one. Mrs Herbert stayed on the periphery and watched. Aha! She does feel something for him-- she can barely move, and she's shaking. This is going to be fun!

Clay spoke first. "Hi, Livy. Mrs. Herbert didn't tell me you'd be here," *which is the truth so help me, God.*

"I understand that. Nor did she tell me." The silence was awkward.

"For heaven's sake, what is the big deal? You two work together, don't you?"

Clay snapped out of his reverie. "No big deal, Mrs. Herbert. We just haven't really seen each other much since we returned from holiday break. I'm sure that Olivia has been busy with her classes, and I've been busy with my meetings, and well, we just haven't had much time to talk." He stole a glance at Olivia, as she looked down at the floor.

"Well, then, tonight should be just fine. But please, don't just talk about work! I had a friend years ago who taught. That was all she could ever talk about when we went anywhere! I'm going to get the salads dished up. You two entertain each other!"

Olivia's eyes widened.

What I wouldn't give to do that!

They both sat down, Livy on the couch, Clay on the chair. Olivia couldn't quit fidgeting, she was so nervous; and she could hardly look him in the eye. They hadn't seen each other since the night of the Fields' party. Finally, Livy broke the silence. "How is your Mom, Clay?"

"She's doing fine, now. She ended up having an emergency appendectomy, and the surgeon told us that it would have been really bad had it ruptured. Once we got her home from the hospital, it was two days before Christmas, and my brother, Eric, his wife, Phyllis and my niece, Chelsea, all came into town. Mom had planned an event almost every single night for Chelsea, and we were all expected to join in. It was that way the entire break."

"Sounds like fun. I'm glad she's okay. Truly."

"Listen, Olivia. I'm really sorry that I didn't call you over break. I planned on doing it several times, but well, every time I tried to get away, somebody needed me around there.'

"Oh, Clay, it's fine. I understand completely. Uh...I hope that you got the note I sent?

"Yes...I got it. But Livy, how about we go back and try this again?"

She shook her head, and quietly said, "I don't think so. Do you know that Derek proposed to me on New Year's Eve?"

"I've heard rumors to that effect," he responded grudgingly.

"Well, then I'm sure you'll understand why we can't go back."

At that moment, Mrs. Herbert, who'd been eavesdropping, called them both into the dining room.

"Come on, you two. Salad is ready and I don't like to be kept waiting!"

Clay looked at Olivia as she rose from the couch, and he stood as well, rising to stand behind her. As she started to walk away from him, Clay placed his hands on both her arms and bent and whispered into her ear. "I'm sorry, Olivia, but I'm not ready to take no for an answer."

His hands, his scent, his voice, his mere masculinity sent chills down her spine. *Oh, my God. I wish I could just lean back and feel the strength of him. I haven't forgotten how good that feels.* But she took a slow inhalation, and stepped quickly out of his reach. "Please, Clay, remember what I asked."

I remember, damn it! But it's not going to work for me! Before this is over, you're going to be mine, Olivia. No one else's.

The salad and bread course was a little awkward, trying to find conversation between them that wasn't about school...or impulses. But Mrs. Herbert steered the conversation onto her family and her growing up years; which then led the two of them to tell their stories. By the time the chicken and noodles came out, in a huge serving bowl, they were all laughing and joking with each other. Mrs. Herbert used a ladle to dip out the thick egg noodles covered in gravy with huge lumps of chicken.

Clay leaned in to catch the smell wafting up from the plate. "Ahh. I had no idea you could cook like this, when I came to ask you to rent this place. Mrs Herbert. But I think I've hit pay dirt! I'll do lots of jobs for you, if you promise to cook once and awhile!" He turned and looked her straight in the eye.

Priscilla was pleased, judging by the look on her face. Olivia was tickled that her landlady seemed to be enjoying their company, as well as the fuss being made over her. Filled plates were passed around, and all three started eating.

"Oh, Lord, this is good! Could you give me this recipe, Mrs. Herbert? It tastes amazing!"

"No, I could not! It's an old family recipe," she said, scowling at Olivia. "But," she added with a glint in her eye, "I can make it again for you!"

Clay had three helpings and both of them teased him about his appetite, but he just kept on eating.

"Now, that's enough. Save room for dessert!" Priscilla had gotten up from the table and practically whisked Clay's plate out from under him.

Olivia stood too, to help clear the dishes. "Let me help you clean up now, Mrs. Herbert." She moved around the table collecting bowls, plates, and glasses.

Olivia moved carefully around Clay, but he just sat still and enjoyed the view of her delicious backside. Olivia felt his gaze on her, and she turned looking over her shoulder at him. The look of raw desire on his face shook her to the core. Then her eyes wandered down to his lips and locked on them.

Clay watched her lick her lips and felt the immediate hardening in his slacks. Quietly and calculatingly he said, "You <u>will</u> be mine, Livy. It may take a while, but I'm staying the course. You want me and I want you, and you can't keep denying it."

She couldn't breathe. Then slowly she broke the trancelike hold, and shook her head. "It can't work, Clay." She left the dining room with a stack of plates.

I'm going to convince you that it can! At that

moment, he devised a plan to play hard-to-get---come within inches of her on as many occasions as possible, and then stop the contact. *It will drive her crazy, and I know, because it will kill me to do it.* He had seen that look in her eyes. He would play her and play her well, until she was begging him to touch her. Once he had her in his arms, he would convince her that she was his, and only his. *To hell with Derek Donaldson! Go find another girl, GQ man! This one's mine!*

Mrs. Herbert, sensing the tension in Olivia as she brought in the dishes, knew something had happened in her dining room. She said nothing, but began to dish up dessert. Olivia was rinsing off the plates, silently

"Olivia? Does Mr. Mitchell make you uncomfortable?" she asked, prying. "If he does, you just say the word, and I'll never invite you over again at the same time."

She glanced at Priscilla and her good upbringing stepped out, denying any discomfort. "Oh, no, no. He's been a wonderful boss and done so much for our school already. It's just...like he said...we haven't really had any conversation since before holiday break, that's all." Changing the subject, Olivia asked, "What's for dessert? As if I could eat anything else!"

"You'd better! I called the Boxcar and got us a couple of slices of that carrot cake! A nice young man delivered it this afternoon, even with all this snow."

Groaning, Olivia and Priscilla laughed.

"Hey, what's all the commotion out there?" Clay peeked around the corner into the kitchen.

"Oh," Olivia began, "when I came over before, I brought Mrs. Herbert a slice of the carrot cake from the Boxcar. Now she's returned the favor...and you'll see, it's absolutely decadent."

Decadent--a perfect word when used to describe other things that are on my mind. "Somehow, I doubt that word would describe a piece of carrot..."

At that moment, Mrs. Herbert shoved a bite into Clay's mouth.

His reaction was immediate. He sighed, saying, "Pure heaven on the tip of my tongue."

That's a perfect description of his kisses. "Isn't it? I absolutely thought I would die the first time I tasted that. Now, as I explained to Mrs. Herbert, I only like to be tempted once a year, but she's already ruined my plan."

Priscilla grinned and ushered everyone back to the table for dessert. They lingered a little longer over coffee, until both could see the signs that their landlady was growing tired.

"Well, I think it's about time for your dinner guests to get a move on. Do you have anything for me to do tomorrow, or do you need anything from the store, Mrs. Herbert. You know, school's already been cancelled again tomorrow."

"No, I think I'm fine, Clay. Will you please see Olivia home? I'm just done in."

Olivia shook her head. "That's not necessary. Dinner was incredible. Thanks so much."

Clay had risen and was grabbing Olivia's coat. Before she knew it, he had turned her back to him and was helping her into the plush black jacket.

She glanced over her shoulder, and said, "Thank you," looking up into his eyes.

"No problem." That delicious smile reached his eyes. Then under his breath, he said ever so softly, "But

I'd rather be helping you out of your clothes."

Olivia's eyes widened and she smacked his arm.

Mrs. Herbert had been watching the two of them nonchalantly. She smiled smugly to herself. *This is a good beginning.* "Get going you two. I need to turn in. I'm so full and tired."

"Night, and thanks again," Clay offered. They both walked to the front door, with her following them. As soon as they stepped out the front door, they could hear her door lock being engaged.

Clay and Olivia smiled and shook their heads.

"That is some landlady."

"Yes, she's a piece of work. She drives Sally crazy... says that she's a meddling old lady. But I just think that she likes to have a little company once and a while."

Here's to meddling landladies. "How about coming over and seeing my place, Livy? I'm not all settled, but it's looking pretty good."

Olivia looked into the clear blue-gray eyes and was so drawn. But she fought the urge and said, "Not tonight, Clay. I don't think it's a good idea..."

"Why? Are you afraid to be alone with me?" They were nearing her front porch.

"Well, of course not!" She turned to face him with a scowl.

Before she knew it, he was so close to her that she could feel the heat off his body.

"Clay..." she put her hands up to his chest. His coat wasn't buttoned and she felt the beating of his heart.

Placing his hands over the top of hers, he said, "Be a sport, Olivia. You know you want me...quit fighting it," and his lips neared their target.

She was so close to throwing caution to the wind. He

was pure sex and her stomach was doing somersaults with him so near. But, at the last second, she gave him a little shove, and said, "I just can't..." *Get in...before you change your mind!* She rushed through her front door and closed and locked it quickly. "Night, Clay..." she said, as she leaned her head towards the door.

Clay turned away at her refusal and began to leave. Quietly he turned back and spoke to the closed door, loud enough that he knew she would hear him. "I'm not done with this, Olivia. Not by a long shot."

24

They were snowed in for three days. No one could remember snow ever coming so fast and furious. It was a beautiful snow, too--heavy, and sticking to the branches of the trees, creating icy statues everywhere you looked, glistening when the sun shone on them.

Olivia had enjoyed the first couple days of relative inactivity, catching up on some grading and doing her lesson plans. In addition, she did a new workout video, caught up on some letter writing to her family, and completed general housekeeping tasks. Her thoughts often flew to the dinner at Mrs. Herbert's house and as always, of Clay; but the flash of her sparkling engagement ring reminded her of the plans for her future. *This back and forth has got to stop...I need to focus on my engagement.* She'd gone upstairs to take a shower, when her phone rang. It was Derek.

"How's my girl?"

"Oh, my gosh, Derek. I was just thinking of you. When did you get back from Texas?"

"Last night. Frankly, I can't believe I got in with this weather.

"I know, it's been crazy. Is it bad up in Townsend?"

"Yes. I've never seen such a load of snow. No one's driving anywhere. I think I'm going to trudge on over to my parents' place and stay the night with them. My Dad's been asking for help with some things around his house; this is as good a time as any to tackle them, I guess. I wish you could come with me."

"I know. It seems like every time we plan on visiting your parents, something gets in the way."

"Hopefully, we'll do it soon. I just wanted you to know that I was missing you, and I'll be really anxious to see you as soon as we can arrange it."

"Thanks, Derek. Now update me. When are you traveling again?"

"I've got a two-week trip to Hong Kong coming up, Olivia. I'm so sorry. We'll have to wait until I return to see each other. Then I'm back indefinitely, and we can begin to make plans."

"Wow! Hong Kong? That'll be incredible."

"Oh, it is. I've been there twice and I'm planning an exhibition in all three galleries of Asian artwork, so I've got a lot of loose ends to tie up. Maybe the next time I go, you can join me?"

"That sounds fabulous! We'll have to go in the summer, though, with my job and all."

"Sure, sure, I get it. Well, I've got to get moving in order to get some work done for my Dad. Take care, darling. It's been great talking."

"You too, Derek. Say hello to your folks and don't fall into a snowbank!"

Olivia hung up the phone with a smile on her face.

But the more she thought of the conversation, the more disturbed she got. It truly did seem that anytime she was to meet Derek's parents, something came up. It was so easy, speaking to him, but she realized that she hadn't really missed him with a great yearning need, and that bothered her. *Shouldn't the man you're engaged to, be the only thing really on your mind? Instead of the man you work for?...* The ringing of her phone made her jump.

She picked it up quickly, when she saw that Sally was calling.

"Hey, girlfriend. I'm so glad you called. I'm going a little stir-crazy over here. Do you want to go somewhere today?"

"Actually, that's why I'm calling. A bunch of us are going to hike down to Raccoon Ravine and go sledding? Are you in?"

"Oh, my word, Sally. We haven't been down there for five years!"

"I know, I know. But we haven't had this much snow in as long as I can remember, and Dave thought that it would be a ball for a bunch of us to head on over there and make a day of it. Do you still have your old sled?"

"Yeah, I actually do. I can't seem to get rid of it when I'm cleaning out the carport--too many memories of when we were kids. I'll go and pull it out and be over to your place in about an hour."

"Sounds great! Oh, Olivia. Swing by Clay's and get him too, will you? He doesn't know where to go!" Sally hung up before Livy could respond.

Great, just great. Livy could feel her temperature rising at the mere thought of Clay Mitchell. *Okay, you can handle this. Just go get ready, and you'll be so busy with everyone that you don't have to hang around Clay.*

She was ready in about half an hour and went outside to her carport to find her sled. Of course, it was as far in the back as it could possibly be in the stack of things that she should have gotten rid of a long time ago. She was moving some boxes to reach it better, muttering under her breath, when a low, resonant voice broke into her rant.

"Anything I can do to help cut down all those swear words coming from those pure little lips?"

She turned abruptly to see a blond-haired, blue-eyed slice of temptation smiling in her direction. She groused, "Just shut up and help me get this damn sled out from behind all of these boxes..." she rolled her eyes, "Please?"

Clay walked over, and with one easy lift raised the sled above all the boxes and extricated it from the corner where it had been stuck. "Happy?" he said, smiling.

She looked up and grinned at his cocky smile, shaking her head. "You are so full of yourself!"

"You can't be serious! I'm just a nice guy helping a woman in trouble!"

"Come on. Sally called and told me that you didn't know where Raccoon Ravine is, so we'd better start walking!"

"How far away is it?"

"It's about twenty minutes out of town; but with this snow, I don't know how long it'll take us to get there."

"Okay. I've got my trusty backpack loaded with a thermos of hot chocolate. I haven't been sledding in twenty years. The last really huge snow I remember was when I was twelve and Dad took Eric and me sledding up in Barton."

She glanced over at him as he reminisced. He was smiling that adorable, crooked little smile, thinking about the past. *He's too cute for his own good--and for mine, too!*

Clay and Olivia talked all the way to Racoon Ravine, about their growing up years, their family lives, and their hopes and frustrations. They both were surprised to arrive at their destination, with conversation still on their lips, a little winded from their fast-walking, but exhilarated too.

The crowd was large--most of the regulars that Clay had met his first night in town at Ojays, including the doublemint twins, Nancy, Donna, Sally, Dave, Bobby, and Tom Moore and Melanie from the elementary school. Hellos were said around, and then they began counting the number of sleds and sledding tubes that were available, so everyone could have turns on the runs. Clay had already decided to avoid Olivia at all costs after their walk over. *I'm playing hard to get to be sure...Olivia doesn't know her own mind right now.*

Olivia thought that it would be a very good idea to hang with someone besides Clay, as she marveled at their easy conversation, and the pull his presence had on her. Sally had come up and given her a big hug.

"Hey, Sal. Do me a big favor?'

"Sure, hon. What is it?"

Whispering, she nodded her head in Clay's direction. "Try to keep me in your group, will you? I shouldn't be around Clay that much."

"Oh, no. Was it really awkward coming over here?" Sally asked sympathetically.

"No, that's the problem!" Livy answered, exasperated. "It wasn't awkward at all. He's so easy to talk to. We laughed all the way over here."

"Gosh...what a terrible problem. You actually like the man! I can't understand it!"

"Okay, Sal. Thanks for the sarcasm. Just keep me away from him if you can."

"Alright, alright. Come on and sled with Davy and our group."

Everyone had a grand time. The ravine was perfect for sledding, and the nearby river had frozen over. Some of their friends had brought along their ice skates. A couple of the guys had built a snow fort and before you knew it, a snowball battle had started up among the crowd.

Olivia watched Clay from afar as he met new people and started up new acquaintanceships. She understood how disarming his personality was, so she wasn't at all surprised when a bevy of the town flirts headed in his direction. She watched as Alexis Anderson, two years her junior, turned the charm on and Clay fell for it--hook, line, and sinker. She gritted her teeth when Sara Neville, twice-divorced, and still fabulous looking, strolled over and put her arms around Clay's neck and spoke to him entirely too closely.

Unbeknownst to Olivia, Clay was watching her too. He noticed the set line of her mouth, when the "girls" came over and he smiled to himself. *She doesn't like the attention I'm getting.. Maybe I'll try and get some more!* Clay grabbed Sara's hand and took her for a little stroll down towards the river, feeling certain that Olivia's gaze was burning into his back.

Grumbling under her breath she said, "Nothing like

getting into someone's personal space, Sara!"

Sally had seen her reaction and just shook her head. "What did you say? Were you talking to me?"

"No, no. I'm fine; I just think that I'm ready to call it a day. I'm absolutely starving. What time is it, anyway?"

"It's almost four. Let me get Dave, and we'll meet you at the shelter house."

The nearby shelter house was the ideal spot to warm up. Inside were big picnic tables, and a log fireplace, kept going during the day by one of the park attendants. Everyone was laughing amicably, as they headed in to get some hot chocolate, take a break, and warm themselves by the fire. Unfortunately, by the time Olivia reached the shelter house, Clay and Sara were sitting by the fireplace, talking quietly, looking really cozy. Their faces were red and flushed from the cold and snow, and yet Olivia did not believe that she'd ever seen either of them looking more...more sickeningly at ease.

Sara looked up and smiled. "Hey, Olivia. Long time, no see!"

Olivia pasted on her sincerest of smiles, and waved at Sara. "Hi, Sara. It's been ages," she replied, strolling in their direction. "I see you've met my boss."

"Yes, and I must say that you are all lucky to have a boss like Clay!" She scooted even closer to him (as if that were possible) and pulled on his ear lobe. "I'm wishing that Mr. Harrison, at the middle school, realized the importance of socializing for our staff, like Clay does."

"Um-hum. Hey, Sara. Whatever happened to your boyfriend...was it Miles?"

Sara looked a little like she might strangle Olivia. "Oh, yes, Miles. Well, after several dates we knew it wasn't the right thing for either of us. So we just decided to call it off." A moment went by and Sara continued. "But what about you, Olivia? Let me see your ring! I heard you'd gotten engaged to that absolutely scrumptious Derek Donaldson over the holiday?"

The look on Olivia's face registered her embarrassment. *Really, how can I be so hateful to Sara and act like some jealous shrew? I am engaged after all.* "Yes, we did; although we haven't seen each other since, with his travels, and now this snowstorm. It seems like every time we're supposed to get together, something changes our plans."

Looking heavenward, Clay thought. *Thanks. Maybe you can keep these "divine acts" continuing and buy me some time.*

Conversation was interrupted by Dave Garrett. "Hey everyone. I'm so hungry I could eat a moose. How about going over to Giuseppi's for pizza and beer?"

Most everyone cheered in the affirmative and began gathering up their things to leave. Sara leaned into Clay. "How was I?"

"You were great. Thanks for laying it on so heavy. Our little secret? Right?"

"Of course, sweetie. I owe you big time for helping get my little boy the reading tutor he needs. We miss you over at Green Lakes. You know," glancing in Olivia's direction, "she doesn't deserve you, Clay."

"No one does, actually, Sara. I wouldn't wish myself on anyone. I'm a monster to live with!" he chuckled.

"Well...maybe you can persuade Miss High and Mighty to look in her own backyard. But if it doesn't happen, you know where I am, big boy!" She leaned in and gave Clay a kiss right on the lips, in front of everyone.

"Woo-Hoo, Sara," Dave shouted. "Got one of those for me?"

"No way, Dave. Sally would knock me out! See you all later. I've got to get home to the boys." As she sashayed by Olivia she spoke under her breath, "What a man!" and she winked as though she and Olivia shared a secret.

Olivia thought she might kick Sara as she exited, but Sally cleared her throat next to her. Olivia turned around sheepishly. "See what I mean? I get all ridiculous around him..." and her voice trailed off.

Bobby and Dave shouted. "Come on, everyone.. I brought the Suburban. We can all pile in there and ride over to Giuseppi's! Grab your stuff and let's go."

Olivia left the shelter house to get her sled, but before she got there, Clay was picking it up for her. "I've got it, Livy. It's the least I can do for you, letting me tag along and all."

"Letting you? You handled yourself remarkably well around Sar...everyone." She turned her back and said, "Thanks."

"Don't mention it!" They both headed over to the vehicle. The guys were loading up the back end with all the sledding paraphernalia and the girls were climbing in.

"How many of us are there?" someone asked.

"I count thirteen. Some of us are going to have to sit on the guys' laps."

"No problem. It's a ten-minute ride."

Suddenly, the vehicle was testosterone-laden and it seemed like the girls were totally overpowered. "Come on, hurry up," shouted Dave. "I can feel myself losing weight, here! Get situated, so I can pull out!"

Before they knew it, girls were climbing onto laps of any available guy. Clay said nothing when Olivia was the last one standing. He actually looked the other way. She turned around, checking for any other options, but then Dave said, "Get in, Olivia, and sit down!"

She looked at Clay expectantly and he nodded. She positioned herself in his lap and the car roared off.

Clay thought he might explode. The tightest little derriere in skin-tight ski pants had just deposited itself into his lap. *I hope that she doesn't feel how happy I am.* He actually started sweating, trying to keep his randy thoughts under control, so that Olivia didn't find herself sitting on a rampant erection....*Jesus! Why does this happen to me?*

Thankfully the ride was short. Olivia could feel her heart pounding the entire time she rode in Clay's lap, trying not to touch him. Every time Dave hit a bump, her bottom bounced on Clay's lap. *How embarrassing! I am getting so hot, and my legs are weak, not to mention, this thong I'm wearing...*

Below her, the bouncing up and down made Clay grit his teeth. *Think mundane thoughts...All I can picture is driving my upright member into Olivia's tight sheath, and making her scream for more.* "How close are we?" Clay asked, sweating.

*Close, so close...*they both thought.

The Suburban pulled into a parking space at the back of Giuseppi's and everyone piled out. Olivia practically jumped out of Clay's lap and didn't turn back to even acknowledge him, and he suspected why. Clay, who was the last out of the vehicle shouted, "Hey, Dave, can you give me your keys! I forgot my wallet in the back. I'll lock up!"

"Sure," said Dave, as he tossed over the keys. "I'll order a couple of pitchers."

"Thanks." Clay moved to the back of the vehicle, and stood righting the front of his jeans, patiently waiting for his penis to realize that it wasn't getting any.

When he entered Giuseppi's, the aroma of bubbly hot pizza aroused his stomach; but the sight of Olivia sitting at the back of the table between Sally and Dave, aroused much more than that!

She deliberately sat between them so that she could avoid sitting by me, but I'm onto her little ploys. I just need to keep working it as though I'm giving her the space she wants.

Clay sat down at the end of the table, and began regaling them with some of his crazy jokes. He could command an audience. He quickly had everyone laughing, nudging each other, and begging him to tell another quip. Before the night was over, it had become a joke fest with nearly everyone trading a joke or two. Finally though, overfed, overserved, and already forgetting the jokes, it was time to pack it up

Dave suggested that he could give everyone a ride home, as his vehicle was loaded with all of their sleds and gear, so they all piled in again. This time, Olivia made a beeline so that she could share the front seat with Sally. Stops came and each person unloaded tubes and sleds and gloves and mufflers. Gradually, Dave's car got emptied, thus providing the remaining riders their own seats and lots more leg room. All that remained in the car were Olivia, Clay, Sally and Dave, and Tom and Melanie.

"Where am I going, Tom? Are you and Melanie going back to your place?' Dave inquired.

Tom glanced at Melanie, and then shot a look at Clay, cleared his throat, and said, "Yeah, Dave, that would be fine. Melanie left some things at my place."

The smug look on Melanie's face made Olivia catch her breath. *Clearly, she and Tom have something going on, or she's trying to move it in that direction. Why am I agonizing over meeting with Clay? Duh--because I'm engaged!*

Arriving at Tom's place, Dave jumped out to help unload.

"So long, you two. See you whenever we get back to work," shouted Sally as she waved good-bye to the couple. As they were heading up the driveway towards Tom's place, Sally turned to look at Clay. "Well, boss, what do you think of that whole thing?"

Clay caught her drift, but smiled lightly and shrugged. "Well, as far as I can see there wasn't a lot of physical contact there, and I have no proof that anything's happening between the two of them, so I'm just going to ignore it. I have a lot more important things to attend to than a little frivolous flirtation between two of my teachers. Of course, if it becomes more involved, then I have to step in...I've been given my orders from Superintendent Graves."

Olivia and Sally looked up, questioningly.

"Well, apparently when Graves was a principal, a pair of his teachers had a fling and he let it go; but then, parents started calling the superintendent, and long story made short, he had to let them both go. He was uncomfortable, but he didn't really have much of a choice, because they lost all their professionalism and neglected their classes, to grab minutes whenever they could."

Dave listened and laughingly chimed in. "You don't

mean minutes do you? You mean grabbing each other, don't you?" Sally smacked him across the arm and shushed him.

Clay glanced sideways toward Olivia, who was looking at him. "I guess I can understand that," she said, speaking quietly. "Did you ever hear what happened with the two of them?"

"Yeah, I guess that once they couldn't sneak around, the excitement kind of lost its luster, and the two of them drifted apart and married other people. So it probably would have ended on its own eventually."

"It's a shame they had to jeopardize their careers to chase after a little excitement," Olivia said.

Clay glanced at the honey-haired dream, sitting beside him.

Olivia continued. "What an awkward issue for the principal to have to clean up. It just sounds like a mess to me."

"Hey, you two, we're at your place," Sally piped in, changing the direction of the conversation.

"Oh, thanks so much. I'm ready for a hot shower and my flannel pajamas," Olivia sighed. She opened the side door and jumped out quickly.

I'd be ready for her flannel pajamas too, if only I could see them, and then get them off her!

Clay was helping to get Olivia's sled out with a couple of other things left in the back end. "Hey, Dave, Sally, thanks for a great day and the ride home!"

Clay and Olivia stood and watched the two drive away, as the remnants of a light snow fell. Clay finally spoke. "Let me help you get your sled back in the carport, Olivia. Do you want me to put it as far in the back as I found it?" he asked impishly.

"Well, no, I don't think so. Maybe I'll need it again this winter, the way things look." Slowly they walked to the carport, and Clay stashed the sled in a more accessible spot.

"Would you like to come in and see my place and have a nightcap, Livy?"

She shook her head emphatically. "I don't think that's a good idea, Clay."

"Livy...I want you to see my pla..."

"Not tonight. I'm ready to get warm and..."

Clay pulled her in towards his body. "I would be more than happy to warm you up, Livy."

As her body met his, strong and virile, warm and so masculine-smelling, she buried her face in his chest and stayed there while Clay's hands stroked her hair.

"God, honey, I could hold you a long time like this. But then I'd want to..." and he slowly moved her hair to expose the nape of her neck, "...do this." Suddenly, his lips were there and he was deftly showering soft kisses up and down her neck, nipping at her earlobe. The skin on her neck tingled and the tingles shot everywhere, down her breasts, her knees, and into the pit of her stomach and then even lower, sending delightful chills up and down her body. Olivia started to melt into his arms, but reality reared its ugly old head, and she broke out of his embrace.

"Oh, Clay, we can't...I can't...this is NOT a good idea! Good night," and she ran to her townhouse and quickly let herself in.

He stood there, bereft of her body, watching to be sure that she got inside alright. Then his shoulders lifted, he sighed, and he headed up the steps to his place. *There's got to be a way, and I've got to find it soon!*

25

Clay laid awake all night trying to think of a way to get Olivia Sheffield permanently into his life. His slow realization that he was in love--not just lust--with her had taken enough time. She was engaged to that pin-up man, and he had to find a way to convince her that she didn't belong with Donaldson. And soon! Up 'til now the odds had been in his favor, he realized as he thought about the fact that the two of them lived miles away and Derek was often out of town on business. But Clay knew that his luck couldn't hold out much longer. *Think of something new, you idiot, and make it work fast, or you'll lose her before you really have her.*

Finally the beginnings of a plan came to Clay. *Let's hope we're back to school tomorrow, so I can talk to Dad and see where this takes me.*

As luck (or a higher power!) would have it, the streets were cleared well enough by now that driving was safer, so school was back in session. When Clay arrived at his office he put a call into his dad, whom he knew would be in the office as well. He listened as his dad related some of the activities that his parents had engaged in while off work.

"Your mom likes to take advantage of having me home, son. All the things that she can't reach, or do, are on my job list on snow days. Can you ever remember so much snow?"

"Not really. A bunch of us went sledding yesterday to an area called Raccoon Ravine. It was great! The last time I remember sledding was when you took Eric and me over to the golf course hills when we were kids."

They both laughed as they got caught up in the memory for a minute.

"What prompts your call, son?"

"Well, I'm reminded about that Educators Conference in Chicago, and I think I'd like to attend it, if you don't have any of the other principals going."

"No actually, we don't. They've all been to it one year or another. It's a great learning environment, with lots of helpful speakers, particularly directed towards principals."

"Yes, that's what I read in the brochure, But it talks about bringing staff members to the conference as well. There are some grant-writing workshops and curriculum explorations that I think would be helpful. Frankly, I'm seeing one of my teachers as a good fit to attend as well, if it can be approved."

"Do you have the money in your school education fund for both you and...?"

"...Me...and Olivia Sheffield?"

"Okay. How do you think her attendance will benefit Brandenburg?

It will benefit the principal! "Well, Miss Sheffield has been working on writing some grants to purchase new reading materials that are expensive, but really look promising. I've seen the pilot grouping, and I think that they would help our curriculum, particularly for the younger kids, say kindergarten through third grade. Furthermore, she's done some amazing things in her classroom, and I'd like to encourage her to do a presentation of her techniques at one of the teacher break-out sessions. I haven't asked her yet, because I wanted to be sure it was even likely that she could attend. If you give me the go-ahead, I'd like to speak with her about it today."

"Sounds like a winner all around, son. Go for it, and see if you can talk her into presenting at the conference. Based on how she works on the District Advisory Committee, I think she'd do a great job."

"Great, Dad. So will you put me down as being out of the building for Thursday and Friday...let's see, that would be February 28 and March 1?"

"Sure. Maybe I'll come over to Brandenburg and check things out for a couple of hours one of those days. The last time I got to your building was the morning I introduced you to the staff. Yes, just plan on that. I can have lunch with the teachers and give them some time to talk to me about their concerns or questions...or settle any complaints about the principal?" He chuckled.

"Oh, a comedian this morning, huh? Okay, this is great, Dad." Looking out the window, Clay saw the school buses rolling into the front parking lot. "Here come the school buses, Dad. Have a great day and I'll talk to you and Mom this weekend."

"Bye, Clay. Good talking to you."

A jubilant Clay Mitchell hung up the phone. *Okay, now my work's cut out for me. I have to convince Olivia to travel with me to Chicago and do a presentation.*

Then I can have her alone an entire weekend. Not to mention that we'll have to work on her presentation at home before we leave. That should give me some time to seal the deal!

Clay headed down the hall to the front lobby to welcome in the swarm of excited students, who had been off school for several days. The kids had become comfortable seeing their principal in the morning, and they shouted their "Hellos" or made comments about the fun they'd had, away from school.

Little Joanie Caswell came in and in her normally loud voice said, "Hey, Mr. Mitchell. I saw you having a snowball fight yesterday at Racoon Ravine!"

"Well you're just lucky I didn't see you, Miss Joanie. I never miss my target, and I would have aimed at you!"

Joanie giggled and moved toward her classroom.

Suddenly, in came Sally and Livy through the front door. They were bundled up and laughing uproariously. Livy looked directly at Clay with those luscious brown eyes and smiled.

"Hey, ladies. Good morning. Why are you coming through the front door, and not the teachers' parking lot door?"

Sally gushed. "Well, my car wouldn't start this morning, so Liv came over to give me a jump..."

Oh, if only...

Olivia continued. "But then my car wouldn't start... so are you ready? We had to call Mrs. Herbert to come and get us, since we knew that Dave was too far away to help, and you were already gone."

"Mrs. Herbert?" Clay asked jokingly with eyebrows raised. "What did you have to promise to get her to do that?"

"Oh, Clay, she's not that bad!" Olivia shot him the eye.

Sally interjected. "Usually I think she's a nosy busybody, but she <u>did</u> get us to school on time. Even though she was wearing her aqua bathrobe and matching slippers. Yikes! What a sight!"

Both Clay and Sally shuddered at the thought. Olivia just shook her head at the two of them.

"Do you girls need a ride home after school, then?"

Sally shook her head in the negative. "Nah, Davy's picking me up. We've got some errands to run this evening."

"Olivia?" Keeping his fingers crossed, Clay tried to sound nonchalant.

"Well...since you're going that way anyway, I could, yes."

"That's great. Just come in at the end of day, and I'll take you when you're ready."

Take me when I'm ready?...I need to get my mind out of the gutter. I have a fiance!

"Thanks," Olivia voiced as she turned and headed down the hallway toward her class.

The lobby was clear now of children and hot-bodied teachers. Clay took his time walking back to his office. When he entered, he strode straight into his office, past Kathy's desk. He smiled and said, "Hey, Kath. I've got a load of catch-up to do today. Use the intercom if you need me, but I'm going into overdrive in my office today." He closed the door.

Around 4:00 p.m., Olivia walked into the office and saw Kathy there, still working. But it didn't really surprise her, because Kathy was usually the next to last to leave for the day, only before Clay.

What <u>did</u> surprise her was the whistling she heard coming from her principal's office.

She looked up at Kathy, with her eyebrows raised. "Is that normal?"

"Not usually. But it has been today!" She smiled, shrugging her shoulders. "Go figure!"

"Did you have some good snow days, Kathy?"

"You could say that. Charlie and I watched four movies, and basically laid around the house in our pajamas. It was fabulous. I read two books and cooked and took my time doing some stitchery. I could use a couple of days off every month, couldn't you?"

"I get it." She stood outside, looking at Clay's door. "Do you think Clay's okay if I knock? He's giving me a ride home, because my car didn't start this morning."

"Oh, sure. Just tap on the door."

Olivia knocked on Clay's office door and she heard the deep baritone, "Come on in. Is that you, Olivia?"

She opened the door, trying to ignore the beating of her heart. As she entered, she looked at the man who totally drew her attention. He was ruffled with a slight hint of five o-clock shadow, his top button undone, and his tie slightly askew. *I don't recall him ever looking more handsome.*

Clay looked up from his paperwork, dragging his right hand through that perfect hair. He smiled warmly. "Hey," was all he said.

"Hey. I hear that you've been working in your office all day, according to Kathy."

"Yep. Just sort of on a roll you could say, and I didn't want to stop."

She waited quietly, twisting a section of the collar of the brown curve-hugging top she wore.

Clay finished up what he was doing, and then said, "Before we leave, could we talk a few minutes? I have something I'd like you to consider." He motioned for her to sit, and she took the chair across from his desk.

Okay, here goes. "I'm not sure if you're aware, but there is an Educators Convention coming up at the end of next month in Chicago?"

She nodded. "Oh, yes, I know. I read about it in my issue of TEACHER'S MONTHLY."

"Good. Well, Dr. Graves has given me permission to attend that conference and is allowing one staff member to go along as well. I'd like that person to be you." *Whew! Got that out. Now for the fireworks. Gotta make it seem legitimate.*

Olivia was clearly taken aback if her facial expression meant anything. She cleared her throat, and lowered her eyes, staring at her lap before she replied. "Well, I'm flattered, Clay, but I hardly think that would be a good idea...considering our...history...and the fact that..."

I can barely keep my hands off you? "Yes, you've told me that you really don't want to be around me that often."

She made direct eye contact upon hearing that comment. In desperation, her shoulders lifted, and she said, "I just don't think that we need to be in a position..."

I'd like to get you in a position! He said nothing.

"...where we might find ourselves..." she wrung her hands, and Clay waited, "...otherwise occupied...in an awkward situation...and well, I'm engaged...and I don't think..." Her voice faded away, leaving her thoughts unfinished.

"Let me paraphrase, Olivia." Clay said in a slightly gruff voice. "Basically, you're telling me that you have no interest in attending a conference with me, because in the past we've been a little too chummy, and you're afraid you won't be able to contain yourself when temptation is so close, and practically breathing down your neck."

She looked up, indignant. "I did not say that..."

"Continuing, if I may. This is a chance for you to attend a lot of great sessions, geared totally to grant-writing, so that you can learn the tools that you need to secure that grant for the Thompson Reading Program. It's a free trip to Chicago with your flight, your room, and all your meal expenses covered. I, myself, will be at most of the principal's sessions, and will probably only see you at meals, but if you think that will be a problem, that doesn't even have to happen. Graves asked me who my first choice would be to go, and your name was the first. But if you're going to turn this opportunity down, I'll just ask Melanie." His voice had been forceful, almost pushy, and exasperated, to make her even more uncomfortable in realizing that she would be throwing away a great opportunity. He watched her carefully, keeping a stern visage. *The part about Melanie is a total bluff. I couldn't stand a day with her, let alone a weekend; but Livy doesn't need to know that.* Clay waited again.

She was blushing now, clearly embarrassed by her apparent rudeness in not accepting the chance given her readily. "I'm sorry, Clay, I...didn't mean to seem so disinterested. I was just so surprised...and for a moment, I thought that you might..."

"Still have designs on you? Create some kind of reason to get you away and alone with me?" His eyes flashed angrily. *God, please don't strike me dead!*

The blush continued. "Forgive me. Of course, I'd love to go, if you think that I would be the best person, *not Melanie, the man-shark,* to bring back most from the conference." She paused for a moment, and then quietly said, "Thank you, Clay, for thinking of me. I won't let you down."

*Actually, I'm hoping to be elevated most of the weekend...on my back...with you on top...*The stern expression he'd worn earlier relaxed a bit. "Good, that's good, Livy. Now there's one more thing. As I was explaining to Dr. Graves about what you've done with your second graders in regards to all of your reading strategies, he" *forgive me* "thought that it would be advantageous if you did one of the presentation break-outs. There are openings for a couple more, and with his recommendation, I know you can get one of the slots. He was very complimentary about how you handle yourself on the District Advisory Committee and saw presenting as a valuable step in your career. Are you interested?"

Now Olivia was shocked. *The superintendent saw something special in what I did on the DAC? He wants me to present at a National Conference?* "Wow, I'm overwhelmed. I guess I could try to pull a presentation together, but there's not much time actually. When is that conference?"

"It's the end of February, about six weeks from now. You'd have to know what you needed for the presentation at least two weeks prior to that, and you'd have to have a firm number of how many participants could attend your session; so roughly, you have about three weeks. I've seen all your hands-on classroom aids though, and I'm willing to help you work on your powerpoint and verbal presentation, plus get you what you need in terms of supplies. Basically, we're going to have to lock ourselves in your house after school and work pretty steadily, if you want to do this." *I feel just a little like the Big Bad Wolf talking to Red Riding Hood. Tamp down your conscience, buddy, and go for it!*

She was nodding in understanding and seemed to hardly notice the "we" word he'd thrown out. Her eyes were lit up in excitement.

"So...can I take it, that's a yes?" Clay rose from his desk and turned his back on Olivia, pretending to look through some files.

"Oh, yes, Clay. That would be fabulous. Would you please tell Dr. Graves that I'll do my very best to give a great presentation and thank him for the chance?"

Clay smiled to himself and turned around to look at his own brand of heaven. "Sure, sure. Remember, I'll be along the entire time helping you to get ready. I've done several presentations in the past, so I know what they're looking for. Why don't you scoot down to your classroom and bring home some of the games, books, and worksheets you've been using, and the tactile stuff, as well. We can get started this evening, if you're available, on the best choices to present. You have to have enough material for an hour session, with a ten-minute break, and questions and answers at the end. Get what you need at least to begin, and I'll get my coat and take you home."

"Oh, Lord," she was laughing, "in my excitement,

I'd totally forgotten that I needed a ride home tonight. I'll hurry, I promise. Be back in a few minutes."

"Take your time. I'm going to book the flights right now and arrange for the hotel rooms."

Olivia hurried out of Clay's office.

Clay waited for her to go, shut his door, and then dialed the Hotel Ambassador, where the Convention was being held. "Hello, I'd like to book a couple of rooms, please. We're coming in for the Educators' Conference on Thursday morning, February 28, and leaving Sunday afternoon, March 3."

The voice on the other end of the phone responded.

"What? Would it be possible to get adjoining rooms? You're checking?" Clay listened. "Oh, that's great, thank you. The name is Mitchell, Clay Mitchell. Could you please sign us up for early check-in as well? If I can get out of town early enough, I'd like to do some sight-seeing before the conference starts. Thanks."

Clay's great mood continued as he pulled out his credit card to secure the room. He hung up the receiver and his shot of happiness, in the form of a second-grade teacher, rushed in the door, out of breath, with two shopping bags overflowing with "teacher stuff".

She looked sheepish, and adorable. "I didn't know what to pick from, so I brought a bunch of it!"

Clay chuckled. "It's okay. We'll sift through it tonight at your place. Let's get going. I got the hotel rooms booked, but still need to call the airlines." He helped her with her coat and waited for her to leave his office, as he pulled on his topcoat, turned out his light, and whistled his way out the door.

26

Clay took Olivia home, and on the way they discussed some planning strategies for their presentation, and what she'd need. When they arrived at the apartments, Clay waited for Olivia to invite him over.

"Thanks so much for the ride. I'm so excited about this presentation that I can barely wait to get started. I don't have much to eat over here because of the weather, but I guess I could throw a sandwich together..."

Clay held up his hand. "Actually, since I haven't been moved in for long, I got out a casserole this morning that Mom made for me. If you're okay with spaghetti and meatball bake, I'll just cook it over here and carry it across about six-thirty?" He could tell that Livy was chomping at the bit to get going, but he wanted her impatient in many ways. He smiled to himself as she made a frustrated frown, but then she nodded.

"Okay. That sounds fine. Come on over then, and we can work." Clay parked in the carport, then helped Olivia to get her bags out of his back seat. "Thanks again, Clay," she said, smiling warmly.

"Don't mention it. See you soon."

Clay let himself into his new apartment and heaved a sigh of relief. *Well, buddy, you have about six weeks to make Olivia realize that she's way more "into" you than she's letting on, so make it good!* Clay decided to keep the "hard to get" act going and stay very professional, while being his normal charming self in his work to help Livy.

He preheated the oven as he entered through the kitchen, then went upstairs donning his comfortable jeans with the hole in the knee and pulling on a tight-fitting navy t-shirt and shoes. He didn't shave, keeping the scruff look going, but took a look in the mirror first to be sure he looked decent. Then he went downstairs, put the casserole in the oven, and set the timer, pulled out a beer, and stretched out on the couch for a quick doze. He was asleep in a minute.

On the other hand, Olivia went upstairs to her bedroom, stripped out of her school clothes, jumped in the shower, and then stood idly by, staring in her closet. It was still cold outside, but she wanted to be comfortable at home that evening, and still look good. Finally, she decided on a black pair of stretch pants and a fuchsia mohair sweater. She liked the relaxed fit of it and the way it looked with her coloring. She touched up her make-up and messed a little with her hair, then hurried to the kitchen to see if she could rustle up some kind of a salad. She pulled out some left-over veggies and luckily had some lettuce left. Then she took out a half-dozen chocolate chip cookies that she'd frozen in the past for dessert. She straightened up the kitchen table and set it for two, and finally when she was satisfied that the meal was taken care of, she cracked open a bottle of her favorite Cabernet and poured a glass. "Ah," she sighed aloud, as she took a sip of the wine. She went to the living room and started laying out some of the reading games that she had made for her students. Six-thirty arrived before she knew it, but Clay didn't, and she was starving.

The oven timer woke Clay. He couldn't believe that he'd slept that long, his beer barely touched and warm on the coffee table. He pulled out the casserole, covered it in foil, pulled on his jacket, and let himself out his front door, heading to Livy's place. He knocked, waiting for her to open the front door. Mrs. Herbert's curtains parted, and she looked out her front window to see who was at Olivia's. Clay saw the motion, leaned over towards Mr. Herbert's window, and winked at her. She smiled knowingly and pulled the curtain back in place. At that second Olivia opened her front door, oblivious to any kind of interaction between her boss and her landlady.

"Oh, my gosh, that smells wonderful! I'm positively starving!" She took the casserole from Clay's hand and yelled, "Let yourself in and take off your coat. The table's set and I'm famished."

I'm famished too...but not for food! He hung up his coat in the hall closet and wandered into the kitchen.

Livy had set a really nice table, with placements, napkins, and brightly colored plates. The room was inviting. She was holding a glass of wine, and she looked up when he came in. "Would you like a glass of wine? Or I have beer, if you prefer."

Lord, is she beautiful. The lights in the kitchen glowed off her hair and the soft sweater she wore had slipped off one of her shoulders showing off her long neck. *What I wouldn't do to nuzzle that...* "Glass of water first, then some wine, I think." He could tell that she was nervous as she poured and handed him a glass of wine, and brought out water as well.

Motioning to the table, she said, "Sit, sit, please. I'll dish up the dinner." She was yammering a little, something he'd noticed that she did when she got nervous. He smiled to himself.

"Did you say that your mom made this casserole? It smells like heaven!" She scooped out portions of spaghetti for each of them and indicated the salad plates on the table. "Help yourself to salad."

Clay did. He was quiet, watching her in her kitchen, taking her swift movements in, watching the roundness of her derriere in those tight little stretch pants, adjusting the front of his own pants which had gotten uncomfortably tight before she turned around. He waited until she sat down and served her own salad, then he lifted his wine glass up, and toasted her saying "Cheers. Here's to a close working relationship and a great dinner!"

Their glasses clinked lightly, and she smiled that dazzling smile. "Can we have the great dinner first?" He laughed and they ate companionably, talking about school, friends, families wherever the conversation led them. Dinner was soon over after Clay's third portion, and Livy jumped up to begin the clean-up.

"Let me help too. We'll get it done faster." He stacked the dishes and the bowls and carried them over to the sink. *Now for a little up close and personal.* He handed her the plates being sure that he made contact with her hand. She looked up in his direction but he acted as though the touch hadn't even happened. *It's like an electric shock every time this woman comes near me.*

Olivia kept working, oddly quiet. She washed the serving bowl and put it in the drainer, and wiped off the table. Clay rinsed out the water glasses and put them in the dishwasher. She straightened the table, dried the salad bowl, and reached up toward the top cupboard to put it away. Clay was directly behind her, not an inch from her backside.

"Here, let me get that."

"Thank you." Olivia didn't turn around. She could feel the heat off Clay's body, and she knew she'd find herself plastered against his front if she turned. *Give me strength, Lord. Don't let him see what he does to me when we're this close.*

Clay stood a minute more without moving; then he backed away and headed toward the living room. "Let's get going on this project. I saw all your stuff out here on the table when I came in."

Olivia shut her eyes and tried to calm her racing heart. "Sure, that sounds great. Would you like any more wine? Looks to be about two glasses left."

"Naw, you finish it. I'm done for the night."

She poured another glass and walked out to the living room.

The two of them talked, first about what Olivia would like to cover in her presentation, then Clay made some suggestions about things he'd seen her do with her students in the classroom. He thought that using a lot of her hands-on manipulatives was a great way to do small groups, after she'd done the major portion of her presentation.

"You need to have several of these games created

for each small group of teachers, so you need to decide exactly how many participants you can comfortably handle in each break-out."

They continued discussing lots of details, and Clay talked about different things he'd seen done at past conferences that he'd attended; things that he thought could be used effectively in hers.

Olivia listened closely and nodded her understanding. She also made some great comments and soon started coming up with creative ideas that would help make her presentation exciting and thought-provoking at the same time.

Clay watched her intently. Her eyes sparkled even more, if that was possible, as she began to see the path she'd take for her presentation. They jotted ideas down as they talked and eventually laid out an outline.

Finally, when the busyness of the day and evening seemed to hit both of them, and Livy started yawning, Clay knew it was time to call a halt. *Okay, keep it light and disconnected, big boy..* "Well, I think it's time to call it a night. We both have to work in the morning. How will you get to school tomorrow?"

She grimaced, looking into Clay's face. "My car's in the shop for the rest of the week. I can call Sally though."

"That's kind of silly when we live across the sidewalk from each other, don't you think? No, I insist. Call Sally and let her know I can get you to school tomorrow. Are you okay with that?"

"Yes, sure. Thanks again…oh, let me get your casserole," and she started toward the kitchen.

He touched her elbow quickly, then dropped his hand instantly. "Leave it for our next session. We've really made some progress tonight. Now we need to let it settle a little before we fine tune the presentation portion of your session. Don't try to plan everything right now. More ideas will continue to come up, and I want you to be open to think about them. Make sense?"

He pulled on his coat as she walked him towards the front door. "Get some sleep! Morning comes fast. I'll be ready to leave at 6:30 if that's okay?"

With a wave and glance back, Clay was out the door. *The room seems so little and empty when he's gone. How ironic, that I'm supposed to be keeping my distance, and now I need to spend more time with him.* She shook her head, swallowed a last sip of her wine, turned out the lights, and headed to her bedroom.

Olivia took off her clothes, setting them down on the overstuffed chair in her room. She thought of Clay and the way he'd helped her understand what she would have to do to really make a good presentation. He had explained everything clearly, had been so sweet when she got excited and loud, and had laughed at her ebullience. *His charm just sort of spills out of him.* It was easy to be around him, especially in the "new" place they had found. *He didn't once try to touch me or look at me with that "come-hither thing" he does that drives females crazy. He's respecting my desire to be professional and work together without attachments.*

She pulled on her warm flannel pajamas, brushed her teeth, jumped into bed pulling the covers up, and closed her eyes. As her body began to relax in its new-found warmth, the one sensation that came back to her was when Clay had stood behind her to put the salad bowl away. A shiver of pleasure ran down her spine.

She quickly put it away in her "professional" zone, and went to sleep in the blink of an eye.

Two weeks had passed and Clay and Olivia had been buried in their planning. They had settled on numbers they needed and let the presentation committee know that title of her presentation and how many partici-pants could attend. They both were pleased with the progress they'd made and were planning to start the PowerPoint portion of the presentation this evening. Olivia had finally agreed to check out Clay's apartment, and she'd been surprised at the way he'd set things up to keep a strong masculine bent, but make it inviting and warm.

"Clay, I really like how you placed that large central photo with all the smaller photos around it. Oh my gosh!" She gasped, as she drew closer to the pictures. "Look how adorable you were when you were little!" She pointed to a picture of two boys at a Fourth of July Parade holding little flags, all dressed in red, white, and blue.

Clay rolled his eyes. "Yeah, Mama Caro and Dad took photos by the dozens, and Eric and I became fairly camera shy after a while."

"So this is your brother, Eric? How much older is he than you?" she asked, all inquisitive.

"Eric's four years older than I am, but after our par-ents were killed, he and I became pretty inseparable. We still talk weekly, and I've told you before about his fabulous wife, Phyllis and my brilliant niece, Chelsea, haven't I?"

Olivia loved to hear him talk about Chelsea. He bragged about her as if she were his child, and as he rambled on, Livy realized what a great father Clay would make when he settled down. Her head tilted to the side a little as she watched him gather some of their paperwork to place in yet another stack. His back was to her, and she admired the masculine physique that stood in front of her, having lost the thread of their earlier conversation.

"Hey!" Clay turned around quickly. "Didn't you hear me? I was asking you what you wanted to do..." Conversation stopped. Clay had turned quickly and caught Olivia staring at him. Her eyes were bright, her face was flushed, and it had clearly taken her a while to get the shell-shocked look off her face. *What are you thinking, little one?* "Are you okay, Olivia?"

She angled her face, and cleared her throat. "I'm fine. Don't know what came over me."

"Was it me?" Clay pointed to himself as he moved closer to her.

She started to back away, but bumped into the sitting room wall. She shook her head, but she didn't make eye contact.

Clay kept coming. He tilted her chin up, until her beautiful brown eyes locked with his. "Livy, I've been nothing but good for the longest time. I haven't touched you. In fact, I've avoided even sitting too close. But a minute ago, you were looking at me with eyes that gave me a different message than you've said in words. And honey, by the way you're trembling when I touch you, I think, no...I hope you might be changing your mind..." His face was barely two inches away. "...and every time I see those lips, I just want to sample them again and again."

His mouth took hers so tenderly, she ached. When she opened her eyes for a split second as he pulled away, her blush extended up her neck. Their eyes met, and suddenly there was nothing else to do. She wrapped her arms around his neck and said in the quietest voice, "More, Clay. I want more."

The groan that escaped his throat surged through both of their souls; then all at once he was kissing her full out. Tasting her, his tongue delving into the sweetness of her mouth, Clay thought he might explode with the urgency of it all. She kissed him back with the full ardor of a woman who was starving.

He lifted her, arms still anchored around his neck, kissing him, and he set her down on the kitchen table. "Oh, my God, Livy, I might die if I don't have you!" He dragged his shirt out of his jeans, trying to unbutton it, but getting all tangled up in his hurry. "Oh, hell!" he ground out, and ripped at the front with two hands, sending buttons flying, exposing his bare chest. Light blonde hair covered his chest and traveled down towards his waist and disappeared below.

Livy looked her fill. "You are an amazingly beautiful man, Clay." She couldn't take her eyes off him.

He watched the naked desire on her face. He swallowed. "Livy...please...touch...me."

She reached towards him and then looked up, and shook her head ever so slightly. "If I do, I'm afraid I won't want to stop."

"God, then don't!" He pulled her tight ass forward on the table towards him and stood between her open thighs, kissing her, making love to her with his lips, his tongue, reveling in her reaction, and the flavor of her excitement.

Suddenly, he felt her hands on his chest. Then she leaned up and circled his nipple with her tongue, slow and easy. His legs went weak, and he dropped his arms and let her touch and taste.

The muscles of his finely toned abdominals flexed as Olivia slid her tongue down his chest, sampling the very essence of his skin. Light fingers grazed through the hair on his chest. She marveled at the way his skin felt, all firm and tight, and warm, like a slowly heating tea kettle about to boil over.

Clay's eyes were closed with the look of someone who was sampling paradise shining on his face. His breathing was low and ragged and all he said was, "God, Livy, you make me feel like I'm a fourteen-year old."

"How is that?" she asked, not taking her eyes or hands off him.

"Like I'm going to come all over the floor in about two minutes, if you don't quit doing that."

She smiled at the apparent power she had over him and his body. *It's nice to be the* one *giving pleasure sometimes.* "Well, maybe you'd better prepare to clean the floor then..." and she glanced up through long-lashed eyes with an ornery smile on her face.

He grabbed her hands and pulled them off of him, capturing both of them in his one, and pulling them above her head. Her beautiful breasts were within his mouth's reach, puckering beneath the tight silk top she wore. He tilted her backward so that she was lying fully on the table, and then he climbed on top of the table, scooting her underneath him more securely.

She felt his desire clearly through the front placket of his pants, settling into the crevice of her own body, which was wet with need. She could feel everything through the jeans she was wearing. Clay began to move, up and down, sliding, friction of skin and fabric, rubbing, slowly back and forth, as though he was fitting his erection right against her, trying to grind into her. It was heaven and hell all at once.

He watched the expression on her face as she savored the contact he was making, and he knew that he could have her, if he just took her. She was open to him, relaxed and ripe for fulfillment. But somehow he couldn't do it. Somehow he couldn't mark her as "his" because he knew that she wasn't yet. He also knew that he wanted her without reservations, without usurping another man's property. And even though it killed him to stop moving against her pliant body, he did stop. Then he said "Olivia, open your eyes and look at me."

The long lashes shivered and her eyes slowly opened. They were glazed over and it nearly killed him with longing.

He spoke quietly. "Olivia, I want you more than words can express. But I don't want you this way. You belong to someone else right now, and I want you for myself--mine totally and completely. Whether you're ready to admit it or not, there is something huge between us--and I'm not just talking sex, either!" He eased himself off her, and she felt a horrible chasm of emptiness.

He lifted her and straightened her top,and slowly smoothed the silken hair. "I need a break from the nearness of you, and you need a break from me."

There was silence and a wide-eyed look of longing.

Don't respond, or we'll be flat on the table again, and bare-butt naked. "You know enough about your presentation that you can do this on your own. I can still help with the PowerPoint portion and develop an outline to help you get going, now that you know what to expect. We'll talk later in the week...at school. I think that's the only place we should meet anymore. Let me get your coat, now. "

She lowered herself off the table, disappointed, sexually frustrated and ashamed at her total lack of control. She couldn't make eye contact with him. *He is totally right. I was ready to give him my body completely, and yet the rest of me is still tangled up with Derek.*

Clay was back with her coat; he turned her around to put it over her shoulders and to help with the sleeves. He leaned down and whispered into her ear, his breath warm and inviting on her neck. "I'm sorry honey. I got so carried away..."

She turned swiftly and finally looked up into his face, touching the stubble of his beautiful cheek. "Please stop apologizing, Clay. I'm the one who owes you an apology. You're too good a man to have a woman who isn't ready to give everything. Please forgive me for my selfishness. And yes, I understand why we should only work at school..." she swallowed a lump in her throat, "...from now on. Thank you for being such a gentleman. " She quietly gathered up her paperwork and went to the door.

Just this once, Clay didn't move. *I'm afraid that if I so much as touch her, I would change my mind. It's a huge gamble to let her walk out the door; but for some reason, I know it's the only way there could ever be a real relationship between us. God, please make her see that there is so much here for us and what she has to do to let it happen.*

Olivia walked out of Clay's apartment, not turning around, and walked down the front steps of his porch heading to her place. The night was crisp and cold, but Olivia was warm and flushed with embarrassment and unabashed lust. She walked through her front door and set her things down, so she wouldn't forget them in the morning. She stretched out on the couch and put her feet up, waiting for sleep to overcome her. *Please God, help me to know what to do. I'm not having much luck on my own.*

In the morning, when the light of dawn broke through her living room windows, she sat up and she knew.

27

Nicole Marshall needed artwork, and she needed it fast. The administrator of Barton General Hospital had called late last night to ask her to help secure artwork for the grand opening of the new pediatric wing. He had asked for "bright and cheerful" via the committee's recommendations, to make the wing visibly inviting for kids who would be visiting or staying there. She grumbled under her breath, looking through her Rolodex of business cards for the name of the man she'd met at the festival with Clay. "I think it started with a...D." Flipping through the cards quickly, she finally found what she was looking for. "Ah, here it is! Derek Donaldson, Townsend Art Gallery." She picked up the phone, dialing the number listed. Gee, I hope he can help and help fast! The opening is scheduled for next Wednesday night. It never ceases to amaze me how these committees neglect to think through a whole process, and then at the last minute make all of us jump through their hoops to finalize things! "No one trained me for this kind of stuff in med school!" she grumbled.

The phone rang and a woman answered.

"Good Morning. This is the Townsend Art Gallery. How may I help you?"

"Hello, my name is Nicole Marshall. I met Mr. Donaldson in the fall; I'm the Head of Pediatrics at Barton General. I'm looking for some artwork for our grand opening, believe it or not, NEXT Wednesday. Do you have anything there that I could possibly put on the walls over here, fast?"

"Let me have your name and number, Ms. Marshall. I'll check with Mr. Donaldson and see if we can arrange anything for you."

"Oh, bless you. I feel absolutely ghastly calling you with this little notice."

The girl on the other end laughed. "It's actually not that unusual. It's just that Mr. Donaldson is out of town right now..."

"Oh..." Disappointment sounded in her voice.

"Well, actually that's not unusual either. But I can reach him, and I promise I'll get back with you hopefully before the day is out."

Nicole gave her cell, office, and home phone numbers, thanking the receptionist for her help. Then she hung up the phone, put on her medical coat, and went about her rounds for the day. She was in the hospital cafeteria when her cell phone rang.

"Hello. Nicole Marshall here...Oh, thanks for getting back with me, Mr. Donaldson. What? Yes, Derek, of course."

She listened to his comments, and then she responded. "Yes, we need something in here right away. Our grand opening is next Wednesday, and we have a lot of big white walls. The committee asked me to find the artwork. Their exact order was artwork that is bright and cheerful for the kids'..."

Again the voice of Derek Donaldson interrupted.

"Really? Oh, that would be simply marvelous! Okay, next Tuesday afternoon? Yes, I'll schedule myself here for the delivery and installation. What time did you say? Okay, I'll put it on my calendar right away, and oh, Derek...I owe you! Thanks so much!"

She turned off her cell, programmed in the date and time for next Tuesday for the art drop-off, and went in to tell Mr. Yates what was planned.

Tapping on his office door, she heard the familiar voice, "Come on in."

Nicole pushed the door open and smiled, "Well, we just got lucky, Don."

Don Yates glanced up at his Head of Pediatrics. "How so?"

"I was able to get an art gallery owner in Townsend to sell us some artwork for the Pediatric Wing Opening. It's being delivered and installed next Tuesday about seven o'clock."

"That's fabulous, Nik. I knew you'd do it!"

"How did you know I'd do it?" she exclaimed, rolling her eyes.

"You know so many people, Nicole; I told the committee you'd get right on it...and as usual you did--and you made it happen!" He smiled annoyingly.

"You might want to wipe that smug smile off your face, buddy, when I tell you what it's going to cost you!"

Don Yates, Barton General Hospital Administrator, frowned, held up his hand, and said, "Wait! Let me sit down first!"

Two secretaries outside Yates' office couldn't help

but overhear the raucous laughter of Nicole Marshall. They both looked askance, their eyebrows raising. "It must be something really good for her to laugh like that!" Both secretaries agreed.

Olivia Sheffield put a phone call through to Derek's direct line. "Hey, Derek, it's Olivia. I'm not sure where you're traveling right now...I've sort of lost track; but could you give me a call, please, as soon as possible? I need to talk to you. I'll be home all evening."

It was Olivia's lunch break, and she'd stayed in her classroom after her students went to lunch to make the call. She'd awakened this morning with a sure sense of what needed to happen, and she was just going to plow on ahead, no matter what. It was only fair.

She turned off her phone and went to meet her kids in the lunchroom. She had indoor recess duty this week. She thought about her upcoming conversation with Derek for a minute, but then she had to focus on Gus Kelley and Johnny Nicols who were getting in trouble over in the game corner. "Alright, gentlemen," she said firmly, "time to break it up."

"But, Miss Sheffield. Johnny and I had the game before Mike and Tony, and they came over and stealed it from us!?" Gus complained.

"Stole is the correct word, Gus." She turned around and looked at a little dark-haired boy. "Is that so, Michael Tomaso?"

Michael hung his head in shame. "Yeah, maybe, Miss Sheffield, but Gus and Johnny get the game every day, and Tony and I want to play."

"Very well. This is easy to solve. Today Johnny and Gus get the game, and tomorrow you two get the game."

Gus put on his mopiest face.

"That face doesn't work on me, Gus Kelley. You know what you're supposed to do, boys! Right?" Olivia gave them one of her sternest faces.

"Sure, sure, Miss Sheffield," said Johnny. "Tomorrow we give the game to Michael and Tony."

"Wonderful, Johnny. I'm proud of you, and I know that you'll all really try to get along during indoor recess. No more pushing and shoving. Are we clear?"

Four little voices echoed, "Yes, ma'am."

"Now you'd better get to your game, or you won't have much time to play." She smiled as she walked away from the foursome and made her way over to speak with some of the girls.

The day dragged by slowly. Olivia thought about all the things she had to do at home tonight to get ready for her PowerPoint presentation. She hadn't seen Clay all day, and she guessed that she wouldn't. She wasn't in the mood to talk to anybody really, so she did her best to appear busy when Sally came over to talk.

"Hey, hon. How's it going?"

"Okay, Sal. Just working on my presentation."

"I understand. You've really been wrapped up working on that thing. I hope you'll show it to me before you go off to Chicago. I can preview it, and give you pointers if you want."

"Sounds great, Sal, but I probably won't be ready until right before I leave. I'm suddenly getting nervous about the whole thing, and wondering why I agreed to do it."

"Oh, now don't start second-guessing yourself, Olivia. You'll do a great job!"

"Thanks, sweetie. Gotta get back to class.The kids will be coming any minute now."

"Mine too. See you later." With that Sally turned her back, waved at Olivia, and walked into her classroom.

Space. I've got to give her space. And here I am. Talking to myself again...I hope this works. Clay had been in the lunch line grabbing a bite, when he heard Livy breaking up the potential altercation with the boys. He'd stayed out of the cafeteria. He really hadn't wanted her to see him, or any kids to see him for that matter, either. He wasn't in the mood to have conversation. His normally positive outlook, didn't seem so rosy today. In fact, he didn't feel so great overall. He walked to his office carrying his sandwich and passed Kathy's desk.

"Kathy, I'm shutting my door. I don't want to be disturbed."

She looked up, surprised. "Oh, sure, boss, I understand. *You've been putting in a lot of hours here at work and then over at Olivia's place too. How's it going?" she asked inquisitively.

"You know Kathy, sometimes it seems that you know a little too much. And I'd rather not get into anything related to Miss Sheffield, frankly."

The comment took her totally by surprise. But as she looked up to question him, the look he shot in her direction dared her to respond.

Kathy Tiffin knew when to leave well enough alone. She puzzled, though, at Clay's behavior and wondered what had happened. About an hour later, Clay came out of his office and remarked, "I'm going home early. I'm just not myself today. I'll be in tomorrow for my meeting with the Administrative Team. See you later." He walked out of the office pulling on his overcoat, leaving quietly.

"Okay. Take care of yourself. If you're not feeling better in the morning, just let me know, and I'll call over to Central Office."

Clay didn't even turn and respond to the comment Kathy had just made. Wow! That was so strange. Over the months since Clay's arrival, Kathy had adjusted to his managerial style and loved the freedom that he allowed her to do her job in the way she saw fit. He rarely second-guessed her, and always took her opinions into consideration when making a decision that might affect her. On top of that, he was always in a jovial mood with both the students and the teachers. He could handle just about any issue that arose and usually resolved most problems quickly. The display that she'd just witnessed was unlike Clay totally. I really can't believe that he said that to me about knowing too many things. And he was curt and rude on top of it. I wonder if he's coming down with something--Oh, everyone has a "black mood" now and then. It's probably nothing. But work was piling up on her desk, so she got back to it. Before she knew it, the final bell for the school day's end rang and it was time to head home.

Derek finally returned Olivia's call that evening. "Hey, Olivia. I'm changing time zones and have no clue when you called me, but I'm finally getting back to you. Is everything alright?"

"Hi Derek. Well, in answer to your question, yes and no. I'd like to come up to Townsend and meet you this week if that's possible."

"Oh, sweetie, I'm sorry. I don't get back in from Hong Kong until Monday evening, and then I need to go over to Barton on Tuesday. I'm taking some artwork over to Barton General for that doctor friend of Clay's, Nicole."

Nicole? I wonder if Clay's still seeing her? He hasn't mentioned it, but really, why should he? "Oh...sure... okay, well...how about next Wednesday?"

"Honey, can we talk on the phone?"

"No, Derek, I don't think so. We haven't seen each other in ages. I'll just plan on driving over to Townsend on Wednesday, if that's okay. I'll probably get in about six p.m."

"Can I arrange dinner out somewhere?"

"Let's just wait until I get there, Derek, and make those plans later. Hope the last leg of your trip isn't too bad. See you next week." Olivia heaved a sigh of relief after hanging up the phone. *Okay, one hurdle overcome. Now for the rest. I only hope that I don't regret what I'm going to do.* Then Olivia got back to work on her presentation. It was coming along nicely, and she was really feeling confident about the organizational side of what she and Clay had been able to accomplish. *I wish I could take it over and show it to him.* But she knew that that was not the way to go.

She straightened up the kitchen after making a light

supper, and then started making six more sets of the reading cards she'd created for her small group activities. Before she knew it, the eleven o'clock news was on, and she tumbled into bed, forgetting to turn off the television.

Kathy arrived in the morning and turned on the answering machine to check all the student absences. There was a message from Clay. The voice was harsh and raspy and hard to hear. "Kathy...Clay here...not coming in today...let Central office know." And that was it.

Kathy picked up the phone straight away and called the superintendent's secretary, Rachel. "Hi Rachel. It's Kathy Tiffin over here at Brandenburg. I was just checking my messages and there's one from Principal Mitchell. He sounds really bad and won't be in today. Will you please let the boss know?... Great....Thanks."

Kathy got a tremendous amount of things done during her boss's absence. She reorganized some files that had been driving her crazy, dusted all the bookshelves in the outer office, and Clay's as well. Then she went through all the kindergarten enrollment forms, setting them up alphabetically. Finally she got the student/ parent information sheets re-labeled. It was great! Best of all, only one kid had come into the office today feeling poorly. That's the real shocker. It's usually like a sick bay around here, coughing, sneezing, running fevers. "...Oh, My word! That's what's wrong with Clay!

He helped Sandy Shields last week, and she was sick as a dog!"

Kathy got on the intercom phone and paged Olivia. When she answered, Kathy asked, "What's the name of your landlady over where you live?"

Olivia responded. "It's Mrs. Herbert. Priscilla Herbert."

"Is there a number to reach her?"

"I'll look it up, and come down to the office." Her students were at recess, so she had time to gather the number. "Here it is, Kath," she said, handing over a piece of paper with the phone number on it. "What's going on?"

Kathy was dialing as she asked, and held up her finger to indicate one minute. "Hello, Mrs. Herbert? This is Kathy Tiffin from Brandenburg. I got your number from Olivia Sheffield. I have a big favor. Could you go over to Clay Mitchell's apartment and use your key to check in on him, please?"

Olivia's head shot up.

"Well, he's been exposed to a bad case of pneumonia, and I don't want you getting sick either, but I'm really worried about him." She listened. "Okay, that'll be fine. Call me back when you know. Thanks." She hung up the phone and began to explain. "Clay spent most of the day with little Sandy Shields last week in the clinic. He read to her and brought her juice and water and kept her company. He hardly did any work that day. Her parents were both out of town and she had a babysitter. They were scheduled to pick her up after school. As the day dragged on she didn't improve at all, so Clay finally ran her over to the emergency room at Burg. She had a really virulent strain of strep that had gone into pneumonia. She's still in the hospital, and they've been pumping fluids into her...."

The phone rang. Kathy picked up. "Oh, okay, thank you, Mrs. Herbert. We'll call you back."

Kathy hung up and looked at Olivia. "Call Dave Garrett, right now. Clay's delusional and burning up with fever; she can't budge him. We need to get him into the hospital ASAP or he's going to be in trouble."

Olivia called Dave, and explained what was happening.

"Sure. I'll get over there as quickly as I can and get him over to Burg," Dave said. "In the meantime, call the hospital ER and let them know we're coming."

"Kathy, Dave suggested calling the ER and let them know what to expect."

"Already done. I also called Jeff Graves to let him know."

"As soon as the kids have been dismissed for the day, I'll head home and stop by Mrs. Herbert's place and get her updated; then I'll wait with Clay until Dave arrives. Do you think we should call the squad?"

"No, Dave's closer to your apartments and we only have one squad available at Brandenburg."

The kids were soon gone for the day, and Olivia drove too fast heading home, but she was really worried and wanted to check on Clay. She called Mrs Herbert and told her that help was on its way, parked her car in the carport, and ran up Clay's front porch, letting herself in the unlocked door. Clay was laying on the couch in a t-shirt and boxer shorts thrashing about, kicking off the small blanket that was laying there. "Wake up, sweetheart. Come on now." She tried to make him open his eyes, but he wouldn't. She tried to get behind his back and lift him to a sitting position, but he was too heavy. "Clay, please. You're scaring me. Come on, now."

Running into the kitchen, she grabbed several towels and ran them under cold water. At the same time she looked in the cupboards and pulled out a plastic glass and filled it with tepid water. *I've got to get some fluid in him and cool him down.*

She ran back to the couch using the icy wet towels to wipe off his neck and his face.

"Ahh!" He moaned.

"Okay, okay. Does that feel good and cool? Wake up, open your eyes. It's Olivia." She mopped frantically at his face, the towels drying almost instantly. *Oh, come on, Dave. Hurry up and get here.* "Here, I brought you some water. Can you take a sip?" she said, as she brought the glass to his parched lips. "Oh, please, Clay. You need to drink some water. Please drink," she pleaded. The act of tending to him seemed to wake him slightly. His normally clear blue eyes were rimmed with dark circles as they opened ever so slightly.

He smiled that adorable crooked smile and said, "Who...are...you?"

She was shocked for a second, but realized that the fever was part of the answer to this question. "I'm here to help you. I'm Olivia. Let me get some more towels."

Sprinting to the kitchen, she wet down the towels again with cold water and then returned, laying them on Clay's neck, and his face. "Can you lift your shirt for me?"

The look on his face was like a drugged man, and he just sat there watching her.

Finally, Olivia lifted his t-shirt away from his abdomen and slapped a wet towel low around his waistline.

"Jesus! That's bitchin' cold. What are you doing to me?"

Good. Reaction. "I know it's cold, but it will help cool you off. Now, I want you to try and drink this for me." She held the cup to his lips.

He shook his head. "Don't want any. Not thirsty!"

"Yes, yes, you need to drink..."

He interrupted. The little smile crept on his face again. "What will you give me if I drink?"

Is he kidding me? She watched Clay a moment, the same clueless look appearing on his face. "Well, I don't know. What do you want?"

The tipsy voice came out. "What'd you say your name was?"

"It's Olivia. Now try to listen and understand. You have a high fever..."

He was grabbing her and pulling her closer to his body as she sat on the couch.

"What are you doing?"

He smiled and looked up at her. "You can sit in my lap...and give me a kiss..." By this time, Clay had pulled Olivia downward towards his lap, and she was trying to fend him off. *No matter what, he seems to have one thing clearly on his mind.*

In her sternest teacher voice, she said, "No, Clay. Not now. You have to drink this while we wait here and maybe in a few hours, if you remember who I am, I'll sit in your lap and give you a kiss. Now drink!" She placed the cup next to his mouth and finally he took a sip, then another, and then a longer drink.

At that moment, Dave got there and opened the door. She had heard him coming up the steps to the apartment. "Olivia, are you in here? Your landlady said you were." He came barreling through the door. "Jesus, Clay. You're a mess, man, and you reek. Come on, pal. We're going."

Clay looked up at all the activity around him, and questioned, "Okay, where are we going?" as though he were in a stupor.

"I'm taking you over to Brandenburg General. Olivia, go upstairs and find some clean clothes for later. They're going to need to douse him to get this fever down, and he'll be pissed if he's in a hospital gown with his ass hanging out."

A not unpleasant picture, Livy thought, as she did exactly what Dave asked. By the time she got back downstairs, Dave had gotten a robe on Clay and his winter coat over it. "I'm taking him this way. He weighs too much to wrestle him into a sweatsuit. Did anyone call the ER?"

"Yes, Kathy did. They're expecting him, and the little girl who probably gave it to him is still in the hospital."

"Okay, buddy, I'm going to take your arm and get you out to my car. Now hold on!"

Clay grabbed his arm, but before they left the room, Clay turned around and pointed at Olivia. "You...don't forget...you promised..."

She smiled and nodded, "Later." She watched as Dave got Clay into his Suburban and pulled away from the curb. Olivia set to work, opening the windows to air out the place, cleaning some dishes in the sink, and generally straightening up, fluffing the couch pillows. She threw the blanket and the pillowcase Clay had been using into the washing machine and got a load of clothes going. Even though it was cold outside, she thought that airing out all the germs wasn't a bad idea, and it did smell a lot better by the time she finished cleaning and closed up the house again. *I'll come over later tonight and move those clothes into the dryer.*

She stopped over at Mrs. Herbert's and brought their landlady up to date, then she let herself into her own place, and went upstairs to take a shower and wash her hair. *I'll go to the hospital later this evening and check in. And maybe, if he 's really good...and knows my name...I might just sit on his lap and give him that kiss.*

28

Clay was admitted to Brandenburg Memorial on Thursday. It had taken several hours to get him into a room there, but the minute they started him on IVs, his body temperature started cooling and his fever began to abate. He was as weak as a baby, and he could hardly stand up to get into bed when they finally got him a room.

Dave had spoken with the nurses about giving Clay a sponge bath to clear the stench. He had laughed uproariously when several of the younger nurses volunteered for that job. He shook his head. "Man, it's just not fair. He's practically comatose and he still gets the girls!"

All of the nearby nurses giggled, except the Head Nurse, Nurse Conner. She moved into the center of the crowd. "Mr. Garrett, is it? I think that you've probably helped your friend as much as possible for the evening; and frankly, you're holding up the work that needs to get done around here." She shot a look at the young nurses, and they scurried to their stations.

"Well, you're probably right, Nurse Conner. I want to wait around for someone to relieve me though. I promise I'll go as soon as someone else gets here."

"Very well, young man. Actually, I'm sure that you have no shortage of young women at your beck and call too; so quit flirting with the nurses."

Dave smiled. "You flatter me...I'll save it all for you!" And he winked.

Nurse Conner looked over her glasses, and rolled her eyes. But he caught a slight smile on her face as she left.

In no time at all, Jeff and Caroline Graves arrived from Barton. Dave told them what had happened with Clay, and then he took his leave.

Caroline had brought clothes to sleep in and was arguing with her husband. "Jeff, you are not going to talk me out of staying here tonight. It took us forever to get here anyway, and I want Clay to see me when he wakes up. After all, he was at my side during the entire appendectomy ordeal."

As usual, Jeff Graves gave into his own little tropical storm. Caroline would drive him crazy if she didn't get her way anyway. "Okay, I'll go stay at Clay's place tonight and come here first thing in the morning."

"That sounds fine, dear. Do you have a key?"

"Yes, I haven't seen the place, but I know where it is. I'll just let myself in and get situated. You call me if you need me to bring anything when I come tomorrow."

"Sounds good. Now get going and leave me here with our baby."

"Dear God, Caro. Don't let anyone hear you call Clay your baby. He'd be mortified!"

"Shhsh," she said as she shooed her husband away

and straightened the bed covers around Clay. "Go away, love. I'll see you tomorrow."

Jeff Graves shook his head, as he planted a kiss on Caroline's forehead. "Night, honey."

Caroline got comfortable and stretched out on the sofa bed in the hospital room. Nurses came and went checking on Clay's IV and vital signs, but he hardly moved a muscle he was sleeping so soundly. When Nurse Conner checked in, Caroline asked, "Is this okay? The way he's sleeping?"

Nurse Conner looked over Clay's chart. "From what I see, absolutely. He probably had a high fever for a day and a half without anyone knowing it. Sleeping is the body's way to protect the brain, once the fever has been brought down. I imagine by morning, you'll see a return to normalcy."

Caroline thanked the nurse and started reading her magazine. She'd just gotten comfortable when a young woman walked in. She headed straight for the bed, staring at Clay. She moved over to check on him and reached out to touch his forehead, having not noticed Caroline.

"Hello, I'm Caroline Graves. Can I help you?"

The visitor jumped and turned quickly, her face registering shock and embarrassment. "Oh, my Lord, you shocked me!" She raised a hand to her chest.

She is absolutely lovely. "Sorry. You came in so quietly that I didn't have time to warn you. I'm Clay's mother. May I ask who you are?"

"Of course. I'm one of the teachers at Brandenburg, Olivia Sheffield," she moved, extending her hand to shake Caroline's.

"Oh, let's not stand on ceremony."

Before Olivia knew it, she was grabbed up into a big hug.

"Thank you so much for helping Clay. Mr. Garrett told us what had happened, and we do so appreciate your willingness to act to get Clay in the hospital. From what we're hearing, he was in a lot of distress by the time he got here."

"Oh, it was definitely a group effort." She glanced at Clay with a frown on her face. "Should he be sleeping like this?"

"Yes, and according to the nurse, that is very good." She watched the concern on the young woman's face, and thought that maybe there was more than a platonic relationship going on here." "It's so nice of you to come down here to see Clay, but I'm surprised they let you in this late. It's usually only family allowed."

Again, the blush. "Oh, I know, I'm...uhh...checking on him for the whole staff, and I promised that I would stay ten minutes maximum. Of course, had I known that there was someone here with him..." Her voice trailed off.

"Nonsense, dear. It's just fine that you're here, but I think that maybe tomorrow would be a better day to come back. Hopefully he'll be more like himself then..."

Clay stirred in the bed. "Mom? Is that you?" His voice was quiet, raspy, and his eyes still hadn't opened.

Caroline jumped up and scurried to the bed. "Yes, Clay, darling. It's Mother. You've been sleeping and sleeping, and I've been so worried...open your eyes, Clay, please."

Slowly, the blue eyes opened, and he was able to squeeze out a wry smile. "Hey, Mom. What is all this shit I'm hooked up to?" he questioned, raising his arm.

Catching the swear word, Caroline said, "Oh, Clay... you're feeling better already!" Caroline turned and looked at someone behind her. "You're in Brandenburg Memorial, Clay, and you have a visitor. Come on over!" and she motioned to someone he couldn't see.

Clay looked up into the big brown eyes of the woman he loved, and smiled. It was one of those fourteen-carat smiles. "Hey, Olivia," he said quietly.

Caroline watched the pair closely.

"Hi." Olivia went over to the bed, and touched Clay's arm every so lightly. "You really scared me...us!" She turned around slightly remembering his mother was in the room, then she stepped back from the bed. "I see that you're starting to act like yourself again, so I think it's safe for me to leave until after school tomorrow. The gang sent me to check on you." She started putting on her coat.

Clay couldn't take his eyes off her, and he wore a sickeningly stupid grin. Caroline Graves watched the unspoken words on her son's face. Wow! He's got it bad!

Olivia went over to Caroline and hugged her this time. "Thanks for letting me stay. I'm sure some of the teachers will stop by tomorrow, but we'll call the hospital first to be sure that he can have visitors. So nice to meet you, Mrs. Graves."

"You too, Miss Sheffield."

Olivia started out the door, but Clay's voice stopped her. "I think I remember through a bit of a fog that you made me a promise?"

Livy turned around, smiling. "Yes, I believe that I did. We'll just have to wait until you're out of here for that, won't we?"

He watched her walk out the door. He called after her, his voice still a little shaky. "I promise it'll be soon!"

Caroline Graves recognized these things, somehow. She'd always been the first to spot romance, wherever it happened. Clay is in love with Olivia Sheffield. And Miss Sheffield loves him back. Oh, dear. I'll just have to keep this from Jeff. He'll blow a gasket if he finds out.

Derek Donaldson arrived home from his travels, determined to stay put for a while. It had been a fruitful trip overseas; he had seen some amazing galleries and gotten even more ideas for both the Boston and New York market. He was tired and his internal clock was askew, but Tuesday morning found him back to the Townsend Gallery, ready to check on business and just be home.

He'd phoned his parents to let them know he had returned. They invited him to dinner but he declined since he'd be over at Barton General for a good part of the evening. He'd gotten into the museum, and checked the storage rooms for the art he'd asked them to set aside. He'd had some pieces sent over from the Boston gallery, and while traveling, he remembered that they were storing a set of nine kids' matching tables and chairs. The New York Gallery had organized a fund-raiser for the museum, asking various artists to paint children's tables and chairs in any style they saw fit. Then they'd auctioned the tables off to raise money, half for the museum and the other half for a Children's Cancer Foundation. Many of the people who'd won the items in the auction donated them back to the museum in the hopes that Derek would one day display them. He knew they would be perfect for the hospital. He'd probably leave them there. After all, they'd get a lot more use in the hospital and people could enjoy them.

After leaving the storage area, Derek was greeted by his receptionist, Rachel. "Hi, boss. Welcome back!"

"Hi, Rachel. I've got to tell you that I'm glad to be home. Do me a favor, will you? Get me some signage, bright lettering but not too big, to take with me to Barton General, so that we get credit for the art display over there. Are you all set with the drivers?"

"Yes, sir. Larry and Tom are scheduled."

"Oh, that's great! When they get in, have them start loading up. I want to take all the pictures that you pulled and the entire Children's Table Collection with us too. Actually, I'm going to head over there about two and just look at the space to see if we need anything else. I'll call you if that's so. Be sure the drivers have all their install equipment as well."

"Sounds great. I love the idea about the table collection going there. That way it won't collect dust, and it will get used and seen."

"Yes, I think it's going to be a great success. Now, I need to get back to my own desk and start clearing!"

"By the way, Miss Sheffield called, wanting to know if you'd arrived safely. I told her you had, and that you'd call her as soon as you could."

"Thanks, Rachel. I'll take care of that right now." Derek returned to his office and thumbed through some of the new paperwork that had piled up. He absent-mindedly hit the speed dial of his phone getting Olivia's cell message. He waited for the beep. "Hey, dear. I'm back, and thanks for checking in on me. Basically my brain is mush right now from all this travel; but it's not far enough gone to forget that we have a date tomorrow evening at six. Just come to the gallery, and I'll be waiting. I'm really anxious to see you. Bye, Olivia. Love you."

Derek worked for four hours steadily and finally stood up to stretch. "Rachel? I'm going down to the cafe to grab a sandwich. What can I get you?"

"Oh, nothing, thanks. I'm meeting my friend for lunch today."

"Okay. I'll be gone when you get back, but keep your cell phone, in case I need to reach you. The drivers should leave to head over to Barton about five-thirty. I'll be waiting for them at the main entrance."

"I'll let them know. See you tomorrow."

Derek grabbed a sandwich at the nearby cafe, then went to the parking garage to get his car. He headed in the direction of Barton, actually enjoying the drive through the snow-covered hills. The heaviest snow had melted and now there was a thick coating of about five inches left. The temperature was mild, the sky was a clear blue, and the sun shone off the snow, causing it to sparkle. It looked peaceful and serene and Derek was glad to be back stateside.

It was an easy drive over to Barton, and when he got to the hospital, Derek parked in the main parking lot and walked into the building. He spoke with the woman at the Information Desk, and she directed him to the Pediatric Wing. When he arrived there, it was an anthill of activity, with the main lobby blocked off, and a lot of people scurrying around. As usual, there were doctors, nurses, and patients wandering around the public area. He stood behind the barricades looking at the area where the artwork would be displayed, picturing it and deciding the best way to stage everything.

He heard a quiet voice behind him. "You, sir, are a life-saver."

He turned and smiled. "Hello, Miss Marshall."

"No, no, no. Please, Nicole."

He nodded, "Nicole."

"What do you think of the space and how it will work?"

"Well, I've got some ideas about traffic patterns for tomorrow's event, but I don't know if you have time to talk about it?"

"Oh, yes. My boss gave me the day off, as he knows I'll be here working late. In fact, this is the first time I've been out of my doctor garb for a long time." She grabbed the crook of his arm and steered him to the left. "Let's go over to my office and do some planning."

They walked together, using the elevator and making small talk. "So, you've been traveling?"

"Oh, Lord, yes. Hong Kong and all around Asia for over two weeks. It's been a whirlwind, and I'm ready to stop for a while."

"I understand that, but don't you just love Hong Kong?"

"It's truly one of the most exciting cities I've ever seen."

"Here we are." Nicole motioned him into her office. "Please have a seat. Would you like a drink? I've got some iced tea or a soft drink or coffee?"

"A cup of coffee will be fine, thanks."

They talked easily, discussing the pieces of artwork that would arrive and the table collection. "I think that maybe it would be nice to get some flowers for each of the tables, since it's the opening night," Derek suggested. "Do you have a local florist nearby? It'll make a more striking presentation, but It'll cost a bit in the middle of winter."

"No problem. I've got this handy-dandy credit card from the hospital." Nicole held it up, her eyebrows lifting. "If only I had this on my days off!"

Derek laughed. "I don't remember you being so sneaky...or charming!"

Nicole shrugged. "Well, the last time we met, I was in new territory. I'd only gone out with Clay once or twice and, if you remember, that was the festival where the little boy got lost."

"Yes, that's right. Both of our dates were gone most of the evening looking for him." He paused. "May I ask?" curiosity getting the best of him. "Are you still seeing Clay?"

"You know we went out a couple of times after that, but our schedules just never seemed to jive well, and now, I guess, we haven't spoken for a couple of months. So I guess the answer would be no. What about you and Olivia?"

"It's kind of ironic that you talk about your schedules, because that is exactly our problem as well. It seems like every time we're supposed to meet, I can't or she can't or weather hits or on and on. Anyway, we got engaged on New Year's Eve, and believe it or not, we haven't seen each other since then. She's supposed to come to Townsend tomorrow to meet me, so maybe we can actually spend some time together then."

Nicole listened attentively. "Well, congratulations on your engagement. I certainly hope it works out for you. Why don't we head on over to the florist…?"

"Great. I think maybe a trip to a fabric store would be good too. We'll drape multi-colored remnants underneath the flowers that we choose, based on the colors of the tables and chairs. My installers will be here right about seven, but I promise you that it will take several hours to get things the way we want them."

"Lead on, sir." They grabbed their coats and went out to Nicole's car. "Let me drive. I know my way around. It'll save us some time."

Companionable discussion about artwork, politics, and parents was the order of the afternoon. Derek and Nicole were totally comfortable in each other's presence, and it was refreshing for both of them to have someone knowledgeable to talk to about a variety of subjects. They bought bouquets of different kinds of flowers, then went to the fabric store and brought back swatches of various materials to match. Finally, they headed back to the hospital to drop the purchases off. "Somehow, I think that if we keep flowers in the car, they'll be dead before tomorrow evening."

"So true. Nicole, can I treat you to a bite of dinner before the install starts? I think it's going to be a late night. In fact, I'm starting to think that maybe I should book a hotel for the night. I think that jet lag may hit me like a brick wall when we're done with this installation."

"Good idea. And no, you may not buy me dinner. I'm buying you dinner. And there's a nice hotel right down the street from the hospital. Let's book you a room, on the hospital of course, and then go out for an early dinner. I know the perfect place."

The dinner and install went off without a hitch.

The drivers arrived on time and Derek oversaw the placement of all the paintings, as well as the table and chair collection placement. Underneath the artwork they worked together draping fabrics to bring out the colors of the pieces; then when everything was in place, they filled vases with fresh flowers that matched the tables. It looked like a slice of summer in the dead of winter. "Oh, my God, Derek. This is positively gorgeous! Everyone is going to love it! I owe you big time."

When everything was finished, the drivers, she and Derek stood back to admire the work they'd done. It was after eleven o'clock. "Oh, no, Derek. Do your drivers need a room tonight? We didn't do anything about booking them one."

Derek looked up at Larry. "Naw, boss, we're heading home. I'd rather sleep in my own bed tonight. Especially since we have tomorrow off...right?"

Derek laughed. "You guys have been great! Yes, take the day off and enjoy it!"

"Thanks. Nice to meet you, Miss Marshall. See you back in Townsend, boss." Both men left.

"Well...it's probably time to call it quits, isn't it?" Nicole looked over at Derek.

"Yeah, probably. The only problem is that when I'm done with a special project like this, I have a huge sense of euphoria. And I'm not the slightest bit tired. Would you be interested in a nightcap in the hotel bar?"

"I'd love it. I feel the same way. I couldn't sleep if I wanted to. Let me get my coat."

Derek helped Nicole with her coat, and they drove over to the hotel. They sauntered into the lounge area and even though they were the only ones in the bar, they sat and talked another hour, sipping on wine and winding down.

Finally, the yawns started coming for both of them. "Okay, I think I could sleep now," Nicole chuckled. "Derek, before I leave, I want to invite you...and Olivia, of course...to the Opening. I'd love you to see everyone's reaction."

Derek shook his head. "Oh, I don't think that'll work, Nicole. I'll just leave it up to you to let me know how it all goes." He stood and said, "Let me get you out to your car. It's late."

He walked her to her car and opened the door. "Derek, I can't thank you enough. This has been a truly wonderful evening; it's been so much fun seeing the transformation. If you and Olivia change your mind, don't hesitate to come over." Before she knew what she was doing, she leaned into Derek, kissing his cheek.

Her fresh scent swirled around him, and he held her there for a minute more than could be considered appropriate. Then in spite of what he should do, he tipped her chin up and gave her a kiss back on the lips. "It's been entirely my pleasure." He helped her into her car and watched her buckle her seat belt. She waved as she drove off.

"God, man. You need a woman." As he walked back to the hotel, he was a little surprised to realize that the picture of that woman was not honey-haired. She was a tall, wispy brunette.

It was Wednesday finally. The weather had calmed down, and there were no more crises, so Olivia left directly after school to head for Townsend. The drive was not normally difficult, just rather tedious, but stopping and stretching a couple of times always made it go faster.

Olivia practiced over and over the words she had decided to say when she saw Derek but the closer she got to her destination, the more nervous she became. This was going to be awkward to say the least; but she had to do it.

She arrived at the gallery and entered the front door. A pleasing bell tinkled as she entered, and before she knew it, Derek was there. He strode to her swiftly and grabbed her in a big hug. "Olivia, it's so great to see you! I'm anxious to get you caught up on all my travels and hear about what you've been doing as well. Let me take your coat and show you around the gallery."

Her coat was off her shoulders, and he had grabbed her hand and was pulling her around the gallery showing her all the changes since she had been there last. "Wait'll you see what I got from Hong Kong!" He ushered her into his office, where framed in a huge shadow box of glass, was a kimono. Additionally, there were insets of a fan and slippers. The colors, the display, the fabric was all breathtaking. "I'm planning an exhibit in the spring of all kinds of art from Asia, and I thought this would make a great centerpiece in one of the entries. What do you think?"

"It's utterly amazing, Derek. What is the time period that this was made?"

They spoke more and he gave her details of his trip; then he brought her over and sat her down. "Look,

Olivia, I brought you back something as well." He presented her with a velvet box.

She looked at it for a minute, but didn't take it. Then she glanced up at Derek and shook her head. "Derek, I'm sorry. I can't accept it. In fact, I can't accept anything else from you."

Derek sat back, a puzzled expression on his face. But somehow he knew what was coming.

"Derek, please listen. This isn't easy for me, and perhaps it will not be easy for you, but I can't go on this way anymore."

"Are you talking about us not seeing each other? Because I'm totally in agreement, and I'm here for a good long..."

She raised her hand and shook her head to stop him. "No, Derek, although that <u>has</u> had an impact on this decision. But, well, the truth of the matter is, I need to...call off...our engagement."

Derek said nothing, waiting for Olivia to continue.

"In the beginning, I was sure that this was the right thing for both of us. We enjoy each other's company, we have much to talk about, and well, what woman wouldn't love being spoiled by you?"

"Apparently, you," he said, pointing at Olivia.

"No, that's not so. You have gifted me with so many wonderful things since our first meeting. In fact you've been overly generous. The truth of the matter is, and I think you will see it too, is that we care for each other; but we're not in love. Every time we've tried to get together, something has stood in our way. After a while, I realized that I was disappointed I wasn't seeing you, but I wasn't going crazy to get together. Clearly, that has to be so for you as well. I just think that two people who are madly in love would not let storms, or students, or work get in the way of seeing each other. And we have."

There was silence in the room. Derek was looking at his lap.

Olivia went on. "Please, Derek, The night I met you, I thought sure that you were my destiny. But time has shown me differently and..."

"It's him, isn't it?"

She looked him directly in the eyes and didn't even try to pretend. "Yes. Nothing much has happened between us; but it's always boling right below the surface. Without being indelicate, he is uppermost in my thoughts. He and I have never discussed this; actually your name is not a subject that I bring up. He doesn't know that I came here, nor what I planned to do. In fact, he's in the hospital as we speak."

There was a passing look of concern. "Will he be alright?"

She nodded her head. "I think so, but Derek, I can't keep living this farce for either of us. You're much too special a person to be tied up with someone who doesn't love you, and whom you don't love. So, please...I'm asking you to take the ring back." She pulled the beautiful diamond off her finger and extended it to Derek.

He took it slowly, looking at it without looking at her.

She tried to fill the quiet space. "I also brought my lapis lazuli bracelet..."

He stopped her with a look. "Olivia, please. That was a gift for you, and I have no desire to have it back."

She nodded quietly. "Please understand that I believe you to be an incredible person, and I wish you the best of everything, but you and I don't belong together.

There's someone else out there for you. Whether Clay and I can ever find a way to be together, or if he even wants to, remains to be seen. I only know that this isn't fair to you...or me. I hope you'll be able to forgive me down the road, and I hope that we can stay friends." She walked over to the couch in the office and quietly picked up her coat. She turned around once, and said, "Take care, Derek. I'll see myself out."

He didn't come after her. She hadn't expected him to. She got into her car and began the drive home. There was sadness, but relief too. As she continued driving, she knew that she'd done the right thing. *I'm glad that I didn't mention this to anyone, including Sally. I'm not even sure when, or if, I'll tell Clay. I just need to sort through all these mixed up feelings and decide what to do next.*

On the way home, she called Jimmy and told him the news. Not about Clay, of course; just that she and Derek had grown apart, and that she knew she needed to end the engagement. Jimmy listened well for a change, and said he understood. "I'll tell Susie when she gets home. Chin up, little sis. You always know the right thing to do, and you're going to be just fine. So will Derek."

"I know that, Jim. Thanks for your support though. It means a lot."

Back at the gallery, Derek sat looking at the ring for several minutes. Then he quietly got up, went to the safe in his office, and placed the ring in there for safe-keeping. Well, that's that, isn't it? What will I do this evening then? He looked at the clock. It was just after six-fifty.

The Opening of the Pediatric Wing was an enormous

success. Nicole had dressed in her most elaborate set of black harem pants and an over-blouse of sheer orange, fire reds and black. She'd let her hair fall on her shoulders and wore the long scrollwork earrings that looked great against her hair. She was in her highest of black cocktail shoes. She felt good, and was enjoying watching the reactions of all in attendance.

The kids and families were amazed. They loved the tables and chairs and were sitting around with refreshments and chatting away. The Board of Directors had complimented her on the artwork, and every time they did, she pointed to the sign from Derek's Gallery. All in all it was an almost perfect evening. At eight-thirty, the entrance door opened, and she glanced up to see an impeccably dressed Derek Donaldson, almost as though she'd conjured him up, standing in the entryway. "He's alone," she whispered to herself, and she sauntered over to where he stood. "Hi," they both said at the same time. And suddenly the evening was more than perfect.

29

Heading home from Townsend, Olivia was glad that she hadn't told Sally about her plans for ending it with Derek. She knew that she'd made the right decision, and didn't really want to get into all of the details. *Details? There are no details, except that I'm in love with my boss; a situation without an apparent resolution that I can see.*

Once arriving home, she made her way towards her apartment. Mrs. Herbert came out, heading for her front door. *She might be a little nosy after all.* "Hi, Mrs. Herbert. What are you doing outside? It's still pretty cold, you know."

"Well, I saw you come in, and I just had to find out how Mr. Mitchell is feeling? Do you know anything?"

Olivia updated her, and let her know that Clay, according to Kathy, would be coming home soon, but was to give it about a week, before returning to work. Then Olivia said, "it's been a long day, Mrs. Herbert. I just drove in from Townsend, so I really need..."

Mrs. Herbert grabbed Olivia's arm. "Olivia...I can

see, even in the porch light. You're not wearing your engagement ring!"

Olivia had no real option. She nodded her head as she glanced at her finger, saying, "I drove over to Townsend to speak with Derek. He's been traveling a lot lately, and he's just gotten back. I just couldn't go on..."

"Are you saying that you ended it?"

Nosy, nosy, nosy. "Yes. I love Derek. In fact I adore him. But it's become increasingly evident to me that I'm not 'in love' with him, and I just didn't want to tie him down to a relationship that is heading nowhere. Do you know what I mean?"

"Yes, actually I do, dear," Priscilla patted her hand. "...I think you made a wise decision and can now concentrate on...other...people?"

Looking up quickly, Olivia asked, "What? Who do you mean?"

Priscilla Herbert turned quickly, shaking her head, deflecting. "Oh, no...one in particular. I need to get inside. It's getting chilly..."

"Mrs. Herbert. I'd rather you not mention this to anyone right now. The news will come out soon enough as it is."

"Of course, dear. No problem." She turned around and opened her door. The fact that her fingers were crossed didn't register with Olivia.

Clay had been released from the hospital, but it surprised him how weak he still felt. Doctor's orders had been to stay home for a full week before resuming his duties, and only as he felt able. It peeved him no end, but he'd actually realized that he was going to have to follow those orders. He didn't have the energy to do anything for very long.

Of course, it was no problem at Brandenburg. The school had run itself in the past, and all the teachers, as well as Kathy, encouraged him to take the time away that he needed, so he would return in full force. One of his concerns was Olivia's presentation, knowing full well that the time was passing swiftly. When he called her to double check how it was going, she told him that all was fine, and she had it totally under control. "In fact, I just emailed all the final information to the Presentation Board and they told me that they had received everything. Clay, please don't worry about this. Once you got me started, I knew the direction I wanted to go. Just rest so you're able to attend the conference. That's when I'll need your moral support more than anything else."

No way I'm missing the one shot of getting her away...and alone! "Okay, then, if you're sure you're alright. Maybe you can arrange to practice part of your presentation at this week's staff meeting? That would be great for the teachers to see what you've done, and it would give you time to see if there are any kinks in the whole thing."

"Oh, I love that idea!"

"I'll tell Kathy to put it on the agenda. There's not much on it this week, so you'll have plenty of time to do your thing."

"That sounds great. By the way, how are you feeling?"

"Better, thanks. Hopefully, I'll be back to school late next week."

"Okay. Well, bye Clay. You take care." She'd thought about going over to check on him so many times, but in the end she chickened out. She didn't know what she'd say if the subject of Derek came up, and well, she just needed to concentrate on the conference right now. *No other outside things... like the man you love getting in the way.*

It eased Clay's mind to know that she was okay. It bothered him like hell that he hadn't seen her, nor had the energy to "do" anything, even if he had seen her. His plan to be alone with her had been a big bust, and a niggle of concern entered his mind about their up-coming trip to Chicago. He knew from Dave that she'd driven to Townsend to meet Derek while he was in the hospital. But Dave didn't know what had gone on at that meeting. *All I know is that I need to get up and out of this bed, soon! I'm going crazy!*

As if in answer to his prayers, the doorbell rang. He peeked through the peephole to see Priscilla Herbert standing outside. He knew he looked like hell, but that didn't matter. He was so happy to have some compa-ny, that he swung the door open quickly. "Wow, Mrs. Herbert! You're a sight for sore eyes!"

His landlady registered a look of shock, but quickly caught herself. "I came to check on you, and to bring you some of my chicken and noodles to heat up. I know that you haven't been able to do much of anything, and little birds have been telling me that you might be go-ing crazy!"

"Hah! That's an understatement. Who told you?"

"Who told me? Mr. Garrett, Miss Litchfield, Mrs.

Tiffin, Olivia...and the list goes on and on. Anyway, is there anything that I can do for you? I need you back in full health! I have work around here." She tried to look tough, but she was holding a casserole dish of food for him.

Clay chuckled. "Thanks for the sympathy, there, ma'am. I'll just take that casserole to the kitchen." He took it around the corner and set it on his counter. Returning, he said, "Anyway, I do want to thank you for your help on the day I went into the hospital."

"Nonsense. I didn't do anything but return Mrs. Tiffin's call after checking on you. Anyone would have done that. But I must tell you, you certainly have a lot of friends for someone who hasn't been in town that long. You're a lucky man, Mr. Mitchell."

"You're right and I know it. Say, you mentioned Olivia? How is she? Have you seen her?"

"She's hardly surfaced since she came home last week...from Townsend."

Clay's head snapped up. "Do you know anything about that?"

"I might...but I thought that you were going to try to win Olivia...your time is ticking..."

"Wait! You <u>do</u> know something? Dave Garrett told me that she went there to see the "poster boy for women", but he didn't know a thing. Please, Mrs. Herbert, I'm begging!" He looked at her with a pained expression. "If you know anything about Olivia and Derek just break it to me easy." He stood with his head down, his hands crossed, almost as though he was in prayer.

"This apparent posturing of...losing...does not become you! Yes, I do know that Olivia went to Townsend to see Mr. Donaldson." She waited until Clay looked up. "And I happen to know that she...broke...off her engagement! It seems she might prefer a lower order of the male species!"

Clay's face said it all. "Oh, my God! Are you kidding? WOO-HOO!"

Before she knew what was happening, Clay had grabbed her in the biggest of bear hugs and whirled her around in full circles. Instantly he felt dizzy. He sat quickly on the couch, apologizing. "Sorry, Mrs. H. I got a little too excited, there."

"Really, Mr. Mitchell," she scolded, "just because this appears to be good news, I think that you still have your work cut out for you; and I think that as soon as you're better, you'd better get to it...we have a deal! You told me that you loved her!" The look of unabashed joy on Clay's face warmed her heart.

"You're absolutely right. This news is going to help me get better faster. I promise you...my one and only mission right now is to get...Olivia...Sheffield."

"See to it that that happens, young man. Now, I need to be going!" She turned abruptly towards the door, and left.

Clay watched her go. For the first time the tightness in his chest eased up, and he saw the way clear to his future.

Another full week passed before Clay was back to work full-time. He'd taken the days he needed, and the rest had done him a tremendous amount of good.

On the first day of his return, the staff had doughnuts and coffee ready in his office. They all assured him that the school was fine, and they were pleased that he was back. There were cards all over his desk, made by the students. Olivia was not there that day. Kathy said she'd taken a personal day to get all of her materials ready for the presentation.

Curiously, Clay asked, "Any news I need to know about, Kathy?"

"Not really, Clay. We've all handled ourselves well in your absence. Uh...except you <u>might</u> be interested in knowing that Olivia is no longer engaged." She turned around, one eyebrow raised, peering over the top of her bifocals.

He peered back, smiling slightly. "I <u>had</u> heard that rumor, and I can't say that I'm disappointed." He winked at Kathy. "Do you have a sub scheduled for Olivia for the conference Thursday and Friday?"

"Yes, that's all set, and Jeff Graves called and said that he'd be over on Friday for the entire day to meet with the teachers and generally hang around the building."

"By the way, what was the response to Olivia's presentation for the staff?"

"From what I heard, they were all impressed. Even the girls who are normally short on compliments were behind her. You know Olivia. She rarely does less than a stellar job!"

"That's great news. I have a truckload of catching up to do, before we head out for the conference, so I'm thinking some ten hour work days are in order this week. If you hear a scream from my office, come and rescue me!"

Kathy laughed. "Boy, am I glad to see my boss back. Get going, bud!"

Clay <u>did</u> work ten hours all three days that week. He was so far behind that he just wanted to get caught up before he left town. *I want no distractions this weekend in Chicago.* He had run into Livy periodically during the three days, but she'd always had an armload of things she was carrying to her car, or been with a group of kids, so he'd never really spoken to her.

Late Wednesday afternoon before the school day was quite over, he headed down to her classroom. The students were cleaning up their desks and generally going through their end-of-day routines. Clay walked into the room breezily. "Hey, boys and girls."

Olivia jumped through her skin. These last few hours, it had been difficult to concentrate on the kids and their needs, as she was trying to think through everything she needed to do once she got home. *And now, to top it off, Gorgeous walks in!*

Little Joanie Coswell ran up and said, "Mr. Mitchell. How you feelin'? You look pretty good, I think," nodding her head.

Indeed he does, Joanie. Olivia glanced up and their eyes met in a smile.

"Thanks for asking, Joanie. I'm so much better. I do have to tell you that if any of you get sick, you'd better listen to your parents and your doctor. Take your medicine and get your rest. Hey, did Miss Sheffield tell you that she's having a substitute tomorrow and Friday?"

Groans escaped the students' mouths. "Yeah, she told us, but we don't like it so much," said Tony.

Clay chuckled, but then put on his serious face. "Well, you're just going to have to deal with it. Miss

Sheffield is doing a really important presentation in Chicago, that'll make our school look really good, so I expect you all to be on your best behavior for the sub." He glanced around the room at them all. "Do I make myself totally clear?"

"Sure, sure," said Tony. Several of the other students nodded.

Clay strolled over to Olivia's desk, leaning in and whispering, "I'll pick you up at six a.m. sharp. The flight's early, but we have time for a little sight-seeing once we're in Chicago. See you in the morning."

"I'll be ready." She looked into the smiling blue eyes, and felt her own light up with anticipation. "I have to admit. I'm getting excited."

"Good." Clay made his exit, waving good-bye to the kids. *I plan on making you more excited, if I have my way.*

The flight to Chicago went off without a hitch, and they arrived at the Ambassador Hotel by 10:30 a.m. Clay went to the front desk to check in.

"Hi. I'm Clay Mitchell and I'm here for the Educators Conference. I've asked for an early check-in?"

"Just a minute, Mr. Mitchell, and I'll be right with you." The clerk was glancing at the computer, and said, "Hah. Here it is. Rooms 1257 and 58. How many keys, sir?"

"Two please. In which ballroom does the conference begin tomorrow morning?"

"They have breakfast scheduled from 6:30 to 8:30

in the main dining room. Then the opening of the conference takes place in the Roosevelt Room and spreads out from there. Here's a map of the hotel. Can I be of any further assistance?"

"No thanks. I've been here before, and I think I'll be okay."

Clay took the keys that were handed to him, and went over to where Olivia was standing. Her eyes were huge with excitement. "My, Lord, Clay. This hotel is massive and the decor is beautiful."

"I know. I've been here before and it's top of the line. Here's your key, Room 1257." As he handed it to her, he gently brushed her fingers.

A shiver went down her arm from the contact. "Thanks," she smiled, tongue-tied.

"Elevator banks are over there," he indicated, pointing. "Why don't you head on up, and I'll be right behind you with your presentation materials."

Wedged into a crowded elevator, Olivia noticed some folks wearing convention name tags. Everyone was loud, all talking at the same time. Livy glanced at the woman next to her in the elevator. "Boy, you can tell a crowd of teachers anywhere, can't you?'" she shouted.

The woman just laughed and added, also shouting, "And to think, these are the people that parents entrust their little darlings to..." She tossed off a wave, as she got off on her floor.

Getting out on the twelfth floor, Livy searched the signs for their rooms. She used the key to open her room, and her eyes widened in surprise.

Clay had just arrived carrying her presentation materials. He set them in her room. Noticing the smile on her face he asked, "What do you think, Olivia?"

"Oh, my God, Clay. This room is incredible!"

There was a huge sitting room with a fully-stocked wet bar, a sectional sofa, credenza, coffee table, and large screen television. A floral arrangement of exotic plants stood on a stand in the center. The windows overlooked the Magnificent Mile and the view was stunning. Livy was so excited that she was running around looking at everything.

"Gee! You'd think I've never been to a hotel before! Eek!"

Clay had opened up the door to the adjoining room and was hanging up his suit coats. He glanced up as his brown-eyed girl turned the corner with a stern look on her face.

"Clay...these are adjoining rooms?"

"Well, yeah, I know. They were the last rooms left when I booked. But I figured it would be fine...and see," he turned the lock, "if you're worried about your big bad next-door neighbor, you can always lock the door!" He turned around and looked at her, wiggling his eyebrows, trying to put on a threatening look.

"You are absolutely crazy, do you know that?" and she laughed outright at his silliness.

He pulled her into his room. "See... the rooms are identical. And wait'll you try the beds. They're amazing! Check it out!" Before Livy knew what was happening, he'd picked her up and tossed her on the center of the king-sized bed.

She sank into the plush bedding, and sighed, with her eyes closed, savoring the comfort of the mattress. Stretching like a cat she said aloud, "I may not want to get out of this bed." She opened up her eyes to see Clay, with a look of pure desire on his face.

He paused a minute, and she wondered if he would come towards her; but he backed away and said, "Maybe you <u>should</u> keep that door locked, Olivia. I'm heading down to get us some ice." And he was gone.

Olivia got up and went back to her room to hang up her dresses in the closet, quietly unpacking her underthings, when Clay entered the room with an ice bucket. "Oh, there you are..." He stopped, as she held a lacy peach bra in her hands. "Are you trying to kill me, here, Livy?" He walked toward her ever so slowly, taking the bra from her hands, and leaning in to say, "I'd like to see you in that bra...but I'd really prefer you out of it." He was there suddenly, stroking the flesh on her arms up and down...up and down in slow motion. She was lulled into a feeling of total relaxation. For a breathless moment, she thought he'd kiss her, as she sensed him drawing nearer, the closeness of his mouth, the curving smile on his lips, the scent of him, swirling around her. At the last minute, though, he pulled away. The thought of being in the same room with him, alone, made her stomach curl in little tingles. He had been so near...and she had been totally aroused by his proximity.

"Hey, you okay?"

She shook herself out of the reverie, saying "Yes, I'm fine." But what she really thought was that she might need a little ice to cool down

Clay continued, "Why don't you finish unpacking while I glance through this City Guide Book and check downstairs with the concierge about a couple of things that I think would be fun? No hurry."

Olivia smiled. He was adorable...and charming...

and already she'd gone from nervous excitement to sexual arousal...to unpredictability. *One thing I have to give him credit for. No boredom here.*

Olivia finished unpacking, and then she and Clay talked about some of the things they could do for their major sight-seeing day. "Tonight is the Welcome Dinner, so whatever we decide on, we need to get back no later than 6:30 p.m. so that we can freshen up and get ready for that. Who knows? You might even want to take a nap before we go to dinner. We've both been to Chicago before, but I'm game for whatever you're interested in doing."

They decided to forego the Field Museum because they'd both been there before. It was a cold day, but not bitter and the sidewalks were well-cleared of snow and ice, so they took a walk to the Art Museum and spent some time looking at the major exhibits on display. After that, they grabbed a quick snack, then went to wait for the bus for the Gangsters Tour. Clay had gone on it once before and had really enjoyed it. The tour basically consisted of a visit to the areas where Al Capone and the gangsters of the "Roaring Twenties" got their start. The tour was cleverly designed with little theatrical and historical elements thrown in along with the sights in parts of "Prohibition Chicago". Following the tour, they returned to their hotel just in time to put their feet up before getting ready for dinner.

"What a ball this has been!" Olivia remarked as Clay

used his key to open his hotel room. Olivia followed him in.

"I know. Those guys were really funny, weren't they?"

"Yes, and so were you. You seemed to have a one-liner to throw their way almost every time they told some gangster story. I think they would have hired you, if they thought you needed a job. I had no idea all that was happening during the Roaring '20's." Olivia plopped down on the sofa.

"Hey, now, don't be messing up my room. And get your feet off the coffee table!"

Olivia had taken off her shoes and socks and was enjoying the feel of the lush carpet underfoot. "Oh, be quiet! I'm just going to stretch out here for a minute and rest my eyes before we need to get cleaned up!"

"Oh, no you don't!"

Before Olivia knew what was happening, Clay picked her up off the couch and took her to her own bedroom. "Rest your eyes there. Then if you fall asleep, I'll be able to wake you up in time to get ready. Anyway, I want to watch the rest of the basketball game out here."

"Ahh...this bed feels amazing. I'm sinking down into the mattress...I think I'm in heaven." She actually had closed her eyes and was lying in the center of the bed.

For a minute Clay couldn't take his eyes off of her. She was rosy from the cold, and her hair shone like strands of gold across the stark ivory bedspread. The words amazing and heaven rang true for him too, but they were in response to what he'd like to do on that bed with Olivia. He shook himself, cleared his throat, and quietly said, "Take a nap. We have time." Then he pulled the door almost closed and went into his room.

He went out to the sitting room and turned on the television to watch the basketball game. He smiled as he thought about their day together. He'd had such a great time. It had been so long since he had actually enjoyed someone's company, someone who was so interesting to be with. Olivia knew about a lot of things, and she could talk to total strangers without a qualm. She charmed everyone's socks off on the tour, and she continued to work her wiles on him, as well. *The more I'm with her, the more I want her. I'm going for it all the way, no matter what happens with my job. I can't imagine my life without her.* He glanced heavenward. *I could use some help here!*

Clay awakened groggily, with someone shaking his shoulder. He'd fallen asleep watching the ballgame and dreaming of Olivia Sheffield. He opened his eyes slowly, only to see a vision looking back at him.

"Clay, you're the one who fell asleep, after all that teasing! I went ahead and got ready myself, since I knew it would take me longer…"

"Sweet Jesus!" Clay sat straight up. "You look incredible!"

She smiled, clearly pleased. "Do you like it?"

"Do I like it? That may be an understatement of some kind."

She was wearing a pale turquoise cocktail dress with a top layer of chiffon. It was cinched below her breasts with some rhinestones of silver. She wore silver heels and silver accessories. It was simple, elegant, and took your breath away. She'd left her hair down tonight, but had styled it with a soft halo of curls. Her eyes were bright, her skin flushed and beautiful, and his hands practically itched to touch her.

He stood up and spun her around, feasting his eyes on her. "Very nice...very...very...nice."

When he'd finished turning her, he was left there, staring down at her. She was staring up at him, almost as though she was waiting. He leaned in and she strained upwards towards him. She closed her eyes in preparation for the kiss that she knew was coming, but he tapped her on the nose ever so lightly and left her abruptly. "Well, I've got some work to do, if I'm to be your escort for the evening." He breezed out of the room, and she heard the water turn on.

Olivia stood quite still, shocked that he hadn't kissed her. She was frustrated to no end that he'd been so complimentary and then done nothing. She could feel the sexual tension building.

Clay strode out into the room once more. He'd stripped off his shirt leaving only his jeans on with the top button undone. "Hey, sorry, I forgot my toiletry bag." Then he turned and gave her a little sight of himself. *So maybe I'm a little narcissistic, but what the hell.* "Hey, you okay? You look a little shell-shocked! Would you like a drink? I can fix you one fast."

Livy didn't say a word. She just nodded.

"Livy...what would you like? He bent down at the wet bar, waiting for her to answer. Strong, sinewy back muscles and an amazing rear end were the view that faced her.

What a fine sight that is! "Gin and tonic, please."

"Okay. We've got the gin and the tonic but no limes, I'm afraid; hey, we'll stop and pick a couple up the next time we pass by one of the nearby markets. Okay?"

She didn't respond, but watched him pour the

liquids over the ice, turn around, then start to hand it to her.

She reached for it.

"Oh, wait. I forgot. Hope you don't mind the stir." He dipped his finger in the mixture and stirred it around, licked his finger and passed her the drink. "Gotta go! My water's probably boiling by now!"

Boiling! Whoo! Something's boiling alright! Looking at him, dressed like that makes me just want to see less clothes, and what those jeans are covering. She took her drink and deposited herself on the couch, pretending to watch the news. All she could really think about was Clay in the shower, and the gnawing ache of desire she felt in her bones.

;

30

The Welcome Dinner was designed to be just that--a way to welcome all the participants into town, give them an overview of Friday and Saturday sessions, allow them a little free time, but still get them back to their rooms by 10:30 p.m. There was a cash bar, but Livy had already had two gin and tonics, so she wasn't interested in more. Clay went off to the bar to get one more beer, and while he was gone, others had begun to take their seats around the assigned tables.

A middle-aged school board member from Iowa sat down with his wife; then a couple of elementary teachers from California came in. A principal from Connecticut with his superintendent appeared; last, there was a lone gentleman, mid-thirties, from Arizona. He was strikingly handsome with dark hair and a goatee, on the lean side; he arrived at the table, smiling and nodding, until he set eyes on Olivia.

"Hello," he drew out. "And who might you be?" in a voice easily recognizable as a guy on the make. He extended his hand.

She took his hand and smiled up into his eyes, tickled by his suave demeanor. *What a devil's glint there!* "I'm Olivia Sheffield from Brandenburg, Indiana. I'm a second grade teacher."

"I'm Josh Combs from Phoenix, Arizona, and I am inordinately pleased to meet you." He nodded at the others and listened to their introductions. He deposited himself in the seat directly beside Olivia and glanced at the empty seat on her left. "Are you alone? Because I am, and if so, I thought," he leaned in close, "that perhaps we might prolong the evening by enjoying a ..."

"Josh? Josh Combs? Is that you?" Clay was striding towards the table, beer in hand.

"Clay, you old son-of-a..." he caught himself before he finished the moniker. "How the hell are you?" Combs rose as Clay got to the table, shaking his hand and patting his back.

Good Lord--seeing two alpha males like these in one room could answer the prayers of women of all ages! Olivia smiled to herself as she looked at the expressions on the faces of the two elementary teachers, who had been stunned into silence by the presence of Clay and Josh.

The men were talking jovially, clearly happy to see each other. Then Josh caught Olivia's eye. Under his breath he leaned in and said, "I see that you are not alone, but I must advise you, I'd be the better choice to spend the evening with!" His so-called whisper was loud enough for Clay to hear.

Clay whispered too, not quietly. "Get your face out of her ear, Combs. She's here with me tonight. I'm protecting her from the likes of you!"

Combs laughed a most contagious laugh and sat

on Olivia's right. "Well, we'll see about that, won't we, Olivia?" He ran the palm of his hand over Olivia's hand.

Clay was no longer smiling. "Josh, keep your hands off...of...her!"

Olivia glanced up in the center of the two men; there was a stand-off happening as they stared at each other. Olivia deflected. ""Really, you two, could we enjoy the evening?" She began to address the remainder of the people at the table, asking them when they'd arrived, if they'd done any sight-seeing, and relating what she'd done. In a minute, she had everyone comfortable at the table and the earlier short-lived tension was gone. "Now, while we have some quiet, how is it that you two know each other?"

Josh jumped in to answer the question. "Clay and I took some administrative classes together in Arizona and eventually got assigned to two schools that were relatively nearby. We're pretty good friends, actually. Right, ol' buddy?" glancing at Clay.

"Yeah, when you're not an ass..."

Olivia kicked Clay under the table.

"Oww!" He didn't even look at Livy, but looked at the rest of the table and apologized for his language.

Josh looked at Clay and Olivia with a quirky sort of smile and for once said nothing.

Dinner was served. There was conversation about schools and policies, principals and superintendents, school board issues and retirees. Everyone took part in the conversation. It was interesting to discover how different and yet alike the schools were from state to state. Following dinner, several groups of students from throughout the Chicago School District performed for the appreciative audience. There was choral music, an orchestra number, and even a skit that the students had written themselves, all pretending to act like teachers. The audience was howling before it was over. Finally, coffee and dessert was served and the evening came to a close.

Everyone said their good-byes, and Olivia looked at Clay, her warm brown eyes, registering a question.

Clay answered her plea. "Are you ready to head up?"

She nodded.

He rose instantly, pulling her chair out for her. "Well, we're going to say goodnight. Olivia has a presentation tomorrow, and I know that she wants to get things set up for that. It's been great meeting you all, and Josh," he turned and smiled, "good to see you again. What session are you attending in the morning?"

They talked a minute more, agreeing to meet for coffee in the early morning. Olivia began to move away from the table, and Josh grabbed her hand as she walked by.

"I'm not sure what you've done to my old buddy, but I have to admit that he looks pretty happy."

She turned, surprised. "Oh, we're not...together..."

Josh burst into laughter. "Tell that to someone who hasn't spent the evening with you two." He was still snickering. "Just a reminder, if you get tired of him, I'm willing to stand in."

Olivia looked up and shook her head, pressing her hand against his chest. "You're remarkably sure of yourself, aren't' you? I imagine that DOES work most of the time; just not with me!" and she strode away.

Clay had been standing right behind her and heard every word they both had said. "Piss off, Combs!" he muttered under his breath, and he laughed all the way out of the ballroom.

The two of them made small talk in the elevator, commenting on how ironic it was that Josh had sat at their table.

"That is quite a man!" Olivia chuckled.

"He's full of himself...and an absolute hoot. But he's one of the best principals I've ever seen in action, and he has a soft spot for kids with disabilities. His younger brother has Downs Syndrome."

"Not attached to anyone?" Olivia questioned curiously.

"Are you kidding? He's usually attached to two or three at once."

She laughed. "I have absolutely no trouble believing that!"

Arriving at the room, Clay opened the door and shut it behind Olivia. She walked on ahead of him rotating her neck as if she was uncomfortable. Clay stepped up behind her, and slowly began to massage her neck.

"Ahh...that feels fabulous! I think I'm working on getting a tension headache. My neck muscles get so tight when that happens."

"Uh-huh." His miracle fingers kneaded into her tense shoulders, then he rotated his thumbs, loosening up the muscles.

"Oh...my...God, that is...heaven."

"Un-huh." Suddenly his mouth was on her neck in exactly the same places that his hands had been. The tip of his left hand caressed the center of her neck moving down her spinal column, then his lips followed the same path.

Somewhere in the haze that held Olivia, she felt him unzipping her dress, and exposing her back, save the turquoise lace bra she was wearing.

His hands and then mouth continued to find sensitive places to touch and taste.

Olivia shivered with the anticipation.

Then he stopped. She heard a quiet sigh. "I'm sorry, Livy. You are so tempting...I'm trying to honor your wishes of staying...away...and keeping...professional."

She turned and the look of raw lust in her eyes almost undid him.

Keep playing the knight in shining armor. Don't screw it up yet...hold on! "Look," he moved away, "you have your presentation tomorrow. Let me help you get everything gathered up and in the right order. Then you probably need to get a good night's rest."

She looked at him and nodded. *Give me strength. I'm about ready to jump his bones!*

"I think I'll change and get into my pajamas, then gather everything up. It's mostly here already, but I'll double check.' She turned and headed towards the bedroom, leaving her dress unzipped.

The sight of her beautiful back bared and the inviting sway of her hips nearly made him howl, but he let her go. He untied his tie and unbuttoned his dress shirt and stretched out on the sectional in his stocking feet. Of course, the crotch of his pants was uncomfortably confining; he gritted his teeth, fighting off the need to ram his erection into a nice, warm...

Olivia had reentered. If it were possible for her to look more desirable, he'd be shocked. The funny thing was she wasn't wearing a negligee or fancy lingerie. She wore a soft-looking robe in a mint-green color that made him want to touch her. She was packing up her things, not looking at him, sorting through each game, each book she'd brought, marking off a list that she was holding, and talking to herself quietly.

He sat up and watched her, fascinated at her focus. *Why hasn't she told me about breaking up with Derek? Maybe she's having second thoughts.* He stood and advanced in her direction. "Do you think you have it all organized?"

"I think so." She didn't make eye contact, but continued gathering stacking crates and putting them in order.

"My plan is to meet Josh for coffee and a work-out early. But if you need me, I can come up and help get this stuff down to the presentation room."

"No, Clay, that's not necessary. I'll call the bellhop and he can do it. Enjoy your visit and work-out. I know that you and Josh will have a lot to talk about." She still hadn't looked in his direction, but appeared to be finishing up her preparation. Finally, she stopped puttering around, and glanced up. Her eyebrows raised. "Well, I guess I'm as ready as I'm ever going to be. Thanks for giving me the opportunity to do this, Clay."

"You're entirely welcome, Livy. I know you'll do a great job. I've got a couple of sessions to attend but I promise I'll be there at eleven to see you." He stepped closer and tipped her chin up. "You're going to be amazing. I just know it," and he placed a fatherly kiss on her forehead.

Her disappointment was palpable. *He didn't even notice my new robe. I think he might have changed his mind about me. I hope that's not right, now that I've finally figured out what I want.* She turned her back and headed to the bedroom.

"Night, Livy. Sleep well."

As if. I probably won't sleep at all. She closed the door slowly and waved a good-night.

Clay watched the door close and ran his hand through his hair. *I can't take a cold shower now, and I don't think I can stay in here with her in the next bedroom.* Eleven p.m. saw Clay heading for the work-out area, so that he could do laps in the pool. He knew it would be closed, but was hoping no one would notice he was there.

Olivia had set her alarm early and it was a good thing she had. She hadn't fallen asleep until at least three in the morning. She showered and shampooed her hair, trying to keep quiet so as not to awaken Clay; when she went out to the sitting room to make some coffee, it was already made, and he was gone.

She went about getting dressed for her presentation, practicing what she planned on saying and generally reviewing her program. Her stomach was full of butterflies and she knew that she couldn't eat anything this morning. She sat down at the table wishing Clay was here to talk to, but knowing that his presence would overwhelm her in ways she couldn't act on anyway.

She'd stayed awake trying to figure out a way to tell Clay that she wasn't interested in "professionalism" any more. Finally, she'd just decided that tonight after all the sessions were over, she'd tell him that she had split from Derek for one reason--him. *If that doesn't work, I'm done for.*

She sipped her coffee, and as she stood up to return to the bathroom to finish her make-up, she saw a wrapped package on the coffee table. There was a small card on it with her name. She opened the note card and in Clay's legible scrawl she read:

I know it's not lapis, but I saw this bracelet yesterday and wanted you to have it. Remember today's date--your first, but surely not your last presentation. Clay

Olivia lifted the tissue and saw a charm bracelet, covered with school charms. There were books, a desk, a globe, eraser and chalk, a schoolhouse, ABC's, and a heart with the word Teacher on it. Today's date was engraved on the back of the heart. It was adorable. Olivia turned it around taking in all the details, then fastened it to her wrist and went into the bathroom to finish getting ready.

She called down to the Main Desk to ask for help in getting her crates down to the conference room. Before she knew it, Jonathan, the bellhop arrived and loaded up everything; together they rode the elevator to the third floor conference rooms.

"Let me take this right in, Miss Sheffield. You're supposed to check in when you get to the conference room, so they know you're here. I'll take all your supplies to the main stage."

"Thanks so much, Jonathan," she said, handing him a ten-dollar bill. He started to decline, but she looked at him with her teacher stare, then she smiled and said, "I insist."

"Thank you, then. Good Luck!" and off he went with her crates.

Olivia checked in and met all the other presenters. They talked about their nervousness and their excitement, as well. The presenters were given assigned seats in the front of the room to watch the presentations, and then more easily make their way to the stage when it was their turn.

Before Olivia knew it, it was her time, and the Board members motioned for her to come on stage. They hooked a lapel mic on her and asked her to check that her PowerPoint settings were correct. Then the announcer introduced her and her school, and she came out onto the stage.

For a moment she stood center stage, looking over the vast crowd, smiling. The lights were bright and hot and she was silent. She took a big breath and started giggling. "Well...can you hear it?" She stared at the audience, expectantly. When no one said anything or responded, she continued. "You mean you can't hear my heart pounding?" The audience broke into laughter, and she was on her way.

Clay and Josh were standing in the back of the conference room. Both of them chuckled under their breath when Olivia tamed the crowd. Then she went on, presenting the most boring information, statistics and graphs and lots of data, in a way that made sense and was somehow worth listening to. To top it off, she made self-deprecating remarks, putting everyone at ease and keeping their interest. The listeners understood in very short order that there was a lot to learn from her presentation, and she made them want to learn it.

"Good God Almighty!" Josh commented. "She makes statistics fun; then you have the added benefit of looking at her." Josh glanced over at Clay who was watching Olivia with adoring eyes. "Well, ol' buddy. I recognize a fallen comrade when I see one!"

Clay looked over with a stupid look on his face. "What?"

"Jesus! Have you told her you're in love with her yet, you idiot?"

Clay glanced in Josh's direction, shaking his head. "Not yet. Tonight!"

"Do it fast, Clay. After today's presentation she's going to have everyone eating out of her hand! Who knows? There might be someone more deserving of her attention, like maybe...me?" He smiled his most annoying smile and jabbed Clay in the ribs.

Clay didn't take his eyes off of Olivia. "Just try it. I've been waiting to wallop you for a very long time!"

Josh laughed low and deep in his throat, putting up his hands. "Okay, okay, I give up. But a word of advice. Lock this thing down..." He added, "See you tonight?"

"Not if I can help it! I've scheduled room service for later, and then I'm hoping..."

"...to provide other services in the room? Right?"

Clay smiled smugly.

Josh shook Clay's hand, slapped him on the back, and said "Good Luck!"

Clay nodded ruefully. *Thanks! I'm going to need it!*

The day had been amazing and so much fun for Olivia. Her afternoon break-out sessions were well-attended. She'd roamed around from station to station, watching the teachers use her games and manipulatives, all the while listening to how they could use the same ideas in their classrooms. She was there to answer questions, if necessary. Mostly she just enjoyed interacting with other teachers and talking about literacy issues.

She had gotten tremendous feedback about her ideas and actually jotted down some notes and comments that she thought would be helpful in the future. She'd shaken hundreds of hands during the day and basked in the glow of the response from the participants who begged her to come back and present again.

She gathered up her materials slowly, making sure that everything was there. One of the conference organizers, Sheila Hass, told her that they would have all of her crates sent up to her room within the hour. "You were fabulous, Miss Sheffield! Congratulations!"

"Thanks so much. I'm pleased that it went so well." Olivia headed up to the room. She was elated and charged with adrenaline, but she knew if she dared to sit down she'd probably collapse. *I know what I'll do. I'll head to the swimming pool, and when Clay gets back, maybe we can have some dinner. I'm starved!*

She changed into her swimsuit, threw on her cover-up, and took the key, heading to the fifth floor Spa and Pool. At the last minute, she jotted a note for Clay telling him where she would be, should he arrive back soon. When she got to the pool no one else was there. She was thrilled, as she really wanted some quiet time to concentrate on doing laps and just unwinding. She threw off the cover-up and dove into the pool. The water was exhilarating, but not too cold. She'd always enjoyed swimming, and it was particularly pleasant to swim in the dead of winter. She began doing laps back and forth, using some of her pent-up energy, and when she felt that she had gotten some good cardio, she took a final dive under the water and came up for air. She brushed her hair out of her eyes, and sitting on one of the pool chairs was Clay.

"Hello there! I've got a glass of Cabernet waiting for you. Are you game?"

"Oh, a glass of wine sounds marvelous." She toweled off and put her cover-up back over her shoulders.

Clay watched as he poured. *That body is the reason two-piece swimsuits were invented.*

Olivia walked over to Clay slowly, almost embarrassed by the silence in the pool area. He handed her a glass.

Then he held his own up and toasted her "You were incredible today, Liv, I've been grinning all day since your presentation; everyone in the crowd loved it! Cheers to you and your hard work! I couldn't be prouder!" He touched the tip of his glass to hers.

She smiled, "It <u>was</u> good, wasn't it? I was so afraid when I stared out at the lights, but then I just thought, "Oh, do it, Olivia, you're prepared; then it just came out of my mouth. Truth be told, I'd prepared, but there were a lot of things I said that I don't even remember planning on saying."

"That's the thing that made it most fun. Your spontaneity. People knew it wasn't scripted or stilted. How in God's name you can make all that boring data exciting, I'll never know, But you did it!"

They sat down at one of the tables around the pool, sipped at the wine, relishing each other's company and savoring the moment.

Glancing up into his blue eyes, Olivia patted her left wrist. "Clay, I absolutely love my bracelet. I put it on the minute I opened it, and now I don't think I'll be able to take it off. It gave me courage and luck, I think. Thank you so much."

He touched her wrist after the comment, stroking the top of her hand and its long fingers. "You have beautiful hands, Livy." Then he touched her ring finger. "But something's missing..." He looked her straight in the eye, waiting.

At that moment, some teenagers entered the pool area, laughing and talking loudly, ready to have a good time together.

She watched his hand on hers and nodded, "Yes. I'd hesitated telling you. In fact, no one knows--not from me, at least. I was sort of waiting to get through this drama before another one unfolded."

Clay held her hand, not looking up.

She started to talk, but then she said, "I think I'd rather go to the room and have this conversation, if you don't mind." She indicated the teenagers over her shoulder.

"Sure, sure. I'll get the glasses. Can you grab the wine bottle?"

They got in the elevator and headed back upstairs to their room. When they arrived, Olivia went to change out of her wet suit, and Clay pulled out some light snacks that he'd picked up during the day, to tide them over until dinner.

Olivia returned, wearing her comfy, close-fitting

ski pants and a short turquoise sweater. Her hair was a little damp, but it laid gently on her shoulders with a little wave.

"Hey--I went out on a limb. I hope you don't mind. I got some snacks for right now, and I ordered a great meal from room service; if you'd rather go out, though, I can easily cancel. I just thought you might enjoy unwinding after the day? Any thoughts?"

"Staying in sounds like heaven. I really don't feel like getting dressed..."

I'd rather you be undressed...and un...der me!

"Good, then it looks like we're on the same track. Have something to eat." He handed her a plate with cheese and crackers and sliced pears and apples.

"I'm famished!" She grabbed the plate and went to town eating and taking sips of her wine. "This tastes great!"

"Don't spoil your appetite. Dinner comes in about two hours. Champagne too, to celebrate your hard work!" His smile was contagious.

"Then I'd better cut off my wine consumption, or I won't be worth anything by the end of the night!"

"Don't be silly. You're fine. Drink up! No one's driving tonight." Clay waited for a minute, and then he broached the subject. "Olivia...what happened with Derek?"

She thought about what to say for a minute. Then she stood and walked away from Clay, turning her back to him. Finally, she started talking. "Well, to be frank, we got engaged on New Year's Eve and hadn't seen each other since. He had a tremendous amount of traveling to do, including Texas and Hong Kong. There were several occasions when we were to meet his parents, but between our weather, my work, and his travels, it just never happened. The more I thought about the whole situation, the more clearly it began to register."

Clay moved up behind her. "So...are you telling me...that...?" he began.

Olivia turned, facing him. "That I ended the engagement. The real truth of the matter is that you can't very well be engaged to one man...when you can't get...your mind...off another." She stood there facing Clay, totally exposed in what she was saying.

Clay's heart soared, and he stepped into her personal space. Suddenly, he was kissing her full out, mouth on mouth, lips meeting, testing, sampling, body plastered to body, grabbing, taking, feeling. "God, Livy, I've waited for this day since the night I met you."

"I know, I know," she was gasping. "Please, Clay... now that we're here...please don't...stop!"

He lifted her up and sat down on the sectional with her in his lap. "It seems I'm remembering a promise you made to me when I was sick." He smiled and wiggled his eyebrows.

"You didn't even know my name at first," she smiled, swatting his shoulder.

"But I knew I wanted you in my lap kissing me, even then...and so you are..."

Her body was perched conveniently in his lap, and she held his face and gifted him with slow, languorous kisses, allowing her tongue to revel in his response, and to feel the broad expanse of his shoulders as she moved her arms lower.

There was a low growl out of him that excited her further, while she fitted her bottom even higher in his lap, so that she was sitting on the evidence of his excitement. "Oh, Clay. I want you...to..."

"God!" He didn't wait. He lifted her off him and laid her gently down on the couch, looking into her eyes. "Olivia...I want to see you...to hear you...come for me... only me." He stripped her of her clothes, pulling her sweater over her head, working to get the ski pants down the slim legs, exposing her beautiful breasts covered by a lace blue bra, with a tiny blue thong that covered very little. His shuttered eyes stared at her for a moment, then he knelt beside her extended form and began to shower kisses in her cleavage and over the mounds of her breasts, one hand toying with her nipples inside the bra, rubbing, abrading against the lace and his finger, then bending down and pulling the nipple into his mouth and sucking. He lifted her breasts out of the bra cups and let them spill over.

She gasped and writhed on the couch. "Oh, my God....more..."

The plea in her voice, undid him. "Not...to...worry, Liv. I want more, too."

Suddenly her bottom was lifted up, her pelvis thrust forward and the thong pulled off. Her eyes opened slightly and he was staring at her, spread open and inviting. As she watched him, he put his hand under her bottom, tilted her mound upward, and he sampled the warm flavor of her arousal.. "My God...I've wanted you in my mouth for so long..." Then he tasted, tickled, circling his tongue around her love lips, and she let him have every ounce of her wet, hot core as she watched him love her.

The pitch of excitement was rising for Olivia. She could hardly breathe. She closed her eyes and let him take her into oblivion. When she thought she would shatter, his mouth left her and he was kissing her again, letting her taste her own pungent flavor, sampling her own erotic taste from his tongue. Then his fingers were inside her, flicking and rubbing, keeping the friction going, and his lips and tongue were teasing her while moving back to her nipple, around and around.

Her breathing was harsh and labored; so was his, but he kept on pleasuring her until he knew she would break. Then he moved down her flat stomach, lifted her thigh, gifting her with tongue kisses all the way down to her honey-colored patch of heaven. "Come...for me... honey, I want to taste your nectar on my tongue."

One...more...circle of his tongue and she screamed, the rosy, pink flesh, filling his mouth, her writhing body savoring the action, reaching, reaching, reaching to hold onto the climax as long as she could. He kept his mouth on her, feeling her come, tasting her rich juice of arousal, arousal that he'd given her, and finally, she started to come back to earth, shivering, her spasms slowing, as the ecstasy started to abate.

They were both gasping for breath, and Clay was dripping with sweat. All of his clothes were still on, but it didn't matter. Only bringing her to the heights had mattered. It had never been like that with any other woman--wanting to give her everything, before he took anything. He gathered her in his arms and held her, warm and secure, stroking her back, her large breasts pressed against his shirt front, still spilling out of her bra.

She was sighing with satiation. "My God, Clay, it's never been like that before." She looked into his eyes with a more than satisfied smile.

"I'm going out on a limb here, darling. There's more

where that came from." He lifted away from her body for a minute, standing, and began to take off his shirt.

A sudden knock at the door and a voice, "Room Service," shocked them both. Clay responded, "Just a minute, please."

He handed Olivia her clothes, shooed her into the other room, and closed the door behind her. He buttoned his shirt, thankful that the tails covered his erection and opened the door for the waiter.

"Where would you like the tray, sir?"

"Here is fine. That looks fantastic. Thank you," passing the waiter a tip, before he left quietly, closing the door.

"Liv, are you hungry, hon?" He was lifting up the lids to check the filets and the meal, but when he turned, his mouth went completely dry.

Olivia Sheffield was standing in the middle of the sitting room totally naked. Large, rounded breasts with raised, aroused nipples pointed in his direction. The perfectly proportioned body with a lush patch of hair covering the path to paradise faced him, and she smiled the smile of a siren.

"I am hungry, Clay...just not for that kind of food. Come and feed me," she turned slowly, and he watched her gorgeous tight ass move toward the bedroom. He followed her like a puppy dog.

When they finally emerged from the bed, three hours later, the food was cold, but neither of them cared. Clay had given her two more orgasms, and he'd finally gotten his cock into her hot, tight sheath and his own climaxes had been earth-shattering. They sampled the food on the room service table, including filets, spinach, baked potatoes and strawberries with cream.

Clay took the bottle of champagne into the bedroom and they had a glass together, laughing, drinking, kissing. Finally, Olivia said, "Clay, you have totally worn me out. I'm going to sleep." With that she buried herself under the mounds of sheets and blankets, and her relaxed breathing was evidence that she was, indeed, exhausted.

"'Night, sweetheart," he said, as he kissed her on the forehead, pulled the comforter around her, and wrapped his arm over her shoulder as the darkness claimed him too.

31

Clay woke Olivia at six in the morning, by sliding the covers down her back and kissing her spinal column all the way to the top of her delectable bottom. She smiled as his hands explored her skin, marveling in how alluring he made her feel just by the touch of his fingers and the sounds that escaped his throat.

"Livy, darling. I've been dreaming of taking you for two hours, and I don't think I can wait any longer! For God's sake, wake up!"

She chuckled quietly. "Do you seriously think that I could sleep with your hands doing that..." Clay's cell phone vibrated on the nightstand.

Clay saw Olivia's horrified expression when she read the letters--DAD.

Reaching across her body, he grabbed the phone. "Hey, Dad...is everything alright?" He listened a minute, and then continued. "Yes, Miss Sheffield presented yesterday and it was well-received..." More listening. "...we've got sessions today and then the awards presentation later on. Thanks for checking in. I'm going to put my phone on silent now, Dad, so I don't forget it during the presentations. See you sometime this week, I'm sure." Clay disconnected.

"Oh, Lord, Clay! What are we going to do?" she groaned, pulling the blanket over her head.

"Now, honey...I don't want you to worry about this...we'll figure it out together when we get back to Brandenburg. Let's enjoy the rest of the day...and night!" and he reached for her, pulling the blanket away from her face, and showering kisses on her, touching her shoulders, her neck, her earlobes with his tongue.

"Oh...Clay...just stop it...now. We need to get out of bed. We have sessions all day to attend!" She tried to get up, but he grabbed her, holding her down.

"Only if you promise me more sessions tonight."

She giggled, as she hopped out of bed. "I believe that I can stand on that promise!" She scooted into the bathroom, turning on the shower. As she washed, she marveled at how relaxed she felt. Her body was like a separate entity, detached from her head, as though she were in some languid floating zone. It had been a long time since she'd had sex, but this was so much more than sex. This was true and potent lovemaking: when two people set out to make the experience the apex for the other person. She knew that if he got her back in bed, she would be ready again for him.

When Clay heard the shower turn off, he arose from the disheveled bed and walked slowly into the bathroom. She was toweling dry and yet she looked so ripe, so pink, so amazing, he actually turned on the cold water, groaning. "Get out of this bathroom right now, or I'll have to take you here on the bathroom floor!"

Her eyebrows raised, and she said, with a sigh of hope, "Really?"

He laughed out loud and swatted her backside. "No...not now...leave something for tonight!"

Leaving the bathroom, she laughed...and then laughed again when she heard Clay shout, "Damn...this water is ice cold! And it needs to be!"

Olivia attended two morning lectures, and a break-out session with an elementary team of art, physical education, and music teachers. It was really fun, and informative, and gave her new ideas that she could use in her classroom. She continued to get lots of compliments about her presentation and a number of people asked for her email address in order to contact her. She was thrilled that some of her games had been so well-received.

After attending the morning sessions, they broke for lunch. *I am absolutely starving. I believe that I can attribute my voracious appetite at lunch to my voracious appetite last night in the bedroom.* She smiled to herself when she thought of some of the things she would do to Clay once they were back in their room. *Paybacks are hell, big boy! You'd better be ready!*

At three o'clock, all the participants were scheduled to head to the Roosevelt Room for the closing reports and awards. She and Clay had arranged to meet in the entry hall of the ballroom; when she arrived it was impossible to miss him standing there talking to Josh. As she approached, Clay's head swiveled in her direction, and he stopped talking to Josh. "Hi, gorgeous," he said, grabbing her hand. She took his and smiled, almost shyly, "Hi."

"Oh, God," Josh declared, rolling his eyes "Could either of you be more sickening?"

"Now, now, Josh. One day, in all that feminine activity you surround yourself with, you'll find yours! So shut up and leave us alone!" Together, Clay and Olivia walked into the ballroom, heading for a table.

Josh strode in behind them, thinking, truth be told, buddy, I'm glad you've found yours. One less man on the make--more women for me! I will admit, though, she's quite a catch. He and Clay had already talked about the marriage proposal that wouldn't be long in coming. He figured that within five or six months, he'd be attending a Mitchell/Sheffield wedding.

Josh grabbed the empty chair near Clay and Olivia, and they all sat down to listen to an overview of the conference. It had been the largest attended conference in a decade and everything had pretty much gone off perfectly. Acknowledgements were made all around for the organizers; then it was time for the awards to be announced.

There were certificates given to all of the guest lecturers first; most of them were college professors or retired superintendents. Then the teachers who'd presented were called up one by one and given a certificate of participation. Finally, a prize was to be awarded for BEST PRESENTATION and no one, except Olivia, was really surprised when her name was called. Not only was she awarded a certificate for participation, but she also received a trophy for the school and a $3,000.00 check to use towards further enhancement of the literacy program.

Josh clapped Clay on the back. "Congratulations, buddy. That'll be a great boon for your school."

And for me! Clay just stood and kept clapping for the love of his life who remained on the stage.

Their final night in Chicago was spent going from nightclub to nightclub, listening to jazz at piano bars round town. Josh and a woman named Stephanie joined them. She was a stunning redhead who lived in the Chicago area; Josh and she had known each other for a while and always got together when Josh was in town.

The four of them enjoyed each other's company. Josh was so droll that one couldn't help but laugh at the things he said. Clearly, they were "friends with benefits", and Olivia thought that seemed okay, but she felt that Josh put on a mask of avoidance when anything got remotely cozy between them, or when Stephanie indicated any involvement in Josh's future.

Saying their "Good-byes" upon returning to the hotel, Josh and Clay shook hands enthusiastically. Then Josh turned to address Olivia. "My dear Olivia, it has been a true pleasure meeting you. Keep my friend here in line; I look forward to seeing you again--soon perhaps?"

Olivia looked at him with a puzzled expression on her face.

Clay shot him a warning glance; Josh cleared his throat and pulled her into a warm embrace. For once

Clay let him do it. "Good-bye," he said, ushering Stephanie forward as they both turned to wave.

Livy asked, "What was he talking about? Is he coming to Indiana or something?"

Clay shrugged his shoulders, nonchalantly. "Maybe, in a few months. We talked about him coming to Brandenburg to see the school and spend some time in town. But we'll have to wait and see if that works!" *Actually, you need to see if the marriage proposal works first, you dimwit.*

"I've been thinking that..." Olivia crooked her finger and stood on her tiptoes to whisper into the ear he leaned her way.

"Sweet Jesus..." was all he said, as he hurried her to the right bank of elevators.

Clay grabbed breakfast for the two of them downstairs in the lobby. While waiting for the order to arrive, he gave his Dad a call to let him know that Olivia had won the Best Presentation Award and the dollars that would be coming their way. His dad had been suitably impressed.

Picking up the breakfast order, he got into the elevator and headed to the 12th Floor. Olivia had heard him coming, and opened the door for him.

"My Dad says to tell you..." he grinned, "...when I see you... that Brandenburg is very proud of you!"

She snorted. "Clay...this is not funny!"

"Why are you laughing then?" He sat their meals on the coffee table, handing her a coffee cup.

"Really, Clay, what are we going to do...about...us?"

"Us? I like the sound of that!" And he squeezed her hand. "Eat your breakfast, Livy; I'll figure everything out when we get home." He winked. "I just need a little downtime from my wild nights, so I can come up with a plan."

Clay and Olivia arrived back in Brandenburg about seven p.m.. He unloaded her suitcase and took it up her steps. "We'll just keep your presentation gear in my car, and I'll drive you to work in the morning." She nodded as he pulled her towards his chest for another kiss. "My God, Livy, you've ruined me this weekend. I'm very doubtful that I can survive more than three hours without you in my bed. Are you sure you don't want to come to my place?"

"It sounds wonderful, but Clay, we've both agreed that until we have this whole relationship/job thing worked out, we can't let anyone know we're together."

"I know, sweetheart...just give me a few days to think about it, and we'll figure it out." He kissed her lips slowly, savoring the reaction he found there.

"Oh, Clay, you are so hard to resist," but she pulled away and moved towards her front door.

"Just keep reminding yourself of that, darling. I'll see you tomorrow," he said, heading for his own apartment.

Olivia set down her suitcase in the entry hall and took her coat off, hanging it in the closet. *No one would believe what a sex-fiend I became this weekend! Stay focused. You just have to figure out the job thing before you can let anyone know that you're head over heels in love...with your boss.*

She headed upstairs towards her bedroom throwing off clothes as she went. *Sleeping alone tonight will be a real trial.* Her phone rang.

"Livy, you didn't lock your door, honey," Clay's voice said over her cell phone.

"How do you know?" she asked, inquisitively.

"'Cause I'm already in your house." The low chuckle that she found so endearing emanated from his throat, and she looked up. He was standing in the hallway outside of her bedroom. "Don't worry, though. I locked it. You're safe now!"

I don't think I'll ever be safe from that devil-may-care look. Clay smiled and wiggled his eyebrows. She laughed and he was on top of her in a second.

32

Clay and Olivia rode to school in the morning; together they unloaded all the materials she'd taken to Chicago. Clay planned on calling an early morning staff meeting in order to announce the award that Brandenburg had received from Olivia's presentation. She started her hand-wringing as they drove, and continued into the building.

"Clay, I don't really think that we need to make a big brouhaha about the award."

"You're kidding, right? Livy, the staff needs to know about your award, and how we'll put it into play next school year. Additionally, the fact that one of our own won, may make someone else on staff want to present next year. All of these are great things for our school and our district. Besides, I'm proud as hell of you, and I want them all to know! Now quit arguing," then he whispered, "and give me a kiss"

"Clay, I thought we weren't..."

He grabbed her in the coat room and said, "Shut up!" as he lowered his mouth over hers and gave her a slow, sexy kiss that made her toes curl. Then he pulled away and smiled. "Okay, that'll do me for a few hours!" and he left. Without turning back, he shouted, "See you at the meeting in half an hour!"

Olivia watched him walk away. *He's done wonders for this building, for the kids, and for the school district. It would be a crime for him to be let go.* She walked around her classroom, straightening desks, picking up a few loose papers that had fallen on the floor, and generally re-reading the notes from the sub. But all the while she was thinking about their predicament. The answer was a simple no-brainer, and Olivia knew the course of action that she would take this evening, when she got home. *I'm a dime a dozen here, but Clay is irreplaceable.* She headed down the hallway to Sally's room before walking upstairs to the library.

"Hey, Sal. How in the world are you?"

Sally glanced at her friend of many years and knew instantly. "Olivia! You look fabulous--all rosy and happy. Anything you need to tell me, even though I already know?"

Olivia stood in shock. "What do you mean you already know? Know what?"

Sally ran over to her classroom door and shut it. "Are you kidding? I know that you won the award for your presentation! I've been following the happenings online, and I saw it late last night! Aren't you excited?" She threw her arms around her friend's shoulders.

Olivia heaved a sigh of relief. "It has been so exciting, Sally. I was so nervous and somehow the words just sort of spilled out and the presentation went really well. Then a lot of people came to the break-outs and loved the games. I'm hopeful that they'll help a lot of other teachers."

"Oh, hon. I'm so happy for you. I can't wait to see the look on everyone's face when Clay announces it this morning. I assume that's what he's planning?"

"Yes, but I told him it wasn't necessary."

"Sorry...but you're wrong and he's right! Well, we'd better head up there, don't you think?" They started towards the door. "Oh, and by the way, Olivia. I know that you broke it off with Derek, and that you're doing the 'nasty' with the boss!"

Olivia gasped, looking Sally in the eye.

Sally just burst out laughing. "Oh...come...on. I know a girl who's getting 'it' when I see one. I must say, 'it' has clearly done you good, girlfriend. Don't worry! My lips are sealed!" and she pretended to zip her lips, even though there was a cute little smile on them. "Come on, come on!" she said, pulling Olivia out the door to the steps.

Before they were down the hall, Olivia started laughing too. "You are too much, Sally!"

"I know. At times, I even scare myself!" They chuckled, walking arm in arm, all the way upstairs.

The teachers had started to converge on the library, and typical Monday morning teacher "talk" was taking place. Some of them dragged in, but most were perky and upbeat. They had surmised that there was some news to tell, since they rarely had morning staff meetings.

Clay was standing at the front desk of the library speaking with Mrs. Holzman, the librarian, about the purchase of more books for the library. She was nodding her head in excitement and understanding. Clay stepped away from the desk. "Excuse me, staff.. I just want to point out that there are some doughnuts and milk and juice left, but you better get over there before Don finishes them off!" Teachers swatted Don on the arm and teased him, but he just grabbed one more glazed doughnut before taking his seat. "We'll start in about five!" Clay finished.

He glanced up with his Livy radar and saw her walk through the doorway with Sally. He stood staring for a second. *She is amazing and has done so much for Brandenburg, these students, and this culture. I can't let her lose her job because I can't keep my dick in my pants around her. I'm willing to give up anything to have her, so I know exactly what I'm going to do this evening.* With a smile on his face and a firm resolve, Clay began the meeting.

"Well, I know it's Monday morning and you all have plenty of things to do in your classroom, but today for a few minutes we're going to celebrate. The conference that Miss Sheffield and I attended in Chicago was excellent, and probably the most organized one I've participated in in a long time. Apparently, it was also the best attended in about ten years. More importantly, Olivia presented her READING FUN-&-MENTAL IDEAS project that she's developed over the course of her teaching, along with her hands-on pieces, and the literature she selected to accompany it. It went over like gangbusters, and she had more participants in her sessions than anyone else who presented. Needless to say, although it shocked her, I was not surprised that she won the BEST PRESENTATION AWARD and $3,000.00 for Brandenburg Elementary to be used for further development of our literacy program. So without further delay, Miss Sheffield, please stand!"

The staff was on their feet cheering and applauding for Olivia. She nodded in appreciation and pleasure, and then sat down quickly.

"As the next few months continue, we will be making determinations about what is best to purchase for our students and our school, so that we can get the optimum use of these unexpected resources. As you're doing work in your classrooms, please jot down notes of places where you see gaps in what we have and what we need. Very soon I will be appointing a committee to join Miss Sheffield and Mrs. Holzman to make these final decisions, so if you want to be on that committee, just let me know. Now I think it's about time to start to work; the kids will be arriving any minute. Have a great day and let's continue with all the fabulous things we do daily here at Brandenburg."

Teachers moved toward the doorway, shaking hands with Olivia, patting her on the back or giving her a hug. Overall, they were truly excited for her success and the good fortune that she had brought to the school and the program as well. It was a great way to start a school week. Clay watched them all as they left. Finally, the library was almost empty, save Olivia, Sally and Wanda Holzman.

Clay walked over. "May I say again, Miss Sheffield, congratulations on your award and the notice it is bringing to our school." He took her hand and shook it, presenting a perfectly professional facade.

"Thank you, Mr. Mitchell," Olivia said, shaking the outstretched hand. "I appreciate your support."

Then he was gone, and she and Sally headed downstairs to their classrooms. "Have a good day, Olivia.

We'll get officially caught up later this week." Sally disappeared into her room.

Olivia stepped into her classroom and opened her palm. In it was a note in Clay's recognizable hand-writing. She unfolded the small note:

I want you naked in my bed at 8:00 tonight!
The Boss

Olivia blushed, chuckled, and tore the note into tiny little pieces before she tossed it into the garbage can next to her desk. But a surge of heat flared down her spine just thinking about tonight.

Clay headed to his office and closed the door, picking up the phone, It rang for a second and then he spoke. "Hey, Mom." Response came from the other side. "I know it's early, but I'm checking with you to see if you can meet me for lunch today?" He listened. "You can? That's great! Why don't we meet halfway between Brandenburg and Barton say...the Touchdown Club at about 12:30?" Another pause and then, "Fine, I'll see you there!"

The morning passed swiftly as Clay worked diligently to get caught up from being off work for two days. *But what days those were! And the nights as well!* When it was about 11:30 he left his office to speak with Kathy.

"Hey, Kath. I'm heading over towards Barton to take my Mom to lunch. Would you like me to bring you back something from the Touchdown Club? I remember you like their food. I won't be back until about 2:30, so it will be late."

Kathy's eyes lit up. "Oh, Clay, I really love their tuna salad sandwich. Could you get me one of those? They're so big, I'll have half late this afternoon, and the other half on Tuesday."

"Will do! See you in a few!" and he was out the door with a smile on his face, whistling as he went.

Kathy wondered what was going on. "Something's up his sleeve again, and I'd sure like to know what it is!"

Clay was waiting in the entryway of the Touchdown Club when his mother arrived. She was a lovely woman of medium height, basically slender, with ash-colored hair. Clay never remembered her looking unkempt; she was always neat and tidy...and charming.

A memory of her cleaning out his closet when he was fifteen flashed through his mind. She had been absolutely furious with him about how messy it was; then she'd pulled out a pack of cigarettes, a dirty magazine, and the skeleton of a dead frog. She'd been upset enough about the cigarettes, but she hadn't said a word about the magazine. Then she'd absolutely railed on him about the frog--poor thing--starving to death in his junk-filled closet.

And when his Dad got home, well, that was another thing. It was a lesson Clay would learn that summer. No one ever crossed his mother and expected to not deal with his dad. He'd been in a lot of trouble that next week, doing all sorts of crap jobs that his dad had found for him, including cleaning the toilets in the four elementary schools in the district. But the most outstanding lesson of the incident was the way his dad took his mom's side and stood together with her in the need for punishment. Clay had always admired his parents for that, and he wanted the same relationship with his spouse that his parents had modeled. That took him directly back to the reason for this lunch meeting.

"Hey, Mom. Thanks for meeting me," he said, giving her a peck on the cheek.

"Oh, Clay, it is entirely my pleasure, dear, and what a nice surprise!"

"They have a table ready for us, and I thought that we could order, and then visit a little. I do have to get back by about 2:30 or so. Oh, by the way, don't let me forget to order a tuna salad sandwich to go. I'm taking it back for Kathy."

"Oh, I do so love Kathy Tiffin, but it's been absolutely ages since I've seen her! Is she well?"

"She's great, Mom; she really keeps Brandenburg humming along."

They both took their seats, read through the menu, and placed their orders. Small talk continued until Caroline Graves took the bull by the horns. "So, Clay darling...what's the reason we're really meeting? By the way, congratulations on the award you just received for Brandenburg. Dad told me about it yesterday. I imagine that you're really proud of Miss...Sheffield, is it?" One eyebrow raised and her eyes had a curious glint.

Clay had seen that look in his mother's eye before. She knew something, somehow, but far be it for him to understand what. He smiled and shrugged his shoulders, speechless frankly, that his mom had thrown in the one name that somehow he needed to talk about with her.

"Go on dear, Spit it out. Time's a-wasting.."

"Jeez, Mom. Do you have ESP or something?"

"Only about the men in my life, Clay," she grinned. "What exactly do you need me to do for you in regards to Miss Sheffield?"

He laughed outright, took a deep breath, and began. "Well, actually, Mom, I'm in love with Olivia."

"Uh-huh." She nodded, totally unsurprised.

"You know this, how?"

"Oh, Clay, I saw her at the hospital checking in on you. I saw the way you looked at her. Furthermore, I saw the way she looked at you. I imagine this love thing is a two-way street."

He looked down at his hands for a minute, and then into his mom's face. "Mom, I never knew falling in love could be this amazingly powerful; but there's a little problem."

Sarcastically, she continued, "You think? Could you possibly be concerned about your Dad's reaction?"

"Mom--Dad is going to have a fit. Frankly, Olivia and I have had chemistry the entire time we've worked together, but we've always done our best to fight it. But last weekend in Chicago..."

"Say no more, dear." Caroline held up her hand. "So you're asking me to smooth it over with your Dad, then?"

"Hell, no, Mom! There'll be no smoothing this over. I'm going home tonight and writing my letter of resignation!"

Shocked, she gasped, "Clay, you can't be serious?"

"Mom," he smiled, a faraway look on his face, "you're going to love Olivia. I've always felt like somewhere out there was a woman waiting for me, and Lord knows, I've tested the waters."

His mom grimaced a little, saying, "No need to go there, Clay."

"I want what you and Dad and Eric and Phyllis have. I can have that with Olivia, but I can't let her risk losing her job. She's done amazing work at Brandenburg, and surely, she deserves to stay there. I'll find another job somewhere in the Midwest, hopefully within driving distance of Brandenburg. But Dad's made it crystal clear that no hanky-panky happens between employees in the same building; and believe me, the hanky-panky's not going to stop. Hell, I plan on proposing to her on Friday."

Caroline Graves had watched and listened to her son; she knew that he was convinced that this was the right path to take to solve the problem. She patted his arm lightly, still thinking. "Alright, Clay. I'll make you a deal. You write the letter, but don't turn it in to your Dad until Friday. I'll plan on being there at his office about the time you take it in. Maybe I can soften the blow just a little. Oh, Clay, dear, I'm so happy for you and Miss Sheffield. Are you certain she'll say 'yes' to your proposal?"

"What man ever knows that, Mom?" Then his ornery smile appeared. "But I can be pretty persuasive when I set my mind to it!"

Caroline couldn't help but laugh. "Order your sandwich-to-go, son. Poor Kathy will be starving, and it's time I took in the idea about getting a new daughter-in-law nearby. Will it be soon, do you think?"

"Jeez, Mom, if it were up to me, we'd be married tomorrow.. We haven't gotten to that conversation. Whatever she wants, she'll have. I only know that I can't see my life without her."

A soft look crossed his mother's face. "Right answer, Clay. That's my boy!"

Olivia had gone home after school and taken a nap. All of her extracurriculars in the bedroom with Clay had deprived her of some serious REMs. *But what a way to lose sleep!*

She was supposed to go to Clay's apartment at 8:00, but until then, she had time to sit down and rough draft her letter of resignation. Never having written one, she thought about it. *Normally I would address it to my principal, but Clay would never accept it. I think it needs to be sent to Dr. Graves and the School Board. Now--for a reason why?*

Dear Dr. Graves and Brandenburg School Board of Education:

I am delivering this, my letter of resignation at Brandenburg Elementary, effective at the end of this current school year, unless otherwise notified.

I have a rare opportunity to work elsewhere next school year, and feel that it is in my best interest to pursue that pathway.

I have enjoyed my years at Brandenburg, and will be happy to work with everyone to ensure a smooth transition for the new hire.
Thank you!
Sincerely,
Olivia Sheffield

She read and reread the brief letter, thinking clearly about what she was leaving. *I know I don't really have a job opportunity, but I'll just get my resume updated and start looking right away. Maybe I can stay fairly close to Brandenburg.*

She looked over the letter again and decided to get it ready to send to Central Office late Thursday afternoon. It would be in Dr. Graves' hands by Friday afternoon. Then she would send the copies to the school board. Once approved, they'd be ready to post the job opening as soon as possible.

She thought sadly for a moment about all her kids at Brandenburg, the ones she had currently, as well as those she'd taught previously. But she also realized that having a relationship with Clay was far more important to her than where she worked. *I know we'll be able to work this out, once I'm not at Brandenburg anymore. This will allow Clay to stay where he needs to be.*

With a surety born of strong conviction, Olivia prepared her letters for Superintendent Graves and the School Board. She personally signed all the copies, folded them, placed them in envelopes, and addressed them. *I'll send the letter for Dr. Graves on Thursday through Interoffice mail. Then on Monday, I'll send the remainder of the letters to the school board members.*

When she was finished, she showered, washed her hair, and put on a top that she personally knew would drive Clay crazy. Finally, she knocked at his apartment door. It was precisely 8:00 p.m. She'd conveniently forgotten her underwear.

Every late afternoon, interoffice mail went through the school district. Usually, it landed in mailboxes early the next morning. Friday was no exception. Jeff Graves' personal secretary, Connie Calloway, carried a large stack of mail into his office from outside the district as well as inside. Usually the mail that came from outside the district was the more important, so Jeff always read those first.

"Thanks, Connie. Hey, could you grab me a cup...?"

"Got it right here, Jeff," she entered, carrying the big coffee mug that Eric had made for him in ceramics class in tenth grade.

"Jeez, Connie. Have you ever seen a bigger pile of mail? What is with all of this today?" he groused, as he scanned letter after letter. Speaking engagements, requests for info about building projects, planning meetings to set the school year calendar for next year, and special meetings with the high school athletics groups were part of the correspondence. He rolled his eyes, wondering how much longer he'd want to keep this job. Caro and he could be traveling all over, if he'd retire. Then they'd get up and see Eric and his family more often, and they could take in some sights they hadn't seen yet.

He knew he was a little grouchy today. It was Caroline. She'd been flitting around a lot lately, baking him his favorite desserts, picking up his dry cleaning, making his doctor appointments. Hell, yesterday, she even bought him a new pair of shoes! He knew she knew that he hated shopping...but a new pair of shoes? Without him there? And they' d actually fit! I mean he appreciated it and all, but usually she'd be telling him that he's not helpless, and to do these things himself. "Oh, Caroline. I know you're up to something--but what?"

The mail kept coming. He'd finally gotten through all the out-of-district correspondence and asked Connie to make a few appointments. Now he started on the interoffice mail which was mostly made up of notes from his principles advising him of issues that were coming up and items for their administrative meeting agendas that needed to be addressed. Another sort of letter appeared in his hand and the envelope was from Brandenburg. He knew it wasn't Clay's handwriting or Kathy's, so he opened it up, curiously wondering what it was.

The letter shocked him. So much so, that he sat down in his large overstuffed executive chair. "Why would Olivia Sheffield resign five nights after receiving a huge award of affirmation of her teaching skills? And what was the mysterious job opportunity waiting for her? Not to mention, she hadn't addressed this letter to Clay, but to him and the school board. Something's fishy around here."

At that minute, there was a knock on his door and in breezed his adorable wife, very nonchalantly. She came straight to his chair, hand on his shoulder, and reached down and gave him a welcome kiss. "Morning, Jeff!"

"Well, hi! To what do I owe this surprise, Caro?"

She was bustling around his office, straightening magazines that didn't need straightening, watering a few plants, and righting books that had fallen on his bookshelf. To top it off, she was humming. He didn't recognize the melody as he had no memory for songs, but it was a spritely little tune and it sounded, well, happy.

He watched her for a minute, and then said, "Caro, darling? I repeat myself. What are you doing here?"

She stopped moving, affronted by his tone of voice. "Jeff Graves, don't you dare take that tone with me! Can't a woman come and visit her hus..."

At that moment, Clay came into the office. "Hey, Dad..."

Apparent surprise, thought Jeff Graves.

"Hi, Mom..."

"Hi, honey. How in the world are you?" Caroline asked Clay.

Jeff Graves was watching the scenario play out, puzzled to no end, but knowing full-well he didn't have long to wait before he found out what they were up to. He hadn't said a word; suddenly they both realized that and stopped their innocuous chatter to look at him. He paused a minute and motioned them toward the chairs at his conference table. "Why don't you both have a seat."

They both did. Neither of them had a particularly worried expression on their faces, but they were certainly intent looks. "Okay, so you want to get me up to speed on what it is we're going to talk about?"

No one said a word, but Clay pulled out a piece of

letterhead and slid it across the table in Jeff's direction.

Jeff looked at Clay, and then Caroline, then he pulled the letter closer, so he could read it. WHAT IN GOD'S NAME IS THE MEANING OF THIS? he roared when he had finished.

"Now, Jeff, remember your blood pressure, darling. You don't want…"

"I asked you about the meaning of this letter," he shouted again at Clay.

Clay stood up, making eye contact with his dad. "Well, it's like this, Dad! I'm in love with Olivia Sheffield. Before I can propose, I want to let you know that I need to be replaced, so that she doesn't lose her job. She's worked too hard at Brandenburg and adds too much to the school community. I know that you wanted me here in the district, and I've loved it. But I won't let her sacrifice herself for my sake…you can find a new principal, and I'll start looking tomorrow for another position."

"Did you know about this?" Jeff's head swiveled over to his wife, as he glared over his bifocals.

"Yes, dear, and I stand behind Clay's decision. Just think, Jeff, a new daughter-in-law!"

Caro smiled that same adorable smile that knocked Jeff for a loop the first night he met her. He was such a sap for that face! He shook himself out of her spell, and continued, "Well, I'm glad you agree, but it appears that, perhaps Miss Sheffield has ideas of her own!" Jeff stood up from the conference table and grabbed a note off his desk, sliding it across to Clay.

Clay reached for the letter, swiftly reading it, and shouted, "Well, I'll be a son-of-a…"

"Son!" Jeff shouted.

"Sorry, Mom. I don't know what this is about, Dad. I never spoke with Livy about my plans to resign, and clearly she didn't speak with me. I don't know what this job is that she mentions, but well, I won't have her leaving Brandenburg unless she really wants to."

Jeff was steaming. "Look, Clay, I thought we had an understanding about workplace romances. Hell, it was you and she that you were asking about by the lake that night, wasn't it?"

"Yes, it was, and dammit, Dad, I almost lost her because I was trying to stay professional. Well, that's not going to happen! I'm not going to let her go, and if she and I can't work together, then I'll be the one to leave!"

Jeff and Caroline looked at their son. Then Jeff smiled quietly, glancing sideways at the love of his life. "It appears our son has made up his mind, Caroline." He paused for a second and said, "Alright, Clay, I accept your resignation. I'll notify the Board, and then post the opening on Monday morning. You'd better start looking soon, son. Mom and I want you in the vicinity!"

There was a knock at the office door. "Mr. Graves, sir?"

"Yes, Connie. What is it?"

"There's someone out here to see you. I tried buzzing you, but I don't think you heard...it's Miss Sheffield."

All three heads popped up. Clay and Caro looked uncomfortable. Jeff smiled. Ah, righteous justice! "Send her in, Connie!"

"Mr. Graves?" Olivia came through the doorway tentatively. She made eye contact with him. Then she glanced around and the look of surprise clearly registered on her face. "Clay?" she squeaked. "Mrs. Graves?"

"Yes, I'm aware of their names, Miss Sheffield. How can I help you?"

"Olivia!" Clay stood, shouting in the same tone of voice his dad had just used on him. "What is the meaning of this letter?"

The three of them started talking at once. Caroline was trying to calm Clay down. Clay was shouting at Olivia. Olivia was arguing with Clay.

I can't make out a word that anyone is saying. Jeff Graves roared, "SIT DOWN--ALL OF YOU!"

They did.

"Now, since this is my office, I believe that I have the floor, so to speak! Miss Sheffield, I received this letter from you earlier this morning. I'm asking you if it's legitimate?"

She glanced at Clay. "Well, it wasn't when I wrote it."

"See, Dad. I told you she'd try to leave, instead of me. I won't have it!"

"Excuse me, Clay Mitchell. I hardly think you have any say in what I do at this moment in time!" Olivia shouted back.

That shut him up.

Good girl! Jeff waited. "Go on, Miss Sheffield."

"Well, the reason I came over today was to tell you that I do indeed have a job offer. It came last night. It's not a full-time job, but the committee that sponsored the conference that we," she pointed to Clay, smiling that enamored smile, "...attended, offered me a job, presenting at conferences around the country." She looked in Clay's direction and her eyes lit up. She continued. "I never saw myself doing anything other than teaching. I've always loved it. But after the convention, well, I really enjoyed the exhilaration of presenting, and I think that I have a chance to help teachers and districts by doing this. So I guess I am officially tendering my resignation."

Jeff Graves stood up and moved from behind his desk, where he'd taken a seat. "Suppose I have an offer for you to consider, Miss Sheffield? Ironically enough, last week I had notified our school board that I thought we needed to create a new position, basically Literacy Administrator. I saw it as an opening for a teacher who could move around the district, training teachers about current, as well as up and coming new literacy ideas. We're still fleshing out the job description; but what if it included the opportunity to present out of district when asked? Would you consider staying in our district, if we could make that happen?"

"Oh, my gosh, yes! That sounds incredible!" Olivia smiled. "You really had planned on that?"

"Yes. It seems rather fortuitous on my part, doesn't it?" Graves said, smugly. He looked around the room at Clay and his wife. He waited a minute, and said, "Well, son. What do you think?"

At that second, Clay dropped down on one knee, and held Olivia's hand in his. "Olivia Sheffield! I don't give a rat's ass what you do for a job, so long as when I get home from mine, you'll be there. Will you marry me?"

"Oh, Clay..." her eyes filled with tears, "Yes, yes. I'll be there. And I'll do my best, Mr. Graves, to act professional when I'm in his building!"

Clay stood up and gathered his honey-haired dream girl in his arms and kissed her silly.

His parents stood there and watched. Caroline dabbed at her eyes with her handkerchief, as she handed Clay's letter to Jeff. Jeff took it willingly, smiled at his incredibly intelligent wife, and tore it up into little tiny pieces.

EPILOGUE

Clay marveled at all the arrangements that had taken place since his proposal to Olivia in his dad's office in March. He had now met Olivia's parents and brothers. The bridal party was set. It included Sally Litchfield, Susie Sheffield, Donna Puckett and the other two sisters-in-law. Groomsmen were Eric Mitchell, Dave Garrett, Jim Sheffield, Jack Kelley, and Josh Combs, who'd flown in from Arizona two days earlier. Clay's niece, Chelsea, was the flower girl, and Gus Kelley was the ring bearer.

Neither Clay nor Olivia had been interested in a mega-wedding; but they <u>were</u> interested in getting married as soon as possible. So rush orders were placed on the bridal gown and bridesmaids' dresses for a late August wedding, right before school started. Mama Caro, Mrs. Herbert, and Kathy Tiffin had been all over town calling in every favor they knew to make the upcoming nuptials special. The town had gone into overdrive to help!

Mr. Henderson at Kipley's Bakery offered the cake

for free and the local florist requested to donate the flowers, as she'd grown up with the Sheffield kids. O'Jay offered his bar for a relaxed rehearsal dinner.

Mrs. Herbert, knowing that Olivia and Clay would likely move within a year, gave them six-months free rent for staying at the apartments. "I need to get all the work out of you that I can, before you move!" she'd said to Clay, winking.

Shock and awe! Even the honeymoon was a gift! Jennifer and Judy (or was it Judy and Jennifer) of the Twin Travel Agency gifted Olivia and Clay with a free trip to San Francisco and the Napa Valley.

Two nights earlier a large package had arrived, while Clay and Olivia were having dinner with Jeff and Caroline Graves. "Oh, my word, Clay--look at this package!" Olivia said, struggling to get it inside from where the delivery truck had left it. Everyone was curious to see what was inside. Olivia tore the wrapping off, and a large mosaic of a Mexican Mariachi Band with a trumpet player in the center wowed them! It was a beautiful piece of artwork and there was a note.

"Best Wishes for your Wedding. We picked this up in Cabo last week! I'll never forget your trumpet playing, Olivia! Clay--don't take her back there, or don't let her drink! Fondly, Derek Donaldson and Nicole Marshall

There would be a luncheon after today's 12:30 wedding and music would be provided by the high school choir. Many of the townspeople were invited and the church was packed with well-wishers. Olivia had specifically declared, if students came, they were to bring no gifts, but books only, to add to the school district's libraries.

The wedding was one for the memory books, and the ceremony was lovely. The entire church broke into applause as Clay and Olivia kissed and turned around to be presented as Mr. and Mrs. Clay Mitchell. Then they headed up the aisle towards the receiving line and the attendees started lining up to greet them.

Little Joanie Coswell, from Olivia's class, was standing in the aisle with her mother, waiting with the crowd. "Hey, Mommy. Can I go over there and talk to Gus Kelley?" She pointed towards the end of the line where the ring bearer had to stand. Her mom nodded her head in the affirmative, so Joannie slithered through the crowd, finally ending up behind Gus in the receiving line.

Gus sensed that someone was standing behind him. He turned, ever so slightly, pulling at the neck of his shirt. It was driving him crazy. "Hey, Joanie."

"Hey, Gus. You look sorta nice in that outfit."

"Thanks, but I can't wait to take it off and put on my t-shirt."

"Say, Gus. Do you remember our bet?"

"Sure do. You owe me two dollars."

"I've got it right here."

"Well, pass it over, then."

She looked at Gus with a smile of longing. "Okay, here." She passed the crinkled bills to Gus.

"Thanks. See I told you I was right. They were holding hands on the ferris wheel, and now they're married. That's the way it happens!" he said emphatically.

Then he glanced over at Joanie, grabbed her hand, and smiled.

CPSIA information can be obtained
at www.ICGtesting.com
Printed in the USA
LVHW090404281021
701751LV00001B/14

9 781977 238283